Peter Tremayne is the fiction pseudonym of Peter Berresford Ellis, ██████ █ authority on the ancient Celts, who has utilised his ██████ ████ ████ ███ ███ and seventh century Irish ██████ ███ate a new concept in detective fiction.

An international Sister Fidelma Society has been established, with a journal entitled *The Brehon* appearing three times yearly. Details can be obtained either by writing to the Society at PMB #312, 1818 North Taylor Street, Suite B, Little Rock, AR 72207, USA, or by logging onto the society website at www.sisterfidelma.com.

Praise for the widely acclaimed Sister Fidelma mysteries:

'The Sister Fidelma books give the readers a rattling good yarn. But more than that, they bring vividly and viscerally to life the fascinating lost world of the Celtic Irish. I put down *The Spider's Web* with a sense of satisfaction at a good story well told, but also speculating on what modern life might have been like had that civilisation survived'                                           Ronan Bennett

'Rich helpings of evil and tension with lively and varied characters'
                                                            *Historical Novels Review*

'The detail of the books is fascinating, giving us a vivid picture of everyday life at this time . . . the most detailed and vivid recreations of ancient Ireland'                                           *Irish Examiner*

'A brilliant and beguiling heroine. Immensely appealing'
                                                            *Publishers Weekly*

'Tremayne's super-sleuth is a vibrant creation, a woman of wit and courage who would stand out in any era, but brings a special sparkle to the wild beauty of medieval Ireland'                Morgan Llywelyn

# PETER TREMAYNE

# PENANCE OF THE DAMNED

**HEADLINE**

First published in Great Britain in 2016 by
HEADLINE PUBLISHING GROUP

First published in Great Britain in paperback in 2017 by
HEADLINE PUBLISHING GROUP

3

Cataloguing in Publication Data is available from the British Library

ISBN 978 1 4722 0838 5

Typeset in Times New Roman PS by Palimpsest Book Production Limited,
Falkirk, Stirlingshire

Printed and bound in Great Britain by
Clays Ltd, St Ives plc

Headline's policy is to use papers that are natural, renewable and recyclable products and
made from wood grown in sustainable forests. The logging and manufacturing processes
are expected to conform to the environmental regulations of the country of origin.

MIX
Paper from
responsible sources
FSC   FSC® C104740

HEADLINE PUBLISHING GROUP
An Hachette UK Company
Carmelite House
50 Victoria Embankment
London EC4Y 0DZ

www.headline.co.uk
www.hachette.co.uk

For Jonathan and Helen Peppiatt

and, naturally, George and Connie

*Si enim nocui aut dignum morte aliquid feci non recuso mori si vero nihil est eorum quae hii accusant me nemo potest me illis donare . . .*

For if I be an offender, or have committed any thing worthy of death, I refuse not to die; but if there be none of these things whereof these accuse me, no man may deliver me unto them . . .

Acts 25:11
Vulgate Latin translation of Jerome 4th Century

# PRINCIPAL CHARACTERS

**Sister Fidelma** of Cashel, a *dálaigh* or advocate of the law courts of Seventh-century Ireland

**Brother Eadulf** of Seaxmund's Ham in the Land of the South Folk, her companion

*At Cashel*

**Colgú**, King of Muman and brother to Fidelma

**Enda**, a warrior of the Nasc Niadh, bodyguard to Colgú

*On the road to Uí Fidgente territory*

**Ciarnat**, an attendant in Dún Eochair Mháigh

**Conrí**, warlord of the Uí Fidgente

**Socht**, his second-in-command

*At Dún Eochair Mháigh*

**Donennach**, Prince of the Uí Fidgente

**Brehon Faolchair**, his chief judge

**Airmid**, sister to Donennach and physician to the court

**Ceit**, *cenn-feadhna* or commander of Donennach's household guard

**Lachtna**, a guard

**Gormán,** commander of the bodyguard of the King of Muman

**Aibell,** wife to Gormán

**Étromma,** mother of Ciarnat

*The religious at the fortress and in the community of Nechta*

**Abbot Nannid,** Abbot of Mungairit

**Brother Cuineáin,** *rechtaire* or steward to the Abbot of Mungairit

**Prior Cuán,** the *airsecnap* or Deputy Abbot of Imleach

**Brother Tuamán,** *rechtaire* or steward to the Abbot of Imleach

**Brother Mac Raith,** a scribe of Imleach

**Brother Máel Anfaid,** a scribe of Imleach

**Brother Éladach,** *aistreóir,* the doorkeeper of the 'Abbey' of Nechta

**Marban,** a millwright and uncle to Aibell

**Deogaire** of Sliabh Luachra, chief of the Luachair Deaghaidh

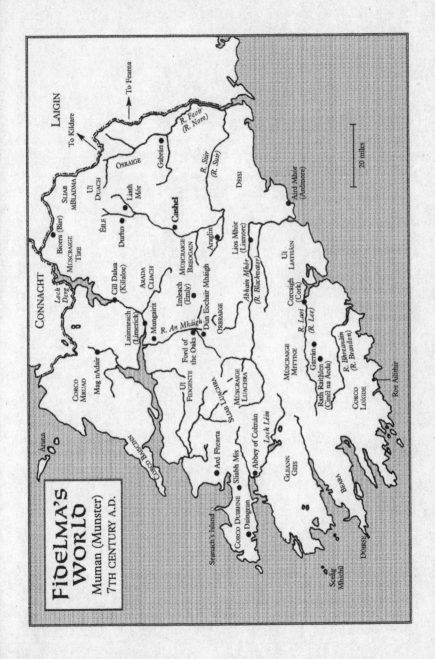

FIDELMA'S WORLD
Muman (Munster)
7TH CENTURY A.D.

20 miles

CONNACHT

LAIGIN

To Fearna

To Kildare

OSRAIGE

Gabrán

R. Feoir
(R. Nore)

R. Siúir
(R. Suir)

DÉISI

Aird Mhór
(Ardmore)

Slíab Mbladma

Uí Duach

Biorra (Birr)

Loch Derg

Múscraige Tíre

Liath Mór

Cashel

Éile

Durlus

Múscraige Breogain

Araglin

Lios Mhór
(Lismore)

Cill Dalua
(Killaloe)

Arada Cliach

Uí Liatháin

Abhain Mhór
(R. Blackwater)

Corcaigh (Cork)

Imleach
(Imly)

Dún Eochair Mháigh

Mungairit

R. An Mháigh

Orbraige

R. Laoi
(R. Lee)

Luimneach
(Limerick)

Corco Mruad

Mag nAdair

Ford of the Oaks

Uí Fidgente

Slíab Luchra

Múscraige Luachra

Múscraige Mittine

Garrán

Ráth Raithlen
(Cinél na Áeda)

R. Bhrcanáin
(R. Brandon)

Corco Loígde

Ros Ailithir

Aran

Corco Baiscinn

Ard Fhearta

Sliabh Mis

Abbey of Coltnán

Loch Léin

Gleann Geis

Beara

Corco Duibhne

Daingean

Seanach's Island

Doirse

Scelig Mhichíl

## AUTHOR'S NOTE

This adventure is set during the month which was called, in Old Irish, *Meithem*, the 'middle month', being regarded as midsummer; today, it is known as June. The year is AD671.

The story follows on from *The Second Death* in chronological sequence. While, like previous Fidelma tales, it is self-contained, some readers may remember the brooding country of the Uí Fidgente in *Atonement of Blood*, together with many of the characters. Some of these characters also featured in *The Devil's Seal*.

Dún Eochair Mháigh, 'the Fortress on the Brink of An Mháigh' – anglicised today as the River Maigue – was the main fortress of Prince Donennach of the Uí Fidgente. Today the site is called Bruree, from Bru Rí – the King's House – in south-east County Limerick. It was so called because it was said to be the one-time capital of the Kings of Muman – Munster. The Uí Fidgente claimed to be descended from Cormac Cas, the brother of Eóghan Mór, the founder of the Eóghanacht dynasty. They also claimed that Cormac Cas was senior to Eóghan, and therefore styled themselves the Dál gCais – Descendants of Cas – with legitimate claim to be rulers of all Muman.

Throughout history there was little love lost between the Uí Fidgente and the Eóghanacht, but it was not until AD963 that Mathgamain mac Cennétig (*d*. AD976) of the Dál gCais was recorded as ousting the Eóghanacht Donnchad mac Cellacháin as King of

Muman. Within a generation, a third Dál gCais King of Muman, Brían Bóruma mac Cennétig (*d*. AD1014), furthered his family ambition by displacing the Uí Néill dynasty to become the High King of Ireland. In AD1005 Brían, who is popularly called Brian Boru, recognised Armagh as the primacy of the Irish churches instead of Imleach (Emly), and is famous for his defeat of the Vikings at Clontarf, being killed by a retreating Viking at the moment of his victory.

Less than 100 kilometres from Dún Eochair Mháigh is Sliabh Luachra, the Mountain of Rushes. In reality it is a range of hills with peaks rising to a height of 500 metres in which seven glens are enclosed. It is a wet area; a rush-filled marshland with dangerous bogs, surrounded by impenetrable woodland and hardly any good arable land to sustain its sparse population. In ancient times it rose as an impregnable natural fortress, which attracted those escaping justice and was ruled by ruthless robber chieftains. In Fidelma's day it was a place to avoid. The most ruthless among these robber chieftains claimed to be 'Kings of Luachra', and would ride forth with their war bands to rob and demand tribute from those who dwelled in the surrounding countryside. It is still a place of much beauty but with a history of sorrow – and always the threat of danger.

Readers might also be interested in the fact that, although the 'Penitentials' are popularly ascribed to the Irish Church Fathers, they originated as rules created by the 'Desert Fathers', the ascetics of the eastern churches. One such rule-maker was John the Ascetic in the sixth century. He was originally from Edessa in Mesopotamia. Many Irish churchmen, such as Finnian, Cummian and Colmcille, certainly adopted these often brutal punishments. It was not until a Council in Paris, in AD829, held under Jonas, Bishop of Orléans (*c*. AD760–843), that the Penitentials were ordered to be discarded and the books containing them to be burned. Bishop Jonas was also known for his work supporting the argument that the Frankish Emperor had authority over the bishops of the Frankish Church in matters of legal authority – a judgement some clerics had tried to reverse in early Ireland.

# CHAPTER ONE

❧

The waters were dark and tranquil, and curiously warm. The slight flow against his body was soporific. The young warrior floated lazily along in the caressing touch of the waters; surrendering his body to their will.

Gentle hands touched his outstretched fingers, and he saw the shadowy form of his mother, gliding along beside him. She was smiling at him, and he felt comforted. On the other side was the lithe, attractive figure of the girl for whom he had left Cashel so that he could come in search of her. *Come in search?* He puzzled over the phrase. Come – to where? Where was he? No matter. The soft current was pulling him on. He had no wish to ask any more questions.

And . . . something stirred within some deep recess of his mind. It was disturbing. It told him he should be doing something – something urgent – and not relaxing here. But where was he – and what was it that he should be doing? There was some errand he had to perform – some warning to be given . . . But what warning?

He turned to the smiling face of the girl, swimming alongside. Her expression was alluring, enticing him to come closer and closer and . . . suddenly her face dissolved and changed into the decomposing, bloodstained features of someone he had known, long ago. Dimly, he recalled that she had been murdered, and he had stood accused. Only Fidelma of Cashel had believed in his innocence. He was not guilty of her murder.

That was it! Murder! He needed to warn Cashel – warn Fidelma of Cashel. But warn them of what?

Even as he brought the thought into semi-consciousness, he became aware of distant sounds, of harsh male voices assailing his ears. He tried to shut them out and yet they grew ever louder, more intense, and close at hand. He also felt a sharp pricking at the base of his neck. Suddenly, his temples began to throb. He groaned, feeling his mouth dry and uncomfortable.

Next, he became aware that his face was pressed against the hard wooden boards of a floor. One arm was outstretched before him. The shouting had not subsided but the jumble of coarse sounds was separating into the form of words.

'Murderer! Foul murderer! You have killed him!'

Gormán blinked again and emerged fully from the comforting safety of the drifting waters of his mind. A man in religious robes stood above him shouting down at him. Beyond this man there lay a bundle of clothes – no, it was a body; a body covered in blood.

Gormán tried to raise himself up a little. It was then that his fingers touched the sticky hilt of the dagger, lying close at hand. As he moved, the pain at the base of his neck increased. It was like having someone standing behind him, pressing on his neck with a sword point.

Gormán groaned again and tried to gather his reason. Where was he? He could recall nothing as the man in the religious robes standing over him was continuing to shout.

'Murderer!'

Gormán licked his dry lips with a tongue just as dry.

'Where am I?' he managed to mumble.

'Where are you?' The voice of the religieux was angry and uncompromising. 'You, warrior, are on your way to Hell!'

\* \* \*

Colgú, King of Muman, halted abruptly in mid-stride. He had been pacing up and down in his private chamber, his forehead creased with agitation, his face set in a scowl at odds with his usual pleasant expression. The knocking on the door caused him to pause and square his shoulders. The knocking continued, but before he could respond, the door opened.

His sister, Fidelma of Cashel, entered and closed the door behind her.

'You sent for me?' she asked, her green-blue eyes registering her brother's anxiety in spite of his efforts to disguise it. 'I see that you have received bad news from Dún Eochair Mháigh.'

Colgú was startled. He brushed away a lock of fiery-red hair – the same colour as his sibling's own locks, and said angrily, 'Has the messenger been speaking to you? I forbade him to say a word about it to anyone. I'll have him punished—'

'Hush, brother,' Fidelma returned calmly. 'He told me nothing, but I observed much. I know that a messenger, under the banner of the Prince of the Uí Fídgente, arrived here and demanded to speak to you immediately. After you had seen him, you then sent for me. Now I find you scowling as if there is a weight of trouble on your mind. What other interpretation should I place on these events except that this messenger brought you bad news, which came from the Prince of the Uí Fidgente who is, according to reports, currently at his fortress of Dún Eochair Mháigh.'

Colgú hesitated a moment and then sank into a nearby chair. It always sounded so simple when his sister explained things. He waved her to a seat opposite.

'It is very bad news indeed,' he admitted gloomily. He turned to a small side table, pouring himself a generous drink from a clay jug, and Fidelma noted with disapproval that it was *corma*, a distilled spirit. It was unusual for her brother to drink intoxicating liquor before the sun had reached its zenith. Colgú motioned towards the jug in silent question, and she shook her head.

'Bad news is better quickly revealed,' she prompted as he took another swallow of the strong liquid.

His troubled blue eyes met his sister's inquisitive gaze, and he sighed, 'Ségdae has been murdered.'

Fidelma stared at him blankly, as if she heard his words but did not comprehend their meaning.

Ségdae was Abbot of Imleach – *comarb*, or successor, of the Blessed Ailbe – Chief Bishop of All Muman and chief ecclesiastical adviser to the King, her brother. Fidelma and Colgú seemed to have known him all their lives. He had been appointed to the position of Abbot on the death of the previous Abbot, Conaing, exactly ten years before. He had advised Cathal, their cousin, when he was King, and now he advised Colgú. Abbot Ségdae had become a pillar of the stability of the kingdom as well as the church.

Her mind flooded with questions, dispelling any immediate thoughts of grief.

'Murdered, you say? Who did this – where and when? And why does a messenger from the Uí Fidgente come with this news?'

'Ségdae had been on a journey to discuss Church matters with some Uí Fidgente clergy. Since Prince Donennach and I agreed a peace in an attempt to end the disastrous conflicts between us, the abbot felt he should take the opportunity to construct some relationship with these clerics at a council at the fortress of Donennach.'

The Uí Fidgente had been long-time rivals of the Eóghanacht of Cashel, claiming their family had equal right to the kingship of Muman. Assassination plots and open warfare had marked their relationship, especially during recent years. Only six months or so previously, Fidelma had been instrumental in averting another Uí Fidgente plot and brokering peace between King Colgú and the Prince of the Uí Fidgente.

'So Ségdae was killed in Uí Fidgente territory?'

'Murdered in the very fortress of Donennach,' confirmed her brother.

'What happened? How was he killed?' pressed Fidelma.

4

'The messenger was not well equipped with facts. He simply reported that the murder happened several days ago, and that Prince Donennach despatched him forthwith to inform us. Abbot Ségdae was attacked and slain in the chamber that had been provided for him in the prince's fortress. The culprit was immediately identified and caught. He was taken before the prince and his Chief Brehon. The facts were heard and there was, apparently, no question of the man's guilt.'

'And who is this man? What was his motive for killing the abbot? Was it some feud from the days of antagonism between our peoples?'

Colgú shook his head in frustration. 'As I said, the facts are sparse. From the messenger, I could learn nothing although I suspect he knew far more than he was saying. Prince Donennach's message was that he wanted me and my Chief Brehon to ride immediately for his fortress. He is concerned with what might be liable to follow in the wake of the pronouncement of guilt of this man.'

Fidelma frowned. 'What did he mean by that?' she repeated, puzzled.

'The abbot's killing has apparently caused an outcry among the Uí Fidgente religious. They are demanding some ritual execution in accordance with the new rules of the Penitentials which have been brought from Rome. Many of the religious are adopting them instead of following our own laws, very probably as a means of asserting their independence from the rest of us. They said that the death of an abbot of Ségdae's standing should be punished in the severest terms according to their laws of the Faith.'

Fidelma suppressed a sigh. 'In one way I can sympathise with them,' she said. 'It is hard to be impartial when it involves the death of a wise old man such as Ségdae. He was like a kindly uncle to us.'

'That is true,' her brother agreed. 'But the argument between those who wish to adopt these rules from Rome and those who want to safeguard our native laws would be yet another tear in the fabric of our society. I have taken oath to protect and sustain our laws, as you have. These arguments between our churches and those of Rome are something that is drawing our people apart, pushing them into opposing camps and threatening our stability. Abbot Ségdae, as you well know, was one of those churchmen who stood unflinchingly behind our laws; laws which we have developed from the time before time. He would be the first to urge us not to abandon them. I fear that this demand of the Uí Fidgente is simply another means to exclude their territories from accepting the rule of Cashel.'

'I see,' Fidelma said thoughtfully. 'How does Prince Donennach propose that this matter be dealt with if, as you say, he and his Brehon have already agreed the man's guilt?'

'He urges me to bring my Chief Brehon and go straightway to his fortress so that we may listen to the details of the matter in person and see how we can appease his religious advisers.'

Fidelma's expression was one of deep suspicion. 'It is hard to trust the Uí Fidgente, even Prince Donennach, who has done much to form this peace treaty between us. I would not recommend riding into Uí Fidgente territory or even responding until we know more.'

Colgú poured himself another drink. 'Abbot Ségdae was my chief adviser on these religious matters. That being so, it is reasonable that I and my Chief Brehon should have all the facts placed before us so that we can endorse the finding of guilt of the person responsible for this evil crime. Prince Donennach and I, as King, must speak on this matter with one voice so that there can be no dissension which might lead to another conflict with the Uí Fidgente.'

Fidelma stared at her brother. 'Do I hear the word "but" in your voice, Colgú?'

'As you know, Aillín, my Chief Brehon, is on a mission to the High King in Tara,' Colgú pointed out. 'That leaves me riding alone into the territory of the Uí Fidgente.'

'Alone? Why not with a *cath*, or battalion, of your Nasc Niadh, your bodyguard?'

'That would be interpreted as a provocative act,' Colgú told her.

He paused and then went on: 'For the time being I shall not leave Cashel. That is why I have sent for you.'

Fidelma stirred uncomfortably. 'I do not understand,' she said, but began to suspect what was coming.

'You are my personal legal adviser. Therefore, I desire *you* to go to Dún Eochair Mháigh to represent both myself and the Chief Brehon, and discover all the facts relating to this matter.'

At once Fidelma protested. 'Even if I have your authority, I do not have the authority of your Chief Brehon. And would it not be argued that I have a personal interest in the punishment of someone found guilty of the murder of such a friend and adviser as Abbot Ségdae?'

Colgú held up his hand to still her protests. 'That same argument would apply to me as well. I have made up my mind, sister. You must represent my authority as you have done, so many times before. You will go as you have the best legal mind in Cashel . . .' A brief wry grin crossed his features. 'I mean, in the absence of Brehon Aillín. Find out the details. Take Eadulf with you, of course. Oh, and you had better take young Enda as escort. After your last adventure, he seems bored with his duties as simply one of the palace guards.'

'One warrior to accompany us into Uí Fidgente territory?' Fidelma did not try to hide her dismay.

'You have travelled into danger often before and emerged unscathed,' her brother pointed out. 'Besides, as I have already said, entering Uí Fidgente territory accompanied by any more warriors could be interpreted in an unfortunate manner; just as it might be if I rode at the head of a battalion of my bodyguards. At this moment, we want no unfortunate interpretations of actions on either side.'

'Has anyone informed the steward at the Abbey of Imleach about the abbot's death?' Fidelma asked, changing the subject.

'The messenger from Prince Donennach called there yesterday on his way here. It seems Ségdae's *airsecnap*, the deputy abbot, and his steward had accompanied the abbot to Dún Eochair Mháigh. They were there at the time of the murder.'

'Since Brother Madagan fell into disgrace when we received the deputation from Canterbury, I do not recall the name of the new steward to the abbot. I think he was a tall man, very muscular, who looked like someone who should have been a *gleccaide*, a wrestler, rather than a cleric. But certainly he was someone full of his own self-importance.'

Colgú was amused at her description. 'That sums up Brother Tuamán right enough. He is the new *rechtaire*, the steward, at Imleach. The deputy abbot is named Cuán. I think he prefers the Latin title *praepositus* or prior. He was also recently appointed and I have never met him.'

'That is unusual. Ségdae would normally have brought him here to introduce him to the court. Prior Cuán . . . is he a relative that we do not know?'

They were both aware that many of the Irish abbeys adopted the same method as for the appointment of chiefs, princes, provincial kings and even of the High King. The method was elective, that was true – but the candidate had to be the most worthy and qualified to fulfil the role. In addition, the candidate had to be of the bloodline that was of the male line related to three generations of the abbot; therefore, a son often succeeded his father as abbot or bishop of a territory. The justification behind this was that an abbot, who was senior to a bishop in the churches of the Five Kingdoms, was usually a member of the royal household, and the members of his ecclesiastic community were regarded as his *fine* or family. Therefore the *derbhfine*, or electoral college, were the community, who acted in the same way as the *derbhfine* of a chieftain, prince or king.

The Abbots of Imleach were related to the kingly line of Cashel, the Eóghanacht. A hundred years before, Fergus Scandal had been chosen first as Abbot of Imleach and later chosen as King of Muman.

He would not be the first or last to hold both high offices. While celibacy was not a tenet of holding high office in the Church, it was a growing matter of concern in Rome where inheritance was becoming a problem. Less than a century before, Pope Pelagius II, had ruled that married religious should not bequeath to their sons any property they had acquired when holding clerical office.

Colgú told his sister, 'The genealogists certainly cannot find him related to our family and it is troubling that Ségdae did not come here to discuss the matter of his appointment. Everything seems to have happened at the wrong time. We should have known something of Cuán's background and qualifications before Ségdae took him to meet with the Uí Fidgente clerics. I know nothing about this man. What if he now expects to be declared as the new Abbot?'

'Ségdae's community would not approve him as *airsecnap*, or prior, unless he held the right qualifications,' Fidelma said. 'Indeed, why would Ségdae appoint him as his deputy unless he is a man of some talent?'

Her brother shrugged. 'Cuán is a common name in these parts. I have no idea of where he comes from.'

'Well, I shall soon meet him at Prince Donennach's fortress and I trust I will have the opportunity to find out more about him then. I just hope that Prior Cuán is not one of those who are supporting the Uí Fidgente clerics' wild idea of executing the culprit.'

'Yes. I can't believe Ségdae would appoint someone who believes in these strange rules that some of the religious are adopting,' agreed her brother.

She looked seriously at him. 'I have heard that many communities are becoming more extreme on such matters. They say that the New Faith approves of maiming and execution for wrongdoers. These punishments are occurring more frequently after the intervention of abbots and bishops who follow the new ideas from the east.'

'That's hardly the principle of our laws. You know more than most that the influence of these insidious Penitentials is growing stronger each year,' Colgú said moodily. 'You have seen for yourself the disturbance they are creating, not just in this kingdom but throughout all the Five Kingdoms.'

'Well, brother, unless the Uí Fidgente purposely intend to destroy the peace that we have made, the law of the Brehons must be made paramount.'

'Here we are, bereft of a good friend and counsellor, and find his death could plunge the kingdom into unrest and conflict,' Colgú sighed. 'Now do you see why it is so important for you to go to the fortress of the Prince of the Uí Fidgente?'

'In other words, you want me to report on the details of the events connected with poor Ségdae's death. You want a report on who the culprit is, assess if he has been tried fairly, discover a way that we can avoid conflict among the religious, stop any talk of execution and bring the Uí Fidgente religious back to the law of the Brehons.' A wry smile formed around Fidelma's mouth. 'Anything else you wish to ask of me, brother?'

King Colgú failed to match her bleak humour when he said morosely, 'Don't think I ask this of you lightly.'

Fidelma wanted to know: 'When do you expect the Chief Brehon to return from Tara?'

'Not before a full month.'

Fidelma sighed deeply. 'It is a bad time for him to be away. Also, it is a bad time for Gormán to be absent.'

Gormán was the commander of the King's bodyguard, the élite warriors of the Golden Collar, the Nasc Niadh. He had been given special permission by Colgú to absent himself to follow the girl, Aibell, with whom he had fallen in love. She had suddenly quitted Cashel, having apparently decided to join Deogaire, a strange young mystic who had once rescued her from being a bondservant in the western fastness of Sliabh Luachra. Colgú and Fidelma had both felt sorry for Gormán, having evidently been deserted by the capricious Aibell. Colgú had, however, given him the opportunity to follow her and attempt to win her back.

'Gormán is a good strategist,' her brother conceded, 'but we have a sound temporary commander in Aidan. We must ensure that no one tries to take advantage of this situation, and so I will ask Aidan to prepare our *catha*, the battalions of our warriors, just in case the worst may happen. I hoped I could trust Prince Donennach, especially after the recent developments. But one never can be sure with the Uí Fidgente.'

'When do you want me to leave for Prince Donennach's fortress?'

'An hour ago.' Colgú then grinned and added: 'Well, as soon as you can.'

Fidelma had risen from her chair. 'I must make arrangements for the care of Alchú, and also inform Eadulf.'

Alchú was her young son. She was at the door when her brother called: 'I have already sent word to Prince Donennach by his own messenger that you will be coming in my place, representing both myself and the Chief Brehon.'

Fidelma turned and said, 'I see. So you were sure that I would go, then?'

Colgú raised a smile at his sibling. 'You forget that I know you too well, Fidelma. It is not often that a mentor of ours, who is Abbot and Chief Bishop, is murdered. I've also told Enda to hold himself ready to accompany you. He will instruct the stables to prepare your horses and provisions for the journey.' Colgús smile vanished and he looked tired and worried. She read the anxiety in his eyes as he gazed into her own. 'Sister, I am relying on you and Eadulf. I can sense some mystery here. Something does not quite add up in the facts that have been related to me. I feel . . .'

Fidelma waited for him to finish, and when he did not, she said quietly: 'I think you believe this might be some Uí Fidgente plot to draw you out of the protection of Cashel and into their territory for a specific reason. I mean, a reason other than to serve the cause of justice for our friend and chief adviser. I think *that* is why you will not go to Dún Eochair Mháigh alone.'

Colgú looked contrite. 'I should never underestimate your powers of perception, sister. That is precisely what is in my mind. If there is some plot, then those behind it will want to overthrow me, the King, not my sister. They would not dare harm you. You enjoy the friendship and support of the High King at Tara, and your reputation even extends to Rome. The unleashing of the Hounds from Cruachán, the Mouth of Hell, would be as nothing compared to the retribution they would face from Tara and Rome. So I believe it is only I who stands in danger if there is any subterfuge arising from this matter.'

'I hope you are right, brother,' Fidelma said tartly. 'If there *is* such a plot, then you are staking my life on your interpretation of it!'

She found Eadulf in the palace library poring over a copy of the *Uraicecht Becc*, a tract on the status of individuals in society. She glanced over his shoulder and saw he was reading about the status of a *midach* or physician.

'You are not thinking of going back to complete your medical studies, are you?' she asked jokingly.

Eadulf looked up with a pensive expression. 'I could do worse. My few years studying at Tuam Brecain have stood us in good stead several times. However, I feel I should learn more.'

'You are thinking of the amputation of poor Dego's arm?' She was aware that this had been troubling him for some time.

Eadulf had indeed been thinking of that very matter. Dego, the warrior in question, had been so badly wounded that Eadulf had been forced to amputate his right arm in order to save the young man's life. Only what he had learned in his short study of the healing arts, his instinct and good luck, had saved the warrior. Ever since Eadulf had studied the healing arts, he had carried a *lés*, a physician's bag, and tried to maintain and extend his knowledge in such matters. He felt he should have been able to perform the task better. Now he answered his wife's question with a quick nod of assent.

'Well, Dego has made a miraculous recovery,' Fidelma assured him gently. 'He uses his left arm with as much dexterity as he used his right. He can ride and indulge in sword-play as well as any warrior with two good arms and hands.'

'That is due to his own ability and perseverance,' Eadulf replied, setting aside the ancient law text. 'Now, what was it that your brother wished to see you about? Did the messenger bring him some important news, as we thought? You said he bore the banner of the Uí Fidgente prince, and we both know that nothing good ever comes out of that people.'

'Come, walk with me and I will tell you.'

She had noticed a few people in the library regarding them with irritation at their conversation destroying the quiet. Outside, she led the way back towards their chambers and, by the time they reached them, she had told Eadulf the dreadful news of Ségdae's murder.

Eadulf was shocked by the death of the old abbot. Although Eadulf was an Angle and wore the tonsure of Rome's St Peter rather than the Irish tonsure of St John, Ségdae had always been a good friend and adviser to him. Indeed, it was Ségdae who had blessed the wedding of Eadulf and Fidelma.

After Eadulf had digested this news, Fidelma went on to tell him of her brother's request. Eadulf was not the best of horsemen and he preferred to avoid long journeys by horseback if possible. Therefore, his expression was momentarily forlorn as he contemplated the journey across the mountains; then he simply said: 'When do we leave?'

'As soon as I have had a word with Muirgen,' she replied. Muirgen was nurse to their son. 'I need to make arrangements for Alchú to be looked after while we are away.'

'At least we shouldn't be gone more than a few days,' Eadulf reflected. 'I must admit, since we were last in Dún Eochair Mháir and nearly met our untimely ends there, I did not think we would be returning quite so quickly.'

'This time we will be there at the invitation of the Uí Fidgente prince, so I doubt we shall be met with quite the same hostile reception,' Fidelma mused. 'But I agree with you that I do not feel at ease in that country either.'

'You say that only Enda will come as escort?'

'Colgú does not want to upset Prince Donennach by implying that we do not trust him.'

Eadulf said wryly, 'But we *don't* trust him, so why hide the fact?'

'Hiding one's real feelings is called diplomacy,' admonished Fidelma. 'Anyway, not all the Uí Fidgente are bad. Look at Conrí, the Uí Fidgente warlord.' They had shared several adventures with the tall warrior, who had become a friend. 'Come, Eadulf. Let us say our farewells to little Alchú and then join Enda who, I am told, is even now preparing our horses for the journey.'

The sun was nearly at its zenith on the day after they had left Cashel when Fidelma halted her grey-white pony, named Aonbharr after the magical horse of the Ocean God, Mannanán Mac Lir. Turning to her two companions with a satisfied smile, she announced, 'It's not far now. If I remember this track well, the fortress of the Prince of the Uí Fidgente is beyond those hills across the valley. We'll soon be there.'

The midday sun was warm. Glancing around at the scenery, Eadulf said: 'Perhaps there is a stream where we could stop awhile and take the opportunity of the *etsruth*?' The *etsruth*, sometimes called the middle meal, was the light snack taken when the sun was highest in the heavens.

Head to one side, Fidelma considered the suggestion. 'You are right. We don't want to arrive at the prince's fortress in a state of hunger and agitation. There must be a stream or spring down in the valley here. We'll stop the moment we find one.'

The day was not unduly hot for the time of year but the sky was blue with only a few fleece-like clouds scudding high above, and it was warm enough to wish for cooling water. They had been passing along the high track across the hills, which was intermittently encroached upon by trees and shrubs. Blackthorns formed a boundary to this stretch, while beyond were the straggling shapes of native pine, with areas of alder and hazel, giving way to glimpses of gorse and bracken. Beyond that were some cultivated areas of barley, the crop somewhat yellow and shrivelled after a cold, rainy spring. They saw areas where a lone farmer was cutting grass and trefoil ready to dry and stack as fodder, and once they encountered a couple of men sawing down a tree. Greetings were exchanged but the trio had not stopped in their westward progress.

As the trees began to thin out into more open countryside, Fidelma recognised the shape of the distant hills and knew they were approaching the southern territory of the Uí Fidgente. Across the valley and beyond the next hill and they would be in sight of the River Máigh and the bend on the river where rose Dún Eochair Mháigh, the fortress of the Prince of the Uí Fidgente.

Sounds from the nearby grasslands – the loud grating 'kerrx, kerrx' cry of the *traonach* or corncrake, startled Fidelma. She turned to watch it rise into the sky, red-brown, with its weak, floppy flight and dangling legs. Its cry reminded her of two rough sticks rubbing together. As her eyes followed the ungainly flight of the bird, they dropped to what she thought at first was an odd cluster of dark clouds around the top of a hill. She soon realised it was smoke.

Eadulf had spotted it as well. 'A farmer must have lit a bonfire atop that hill. It's an odd time to burn crops.' Then it occurred to him that no farmer would burn crops on a hilltop.

Enda chuckled. '*Breo telchae*,' he grunted.

Eadulf had not heard the term before and asked what it meant.

'It's a signal fire on a hill. But what it signals and to whom, I do not know.'

'The smoke seems to rise in regular little puffs,' Eadulf observed.

'Lady!' Enda's cry was a low warning. The young warrior moved forward slightly, his hand falling to his sword hilt as his eyes narrowed to focus down into the valley before them. 'A rider is coming this way at a gallop. He must have been hidden by those rocks below us.'

Fidelma and Eadulf peered down the long, low slope into the valley.

'It doesn't look like a warrior,' Eadulf said, screwing up his eyes.

'The rider is coming from the direction of Dún Eochair Mháige,' said Enda. 'Whoever it is, they are in a great hurry.'

'And certainly punishing that poor horse.' Fidelma disapproved. As a good horsewoman herself, she knew that forcing a horse to a gallop up a steep hill for no apparent reason was good for neither man nor beast. Why was the rider in such a desperate rush anyway? There were no signs of pursuit; no cause for him to punish the beast to such an extent.

They decided to halt and wait for the rider to come to them. They soon realised that it was a woman – no, more a young girl – crouching low over the neck of the beast.

'That girl seems familiar!' Eadulf exclaimed as the figure drew nearer.

'It's the friend of Aibell whom we met at Dún Eochair Mháigh,' confirmed Fidelma in surprise. 'What was her name?'

The girl was almost on top of them when she drew rein on her horse. It came to a halt, rearing back on its hind legs, lashing out with its forelegs before dropping back to the path on all fours, snorting and blowing from its exertions. The rider was little more than twenty years of age and her bare head was a mass of black hair; her skin fair and with pretty features which now seemed to be moulded into an expression of relief. Yet along with that relief was still something tense about her expression.

'God be thanked, lady!' she cried, moving her horse closer to Fidelma. 'One of the Uí Fidgente guards told me that the signal fire meant riders from the east were approaching. I was hoping it might be you. I wanted to intercept you before you reached the fortress.'

Fidelma glanced in astonishment at Eadulf before she replied, 'Why would you think it was me on this road – and why would you want to meet me before I arrived at the fortress?'

'I was instructed that I should do so.'

'By whom?'

'By Aibell, of course. We prayed that you would come, lady.'

Fidelma exchanged another quick look of surprise with Eadulf before turning back to the girl.

'I have no understanding of what you are saying. Aibell and you prayed that I would come – but why?'

'Have you not heard?' the girl almost shouted in her anxiety. 'Abbot Ségdae has been murdered.'

'I know – that is precisely why we are on the road to the fortress. What has this to do with Aibell?'

The girl gave a loud, sobbing gasp.

'Have they not told you? Do you not know who has been judged guilty of the abbot's murder?'

'No, I have not been told,' Fidelma responded quietly. A thought suddenly came to her. 'Are you saying that it was Aibell who killed Abbot Ségdae?'

'Of course it was not Aibell!' Had the girl not been on horseback, she would have doubtless stamped her foot. As it was she made an expressive movement with her arm. 'It is Gormán who has been found guilty,' she snapped. 'Gormán, the warrior who accompanied you to Dún Eochair Mháigh when we first met. It is Gormán who has been charged with the murder of Abbot Ségdae. Gormán whom they are going to execute.'

# CHAPTER TWO

They found a small spring by which to rest and water their horses, within the shelter of some woodland not far from the main track. Fidelma, after fighting to control her flood of questions following the shock of the girl Ciarnat's announcement, had managed to also calm the reactions of her companions and the near hysteria in which Ciarnat had given them the news. No more should be said, Fidelma insisted, until they had found a spot to relax and could hear the whole story from start to finish.

It did not take Enda long to find the rock pool, fed by a spring and protected on one side by a clump of hazels with their wide green leaves forming a natural windbreak. Most of the nuts had vanished, probably removed by mice, birds or perhaps even passing people, for the nuts had long been regarded as a delicacy as well as the ancient and mystical source of knowledge. This was a good spot because it also gave the travellers a view through the trees of the track across the valley towards their destination.

Their horses had to be attended to first; given water and something to graze upon. Only when that was done did they turn to their own needs. Fidelma handed the container of strong liquor that Enda carried to the still-shaking young girl. She took a long draught and it seemed to steady her nerves. They sat by the spring on convenient boulders and, by common consent, allowed Fidelma to start the questions that needed to be asked.

'Firstly, where is Gormán now and in what condition?' Fidelma tried to make her voice devoid of emotion but it shook slightly. Gormán was the only son of her friend Della, as well as having served in her brother's bodyguard for many years. The warrior had faced danger and hardship on many of her travels with Eadulf.

'He is imprisoned in Prince Donennach's fortress.' Ciarnat spoke with some hesitation as if first gathering her thoughts. Her mouth quivered but she was able to hold her feelings in check and to answer clearly. 'He is physically well and has not been ill-treated . . . well, perhaps a little when he was handled roughly on being taken a prisoner by the prince's guards. But the prince's judge, Brehon Faolchair, is a scrupulous man and I think it was he who advised the prince to send to Cashel to report matters before uttering sentence.'

Enda said angrily, 'Whoever he sent failed to tell us that the commander of the King's bodyguard was being held for murder.'

Ciarnat turned to the young warrior: 'He is innocent! He did not do it.'

'I could have told you that without knowing the details,' growled Enda, who had long admired his comrade and commander. 'We are warriors of the Golden Collar, sworn to the warrior's code, not murderers!'

Fidelma interrupted with a quick gesture of her hand. 'Ciarnat, I think we had better start from the beginning. You say that you were instructed by Aibell to come and greet us. What has Aibell to do with this matter? A few months ago, just after the feast day of Brigid, Aibell departed from Cashel. She did so at the same time as a young man called Deogaire – the nephew of old Brother Conchobhar, whose sister had married a man from Sliabh Luachra. Deogaire decided to return to the west, and Aibell left Gormán, who was in love with her. Perhaps it is at that point you should commence your story?'

The girl sat with bowed shoulders and gave a deep sigh. 'There is little in the telling,' she said quietly.

'Such as there is, let it be told,' advised Fidelma.

'As you know, my friend Aibell had reason to be grateful to Deogaire. He helped her escape from the evils of Sliabh Luachra where she had been sold into bondage by her own father. Perhaps because of that, she felt that she owed him something. Perhaps, for a while, she even thought that she was in love with him. But that was a false love, merely gratitude. She did not mean to harm Gormán.'

'What is meant and that which results are often opposite matters,' Eadulf observed dryly.

Fidelma stirred uncomfortably, remembering something of her own past relationship. Then she said: 'Go on.'

'What Aibell told me was that when you came back from the Land of the Uí Fidgente, bringing a resolution to her story, she was never happier. She was living at the farmstead of Gormán's mother, Della. Gormán and she grew close. Then Deogaire appeared at Cashel. She remembered what she owed him; that she would not be free and happy, had it not been for him. She also had a longing to visit her mother's home on the banks of the River Máigh. I think she wanted to see where she had been raised, to pay her respects to the shades of her mother. She also wanted to see me again as we had been the closest of friends when we were young. It was wonderful to renew that friendship. In addition, she planned to visit her uncle Marban.' Ciarnat paused, adding, 'It is hard to grow up with only distant memories and without truly knowing any members of one's own family. When Deogaire said he was going back to Sliabh Luachra – since Fidaig, the evil chieftain in whose house she had been in bondage, was dead – Aibell told me that she felt the urge to travel back with him.'

'Do you know if she had explained all this to Gormán?'

'She said tried, but, he was too angry to listen. He did not understand. He thought that she was going with Deogaire because she was in love with him.'

'And she was not?'

'No, she was not. She simply travelled in his company. When they arrived, they came to find me. As you know, I serve as an attendant in the fortress of Prince Donennach. I was so happy to see Aibell again. They then journeyed to the mill of her father's brother, Marban. She knew, from you, that Marban had killed her father. But she also knew that it was her father who was responsible for the ills suffered by her poor mother, Liamuin – that it was her own father who had sold her as a bondservant to the tyrant Fidaig of Sliabh Luachra. Aibell wanted to know something of her real history. It was only natural. Most of all, she wanted to see where her beloved mother was killed near Rath Menma.'

'Surely Gormán would have understood this if she had explained it to him?' Eadulf said, puzzled.

'She told me that she did not get beyond the fact that she intended to travel with Deogaire to Sliabh Luachra. Gormán refused to listen to the rest. He had made up his mind that she preferred Deogaire over him and closed his ears to her true reasons for leaving Cashel. She, in turn, became so angry that she did not bother to challenge him. So she left feeling furious and thought that she would take pleasure in punishing him for his arrogance.'

'Did you know that he was desperately unhappy when she left? He could not bear her absence, to the point that he asked permission from the king to set out after her?' Fidelma said.

The girl shook her head. 'She did not know then, but found out later. But I suppose that she had her pride, as did Gormán.'

'So are we saying that pride on both their parts caused his lack of communication between them? That it was all a misunderstanding?'

'Put like that, it sounds silly now, but—'

'It is not uncommon,' Eadulf observed. 'Many of the disputes between men and women begin the same way. Misunderstanding followed by pride. Lacking the ability to climb down and admit to one's own faults. Each one seeking to hurt the other in retaliation for his or her own hurt.'

Fidelma made a familiar impatient gesture with her hand. 'So she left with Deogaire. We know that Gormán decided to follow her. You said that she found out about Gormán later. I presume that means that they must have met up with one another?'

Ciarnat smiled brightly and nodded. 'Yes, they did. Aibell and Deogaire set out for Marban's mill, and none was more surprised than I when, nine days ago, Aibell and Gormán arrived at the fortress of Prince Donennach, reunited and happy in each other's company.'

'Did she tell you how this came about?' Fidelma queried.

'Aibell told me that she arrived at Marban's mill in safety. The old man was pleased to see her and had a lot of stories to tell about her mother, Liamuin, and her family and that of her father, Escmug. I understand that most of it confirmed what you had told her when you returned to Cashel.'

'So she stayed with her uncle. What happened to Deogaire?'

'He left her to travel on to his own home in the mountain fastness of Sliabh Luachra.'

'Was it at Marban's mill that Gormán caught up with her?' prompted Fidelma.

'Aibell told me that one day, Gormán came riding up to the mill,' Ciarnat said. 'Aibell was beside herself with joy. When I saw them together, I could see that the hurt and anguish between them was soon mended.'

'Then why did they not return to Cashel?' intervened Enda.

'Simple enough. They were married.'

'Aibell and Gormán are married!' exclaimed Eadulf.

The girl glanced at him defiantly. 'Was there any reason why they should not be?'

'Except that Della, Gormán's mother, and his close friends and comrades would have liked to have been there to wish him well,' Enda said crossly. 'It is unlike Gormán to ignore his family and friends.'

Fidelma found herself in agreement with him. 'Gormán is Della's only son,' she added gently. 'It is unusual.'

Ciarnat nodded slowly. 'I do not think that Aibell and Gormán made their decision lightly. Yet Aibell felt it right and Gormán has a great heart and believes deeply in the spirit of place.'

'I am not sure what you mean.' Eadulf was trying to understand. 'Marriage is marriage. What has spirit of place to do with it?'

'They decided to go up to Rath Menma, where Aibell's mother, Liamuin, hid for a while and then met her death. Old Marban went with them to show the way – although, of course, Gormán had also accompanied you there when you went to investigate. They found the farmer and his wife, the old couple, Cadan and Flannair, whom you met. They even found the half-crazy woman, Suanach, who had witnessed Aibell's mother being killed. The couple sought a local Brehon, and it was there in the ruins of Rath Menma, before those witnesses, that they were joined. I am sure Aibell's mother in the Otherworld looked down and gave her blessing.'

Ciarnat's eyes were unusually bright with emotion as she recounted this. After a moment's pause she continued: 'Aibell told me that they had spent some time exploring the territory of her ancestry. Finally Gormán announced that they must return to Cashel. He had his duties to fulfil with King Colgú and Aibell wanted to start a new life as his wife to help his mother, Della. Gormán also felt they should receive a blessing at the chapel in Cashel in front of his mother and his friends. He hoped that they would understand why the ceremony at Rath Menma had been so important.'

There was a short meditative silence before Eadulf asked: 'How did things go wrong? How is it that Gormán is now claimed to be guilty of Abbot Ségdae's murder – and what is Aibell's role in this?'

Ciarnat took a deep breath. 'It was after they left Rath Menma that they encountered some merchants on the road and heard some news from them which was apparently so disturbing to Gormán that he decided to head for the fortress of Prince Donennach to warn him before he journeyed on to Cashel.'

'To warn him of what?' Fidelma asked. 'What news was it that so disturbed him?'

'He was told that someone called Gláed was leading the hordes of Sliabh Luachra and intent on vengeance.'

'But that's not possible!' Eadulf objected. 'When the judgements at the Abbey of Mungairit were announced, Gláed of Sliabh Luchra was given into the keeping of his brother Artgal to be taken back to his people for trial and punishment for murdering their father Fidaig, who had been chieftain of Sliabh Luachra.'

'The merchants told Gormán that Gláed had escaped, murdered his brother Artgal and had declared himself chieftain of Sliabh Luachra.'

Fidelma sat back, staring at the girl in incredulity. When she had issued her judgements at the Abbey of Mungairit, after her investigation into the attempted assassination of her brother, King Colgú, she had also found that Gláed, son of Fidaig, was involved in conspiracy; the blood of many was on his hands. She had indeed handed him over to his own brother, Artgal, the new chieftain, who had promised to take him back for trial by his own people.

Eadulf's features were unusually pale. 'The fourth shock in two days,' he said. 'Ségdae dead, Gormán deemed guilty, Aibell and Gormán married and now Gláed is loose in Sliabh Luachra and claiming to be chieftain of those people.'

'Worse still, the merchants said that Gláed was raising a band to raid the territory of the Uí Fidgente in order to exact revenge.'

'The dwellers of Sliabh Luachra have been thieves and robbers since time began,' Enda interrupted in disgust. 'Gláed's father was a thief and murderer – and now Gláed has excelled him by killing him and now his brother, Artgal. They are all vile murderers and brigands.'

'That is true,' Eadulf agreed slowly. 'However, Gláed was in league with Lorcán, the son of Uí Fidgente Prince Eóghanán, who met his death on Cnoc Áine. It was thought Lorcán died alongside his father. He did not. Lorcán was a cruel and ruthless man. He killed his own twin brother, Brother Lugna, to take his place and hide in the Abbey at Mungairit while trying to organise the overthrow and death of his cousin Prince Donennach who brought peace to the Uí Fidgente. Gláed was an essential part of that conspiracy.'

'But didn't you and the lady Fidelma uncover this Lorcán – and wasn't he handed over to be incarcerated in Prince Donennach's fortress to await judgement?' Enda asked. 'If Gláed escaped judgement, do not tell me that Lorcán has also escaped!'

There was some relief when Ciarnat made a negative gesture.

'He did try to escape from the fortress – with the help of sympathisers. But the guards, those loyal to Prince Donennach, were on the alert, and he was mortally wounded in the attempt. He died within a week in spite of the best efforts of our physician.'

Fidelma was regarding Ciarnat with some concern. 'What else did Gormán learn about Gláed? Is he really being accepted by the people who once supported his father and brother?'

'Gormán was told by the merchants that many had come to accept Gláed, there being no other leader among them to stand against him. Apart from that, there were rumours going round that Gláed had vowed vengeance against all those who had failed to support him.'

'So, having gained this information, Gormán determined to deliver it to Prince Donennach. What then?'

'As I said, they arrived at Dún Eochair Mháigh.'

'And that was nine days ago?' Eadulf queried.

'Yes. They had left Marban at his mill and came to the fortress.'

'Nine days . . .?' Fidelma was beyond surprise after the many revelations she had heard. 'That is a long time in the circumstances. So they arrived at the prince's fortress. How did Prince Donennach react at the news?'

'Apparently, the prince was dismissive. He felt that he could not consider Gláed as a threat, or not as a serious one, and that to him, the people of that mountain fastness were just ill-bred robbers without leadership. He said that if he ever found out they were raiding outside of the mountain lairs, then he would take a band of his warriors and punish them.'

Enda was nodding his head. 'I think that was probably a reasonable assessment, lady. Based on all I have heard of them, they have always been thieves and cut-throats and would be no match for even one company of trained warriors.'

Eadulf did not look convinced. 'It was a different story when we unravelled the mystery at Mungairit Abbey. Thieves they might be, but they can also supply fighting men,' he commented dryly.

'So what happened next?' Fidelma urged.

'Abbot Ségdae of Imleach and his party had arrived to take part in some council.'

'Do you know the reason for this council?' Fidelma asked. It was unusual for the chief religious adviser to the Eóghanacht Kings of Muman to visit Uí Fidgente. The latter did not recognise the Eóghanacht as legitimate Kings of Muman, let alone bow to the authority of the Abbey of Imleach and its abbot.

Ciarnat shook her head. 'I know nothing of these matters, lady. All I do know was that some council had been arranged between Abbot Ségdae and Abbot Nannid of Mungairit. I was not interested, but when Gormán learned of the presence of Abbot Ségdae he went to see him.'

'Is our old antagonist, Abbot Nannid, at the fortress?' Eadulf queried in surprise.

The girl nodded and went on: 'They say that Gormán was in an angry mood about the reaction to the news he brought. He arrived at the abbot's guest-chamber, there was an argument and they say he killed him.'

'You were in the fortress at the time?'

'No, I was in the township with my mother.'

'Then tell the story as it was told to you.'

'I heard it from Aibell a day or two later. She and Gormán had been allocated a room in the hostel for warriors. Gormán had gone to see the abbot, it being evening. Aibell had fallen asleep when suddenly she was aroused by a great disturbance. The door crashed open, men came in shouting. As she struggled awake, the guards started to drag her out of bed. She didn't know what was happening. They threw her in a cold, dark cell. She was not taken out until morning when the guards manhandled her before Brehon Faolchair, Prince Donennach's judge, who started to question her. She told me that she did not understand any of his questions at the time. It was only later that she understood, and perhaps she should be thankful because her ignorance and stupidity in answering finally convinced them that she knew nothing of what had happened and was innocent of any complicity.'

They waited as Ciarnat paused again, glancing from one to another as if seeking permission to continue.

'And did you discover what had happened?' pressed Fidelma.

Ciarnat took a deep breath before resuming her story. 'We knew nothing until Brehon Faolchair convened the hearing and the details were revealed. Aibell had not even been allowed to see Gormán before then.'

'You attended the hearing? So what was the evidence presented?'

'According to the abbot's steward, Brother Tuamán, Gormán had arrived at the abbot's chamber in an angry mood. The steward left the chamber, to give the two men some privacy. A little while later, he heard a cry from the abbot's chamber and some sound of upheaval. He rushed to the door but it had been locked. He called one of the guards and together they broke in and found the abbot lying dead on the floor. He had been stabbed twice in the chest. By the abbot's side lay his staff of office. Just in front of his body, Gormán also lay on the floor, as if he were just recovering consciousness. There was a knife, still bloodied, in his hand. A point made by Brother Tuamán was that the door of the chamber had been locked on the inside. There was no other entrance or exit than a high window. So the only means of ingress and exit was the door by which the abbot's steward and the guard had entered. It was immediately concluded that Gormán had attacked and stabbed Abbot Ségdae.'

'I presume that the guard confirmed the steward's account?'

'He did. It was argued that the abbot, having been stabbed once by Gormán, managed to strike him a blow with his staff, catching him on the side of the head. Gormán was able to stab him again, fatally, before falling unconscious from his own wound. The steward said that only a short space of time had elapsed since the cry, the noise and his trying to force the door.'

Fidelma exchanged a grim glance with Eadulf. 'From the account that you give, the matter looks very bad for Gormán. You say that there was no other way in or out of the chamber?'

'That was the telling point. However, Aibell is sure that he could not have murdered the abbot, lady. That is why she instructed me to come and meet you and tell you these things before you reached the prince's fortress,' the girl declared fervently.

Fidelma laid a comforting hand on her arm. 'If he did not do it, then we shall do everything in our power to discover who did. How did Gormán defend himself before the Brehon?'

'He told Brehon Faolchair that he had been in the abbot's chamber, speaking normally with him, when he felt a blow on the back of his head. It is true that his head had a bruise and some swelling on the right side. When he recovered consciousness, the abbot's steward and one of the prince's guards were bending over him. The abbot was dead and Gormán was being accused of killing him. He could not explain the bloody knife in his hand.'

'Let me be clear,' Fidelma said. 'You say Gormán had a bruise and a cut on the right side of his head and yet he claimed he was struck from behind, on the *back* of the head. Is that so?'

Ciarnat nodded quickly. 'Brehon Faolchair made much of that. The blow, he argued, was consistent with the abbot striking him as he was attacked. It was *not* consistent with some unknown assailant having hidden himself in the chamber, creeping up behind him and knocking Gormán unconscious before killing the abbot. Ségdae would surely have warned Gormán if someone was behind him before the blow was struck.'

'It is a logical argument,' Fidelma conceded.

'But he is innocent,' the girl replied doggedly.

'Belief is not evidence,' Fidelma told her.

'I was denied the chance to give evidence on his behalf.'

'What evidence would you have given?' Fidelma wanted to know 'You were not a witness.'

'The guard who took food to Gormán's cell passed on a message from him to Aibell. The message said he was innocent and that he was knocked unconscious and only came to his senses after the murder. He did say one thing which was curious. Apparently, while he was talking to the abbot, the abbot suddenly looked at the table where there were some papers and said, "Oh yes, you will be wanting these." It was at that moment that he felt the blow on his head.'

'That is not evidence,' Fidelma said after a moment's thought. 'I am afraid Brehon Faolchair was quite right. That is merely repeating what Gormán told someone, who then told you. Anyway, the *Berrad Airechta* states that reporting something which is heard from someone else is automatically excluded from evidence. Did Gormán state this at the hearing?'

'He did – but said he had no idea what the abbot meant. Brehon

Faolchair didn't let Aibell and me testify for Gormán at all,' protested the girl.

'I am afraid that is also right, for Aibell's relationship to Gormán, and the fact that you are her friend, places you both as an *anteist* or untrustworthy witnesses,' Fidelma explained. 'As a wife it would be seen that Aibell would naturally wish to protect her husband. You are her friend. Therefore, neither of you could be trusted to be impartial when giving evidence. In addition, your "evidence" would merely be repetition, since the facts had already been made known.' Almost as an afterthought, she added: 'Gormán said he did not know what the abbot meant about wanting something among his papers?'

'That's right. He had no idea what it was that the abbot felt he should want. There were some papers on the desk but they had not been referred to before.'

Fidelma thought for a moment and then said, 'Brehon Faolchair found Gormán guilty of the killing?'

'Both the steward and the guard had taken oath that there was no way anyone else could have entered or left the room. Brehon Faolchair pronounced, on the evidence that he had heard, there was no other explanation than that Gormán was guilty of the crime.'

'What was suggested as to a motive?' asked Eadulf, winning a quick glance of approval from Fidelma.

Ciarnat shook her head. 'No one could supply a reason why Gormán should attack and kill the abbot. According to Brother Tuamán, the abbot's steward, Gormán had arrived in a bad mood – but that is no motive for murder.'

Fidelma pursed her lips thoughtfully. 'That certainly is the weak point in this matter. It just doesn't make sense.'

'They will not dare to execute him, will they, lady?' The girl began to sob, overcome by emotion again.

Fidelma compressed her lips into a thin line. She was determined to prevent this; it was all she had been thinking about since she had heard of the situation from this young woman.

'Do you know how the threat of execution arose?' she asked.

The girl tried to explain between sniffs. 'Abbot Nannid, who is the senior abbot and bishop of the Uí Fidgente, as you know, is the main advocate of these new rules of the Faith. Now many of our bishops and abbots have adopted them.'

'Abbot Nannid of Mungairit!' Eadulf exclaimed the name bitterly. 'He must have changed his views since last we parted from him. I did not think he was so strong an advocate for these new so-called Penitential rules.'

The girl looked puzzled but Fidelma felt that now was not the time to explain.

'Do you know why Abbot Nannid is arguing for punishment under the Penitentials and not under the law of the Brehons?' she asked.

'I heard him say that it is because Ségdae was an abbot and bishop of the Faith. Abbot Nannid claims that the murderer must suffer punishment as prescribed by the Faith.'

'You say these events happened about nine days ago, so why was there such a delay between the killing of Abbot Ségdae and Prince Donennach informing us at Cashel?'

The girl did not understand, so Eadulf rephrased the question. 'Many days have passed between the murder and Cashel being informed of the death of the abbot,' he said.

Ciarnat gave an expressive gesture with one shoulder, letting it rise and fall. 'I assume that Prince Donennach waited until the hearing was conducted by Brehon Faolchair and the confirmation of his decision that Gormán was responsible. That was four days ago. Then a messenger was immediately sent to Imleach and then to Cashel. As I said, Aibell knew of your reputation and we were hoping Cashel would send you to save Gormán.'

'The verdict has already been pronounced,' Fidelma said sombrely.

'But not the sentence,' replied Ciarnat, wiping her eyes. 'Aibell and Gormán believe that you can prevent this as it is our laws which must judge him, not these new foreign ideas.'

'And you have been waiting on this road hoping to intercept us?' Eadulf was curious. 'That was taking a chance.'

The girl shrugged again. 'Aibell and I reasoned that if you rode from Cashel soon after the prince's messenger reached there, it would likely be some time this morning that you would be coming along this road. There is no other direct route from Cashel. Therefore, this morning, one of the fortress guards showed me the signal fire and what it meant, and I rode out to wait for you.'

'What *was* the meaning of the signal fire?' queried Eadulf.

In response, the girl pointed to a distant hill behind them. Wisps of smoke still hung over it. Before she could speak, Enda gave a groan of self-recrimination.

'Of course! The signal fire was lit to announce our entry into the Uí Fidgente territory. I should have realised that.'

Eadulf glanced to where the smoke was still drifting on the high wind. 'It is slightly unnerving to know that we are being watched from afar.'

'The *teine caismberta*, or signal fires, are as old as the time people first sought to defend themselves,' Enda told them, standing up and collecting the remains of the meal and the utensils. 'Since the fortress knows of our approach, perhaps we should move on now?'

The hint was not lost on Fidelma. 'I am surprised that no warriors have already come to escort us to the prince's fortress,' she said.

'You are right – and I have tarried long enough,' the girl muttered, getting hurriedly to her feet and moving towards her horse. 'Do not say I have met with you, lady. There is much evil at Dún Eochair Mháigh. I will make my way back by another route. All Aibell wanted, without being overheard, was to warn you of this evil. Look for untruth in the answers to your questions, believe only what you see . . . or perhaps it is better to believe only half of what you see.'

Then she had mounted and moving off at a rapid trot through the trees at right angles to the track.

Eadulf gave a cynical laugh. 'Curious, eh? A warning of what we shall encounter.'

Enda had become suddenly still, looking down the sloping track into the valley, towards the hills beyond which was their destination.

'What we are about to encounter is half-a-dozen warriors,' he said without raising his voice.

They looked at him in astonishment for a moment before turning to follow the direction of his gaze.

Coming along the track from the direction of Dún Eochair Mháigh was a group of six horsemen, riding two abreast, their shields and armaments not only proclaiming them as warriors but bearing the wolf insignia of the Uí Fidgente. One of the two leading riders carried aloft a banner of red silk with the image of a ravening wolf on it.

Enda started to move towards his horse, his hand slipping to his sword hilt and easing it to ensure it was loose.

'Remember, these are not hostile warriors, Enda,' Fidelma said hurriedly. 'From that insignia they wear, they are warriors of Prince Donennach's household. We are in their territory by invitation of their prince. So let us show no signs of hostility or reveal our anxiety.'

Enda stopped still. 'As you please, lady,' he said almost sulkily.

'I would continue to pack away the remains of our midday meal and behave as naturally as you would when strangers meet on the highway,' Fidelma added.

The column of warriors approached the group easily without any sign of aggressive intent and came to a halt before them.

'Well, well,' greeted their leader with a loud bellow of laughter as he sprang from his horse. 'You are once more welcome in my country, lady, and you too, friend Eadulf of Seaxmund's Ham. I confess though, in all our encounters, I just wish the circumstances were more pleasant but Fate, it seems, always designs our meetings at times of crisis between our peoples.'

The speaker removed his burnished silver war helmet and gazed at them with a broad smile on his face.

Fidelma returned the smile of their old acquaintance. 'I should have known that Conrí, the King of Wolves, warlord of the Uí Fidgente, would be among the first to come and escort us to the fortress of Prince Donennach,' she greeted him courteously.

# CHAPTER THREE

T he warrior carrying the red silk banner turned out to be
Socht, the warlord Conrí's comrade in arms. After the greetings
and introductions, for Enda had encountered neither Conrí nor Socht
before, it was decided not to waste any more time but to set off
immediately for Prince Donennach's fortress. Fidelma rode alongside Conrí at the head of the column, with Eadulf and Socht behind
them. After them came Enda and one of Conrí's men, with the rest
of the horsemen following two abreast.

Fidelma immediately began to question the warlord as Conrí
obviously expected her to do.

'Do you know any details of this terrible affair?' she asked.

'None that I was not told, lady,' he confessed. 'I was not at the
fortress when it happened, so I only know what others have passed
on to me. I came to the fortress because I received a message from
Prince Donennach to say that Gormán had arrived to warn him
about Gláed. It seems that Gláed had somehow escaped from the
custody of his brother, Artgal, had killed him and set himself up
as head of that band of thieves and cut-throats who dwell in the
fastness of Sliabh Luachra.'

'The message did not mention that Gormán was charged with
the killing of the Abbot of Imleach?'

Conrí shook his head. 'No. I was at my own fortress at the Ford of Oaks and knew nothing of that until the next day when I arrived at Dún Eochair Mháigh. It was then I heard that Abbot Ségdae had been stabbed to death the previous evening and that Gormán stood accused. I found it impossible to believe that he did it! I knew from previous encounters that Gormán honours the warriors' code. He would never strike down an unarmed man – let alone a churchman. Yet, lady, I sat through the Brehon's hearing and heard the facts presented. One cannot argue with facts, it seems.'

'Although one *can* argue with the interpretation of the facts,' Fidelma pointed out swiftly.

'It would take a sharper mind than I possess to see how they could be interpreted in any other way,' the warlord observed. 'Anyway, I have tried my best to help in the circumstances. I listened closely to Gormán's defence. I felt sympathy for his young wife.'

'So there is little that you can tell me from your own knowledge of the details of the killing?'

'Nothing at all.'

'I gather the murder was uncovered by the abbot's steward and by a guard of the household. Do you know him? Is he a reliable witness?'

'Certainly. His name is Lachtna, and he has served in Prince Donennach's personal guard for over a year or so. He is a good man in battle but has to be directed, if you understand my meaning. He is not imaginative and sees everything in terms of black and white. To him, the bottle is half empty. It is not half full.'

Fidelma sighed. 'Such people often make the best witnesses for they do not let imagination interfere with what they see, nor do they speculate with interpretation.'

'That makes it more awkward for Gormán,' Conrí acknowledged.

'The task is to discover the truth, however unpalatable. And what about Abbot Ségdae's steward, Brother Tuamán? He was newly appointed and I have only seen him at a distance. Did you form an opinion about him?'

Conrí managed a grin. 'I saw him at the Brehon's hearing, and to me, he seems to be following the wrong calling. He is taller than I am and has the build of a warrior, being strong and muscular. However, I would say he possesses the fault of vanity.'

'Vanity?'

'Yes. He is full of his own importance.'

'I suppose a man who becomes steward of the Abbey of Imleach has earned some degree of status,' Fidelma conceded. 'So, you have formed no opinion on the abbot's death other than listening to the facts that were presented to the Brehon?'

'As I said, lady, the facts were such that I could not see a way of contending with them. Even Gormán offered no real defence or explanation other than stating that he did not do it. If I had not known Gormán before this, I would have said that there was no question of his guilt.'

'But you are uneasy?'

'It is not only because the man I knew would not be capable of such a crime against an unarmed cleric. There is something else.'

'What is it?'

'Something that you taught me, lady. You once said, find a motive and you will usually find a culprit. There seems no motive here.'

'*Cui bono*?' Fidelma mused.

'Pardon, lady?'

'It is something a Roman lawyer named Cicero once said. "To whom is the benefit?" And you are right. What gain was there for Gormán in killing the abbot? Abbot Ségdae was known to him as a friend and mentor, as he was a friend and mentor for many of us at Cashel. Also, Gormán had come there by chance to warn the prince about Gláed.'

'I heard that he was in an ill temper when he went to see the abbot.'

'Why would that be?'

'There was some gossip suggesting that his warning about Gláed was not taken seriously by Prince Donennach, and that Gormán went to complain about this to the abbot. It was strange, because the prince had already sent for me.'

'So Prince Donennach *did* take the warning seriously . . . What has been done about Gláed?' Fidelma asked.

'Prince Donennach's intention was for me to lead a punitive raid into Sliabh Luachra to see if we could capture Gláed and discourage his followers. My opinion was that Gláed, having killed his own father, Fidaig, and then his own brother, Artgal, would be at the mercy of many of his own people who would be inclined to join us against him. They might be concerned about who Gláed would turn on next.'

'What happened about this raid?'

'That matter was delayed while Donennach deals with this greater threat and attempts to resolve it. I merely posted sentinels along the western routes to ensure we had warning of any hostile movement from Gláed.'

'You call it the "greater threat"?' Eadulf put in.

'The growing insistence of the Uí Fidgente clerics, led by our old acquaintance, Abbot Nannid, demands that Gormán should be punished by execution under their Penitential rules,' the warlord told him bleakly.

'But Gormán was not tried by an ecclesiastical court of the abbot and bishops of the Uí Fidgente,' Fidelma objected. 'And the crime actually happened in the fortress of the prince whose Brehon has heard the matter. Irrespective of guilt or innocence, the Brehon and the prince are representatives of the law of this kingdom, of all the Five Kingdoms, and the law of the Brehons is still the law.'

'That is true,' nodded Conrí, 'but Nannid has many followers and he is now a great advocate of the Penitentials.'

'Are you saying that he is powerful enough to even dictate law to the prince's Brehon?' Fidelma asked, shocked. 'Surely Donennach supports his Brehon? The judgements and punishments given by him must be in obedience to the Council of Brehons of Muman, submissive to the kingdom and also to the entire Five Kingdoms under the Chief Brehon of the High King.'

Conrí's expression was one of resignation. 'When I said the "greater threat", I meant it. You know our diverging history, lady. The Eóghanacht of Cashel and the Uí Fidgente do not always see the world from the same mountain top.'

'We have recently concluded a peace between us – an amicable peace – and have re-entered a community of spirit in one ancient kingdom,' she reminded him.

'Except that such a matter as this may well turn into another crossroads where our paths may once more diverge.'

'That they must not do,' Fidelma said.

'I'll put it bluntly, lady,' returned Conrí. 'Our clergy knows your brother vehemently opposes the growing influence of these Pententials. That is the very reason why Abbot Nannid is demanding these ecclesiastical punishments.'

'But Abbot Ségdae was a foremost advocate for keeping to our native laws. He would never have condoned the use of these Penitentials to replace the laws of our kingdom!'

'That is not Abbot Nannid's logic,' Conrí said. 'The situation is thus: Prince Donennach finds himself sitting on a knife-edge. You, above all people, will know just how fragile is the peace between our people. A word out of place, a jibe, a threat – and all may be blown away like a house of straw. If Donennach defies his clergy he may face another attempt to oust him as ruler of the Uí Fidgente or, at best, face an internal war among us. If he accepts the demands of Abbot Nannid, then he risks war with Cashel and even retribution from the High King. Either way, there will be bloodshed.'

Fidelma's mouth tightened at his words. 'I am well aware of what is at stake here,' she said. 'Abbot Nannid doubtless still chafes at being rebuked for the conspiracy we discovered at his Abbey of Mungairit, even though he was not directly involved.'

'He may well feel resentment, but proving that is his sole purpose in demanding the death of Gormán would be difficult. Even before this happened he has spoken out in support of these new rules of the Faith.'

'It might be difficult to demonstrate any personal vengeance in him but he certainly would not be squeamish about applying the new rules of punishment on one he sees as an enemy, if it furthers his cause.'

'There is also a whisper among Abbot Nannid's followers that Abbot Ségdae's successor, at Imleach may not be too rigorous a supporter of the old laws,' Conrí added.

'Have you met the Prior of Imleach?'

'I have. I suppose you would describe him as a scholarly man of middling years. He does not appear to be a strong man, either physically or in personality. Frankly, he did not make much of an impression on me. But then, who am I to judge?'

'I wondered if you had discovered anything about his background. He is newly appointed to office and I do not know him,' Fidelma explained.

Conrí shook his head. 'Like you, lady, I know little of him and you will have to judge for yourself. Doubtless you will meet him tonight as the prince expects everyone to attend the traditional welcome feast. You have accommodation in the personal guestrooms of the prince as befits your rank.'

'Where is the delegation from Imleach accommodated then?'

'They are in a guest-house within the fortress grounds. It was where the murder took place.'

'And Abbot Nannid and his party?'

'Abbot Nannid has decided to quarter himself in the Abbey of Nechta.'

'Where is that?' Fidelma had not heard of such an abbey before.

Conrí actually smiled. 'There was a small religious community in the township. It was part of the township but is now enclosed behind newly erected walls. Abbey Nannid has used his authority to call it an abbey.'

Fidelma let out a long breath. 'Often, Conrí, I feel that life is just one long game of *fidchell* in which we are forced to move our pieces on the boardgame of life – not as we would wish to, but only as is dictated to us by the events.'

'That may well be, lady. But you must admit that there is only one important event which dictates this particular game.'

'The murder of Abbot Ségdae?'

'Indeed. However we come to that event, come to it we must,' the warlord said solemnly.

They rode on in silence, crossing a few hills before coming into more gently sloping lands, descending towards the river plain. There were cultivated fields with crops of barley not quite ripe for harvesting next to fenced fields in which rusty red and white cows were grazing – long-backed 'bald cows' as they were called because of the distinctive mound on the head. Such cows did not grow horns like other breeds. Conrí noticed her looking at them.

'That's part of Prince Donennach's own herd,' he told her. 'Good for beef as well as milking.'

They skirted an area of stony ground, identified by Conrí as An Clocher, the Place of Stone. On some of the heights Fidelma could glimpse the dark figures of sentinels keeping watch on the approaches to the fortress. The road led over a small rise and below them lay the river's bend, along which the principal trading settlement of the Uí Fidgente stretched. Dominating all, set atop a prominent hill above the river, stood Dún Eochair Mháigh – the Fortress at the Bend of the River.

Once again, Fidelma found herself thinking, as she had when she had first seen it, that the fortress of Prince Donennach of the Uí Fidgente was surprisingly small and drab for a ruler who claimed an ancestry greater and richer than the Eóghanacht. There was nothing particularly awe-inspiring about the dreary, grey stone stronghold towering above the eastern bank of the river. Fidelma had seen better hill forts raised by local chieftains guarding many small farming communities. However, the buildings were spread in fairly extensive grounds and fortifications.

On the previous occasion of her visit with Eadulf, they had approached the fortress from the western bank and crossed over by a newly constructed wooden bridge. The township, which lay before the main gates, had been busy then as it was now. Many boats were moored along the River Maigh. The township was a trading centre for the merchants who plied their boats along the river. The waters rose in the hills to the south then pushed their way northwards, passing the Ford of the Oaks where they became tidal yet continued to drive on towards the great sea inlet not far from the Abbey of Mungairit.

Now, approaching from the east, the party followed the path down the hill into the sprawl of buildings surrounding the market square. The banks of the river were edged with wooden quays a-throng with wagons filled with produce brought by the river vessels. These would eventually be driven to other inland settlements. There were several blacksmiths at work; the stables were full and business was good. The township was crowded but, if Fidelma's memory was correct, not unduly so. Most people did not give them a second glance although one or two – and she noticed that these were mainly in the robes of religious – did halt and stare at them as they rode by.

What caught her particular attention was the newly constructed wooden walls erected along the southern side of the market square – almost as if in confrontation with the fortress on the hill opposite. She frowned. The last time they were in this township, this area had just consisted of a number of homesteads built close to the local chapel.

The inhabitants of these homesteads were all devoted followers of the New Faith and had formed their own small community. These men and women, with their children, worked at their own trades but supported the chapel that was regarded as their centre. The area had once been an integral part of the township itself, but now, as Conrí had said, they were separated by walls rising to the height of two tall men standing upon each other's shoulders.

'Is this what you meant by the Abbey of Nechta?' Fidelma commented to Conrí.

The warlord glanced at the wooden walls and closed central gate before saying, 'It is, lady. The walls have been set up in recent months, at the order of Abbot Nannid. The community takes the name of Nechta as she was the mother of the Blessed Ita, who had brought the New Faith to this area a century ago.'

'He ordered them to build the walls? I suppose Abbot Nannid has jurisdiction over the people of the Faith in this area?'

'That he does, but he is not a person who endears himself to the local people – religious or otherwise.'

Without further comment, Conrí led the way from the square up the broad sloping track in the direction of the fortress gates, which now stood wide open. Just before the gates, on the left-hand side of the track, loomed a tall pillar stone on which some writing in the ancient form of Ogham was inscribed. It was a simple text announcing the place to be 'the king's house' – and Fidelma was again reminded of the Uí Fidgente's long claim to the kingship of Muman. As in her previous visit, she was aware of the watchful sentinels on the walls, and she also noticed two warriors on guard at the gate. Conrí's red silk standard brought a respectful salute, and the warriors moved aside as they entered. Stable lads were already running forward to take their horses as they halted in the main courtyard.

Conrí dismissed his men to the charge of Socht as two male servants approached to take the *setan* or saddlebags from Fidelma and Eadulf and, of course, the *lés*, or medicine bag, that Eadulf had become accustomed to carrying with him everywhere he went.

'Prince Donennach will officially greet you at the evening meal,' Conrí explained. 'The *fothrucad*, the baths, will be prepared, and you must rest from your wearisome journey. These attendants will conduct you to your chambers. We shall all gather in the great hall when you hear the striking of four bells.'

Eadulf had learned by now that it was customary for people to bathe daily and generally in the evening. Cleansing was a ritual, and even for travellers arriving in such extreme circumstances, it was against all protocol not to go through the ritual before meeting the prince. There were baths for visitors in every guest-house of a palace, abbey or even a tavern.

Conrí turned with a friendly smile to Enda. 'I will show you to the *laochtech*, the house of the warriors, where we have our quarters. There you may also refresh yourself and rest.'

But Fidelma was still lingering. 'It might be advisable for me to speak immediately with Gormán, before I go to my chamber,' she said.

Conrí glanced at her in disapproval. 'Lady, even in these circumstances, the protocols must be observed and respected. Having arrived in the prince's palace as his guest, you and Eadulf must first bathe and then meet with him to discuss matters. Afterwards, Gormán may have your full attention.'

Fidelma knew that to behave in any other fashion would have been a slight against the honour of the prince. When she expressed her acceptance of the situation, the warlord relaxed.

'Excellent. Follow these attendants and they will show you the way to your quarters. Having been here before, I think you will find the surroundings familiar. I will be attending in the great hall when the bell rings for the feasting.'

As Fidelma and Eadulf followed the attendants into the main palace complex, Eadulf shivered slightly. It was not so long ago that they had been under this very roof, little realising that their host at the time was one of the conspirators who, had he known what they were about, could easily have had them killed. They walked across the same great hall, made more impressive on its inside than the outside walls. Huge tapestries covered the walls, and around the lower parts hung shields bearing the symbols of their owners who had once used them in battle. Swords of many varieties were displayed along with the shields; some were ornate and bejewelled, indicating the wealth of their owners.

At the end of the hall was the prince's chair of office, an elaborately carved piece of oak with the icons of the Uí Fidgente inscribed on it. It was placed on a small raised platform overlooking a long oak table. Next to it, at a slightly lower level, was a smaller chair – presumably for the heir-apparent of the prince. The table was the very one where they had once dined under the watchful eye of the renegade steward, Cuána.

It was amusing to find they were being led to the same guest chamber that they had occupied at the time of their first visit. This was where the young attendant, Ciarnalt, had warned them of the steward's treacherous nature.

The attendants laid down the visitors' bags in the chamber and the elder of the two, a gentle-looking man with white hair and sharp blue eyes, bowed and announced, 'I shall order water to be heated and the *dabach* filled for your pleasure. One of the females will attend you, lady, with soap, scents and linen towels.'

The *dabach* was a large tub or vat-like affair in which heated water was poured and into which bathers could climb. There, with the aid of *sleic*, or soap, they would cleanse themselves ready for the evening meal.

'We have a separate facility for you, brother,' the man added to Eadulf. 'You will be called when all is ready. Is there anything else that you require in the meantime?'

There was nothing they could think of and so the attendants withdrew.

They had luxuriated in the hot baths, with spices and scents.

Fidelma had half expected Ciarnat to appear as her attendant but another young girl helped her. It was when she had been at the fortress last and bathed in exactly the same bath-house that Fidelma had met Ciarnat for the first time. When she enquired after her, the attendant – a young, fair-haired girl – had explained her absence.

'Ciarnat is not in this household today, lady. She has an elderly mother in the township and some days she goes to take care of her.'

Having bathed and rested, they found the summer sun was lowering and beginning to cast shadows across the courtyard and buildings; lanterns were being prepared for the coming darkness. Finally, a distant bell resounded four times and there came a discreet knock on their chamber door. It was the male attendant come to escort them to the great hall.

To their surprise, having arrived at the fortress with hardly a sign of anyone to greet them, the hall was athrong with many people. Fidelma noted that there were very few females present – apart from the attendants. The only immediately familiar face belonged to Conrí, who came forward to greet them at once and explained that he would act, for that evening at least, as the prince's *rechtaire* or steward. He then led Fidelma and Eadulf to the dais on which the prince's chair of office was located.

Prince Donennach rose from his seat and took a step down to the same level to greet Fidelma in recognition of her rank. He was a tall, broad-shouldered young man in his mid-twenties, standing with legs spread slightly apart in the manner of a warrior. His grip was firm, an indication of the power of the muscles behind it. His features were not exactly handsome, but pleasant, and his light grey eyes seemed to regard everyone with amusement. The prince's hair was fair with a dusting of red in it as, indeed, was the long moustache that dangled either side of his mouth – the only facial hair on an otherwise cleanshaven face.

'You are welcome, lady. Or should I call you Sister Fidelma?' He greeted her with a genuine smile of recognition.

Fidelma returned his greeting with a bow of her head. 'I have left the religious, Prince Donennach, and now serve only as adviser in law to my brother.'

'And yet I find it strange not to use that prefix "Sister". It is the title by which your reputation precedes you throughout the Five Kingdoms.'

'Nevertheless, it is a designation I no longer have and so, in proof of the one I do have, I present this.' She produced the hazel wand of office which she carried, bearing the silver mounting of the stag rampant. This was the symbol of her authority as representative of her brother, the King.

'Your credentials are without question, Fidelma of Cashel,' Prince Donennach said. 'Your reputation precedes you under whatever title you use – as, of course, does that of Eadulf your husband. Welcome, friend Eadulf. It has been some years since I was a young visitor to Cashel when we tried to negotiate a peace. I was glad of your healing knowledge then, my friend.'

It was true that Eadulf had taken the arrow from Donennach's leg during an incident when Fidelma and he were investigating the mystery of a vanished member of the Abbey of Imleach. Eadulf had almost forgotten the event. He inclined his head gravely in acknowledgement. 'That's right. You were wounded by an arrow from a would-be assassin.'

'And was nursed back to life by you,' Prince Donennach said warmly. 'Your powers helped me to recover.' He paused and then continued: 'Indeed, you are both welcome here, although in the circumstances I had hoped your brother and his Chief Brehon would be represented.'

'I am here in their place. My brother, the King, whose regrets I bring to you, is detained with pressing matters . . .' She noticed Donennach's mouth lift slightly in a cynical gesture. 'Aillín, our Chief Brehon, is also on an embassy to the High King in Tara. As this seems a matter of urgency, and one of very serious consequence, I am here to represent both their offices.'

'One of those offices on your shoulders would be an enormous responsibility,' said a new voice, 'but to have to represent both . . .'

Fidelma turned towards the man who had made the observation.

'This is my Brehon, Brehon Faolchair,' the prince said.

'We have not met.' Fidelma regarded the man of middling years who took his place at the side of the prince. His hair was an unruly mass of ginger curls, his cheeks bright red above the pale white flesh around his neck. He looked to her as though laughter was more the normal expression on his features than the rather sombre cast of them now. 'I hope I will be able to demonstrate to you that I am capable of sustaining both such offices,' she said with dignity.

'I am sure that you will, lady. I have heard much of you, Fidelma of Cashel, and,' he gave a slight bow of his head to Eadulf, 'much of your husband Eadulf of Seaxmund's Ham. Your counsel in the predicament we now find ourselves in will be greatly appreciated.'

There was an ill-concealed snort of disdain from someone within a group of clerics to one side.

Without looking in the direction of the sound, Fidelma observed coldly: 'Evidently, some do not see this either as a predicament or feel that my counsel should be appreciated.'

Prince Donennach looked at the group of clerics and said with weary resignation: 'I believe that you have already met Abbot Nannid?'

# CHAPTER FOUR

Fidelma watched as the tall, gaunt figure of the Abbot of Mungairit moved forward. His pale face was unfriendly, the thin red lips twisted in a curious scowl, which suited his demeanour well. The man's eyebrows met across the brow – a feature which Fidelma had long seen as a sign of a bad temper. His tiny ice-cold eyes bored into her with dislike.

'We have met,' Fidelma acknowledged quietly.

'I see that Brother Eadulf is still your companion.' The abbot emphasised the term 'Brother' as a subtle sneer.

'As well you know, Abbot, Eadulf is my husband under the law,' she returned, equally coldly.

'I also see that Brother Eadulf still wears the tonsure of the Blessed Peter, which proclaims his allegiance to the rules and rituals of Rome. That allegiance seems strange in one who is now an obsequious servant of Cashel.'

Eadulf met the abbot's mocking tones with an easy smile. 'And I see that you still wear the tonsure of the Blessed John. Thus you proclaim your allegiance to the churches of the Five Kingdoms and the Faith that exists under the approval of the kings and laws of those Five Kingdoms. I personally find that strange in one who, I hear, is trying to abolish the laws of the Five Kingdoms in obsequious obedience of these curious rules from the east.'

Abbot Nannid's lips twisted even more angrily. He was about to make some unpleasant rejoinder when another man moved forward to intervene. He walked with a slight limp, and leaned heavily on a blackthorn stick.

'If there is a predicament here, lady, then let us pray that it is one we may resolve together,' he said, his tone gentle but firm. Fidelma detected an iron quality in the voice and examined the newcomer with interest.

He was a short man, inclined to be fleshy, with nondescript brown hair and dark eyes. He wore the robes of a churchman and his hair grew in unruly tufts around the tonsure of the Blessed John. In spite of his plump build, his features were long and mournful – like a breed of dog that knew it had done wrong in the eyes of its master and was now waiting for some sign of forgiveness. His appearance was totally at odds with that tone of authority in his voice.

'I am Cuán, lady,' the man introduced himself before she could articulate the question. 'Cuán of Imleach where I serve as *airsecnap*.'

'We meet under trying circumstances, Prior Cuán,' Fidelma greeted the man. He appeared to be half a head shorter than her and had to raise his dark eyes to meet her own. She wondered if the shortness was caused by him leaning so heavily on his stick. The prior saw the direction of her gaze and hastened to explain.

'This is the result of an argument with a horse, lady,' he told her. 'I broke my leg some years ago when I fell from the beast. The break did not heal well and I was left with a limp and this stick as my permanent companion.'

'I am sorry. Does it give you much discomfort?'

'No discomfort, lady – just frustration that nowadays I have to limit my travels and confine myself to transport by a mule cart.'

'Ah, I see. My brother and I were wondering why you had not yet come to visit us at Cashel.'

The prior hunched his shoulders in an expressive gesture.

'It seems there has not been a suitable opportunity in the short time since I was appointed Abbot Ségdae's deputy.' He hesitated and then added: 'I must advise you, lady, that I was only appointed in a temporary capacity. It will be up to the *derbhfine* of the abbey to approve of me before the king and his council are then asked to endorse their decision.'

'Of course. Yet you now stand in line to become abbot of the kingdom's oldest and most influential abbey,' she said.

Becoming aware of a certain restlessness in the atmosphere as the others waited for greetings to be exchanged, Cuán now turned to the man at his elbow. 'Let me present the steward of Imleach, Brother Tuamán.'

Conrí had called Brother Tuamán vain, Fidelma recalled, and the man who greeted her now was certainly overbearing. He was as tall as Conrí and, if anything, of a more muscular build even than the warrior. In fact, his physical presence was enough to cause awe in anyone he met.

'I think I recently saw you at my brother's court,' Fidelma said pleasantly. 'But we were not formally introduced.'

'You are most kind in remembering such a fleeting encounter,' the tall steward said in a deep voice. 'I attended Abbot Ségdae on only one occasion when he visited Cashel.'

'I believe that you succeeded Brother Madagan as steward after he was disgraced?'

Brother Tuamán was eager to explain his position. 'That is so. I have now agreed to continue to act as steward to Prior Cuán during these difficult days, as it is felt that continuity is essential.'

Prince Donennach interrupted impatiently. 'There will be plenty of time later for getting to know one another better. However, I was hoping that before we sit down to the evening meal, we could engage in a short discussion in order to outline the problem that brings us all together. I feel that we should take the opportunity to state our respective viewpoints as this will prepare us for a more informed debate on the matter tomorrow.'

'Our respective viewpoints?' queried Fidelma.

'There is a suggested difference in the application of law.' It was Brehon Faolchair who explained. 'Brehon Law or these new rules of the Faith.'

Fidelma glanced at the empty seat by Prince Donennach. 'Is your *tanaise*, your heir-apparent, not in attendance?' she asked. 'In a discussion of problems arising about the law, then your heir-apparent should also have a voice.'

Donennach shook his head. 'My *tanaise* is my sister, my *banchombarba*, and she has been called to attend on an urgent matter. I apologise for her absence.'

Eadulf knew that a *banchombarba*, a female heir, was not unknown. However, it was not often one found a female elected to the rigours of chieftainship. The *derbhfine*, the members of a family, usually elected the person best suited to be head of the family from the male line – unless there was no suitable male candidate.

They were directed to seats at the long table. Fidelma noted that most of those present were merely advisers and onlookers. Only the principal participants sat at the table. Prince Donennach took his official chair. Standing behind the chair, slightly to his left, was Conrí who, as warlord of the Uí Fidgente, was the only warrior officially allowed to wear his weapons in the great hall of the prince. Just below the prince sat Brehon Faolchair as the prince's legal adviser. Fidelma and Eadulf were placed immediately below him on the right side of the long table.

Next to them, a little further down the table, Prior Cuán sat with the tall steward, Brother Tuamán, and another religious equipped with a wax-covered tablet and stylus. He was of average height with straw-coloured hair and deep-set light eyes that seemed almost colourless. His features were pallid and gaunt, as if he did not eat well. His brows were drawn together in what they discovered was a permanent frown. The man had been briefly introduced as Brother Mac Raith, a scribe of Imleach.

Almost opposite them, on the left side of the table, sat Abbot Nannid. At his side was a familiar-looking cleric. The latter also had a wax-covered tablet called a *ceraculum* on which to make notes with a *graib* or stylus. The bald pate, fleshy features and unfriendly expression reminded them of someone . . . but it took a moment or two for both Fidelma and Eadulf to recognise another old antagonist, Brother Cuineáin, Abbot Nannid's steward. Fidelma noticed that the cleric still had the curious habit of rubbing his right wrist with his left hand.

Prince Donennach sat back, nodding to his Brehon with a signal to begin.

Brehon Faolchair cleared his throat. 'Abbot Ségdae of Imleach had come to this place to discuss with our leading cleric, the Abbot Nannid of Mungairit, how the churches of our two peoples could better work together in view of the peace that has been agreed between the Uí Fidgente and the King of Cashel. Abbot Ségdae was murdered. I shall go into the details as Fidelma of Cashel was not present at the hearing which investigated that murder.'

The Brehon went on without waiting for approval. He listed the details – which were the same that Ciarnat and then Conrí had given – of how Brother Tuamán and the warrior named Lachtna had discovered the body and found Gormán with the murder weapon in his hand. There being no other means of entering or leaving the chamber, which had been locked from the inside, the Brehon had to come to the inevitable conclusion that Gormán was responsible for the crime.

At this point, Fidelma interrupted. 'Did Gormán admit to the crime?' she asked.

'He did not,' replied the Brehon at once.

'What explanation did he offer?'

'None that could be believed,' Abbot Nannid sneered.

'I am not asking for an opinion but fact from the judge who heard this matter,' Fidelma hissed, with a sharpness that caused the abbot to blink rapidly.

'He said,' Brehon Faolchar went on in a slightly louder voice, 'he said that he had been talking to Abbot Ségdae when he was struck from behind and fell unconscious. When he came to, Brother Tuamán and the warrior, Lachtna, were standing over him. The abbot was dead and the murder weapon lay close to Gormán's hands. That is all he could tell us.'

'And this was investigated by you?'

'Of course. I examined the chamber and found there was nowhere that any assailant could possibly have hidden. Brother Tuamán told me that he was outside the chamber the whole time until he heard the commotion, tried to enter and discovered that the door had been locked from the inside.'

'This is true, lady.' Brother Tuamán felt he should say something at this point.

'A waste of time checking,' grunted Abbot Nannid. 'It was a pathetic defence which no one could believe,'

Fidelma did not bother to look at him as she hit back with: 'So pathetic that no intelligent man, such as the commander of the warriors of the Golden Collar, would have used it and expect it to be believed.'

'I offered him every means to amend his story,' Brehon Faolchair replied sadly.

'I am sure you did,' Fidelma said. 'I am not questioning your thoroughness in the matter. Yet he could only amend it if it was not true in the first instance. I wondered if you made any deduction as to why Gormán would have killed the Abbot of Imleach and in circumstances that left no other suspect.'

'Because he is not as clever as you think,' came Abbot Nannid's spiteful comment.

'Again I have to point out that I am asking a question of the learned Brehon!' Fidelma rapped out.

Brehon Faolchair spread his arms. 'Are you asking whether I found a motive for the killing?'

'Exactly that,' she confirmed.

'I have to admit that I did not, and even when Gormán was judged guilty of the crime and given an opportunity to state his motive in case some means of justification might be found in it, he refused to offer any reason.'

'Do you mean he refused or *could not* offer a reason.'

Brehon Faolchair sighed. 'He could not offer one.'

'While still maintaining his innocence?' Fidelma pressed.

'While still maintaining his innocence,' conceded the Brehon.

'This is just time-wasting!' denounced Abbot Nannid, anger now replacing his sarcasm. 'We did not come here to listen to the sister of the King of Cashel try to mislead us by displaying her legal aptitude.'

'I have seen no sign that Fidelma of Cashel is trying to mislead us.' It was the Prior of Imleach who spoke up. 'I can understand the questions that have been asked because those questions needed to be asked and I, whose knowledge of law is probably the equal to my learned brother, the Abbot of Mungairit . . .' he paused to let the words sink in '. . . I would have wanted those questions to be put and to be answered.'

Eadulf glanced at Fidelma to see whether she acknowledged that they seemed to have an ally in the prior, but her face was impassive.

'Questions that are irrelevant,' Abbot Nannid returned sourly. 'We have heard that Brehon Faolchair, Prince Donennach's own judge, has investigated and heard all the evidence. This man Gormán remains guilty of having killed Abbot Ségdae of Imleach. There is now just one question left: does Fidelma of Cashel claim that Brehon Faolchair has made a mistake in his judgement?'

'Fidelma of Cashel,' she replied coolly, 'concedes that Brehon Faolchair has made an investigation and has, on the given evidence, formed the opinion that Gormán was responsible for the death of the abbot.'

'Hah!' ejaculated Abbot Nannid. 'We have already reached a verdict. The man is guilty and the only reason we are here now is to discuss the punishment.'

'A punishment which is clear in the laws of the Fénechus, the laws passed down by the Brehons, the judges of our people,' said Prior Cuán. 'Our law allows for someone guilty of murder to atone for their crime by payment of prescribed compensation and a fine. That has been our law since the time before time.'

'The time beyond time when we were savages; pagans and not bathed in the light of the New Faith!' Abbot Nannid countered. There was a muttered agreement from his steward. 'Are we now not all of the one Faith and should we not obey the one law – the law of God?'

'It seems that we may have one Faith but already there are many interpretations of it,' replied Cuán.

Abbot Nannid rose dramatically from his seat. 'There is only one interpretation. The law of the New Faith is clear in the words of the ancient scriptures: *non misereberis eius sed animam pro anima* . . .'

'Show no pity for the guilty!' translated Prior Cuán, continuing to recite the scripture. 'The rule should be life for life, eye for eye, tooth for tooth, hand for hand, foot for foot.'

Abbot Nannid sat down, smiling triumphantly. 'Therefore you know the law of the Faith as well as I do. Abbot Ségdae was of the Faith. So we of the Faith demand that the man who killed him should also be killed in accordance with the law of the Faith.'

All eyes now turned to Fidelma rather than to Prior Cuán.

She herself looked to Brehon Faolchair. 'Is this demand from Abbot Nannid deemed worthy of a response?' she asked coldly.

Abbot Nannid flushed and was about to make some angry retort when Prince Donennach held up his hand to still him.

'I am afraid it is, lady. The purpose of this gathering before our meal is to discuss our opinions about the conflict of these laws.

Abbot Nannid will argue that the religious communities in my territory have all adopted these Penitential rules that have come to us from the east with the incoming New Faith. It is argued that these are the laws of the New Faith which we must accept and therefore they must be adopted as governing our people. I would hear a discussion on this matter. Having but recently agreed a peace with your brother, Colgú of Cashel, and acknowledged the kingship of Muman as residing in Cashel, I would not wish to act in any other but a logical way.'

There was a subdued muttering from across the table while Fidelma sat silent for a moment before speaking slowly and clearly.

'It is true that we have adopted a New Faith from the east. In many ways it is different to the Faith of our forefathers, which was followed from the time before time, and so, even in the area over which you claim authority, Donennach of the Uí Fidgente, there are some who have yet to embrace it.'

That caused an angry rumble from Abbot Nannid but Fidelma's eyes flashed.

'Is it denied that, less than a day's ride to the western mountains, you will find that the old gods and goddesses are still revered? Speak, anyone who denies it!'

There was a silence before Abbot Nannid said roughly: 'Come to the point.'

'That point I shall now attempt to elucidate. The people of Rome and, indeed, in the east – in the very land where this New Faith was born – followed their own religions until they were converted to this New Faith. Many saw the New Faith as but an extension of their old one. They continued to adhere to their native laws – laws from their religions which, it must be admitted, were punitive and unlike our more enlightened laws. The very words enunciated by Abbot Nannid are taken from the old texts of their religion, and were *not* born out of new interpretations.'

'That is sacrilege!' Abbot Nannid cried.

'Let me continue.' Fidelma raised her voice above the muttering of outrage. 'The place where the New Faith was first taught was a desolate and desert country. Into this desert, groups of religious wandered in search of tranquillity and formed communities dedicated to the contemplation of their Faith. It was a harsh life indeed. In order to survive, these groups had to have a strict discipline. Among these groups was a man called John the Ascetic.'

'When was this, lady?' asked Brehon Faolchair, intrigued and wondering where her story was leading.

'A little over two centuries ago,' she replied confidently. 'He joined a community of the New Faith who decided to establish themselves in a place called called the Desert of Scetis, which is in Egypt. There he realised that, in order to survive, he needed to enforce discipline upon the community. This John the Ascetic set down a number of rules for the community to follow, a list of rules of behaviour which, if transgressed, were called "sins" and were punished in the manner in which his people had punished wrong-doers from their ancient times. They were the punishments of the laws of his people – *not* our people,' she added with emphasis.

'How would you know this?' Abbot Nannid scoffed.

'How do you know anything but by seeking after knowledge?' she returned.

'You are no longer a religious, even though some still call you Sister.' Abbot Nannid made it sound like an accusation.

'True, I have left the religious – which is not to say that I have left the religion,' she replied. 'And I am not responsible for what other people call me. I will say, however, that in pursuit of the New Faith I have opened my mind to learning, not closed it.'

'This is a long and weary way to make a point,' dismissed the abbot. 'That is, if you have any point to make.'

'*You* seem to find it weary. However, I shall continue. John the Ascetic left his community in the Desert of Scetis and travelled to Gaul. He was to die in the city of Massilia, a place I have visited during my travels to Rome. It was near there that he set up another community, and he used the same harsh rules to govern it as he had with the community of Scetis – rules that little reflected the change of attitude and law of the people in the area in which he now settled. Yet his rules were to have an influence on Martin of the Turones and his community. They also influenced Benedict, whose rules for the communities of the Faith have now been officially adopted by Rome.'

This time it was Prince Donennach who interrupted.

'This is a fascinating history that you recite, Fidelma, but I am at a loss to understand the purpose, except that you say that the rules now being adopted by our churchmen are, as they already claim, being spread by the Faith.'

'I am not denying this,' she rejoined. 'What I am saying is that we have missed the intention of these rules. These Penitentials listed penances and punishments based on foreign laws. Even when accepted by religious communities, they were never meant to supersede the laws of different kingdoms. They applied only to those who had voluntarily joined a religious community that had voted to accept them. Finnian of Cluain Ioraird, then Cummian, and then others, like Abbot Nannid, may have accepted those rules for their communities but not for the Five Kingdoms. They cannot enforce them on all the peoples.'

There was a short silence when she had finished speaking.

Then Abbot Nannid rose again, his voice tight with anger. 'You have listened to the beguiling voice of a lawyer. A lawyer who has an interest in ensuring that you reject the teachings of the New Faith. The fact is that she was once a member of the religious herself but now acts as her brother's legal adviser; a woman who cleaves to the ancient laws that were devised and transmitted from pagan times. I am no lawyer. I am a plain and simple man who maintains that the words of the Faith must be obeyed. What I say is this: the Penitentials have been brought to our land as part of the Faith which we have adopted and, notwithstanding our past, these rules must govern our behaviour now and in the future. That is why we, we of the Uí Fidgente, are leading the way in the Faith by the fact that our abbeys and churchmen accept the Penitentials as the law to be obeyed above all other law.'

Prince Donennach again had to raise his hand to silence the hubbub that followed.

'There is much to be considered here. I must, however, point out that *I* rule here under the law of the Fénechus. How then can I give judgement under the rules of the New Faith?'

'That is a matter for the council of chieftains to decide, which council must sit with the bishops and abbots of the Uí Fidgente who have equal rights as the nobles of the people,' Brehon Faolchair declared. 'But as I understand Abbot Nannid's immediate argument – the argument he has continued to press – Abbot Ségdae was a leading churchman, an abbot and a bishop. Therefore his killer should be punished under the laws of the Church.'

Prince Donennach turned with a questioning look at the Prior of Imleach.

'What is your response, Prior Cuán? You now stand in place of the Abbot of Imleach and are now senior churchman of the King of Cashel. Do you agree with this?'

The cleric painfully rose to his feet, leaning his weight on his blackthorn stick. 'Imleach is not governed by the Penitentials. Abbot Ségdae, may he rest in peace, believed in the old laws and would not wish his death to be a cause of such changes in any part of the Kingdom of Muman, of which he was Chief Bishop.'

'You know this for a fact, brother?' Abbot Nannid called out rudely. 'After all, Abbot Ségdae is dead and not able to come forward, is he, to affirm what you say.'

Fidelma exhaled sharply in exasperation. 'I think there are enough people who knew Abbot Ségdae during his lifetime to confirm his beliefs.'

'I refer to witnesses who are without bias,' Abbot Nannid replied complacently. 'You are an Eóghanacht and an advocate of those laws you uphold over the rules of the Christ.'

Fidelma was once more on her feet, her eyes flashing with fury.

'I was not aware that these rules were laid down by anyone other than those men who decided that their isolated communities needed guidance – many years after Christ was crucified! You should know enough of the law of your people – the law you now want to reject – to know that the oath of the Brehons is to maintain the truth, and pledges are given which are forfeit if their judgement is found false. I am, indeed, an Eóghanacht and have long known that the very term is considered a badge of antagonism to one of the Uí Fidgente!'

'Fidelma!' The quiet word from Prince Donennach was enough of a warning not to let her temper overstep the mark. She sat down, biting her lip, trying to ignore the broad smile on Abbot Nannid's twisted features.

Prince Donennach had caught sight of the expression on Eadulf's face. He gazed at him thoughtfully. 'You look as if you want to contribute a comment, Brother Eadulf?'

There were some startled gasps from the company and even Fidelma looked surprised at the invitation.

'He is a foreigner and has no right to speak here!' Abbot Nannid immediately asserted. 'Even if the sister of the King of Cashel has married him, he has no such right.'

Eadulf coloured and would have remained silent but Prince Donennach took no notice of the abbot's protest.

'I am inviting Brother Eadulf to speak here and he does so under my authority,' he said quietly. 'I remember how Eadulf used his healing skills on me many years ago when a would-be assassin shot an arrow into my leg. No one asked then if he had a right to do so.'

'He will only say what she wants him to say!' the abbot interrupted again, causing Fidelma to start to rise from her seat.

But Donennach replied sharply: 'I know, further, that when he speaks he will speak with his own voice.'

Eadulf stood up slowly.

'Indeed, I will speak on my own terms,' he began. 'I represent no one in my opinions but myself. Had I sought to ingratiate myself with the views of my wife or her family, the Eóghanacht, as Abbot Nannid implies, then you would be seeing me here with the tonsure of John on my head instead of that of Peter. I have continued to wear it to indicate my religious allegiance for many years. Unlike some, I do not wear the tonsure of John yet uphold the rules of Peter of Rome, Abbot of Mungairit. I am no fawning dog who will do what pleases the moment.'

This was said in an even tone, devoid of rancour. Some of those attending suppressed chuckles while Abbot Nannid's face whitened.

'So how do you see this predicament, Brother Eadulf?' enquired Prince Donennach before the abbot could gather his wits to respond.

'I see no predicament in the matter of law. In my own country I was an hereditary *gerefa* before I enter the religious. I came and studied in this land of the Five Kingdoms before travelling to Rome, where I embraced the theology of Rome. I have travelled to many lands in which the New Faith was adopted, but in all of them they have kept their own laws so long as they were compatible with the New Faith. You have your own laws without which you would not have existed, these countless centuries. Rome has no more changed her native laws in favour of John the Ascetic's rules for his community than you should. That is all I have to say.'

'Such comments are appreciated, Brother Eadulf.' Prince Donennach sighed gently. 'However, I am still left with a choice of two possibilities. One is that I authorise the punishment of Gormán to be given under the laws of the Fénechus, in accordance with the wisdom of our Brehons. In that case I court the disapproval of my clergy. The second choice is that I do as the abbot demands and prescribe punishment under the Pententials. In the second case the punishment is extreme and would bring conflict to this land.'

Abbot Nannid was smiling thinly. 'You must think well on this matter, Prince Donennach. The first choice also leads to conflict.'

'Conflict in what manner?' demanded Conrí, the warlord, belligerently.

The Abbot of Mungairit gave him an amused glance. 'I did not hear that a warrior was invited to express opinion here or ask questions.'

'Nevertheless, the commander of my warriors has a pertinent question even if it is not protocol for him to ask it. I shall then ask it in his stead. You may answer to me, Abbot Nannid.'

'All I say is that many of the Uí Fidgente are prepared to defend their Faith – with the sword if necessary. Prince Donennach, the fate of the Uí Fidgente has passed into your hands. After the Eóghanacht defeated our armies at Cnoc Áine and Prince Eóghanán was slain, you have steered a course of peace for our people. Some have whispered it was peace at any cost. You recently went to seek the approval of the High King for the course you have pursued. But remember that you rule by the will of your *derbhfine* and the approval of all your people. The Church has, through me, formed an opinion about what should befall the murderer of one of the leading churchmen of the Five Kingdoms. That opinion would be ignored at the peril of undoing all your strivings for peace.'

Abbot Nannid resumed his seat, sitting with folded arms and a smug look on his face.

An obvious threat was implied. Unless Gormán was turned over to punishment under the terms of the Penitentials – and that meant certain death – then Abbot Nannid believed that a civil warfare could be unleashed among the Uí Fidgente. Abbot Nannid must be sure of his support, Fidelma thought, otherwise he would not have dared to speak so openly and in such terms to the prince.

Fidelma rose to her feet again. 'I think we have reached a

conclusion about where we all stand,' she said. 'Prior Cuán and I, representing the King of Cashel and his Chief Brehon, agree that the laws of these kingdoms are the laws we must use. Whereas Abbot Nannid, saying he represents all the churchmen of the Uí Fidgente, implies that in accepting the New Faith we must also accept the Penitentials as the law of that Faith. He suggests that Prince Donennach should convene a council to discuss whether the laws of the Uí Fidgente be changed from the laws of the Brehons to the laws of the Penitentials. That is a great task and one which, undoubtedly, will threaten repercussions not only in Muman, but in Laighin, Connachta, Ulaidh and even in Midhe, the Middle Kingdom of the High King.'

She looked around at all those present.

'That will be the choice facing the Uí Fidgente – and no one can tell you which choice to make. However, we are not really here to discuss the right of the Uí Fidgente to hold a council to decide such a matter. We are here to discuss a matter that is more specific: should Gormán of Cashel, in the current circumstances, face punishment under the laws of the Fénechus, the judgement of the Brehons, or face punishment under the rules of the religious community as advocated by Abbot Nannid? Is that not the basic question?'

There was some further muttering and then Prince Donennach uttered a tired sigh. 'Put like that, lady, it *is* the main question.'

'Then we are not considering it correctly.'

There was a silence while everyone stared in bewilderment at her.

'Not considering it correctly?' queried Brehon Faolchair. 'How so?'

'It is simple. We are looking at the sentence before the hearing.'

A frown crossed Brehon Faolchair's features. 'I am Prince Donennach's Brehon, and I enquired into this case. A hearing was held under my jurisdiction and attended by the prince. How is that not correct?'

'You examined the witnesses and then you constituted a formal hearing at which you judged the accused as guilty?'

'I have said as much. That is the normal course of events.'

'Indeed it is,' Fidelma confirmed solemnly. 'And as this was a serious matter of homicide, advocates and others are usually invited to attend. *So who represented the prisoner*?'

The question was asked with sudden emphasis and Brehon Faolchair blinked for a moment.

'The prisoner represented himself. No other advocate was here to receive the *lóg mberla*,' he said, referring to the payment that was given to an advocate to represent the defence of an accused. 'But as well you know, a prisoner can represent himself.'

'And was this explained to Gormán?' she asked. 'Did he know the rights of an *aintengthaid*?' The legal term meant a 'tongueless person' who was not qualified to plead in law, but nonetheless could do so at the invitation and advice of the Brehon. 'I was not aware that Gormán had knowledge of law to enable him to know his rights and make the right decision.'

Brehon Faolchair stared at her, a look of dawning comprehension on his face.

'I did not think it necessary to inform him of his rights, being that he was in the service of the King of Cashel and I presumed he knew them.'

'Even though there is a legal obligation on you to do so? And did you, Brehon Faolchair, go through the necessary formalities by depositing five *unga* of silver, in whatever form, to serve as a pledge for the support of your judgement if that judgement was subsequently challenged?'

Even Eadulf, who knew an *unga* was equivalent to an ounce, began to understand her thinking. She was moving towards an appeal against the judgement. He remembered that the law texts said a judgement had to be defended by pledges in case of an appeal.

'I did not put forward such a pledge,' admitted Brehon Faolchair. 'I have to admit that no such judgement has yet been formally given.'

'Are you saying that there has been no such judgement?' Fidelma was astounded. 'I thought that it was that very judgement that was the reason for our gathering here. You must explain this to me.'

Brehon Faolchair did his best to look contrite but there was a hidden smile on his lips. 'A hearing was held at which the evidence was heard. It seemed that there was little defence for the accused to be made. But as for a formal judgement, it was felt that this should be delayed until we could discuss the merits of the system under which the accused could be judged. This is the conversation that we have been pursuing.'

Fidelma realised that Prince Donennach and his Brehon were either displaying a lack of knowledge of the law or that they were playing a secret game in which they were enticing her to use her knowledge of law to outwit the arguments about which law the punishment should follow.

She spoke up. 'A hearing is subject to the law as it stands. Therefore I shall claim the *faircsi dligid*, the appeal before the law, that this case has not been properly heard, let alone judged. That being so, Gormán's guilt or innocence has yet to be decided.'

# ChAPTER FIVE

A bbot Nannid was on his feet, his face contorted and red with
anger.

'This is ridiculous! We know the man is guilty. Are we going to
waste time going through the matter all again?'

Fidelma continued to keep her focus on Brehon Faolchair.

'According to the *Bretha im Fuillema Gell*, the Law of Appeals,
I make my formal submission to Prince Donennach and his Brehon. I
argue that the case against Gormán must now be heard with all due
legal formality. I will give my own pledge of five *unga* of silver to
represent Gormán for this hearing.'

'This is nonsense!' shouted Abbot Nannid. 'Gormán had time
to make his own appeal and did not do so. He remains guilty.'

'Am I in error of the law, Brehon Faolchair?' Fidelma asked.

Brehon Faolchair, who clearly had no respect for Abbot Nannid,
did not hide his smile as he answered. 'You are not in error, lady.
I accept that the proper procedures were not observed and therefore
no legal hearing was made and so no judgement was given. You
are therefore entitled to question all the witnesses and prepare a
defence for Gormán before a new hearing.'

'The facts are known.' Abbot Nannid almost bellowed. 'There *is*
no defence. Can it be that an Uí Fidgente prince is simply afraid of

facing Eóghanacht displeasure? We demand the pronouncement of the punishment!'

Prince Donennach rose and the room gradually fell silent.

'I will forget those words, Nannid of Mungairit,' he said in stern reproof. 'Had they been spoken by any other than a churchman of your rank then you would expect to defend them by sword for daring to question my honour. I am minded that you are a distant cousin to me, so I will say this to you: when the correct legal procedures are carried out, then – and only then – shall a judgement be rendered in accordance to the law. Do I make myself clear?'

Abbot Nannid held himself back for a moment and then the habitual sneer reappeared.

'You have made yourself perfectly clear and I will await the outcome of such a new hearing when doubtless our distinguished guest from Cashel will find a means to prove that this warrior was nowhere near this fortress when the murder took place and that—'

'Abbot Nannid! You presume upon your office!' It was Conrí who moved forward with his hand on his sword hilt. Prince Donennach waved him back.

Only then did Abbot Nannid seem to realise that he might have gone too far. He bent his head. 'I apologise,' he said, his voice not conveying the meaning of his words. 'I allowed strong words to reflect my concern that a killer of a saintly abbot might find escape through an advocate with a smooth tongue. With your permission, I will withdraw from the evening's meal and proceed to the abbey so that I can spend the night in contemplation and prayer for the hope that those guilty of crimes may receive their due.'

'In the circumstances, it would not be of benefit for you to continue here when the purpose of this meal was to sit and drink and eat in friendship prior to discussing ways of coming to an amicable agreement on this matter of contention,' agreed Prince Donennach without emotion.

Abbot Nannid turned and, followed by his steward, Brother Cuineáin, he left the hall.

There were a few moments of silence before the prince resumed his seat and looked sadly at the newcomers.

'I extend my apologies to you, Fidelma of Cashel, to you, Eadulf and to you, Prior Cuán. However, you see demonstrated the dilemma that I find myself in. Gormán must be tried by the law of the land. Frankly, I can see nothing so far that gives me any sign that we have over-estimated his guilt in the matter. I am still left with the final judgement – a judgement under the law of the land. If guilty, then we must return to this vexed matter of punishment, and whatever path is chosen there will be conflict.'

'Well, at least the lady Fidelma has provided us with some respite,' Brehon Faolchair pointed out. There was relief in his voice but no happiness. He turned to Fidelma and forced a smile. 'Thankfully you seized the opportunity that I allowed by purposely failing to fulfil my legal obligations. You have now bought us several more days to consider the matter before a decision is made and we are plunged once more into argument and aggression.'

While Eadulf was surprised by Brehon Faolchair's admission, Fidelma was not. She had suspected that a Brehon of Faolchair's standing would not have neglected the legal rules. Obviously, he had been hoping that she would recognise the legal point to give Prince Donennach some extra time to consider if there was a solution that would avert trouble.

Fidelma inclined her head in acknowledgment of the Brehon's sleight of hand. 'Then tomorrow I will begin to question the witnesses to this matter.'

'You will want to see Gormán first, no doubt?' asked Brehon Faolchair.

She shook her head. 'As Gormán is the accused in this matter, it is often best to hear from those who have witnessed what he is accused of; to hear their stories first. This puts an advocate in a better position to examine the accused. I shall visit him after I have seen the witnesses.'

'Well, there are only two witnesses to the event. Brother Tuamán there and one of the warriors called Lachtna.'

'I am at your service, lady,' the tall steward of Imleach offered.

'Thank you. I shall also need to examine the place where the murder happened.'

'It was in the guest-house where we are staying,' supplied Prior Cuán. 'It is within the fortress, just across the courtyard.'

'Who else is staying there?' asked Eadulf.

'Only our delegation,' replied Prior Cuán.

'Which consists of . . .?'

'Myself, the steward and two of our brethren – Brother Mac Raith here,' he motioned to the scribe, 'and Brother Máel Anfaid.'

Seeing a thoughtful frown crossing her features, Brehon Faolchair added: 'The chamber in which the abbot died has not been touched. We felt this should be left as it was because of the circumstances.'

'Your foresight shows excellent judgement, Faolchair,' acknowledged Fidelma.

Prince Donennach finally seemed to relax in his chair. It was clear the stress of the events was affecting him. 'Let us leave these difficult concerns until tomorrow. Tonight was destined to be a means to welcome our distinguished visitors.' He turned and signalled to one of the attendants. 'Now is the time to eat, drink, listen to the singing of the bards and discuss the more pleasant matters of life.'

On the following morning, when Fidelma and Eadulf left the private guest chambers of the prince's palace, they found Ciarnat waiting for them at the steps leading down to the main courtyard. She appeared agitated. Enda was at her side, attempting to pacify her.

'You have been to see neither Gormán nor Aibell,' Ciarnat greeted them in angry accusation. 'They think that you have abandoned them.'

'I am afraid that we are prisoners of protocol, Ciarnat,' Fidelma said, in an attempt to reassure her. 'We had to see Prince Donennach first and then were obliged to discuss certain matters. You live in this household and therefore you will know something of the rituals of hospitality. After the meal, I sent one of the attendants to find either you or Aibell, to tell you both that I would come to see you as soon as I was able to, later today.'

The girl was not appeased. 'The attendant spoke to Aibell but simply said that you would not be seeing her or Gormán immediately.'

Fidelma expressed her irritation. While it was not wrong, the message did not convey her meaning. 'The reason for the delay was that I had to point out flaws in the previous hearing. This will allow me time to examine the witnesses myself and arrange for a new hearing. *That* was the message that was intended to be conveyed to Gormán and Aibell.'

The girl started a little in surprise. 'That was not explained to us.'

Enda seemed delighted. 'That is good news indeed, lady.'

'At least it is something. You go back to Aibell, Ciarnat, and inform her of this. You go with her, Enda, as I shan't need you for a while. Make sure that the news is passed on to Gormán. My investigation now demands that I have to see several people first as well as inspect the chamber in which Abbot Ségdae was killed. After that, I shall pay a visit to Gormán.'

'People will say exactly what they said before,' Ciarnat stated gloomily. 'No one believes Gormán.'

'It will be my task to ensure that he is fairly heard,' Fidelma promised her.

'But what of the demands for his death?'

72

'One thing at a time. No one outside Abbot Nannid and his supporters would be happy that our law is changed for these church rules. We will argue that matter when, or if, the time comes to do so.'

The girl nodded slowly. 'Very well. I will go with Enda and inform Aibell of what you say.'

'You must tell her and Gormán to be of good cheer,' added Eadulf. 'Make sure of that.'

'You can rely on me to tell them that,' Enda said fiercely.

The girl allowed herself to be led away by Enda, walking across the sloping courtyard towards the stone buildings by the fortress gates that were clearly the *laochtech* or warriors' barracks.

Eadulf turned to Fidelma. 'I wish I felt more confident about this.'

He expected a rebuke but she agreed glumly. 'Everything seems to be weighted against Gormán. A locked room and witnesses to testify that no one could have gone in or out during the time he was there. On top of this, Abbot Nannid seems intent on getting his revenge. I never thought I would feel sorry for a prince of the Uí Fidgente, but Donennach's two choices will lead to trouble whichever one he chooses.'

There came the sound of a stick tapping on the flagstones nearby. They looked round and saw Prior Cuán limping towards them, leaning heavily on his blackthorn stick. He smiled and nodded a greeting to them both.

'I am going to the hall to meet with Brehon Faolchair and break my fast,' he said. 'Have you eaten?'

'We have, indeed. We are now heading for the guest-house,' Fidelma answered.

'Ah, yes. Let me congratulate you on the mastery of law that you displayed last night. It was impressive.'

'There was something I meant to ask you,' replied Fidelma, ignoring the compliment. 'You are clearly a man of experience,

Prior Cuán, otherwise I doubt that Abbot Ségdae would have chosen you as his deputy. But I am sure that you were not always at Imleach.'

The prior shrugged. 'When I was young I joined the community of Cluain Eidnech and received my learning there. I have but recently joined the community at Imleach.'

'Cluain Eidnech?' Fidelma's eyes widened. 'Isn't that in the north of Osraige territory, towards the east of the mountains of Sliabh Bladhma? It has a reputation for scholarship. Indeed, it has been famous ever since Fintan, son of Gabhran, founded it a century ago.'

'That is so, lady. You are well versed in the history of my old community. We must continue these reflections later, however, as I promised to meet with the Brehon. And you have yet to conduct your investigation. I pray that you may come up with something that we have all overlooked.'

He turned and limped towards the feasting hall. They stood looking after him for a moment or two before Fidelma straightened her shoulders and said, 'Come – let us find the room where Abbot Ségdae met his death.'

They had barely crossed the courtyard when Conrí hailed them.

'We are trying to find the hostel where the abbot was killed,' Eadulf replied when he asked their intent.

'I have ordered that the warrior Lachtna make himself available.'

'That is good thinking.'

'May I accompany you, unless it would not be deemed proper according to the procedure of law?'

'You are welcome, Conrí. There should be no secrets in the gathering of information in this matter,' Fidelma told him.

The hostel was a two-storey stone building, rising beside the main warriors' barracks. It was not very large and, to their surprise, many of the windows had iron bars across them. It seemed more like a prison than a hostel for guests. A warrior stood outside the large oak door which appeared to be the only entrance into the building. Fidelma stopped and was examining the exterior with a critical eye. Conrí caught her expression and smiled.

'I know what you are thinking, lady. I will explain. This used to be the quarters for the commander of the guard, a couple of warriors and any prisoners that needed to be confined. When Abbot Ségdae arrived with his small party, he expressed the need for them to be housed together. The prince's palace is not so extensive with its buildings. Therefore, it was considered that, with some modification, this entire building could be handed over to Abbot Ségdae and his delegation.'

'But Abbot Nannid is staying in this newly built Abbey of Nechta in the township. Why was the delegation from Imleach not sent there?'

'That you will have to ask of others,' Conrí replied. 'As I said, I was not here until the day after Abbot Ségdae's murder.'

'But it seems a curious arrangement for delegates to a council on religious matters to be so divided,' commented Eadulf.

'You forget the tensions between the Uí Fidgente and the Eóghanacht, friend Eadulf,' Conrí answered dryly.

Fidelma made no comment and Conrí turned to wave the warrior forward.

'This is Lachtna, who was on duty the night the abbot was killed,' he said, introducing him.

Fidelma gazed at the man. The name suited him well because it meant fair of skin – literally, 'milk-like'. It was a popular name among the Uí Fidgente.

'This is the dálaigh who will question you,' Conrí told the man. 'Give your answers truthfully and without fear.'

The young warrior stiffened before his commander. 'I am at your service, lady.'

'What were you doing on the evening that Abbot Ségdae was killed?' she began.

'I was on duty at the door of this hostel.'

'And the abbot and his party were inside?'

'Well, the abbot and the abbot's steward . . .'

'Brother Tuamán?'

'That is so. There were two other brothers from the Abbey of Imleach but they were not at the hostel. I can't remember their names. They were scribes, I think – those who waited attendance on the abbot.'

'Where were they if not in the hostel that evening?'

'I was not told, lady. I think that they were in the township and had not returned to the fortress. It was not late.'

'So you were at the door of this building on guard duty?'

'It was a hot night, lady. I was outside and I didn't mind as I had a seat to rest on.' He pointed to a bench nearby. 'The guard was not arduous because out here, no danger threatened.'

'A danger did threaten,' Conrí said reprovingly, 'otherwise the abbot would not lie dead.'

The young man shifted his weight uneasily. 'That was a danger within, Commander. One cannot guard against that.'

'A guard should be prepared for any danger,' Conrí responded.

'It was a danger that no guard could be prepared for, unless he was standing next to the abbot,' Fidelma interrupted. 'Now, let us proceed. Tell me what you know, Lachtna.'

'When I took over my shift on guard duty, I was told that a warrior from Cashel had arrived at the fortress. He had seen the prince and then tried to see the abbot, who had been in council with other churchmen. The abbot's steward, Brother Tuamán, told the warrior to return later.'

'Go on,' prompted Fidelma when he paused.

'This Cashel warrior did return that evening. It was not yet dark but many had taken the evening meal by then. He approached me and asked to see the abbot, Abbot Ségdae. I opened the door to the guest-hostel and called for Brother Tuamán. The abbot's steward was in conversation with another religious but he invited the warrior inside. He was, of course, expecting him to return.'

'Do you know who this religious was – the one he was in conversation with?'

'I think it was the steward from Mungairit. Brother Cuineáin is his name.'

'Very well. And then what happened?'

'The door closed and I remained outside on guard. Time passed and I heard the sound of yelling. It was—'

'Just a moment,' broke in Fidelma. 'How long was it between the warrior going into the hostel and the time that you heard this disturbance?'

Lachtna put his head to one side as if calculating. 'Not very long,' he said at last.

'Immediately?' Fidelma pressed.

'Not immediately.' Then Lachtna's face brightened as he remembered. 'Long enough for me to have walked to the gates,' he pointed across the courtyard, 'paused and walked back to my post.'

'Then you heard yelling – can you describe it?'

'It was the anxious cries of Brother Tuamán, the steward, who was calling my name. I rushed in and—'

'You mentioned that the steward had been engaged in discussion with Brother Cuineáin, steward to the Abbot of Mungairit.' It was Eadulf's turn to interrupt. 'Where was he when you came rushing in?'

It was a point Fidelma had nearly forgotten about, and this made her cross with herself.

'Oh, he had left by then,' the warrior said. 'He left as soon as the warrior arrived. Only the steward, Brother Tuamán, was here. So, as I was saying, I rushed in and—'

'Excuse me.' It was Fidelma again. 'The best method is to show us. Take us inside and show us where you went.'

Behind the large oak door was a communal room with doors on

either side and, at the far end of the room, a wooden staircase leading to the first floor. Conrí took it upon himself to explain the lay-out.

'When this was used as the main guardhouse, the rooms for the guards were on either side of the ground floor here. The two brothers you were enquiring about have their quarters here now.'

Lachtna then pointed to the stairs.

'I came in and, hearing the voice of Brother Tuamán shouting for help from above, I rushed directly up the stairs.'

He led the way and on the next floor they found themselves in a small ante-chamber with four doors leading off it. One of these doors was hanging on one hinge with the woodwork splintered.

'It was Brehon Faolchair who suggested that things remain untouched until a decision on this matter was made,' explained Conrí.

Lachtna pointed to the door. 'When I came up the stairs, I saw Brother Tuamán standing outside this door, which was the abbot's chamber. He told me that he feared something was wrong. He had heard a cry from within and a noise, like something falling. He had knocked on the door to see if the abbot needed assistance but, having received no answer, he tried the door and found it was locked. It was locked from the inside.'

'One moment,' Fidelma said. 'I just want to make sure that I know what other chambers are on this floor. This is the abbot's door. So who occupied the other three chambers?'

Lachtna turned and indicated with his hand. 'That one opposite is the steward's chamber. That at the far end is occupied by the abbot's deputy, Prior Cuán. The one next to the abbot's room is an empty chamber. I can assure you, lady, that there are no means of reaching the abbot's chamber from any other.'

'And you say that the two scribes have their chambers below stairs?'

'That is so, lady.'

'We know the steward was here, outside the abbot's door – but where was Prior Cuán at this time?'

The warrior was diffident. 'He was not here, lady. Nor do I know where he was.'

'So let us return to what happened. You say that the door had been locked from the inside. Why do you say that?'

Lachtna blinked for a moment and then gathered his thoughts. 'There was no key on the outside, lady. Brother Tuamán and I put our shoulders to the door and managed to smash the lock.'

Fidelma glanced at the lock where it had been splintered. The metal of the door lock had clearly been wrenched from the surrounding wooden holdings by force from the outside. 'Continue.'

'Well, we burst into the chamber. I saw the warrior first. He was sprawled on his face, one arm flung out with a bloodied knife near his hand.'

'Near his hand?' Fidelma queried.

'Yes. His fingertips were barely touching the handle, as his fingers were splayed out. I presume he dropped the knife as he fell forward.'

'And what sort of state was he in?'

'He was groaning as if coming to his senses.'

'Anything else?'

'Well, I then saw the body of the abbot. He lay slightly forward as if he had been facing the warrior, crumpled up and covered in blood from stab wounds. Oh, and near his left hand was his staff of office. That had fallen by his side.'

'But you are certain the door was locked from the inside?' she asked again.

'It clearly was, lady.'

'Do you know that as a fact, or is it an assumption? This is important. Could someone not have slipped out of the door and locked it unseen to Brother Tuamán?'

The warrior shook his head. 'I know it was locked on the inside for, as we burst into the room, I felt something hard under my foot.

I looked down and saw the key on the floor. Then, of course, I saw the warrior and the body of the abbot.'

'How do you think the key came to be on the floor?'

'I believe it was probably in the lock on the inside and, as we smashed open the door, the force of our blow must have jolted it from the lock and it fell.'

'Show me where.'

The young man pushed open the smashed door and pointed to an area immediately behind it. The spot was slightly to the centre rather than immediately under the lock.

'Where is the key now?' she asked.

'It was handed to Brehon Faolchair.'

Fidelma cast her eye over the door. It was a stout oak door although there were some knots in the ageing wood, and cracks. Indeed, a couple of the knots had simply disappeared with age and wear.

'Are there keys to the other rooms?'

'There are, lady.'

'Would any others fit this lock?'

'I doubt it,' replied Lachtna. 'This place was originally built to hold prisoners as well as the guard. I was told that our locksmiths made all the keys of different shapes. That was back in the days when Óengus son of Nechtan was our prince and very wary of his enemies. He felt the differences in locks and keys were a better security than . . .'

Fidelma held up her hand to stay the other's sudden enthusiasm for the subject. She entered the room and looked about.

It was fairly small chamber. A window gave light but it had iron bars inserted in such a way that no one could use it to exit or enter. A cot bed, a cupboard, a chest and a desk with two wooden chairs comprised the furnishings. She saw nothing that gave her any ideas of how someone could conceal themselves in the room.

'In your opinion, Lachtna, is there any way someone could have entered this chamber, knocked out Gormán, the warrior, and killed the abbot in the manner Gormán claimed?'

The young man shook his head. 'Not unless they were a *púca*, a shape-shifter, lady, and could move through solid walls. Look, even the one window there is a full storey high above ground and has iron bars across it. The windows were barred to hold the prisoners in the old days.'

'But there is a closet in that corner and a chest under the window. Could an assassin have hidden there?' Eadulf asked.

'Anything is possible.' The young man walked to a position before the desk-like table. 'The Cashel warrior claimed he was attacked from behind. From the position where I found him, he was on the floor at this point. The abbot was lying in front of him. From where I am now standing, lady, if a nameless assassin was hiding either in the closet or the chest, how could he not have been observed emerging from these hiding places? How could he come round to strike the warrior from behind without being seen? The chest is there, under the window to the warrior's right. He would have seen the lid opening and the assassin having to climb out from a horizontal position. He did not. And the closet is almost directly behind the abbot, slightly to the left shoulder of where he stood. The abbot might not have seen an assassin emerge from that but the warrior would have done so and presumably raised the alarm.' He paused. 'That is, if his story is true.'

Fidelma was silent for a moment or two, examining the positions indicated by the young warrior.

'You have a keen eye for observation, Lachtna,' she praised him.

'It is my training,' Lachtna admitted modestly. 'I notice things. It is why I noticed the key on the floor behind the door and why I then ensured that it was presented to Brehon Faolchair because Brother Tuamán had failed to see it. The key is the confirmation that the door had been locked on the inside – and that is essential evidence.'

'True,' Fidelma agreed. 'What do you think of Gormán's claim that he had been hit over the head and that he was not the killer?'

Lachtna looked uncomfortable. 'I know you have come here to defend him, lady. That is the talk among the household guards here. I hear he is the commander of the bodyguard of the King of Cashel.'

'Don't let that influence your opinion,' Fidelma told him. 'Just tell me what you think.'

Lachtna spread his arms. 'If I had discovered a fox in a chicken run with feathers in its mouth and a dead chicken before it, it would be hard not to believe that the fox was guilty of killing the chicken.'

# chapter six

⁓

'So there is absolutely no doubt in your mind, speaking as one of the chief witnesses to these events, that he is guilty?' Fidelma was expecting the answer but she had to put the question.

'With respect, lady,' answered Lachtna, 'there can be no other conclusion. It is as if Gormán wanted to be found guilty! If he had planned to assassinate the abbot, why do it in such a manner? Why not wait for some lonely spot in the dark of the night?'

'That argument is of itself one in support of innocence,' pointed out Eadulf.

'I did not see the dagger being plunged into the body of the abbot, brother, but the circumstances indisputably show that he was the only person in the room apart from the victim. I cannot say anything other than what I have seen.'

'That is all we can ask of you, Lachtna,' Fidelma observed gently. 'Now, where is the abbot's staff, the one which is said to have caused the wound on Gormán's head?'

There was a movement at the doorway. Fidelma glanced over and saw the tall figure of the steward framed in it.

'You come at an opportune time, Brother Tuamán. I was about to send for you,' she said.

When Brother Tuamán strode in, his body language assertive, once again Fidelma had the impression of a wrestler going into a contest rather than of a scholarly religieux. She dismissed Lachtna, and the young warrior left with a half shrug at the newcomer.

'I am prepared to answer your questions,' the steward announced, and the condescending tone in his voice irritated Eadulf. It was true what Conrí had previously observed: the steward seemed to have a high opinion of himself, which was unusual in a tall, muscular man. Such men had little need to prove themselves to others.

'That is good because it is your duty to answer the questions of a *dálaigh* and a refusal would bring penalties,' Fidelma replied sternly. 'But I don't need to tell you that.'

Brother Tuamán blinked. Eadulf wondered if he realised that his pomposity would not succeed in elevating his status with her.

'As I mentioned before,' Fidelma went on, 'when Abbot Ségdae visited my brother at Cashel, I recall that you were in his company. However, we did not really talk at that time. I am wondering where you are from . . . before Imleach, that is?'

'From Loch Léin.'

'I meant, at what abbey did you train?'

'For ten years I served in the Abbey of the Blessed Finnian Lochbhair on Inis Faithlian. The abbey is on the island in Loch Léin,' he added condescendingly, as if she would not know this fact. 'I grew up on the shores of the lake and that is why I joined the community there.'

'Inis Faithlian is an abbey of high learning,' Fidelma conceded. 'What did you study there?'

'Penmanship, for which I received much praise as well as my renditions of Latin, Greek and Hebrew characters.'

The man was certainly not impeded by a lack of egotism and Fidelma's irritation now gave way to one of amusement.

'Do you also transcribe our own tongue?'

'*Res ipsa loquitor*,' replied the man pretentiously as if it were obvious.

Fidelma looked at Eadulf with lowered brows and tried to hide her smile. 'Sometimes I find it better not to presume knowledge. Many things that one thinks should go without saying, should be clarified,' she said.

The steward flushed but did not respond.

'I am told your delegation consisted of Abbot Ségdae, his deputy, yourself and two other brothers from Imleach,' Fidelma continued.

'That is so. Brother Mac Raith, whom you met yesterday, and Brother Máel Anfaid.'

'And their positions?'

'Assistant scribes to make a record of our discussions.'

'The purpose of this journey was to meet here with clerics of the Uí Fidgente to discuss how our churches and the leaders of the religious communities might come into a better communication with one another after the peace made between the Uí Fidgente and Cashel. Is that so?'

'It was only a preliminary meeting,' the steward replied. 'The Abbot of Mungairit called this council and suggested it be held here at the Abbey of Nechta.'

'So the council is being held in the new abbey?'

'It is logical that the council be held in the religious community. But, it being only recently constructed, they do not have a guest-hostel fit for our delegation. Therefore Prince Donennach offered hospitality.'

'How far had these discussions proceeded with Abbot Ségdae?'

'We had only had two days' preliminary discussion. It was the evening of the second day that this catastrophe happened.'

'What churchmen of the Uí Fidgente have attended this council?'

'Abbot Nannid and his steward are the only senior clerics to attend. No one else, for these were exploratory talks. Had they been successful then a full council of senior clerics would have been called.'

'I wish to talk about the day that Abbot Ségdae was killed. I was about to ask to be shown the abbot's staff of office with which he was said to have knocked Gormán unconscious . . . No, wait! We'll come to that in a moment. While we are in this chamber let us continue the account of that event. I am told that Gormán had called to see the abbot earlier that day. Is that right?'

'He did,' affirmed Brother Tuamán. 'I was here but the abbot was not. I told him that the abbot would not return here until after the evening meal. So it was later in the evening when Gormán arrived again to see him.'

'The guard mentioned that one of the religieux from Mungairit was here at that time as well. I think he said it was Brother Cuineáin.'

Brother Tuamán seemed momentarily surprised. Then he nodded. 'Indeed, Abbot Nannid's steward came to go over some essential details with me for the next session of our discussions the following morning. We had just finished when the warrior arrived, demanding to speak with the abbot.'

'Demanding?' Fidelma seized on the word. 'I thought he had earlier made an arrangement to see the abbot. Why would he have felt he had to demand to see him?'

'Perhaps I chose the wrong word,' muttered the steward. 'He asked to see him.'

'In what manner did he arrive?'

The steward frowned, obviously not understanding.

'How did he seem in manner?' Fidelma clarified. 'Was he excited? Was he anxious? What?'

The steward considered and then shook his head. 'I couldn't say.'

'Did he look like a man intent on killing someone?' Eadulf snapped, annoyed by the man's attitude.

'How does such a man look?' Brother Tuamán countered.

Eadulf accepted the point. 'We merely wanted to ascertain if there was anything unusual about the way Gormán presented himself. We have previously heard that he seemed moody.'

'I would agree that he seemed somewhat short of temper.'

'Angry?' Eadulf asked.

'Not in a good humour,' replied the steward.

'What happened when he arrived?'

'I left him in the hall while I came up here to ask the abbot if it was convenient for him to see the warrior. The abbot asked me to bring Gormán to his chamber immediately. They greeted one another as friends. Therefore I left them alone together.'

'Closing the door of the chamber?'

'Closing the door of the chamber,' echoed Brother Tuamán.

'And then you went back to continue your discussion with Brother Cuineáin?'

'There was nothing much more to discuss. He had already left.'

'Then what did you do?'

'I returned to my own chamber to work on my notes. It is over there,' he pointed across the hallway to the opposite door. 'A short time passed and then I heard raised voices coming from the abbot's room. There was a loud cry, as if of alarm, followed by a tremendous crash. I left my chamber immediately and hastened over here to the abbot's door. I called out, asking what was wrong. There was a silence. I tried the door but found it locked. It was not the abbot's custom to lock his door.'

'There was no response to your call?'

'None. I shouted for the warrior who was on duty below. That was Lachtna, whom you have just seen.'

Fidelma suddenly looked at Conrí, who had remained silent during her questioning. 'I meant to ask you – was it unusual for a warrior to guard the hostel when its occupants were a religious delegation?'

'Not in ordinary circumstances,' Conrí replied cautiously. 'You would have to ask the commander of the household Guard. I was not here at that time.'

'Not in ordinary circumstances,' repeated Eadulf. 'What could be extraordinary circumstances?'

'This is not an abbey,' Conrí reminded him. 'I would imagine that Prince Donennach might have some concern about the safety of the abbot. After all, this is the principal fortress of a people who had conflict with Cashel, and Abbot Ségdae was the principal adviser to the King of Cashel on religious matters.'

'A good point and one we shall check,' conceded Fidelma. She returned her gaze to the steward. 'What happened then?'

'Lachtna joined me and tried the door. We agreed to break it in. As you can see,' the steward added, gesturing at the condition of the oak door.

'I have seen,' Fidelma nodded. 'Which reminds me, when you came to the door, received no answer, found it locked and were fearful for what had happened, did you, in the short time you had to wait for Lachtna to join you, think to peer through one of those knot-holes that I see age has put into the wood?'

'No, I did not think of such a thing.'

'Come into the hall with me a moment.' They went out and Fidelma drew the door shut. She told them: 'I noticed one knot-hole especially – the one that is just below eye-level and shaped like a diamond. It is the length of a person's little finger. By pressing one's eye to it you could see roughly into the chamber. Try for yourself.'

Brother Tuamán moved forward and, following Fidelma's instruction, peered into the gap. Then he stood back and shook his head.

'I doubt that anyone would have seen very much. I can only see the abbot's desk but not where he was lying on the floor, nor can I see where the warrior was. However, lady, this did not occur to me.'

'I thought you might have made an attempt to look,' she said mildly. 'There seem to be a few new scratch-marks around the knot-hole. No matter.' She reopened the door. 'So . . . you and Lachtna burst into the room – and what did you see?'

'I saw the abbot's body first. There was blood soaking his robes and staining the floor. He had probably tried to use his staff of office as a means of defence for it was lying by his left hand. Before him, groaning, was the warrior. He was also on the floor. I saw the bloodied dagger by the warrior's right hand. It was obvious what had happened.'

'Which was what?'

The steward smiled thinly. 'The man had attacked the abbot and stabbed him. The abbot, perhaps in his dying moment, had swung his staff of office at his attacker. You may know it bears a heavy cross of silver on the end. This caught his attacker on the side of the head, knocking him unconscious for a while and allowing us to apprehend him.'

'I see. You felt that, had Gormán not been knocked senseless, he would have contrived to escape somehow. Surely the obstacles were many to such a flight in the circumstances.'

The steward thought and found no answer.

'You were going to show me the abbot's staff,' Fidelma reminded the man.

'It was cleaned before being given to the prior. After all, it will be his once he is confirmed as the next abbot.'

'I would still like to see it,' she insisted.

'The prior is not in his chamber . . .' prevaricated the steward.

'I presume, however, that the staff is?' cut in Fidelma.

The steward reluctantly led the way across the passage and opened the door. The room was sparsely furnished: a desk, with a candle and a tinder box on it and a vellum-bound parchment book. To Eadulf, it appeared to be a book of liturgical matter. There was a wooden chair, a bed and a cupboard which revealed only a change of robes and a pair of sandals.

'Prior Cuán certainly believes in frugality,' murmured Eadulf as he examined the belongings of the absent occupant.

A staff with a polished silver crucifix of intricate design was leaning prominently in one corner. It was shining and clean. Fidelma had vague memories of seeing Abbot Ségdae with it, but she had never taken much notice of it before. It was Eadulf who went over and picked it up. As he did so, a shorter stick next to it, a chestnut walking stick, was dislodged and clattered to the floor.

'It is the prior's walking stick,' the steward said, bending down to retrieve it and place it back against the wall.

Eadulf was turning the staff of office over in his hands and examining it carefully. Then he shrugged and put it back.

'You are right, Brother Tuamán,' he said. 'It has been well cleaned and polished. Did it have much blood on it?'

Brother Tuamán looked startled. 'Doubtless the physician would have such details.'

Fidelma tried to prevent a look of surprise from crossing her features. A physician? There had been no previous mention of any physician attending the scene. She felt annoyed with herself. Of course, she should have remembered that the attendance of a physician would be obligatory, given the death of an illustrious guest. Also, someone must have attended Gormán as his defence rested on a claim of having been rendered unconscious.

'Who was this physician?' she asked.

Brother Tuamán shrugged. 'I can't remember the name. They did not appear at the hearing.'

'The lady Airmid is the only physician in the fortress,' Conrí said. 'I'll take you to her apothecary, if you wish.'

'Before that, there is one thing I am curious about,' Eadulf said. 'It appears that the prior and Brother Mac Raith and Brother Máel Anfaid were not here when Abbot Ségdae was killed. Where were they?'

'I think Prior Cuán had gone to see Brehon Faolchair, but Brother Mac Raith and Brother Máel Anfaid were attending some service in the chapel in the Abbey of Nechta. They have a relative who serves in the community there.'

'A relative?' Eadulf was surprised. 'Are you saying that they are of the Uí Fidgente?'

'I thought they were of the Muscraige Mittine,' the steward

replied, mentioning a clan who dwelled south of the Abhainn Mhór, the big river that almost divided the kingdom. 'But they did mention a relative who serves at the abbey.'

'You don't know who?' Eadulf asked.

'It is not my position to question the personal lives of the brethren,' the steward said repressively.

'Very well.' Fidelma sighed. 'You have heard Gormán's claim that he was talking to the abbot when he was struck unconscious while standing with his back to the door. What do you have to say to that?'

'That the man is a fool and a liar.'

'And why would that be?'

'He was alone with the abbot in his chamber. The door was locked. At first I assumed that Abbot Ségdae might have locked it, but now I think it more likely that the warrior locked it so that he would not be disturbed in his plan to kill him. The notion that someone could have entered, knocked him out, killed the abbot, arranged the bodies, and then left, locking the door from the inside before disappearing, is nonsensical. Don't forget, I heard the voices raised, the thud of the falling bodies and was at that locked door within moments. No one could have entered or left the room. So the man is a fool to present so ridiculous an excuse and an obvious liar to boot.'

'That is the conundrum,' Eadulf observed aloud. 'Gormán is no fool – so why would he tell such a story if it did not happen as he said?'

'There was no third person,' the steward firmly assured them. 'You have examined the chamber. There is nowhere to hide without either the abbot or the warrior seeing them. And there is nowhere to enter or leave except through this solid oak door. Perhaps you would like to examine the window more carefully . . .'

'We have seen the iron bars,' Eadulf cut in. 'Anyway, it would have been difficult enough for someone to climb up or to climb down the outside wall – even if they *could* get in or out through the window.'

'Then you will agree with me.' Brother Tuamán's tone was again arrogant. 'The idea that anyone else could have killed the abbot is preposterous. Even Brehon Faolchair pointed out that the abbot was standing in front of the warrior. Had someone crept up behind Gormán to deliver the blow, the abbot would surely have seen and given warning of the attacker. Unless,' the steward said insolently, 'you will argue that the abbot connived in his own murder by having the warrior knocked out first?'

After they left Brother Tuamán, Conrí conducted them to a group of single-storey stone buildings to the far side of the fortress and took them into the centre of a well-cultivated herb garden.

'You'll find the lady Airmid there,' he said, pointing to one of the buildings. 'It is where she prepares her concoctions. She is usually there at this hour. I'll leave you here as I have business at the *laochtech*. Should you need me, any warrior will know where to find me.'

The woman who greeted Fidelma and Eadulf as they entered the small apothecary was tall – as tall as Fidelma. Her fair hair had a reddish tinge, making it almost copper. She regarded Fidelma and Eadulf with curiosity. Her features were pleasant, while her shapely mouth had a humorous quality to it. The couple paused a moment on the threshold to allow their senses to adjust to the pungent smells of the spices and herbs of the apothecary. Eadulf was immediately reminded of Brother Conchobhar's apothecary in Cashel, except here a little grey terrier ran up to them and sniffed excitedly at the new scents they had brought with them. The woman had to shout an order and the dog immediately desisted and went off to examine other things.

'Come in, I have been expecting you.' Her voice had an attractive musical quality. 'I heard that you had arrived in the fortress last evening but I was unable to attend.'

Fidelma stared at the familiar face of the woman for a moment. 'Have we met before?' she asked.

The woman chuckled. 'We have not, but people often see in me a reflection of my brother, Donennach.'

Eadulf recalled that Donennach had mentioned his sister. 'Then you are also his *tanaise*, his heir-apparent?'

'I am Airmid. I prefer to be known simply as the physician to this household.'

'It is an appropriate name for one of your calling.' Fidelma returned the woman's smile. Airmid was the legendary daughter of Diancecht, the old pagan God of Medicine. Her father had been a jealous god. He had killed his own son Miach, who had begun to outshine his father's healing knowledge. Airmid had then collected all the 365 healing herbs that had grown from the grave of her brother, and arranged them so that everyone would have knowledge of their use. However, Diancecht, in a temper, then destroyed the arrangement of her collection so that the secrets would become lost for ever.

The physician grimaced. 'Much sport was made of my name when I was studying at Inis Faithlcann. I rather think my professor hoped I would fail to qualify because of my name. However, I should apologise to you, lady.'

'For what reason?' Fidelma frowned.

'I could not attend the feast to welcome you last night for I was called to attend an injured man in the Abbey of Nechta. One of the brethren had contrived to break his arm and it needed to be set. Thankfully, it will heal well,' she added. 'Now, how may I serve you? I know you are investigating the circumstances of Abbot Ségdae's murder.'

'I was told that a physician had examined the abbot's body,' explained Fidelma. 'Conrí conducted us here.'

'I am that physician,' Airmid confirmed easily and indicated a bench for them to be seated while taking a stool opposite. 'This is a sad event, and one that has upset my brother considerably. He was hoping to strengthen the peace that he has made with your brother. This murder has provided an opportunity for Abbot Nannid to pursue his ambitions.'

'Abbot Nannid has ambitions?' Eadulf asked in surprise. 'So far as I am aware, Mungairit is the largest abbey among the Uí Fidgente. He is its abbot. What other ambition could he have?'

'The abbots of our kingdoms are usually of the royal families. Abbot Nannid is a cousin of Crundmáel of the Ua Coirpri. Crundmáel's son, Eóghanán, led the Uí Fidgente against Cashel at Cnoc Áine where Colgú defeated him. If anything happened to my brother, Nannid could have a legitimate right to claim that he be ruler.'

'I did not know that,' admitted Fidelma. 'But you are Donennach's heir-apparent.'

'I hold the office only on sufferance; that is, until someone better qualified in the eyes of the *derbhfine* emerges,' smiled the physician. 'My brother's son is not yet of the age of responsibility but it is hoped that he will prove himself a worthy successor. However, Nannid's ambition is one that concerns us. If my brother stands against Nannid and his newfound views, then who knows what might happen?'

'Newfound views?' Eadulf picked up the phrase.

'It was not that long ago that Nannid decided to become a champion of the Penitentials, claiming that they superseded the laws of the Brehons. Having now claimed the role of spokesman for those who believe this, Nannid is making himself very popular among several of our clerics.'

'And this is why your brother finds it hard to challenge him about Gormán? I see . . . Nannid has decided to make this an issue of magnitude.' Fidelma could understand Donennach's dilemma.

'Whichever choice Donennach makes, I am afraid it will mean war and perhaps the destruction of our house.'

'Let me finish my investigation first before the sentence is given on punishment,' Fidelma advised. 'Gormán has yet to be proven guilty beyond all doubt.'

Airmid looked sceptical. 'Well, I do not think that I can help you.'

'What do you mean?' Eadulf demanded.

'Oh, it is not that I won't,' Airmid explained hastily, 'but I can't present you with any magical evidence that would prove your warrior friend is innocent as he has claimed. I was summoned to the abbot's chamber and found that he had been stabbed several times in the chest and in the neck. The wounds were such that they seemed to have been struck in a frenzy of anger.'

'Did you also examine Gormán?'

'Only afterwards, when he had been dragged to the cells and handled roughly by our guards. I could discount the superficial bruises from that beating. He maintained that he had been struck from behind and rendered unconscious, as you already know. He had certainly been struck on the head,' Airmid told them. 'There was evidence of a blow on the right side of the skull.'

'Had the skin been cut there?' Eadulf asked.

'The bruising and swelling could have been made with a staff striking the area above the right ear, with some force. But there was no sign of the skin being perforated and bleeding.'

'No blood?'

'None. Is that important?'

'It is claimed that he was struck with the abbot's staff,' Eadulf pointed out.

'So I was told,' she nodded. 'It seems logical that the abbot would use it to defend himself with.'

'And was the staff presented in evidence to Brehon Faolchair at the hearing?'

Airmid grimaced. 'The circumstances and events were considered obvious and so I was not summoned to any formal hearing. My opinion, when I gave it to Brehon Faolchair, was not deemed to be at odds with the rest of the evidence. I could only say what I observed of the injuries, no more, no less.'

'And for that we are grateful,' Eadulf said, with a glance to Fidelma to signal that he had finished.

They left Airmid's apothecary, but before Fidelma could question Eadulf, they found Brehon Faolchair coming towards the building.

'Lady,' he greeted her. 'Conrí said that I might find you here.'

'And you have found me,' Fidelma replied.

'Conrí told me that you were interested in the key of Abbot Ségdae's chamber. It was found by Lachtna when they broke in. It was lying on the floor, which was proof that the door had been secured from the inside.'

'So I am told.'

Brehon Faolchair fumbled in his *bossán*, the pouch he wore at his waist, drew out a bronze key and offered it to her.

'This is the key to the abbot's chamber. Lachtna and Brother Tuamán confirm that it was found inside the room.'

Fidelma took it and turned it over. It was unremarkable. Keys and locks were common enough and certainly varied in design thanks to the mastery of the locksmiths, who often chose between bronze and iron to make their locks and keys.

To the obvious surprise of Brehon Faolchair, she closed a hand around the key and said: 'Forgive me if I keep this for just a short while until I check that it does fit in the lock.'

'You have my word it fits the lock,' he said, and bridled a little.

'I do not doubt your word, but first-hand knowledge is always better.'

The Brehon gave a snort and turned away, saying; 'It will soon be time for the midday meal. A bell will ring. You will find me at that time in the great hall.'

Eadulf seemed as eager as she was to retrace their steps back to the guest-hostel, Fidelma noticed. Her reason was that it would be a good opportunity to try the key, but she wondered why he was so keen. This time there was no guard outside the building and so they entered freely. Brother Tuamán was still there, apparently just leaving the building. He seemed surprised to see them again.

'You seek me, lady?'

Fidelma shook her head. 'I just needed to check something. We will not detain you.'

The steward hovered uncertainly as Fidelma and Eadulf quickly climbed up to the next storey. Eadulf waited as she inserted the key into the damaged lock. It fitted and even turned easily, for it was only the wood around the lock, where it had been fitted to the door, which was splintered.

Eadulf was suddenly aware that Brother Tuamán had followed them up the stairs and was watching them with curiosity.

'Are you sure you do not need my help?' he enquired when he saw that Eadulf had spotted him.

'We don't want to delay you when you were so obviously leaving,' Eadulf replied pointedly.

The man hesitated before turning and descending the stairs. Eadulf looked round to find that Fidelma had already entered the chamber and was bending to pick up the key from a spot behind the door.

She looked up and told Eadulf: 'I just wanted to check the position where Lachtna said that he had found the key when they burst into the chamber.'

As she straightened up, Eadulf placed a finger against his lips and nodded to the chamber that was used by Prior Cuán. He moved across and cautiously opened the door. Fidelma followed him with a puzzled frown. Eadulf entered and gestured to the abbot's staff which stood in a corner, still resting against the wall.

'I cannot accept that this was the weapon that knocked out Gormán,' he whispered, 'or inflicted the wound described by Airmid just now.'

'Why not?' Fidelma asked.

Eadulf took the staff and indicated the heavy silver crucifix at the top.

'If the abbot had struck Gormán with this staff, the sharpness of the metal would have lacerated his skin. There would have been a great deal of blood and the wound would have been noticeable and needed treatment. No one has mentioned bloodshed. The physician said it was merely a bruise, an abrasion but not a wound.'

'Maybe the blow could have been delivered with the wooden shaft?' Fidelma suggested.

'Had it been so, this staff would not have been sufficient to knock senseless a warrior like Gormán.'

'Because?' queried Fidelma, peering closely at the wooden staff. She realised what he meant even before he explained.

'The wood of the staff is a thin yew and would have shown some degree of damage from such an impact. To knock Gormán out would have taken something harder – perhaps a cudgel or a stick.'

By the time they descended to the lower floor, it seemed that Brother Tuamán had departed. Eadulf saw that Fidelma was deep in thought so he did not speak as they walked back towards the main building of the fortress. It was only when a bell rang out briefly that Eadulf broke the silence.

'Where now?' he asked. 'Should we not go to see Gormán?'

To his surprise, Fidelma shook her head, glancing towards the sun. 'I think that was the bell for the *etar-shod*, the midday meal. We will attend to that before we speak with Gormán. I need a little more time to digest things.'

'It does not look good for him, does it?' Eadulf sighed.

'There are some things that need more consideration,' she replied in a solemn tone. 'Several questions that need an answer.'

'We spoke about a lack of motivation,' Eadulf said. 'That is a matter we must pursue with Gormán after we have had our meal.'

'He does not admit to the act, let alone confess to a motivation,' Fidelma said rather impatiently.

'You misunderstand. I meant that . . .' But Eadulf realised that he did not know what he meant, only that he felt at a loss; unable to see any other explanation.

Several of the household and guests were assembled in the great hall and were sitting down to the light midday meal. Fidelma went to Brehon Faolchair and handed him back the key with a smile of thanks before she joined Eadulf and they seated themselves at the table. Prince Donennach was absent, as was his sister. But Abbot Nannid and his steward were there, along with Prior Cuán. Conrí entered and seated himself beside Fidelma.

'How is the investigation proceeding, lady?' he asked in a hopeful tone but lowering his voice so that Abbot Nannid at the far end of the table did not hear.

'Slow and difficult,' she confessed.

'Was Airmid helpful?'

'So far as she was able.'

'She is a handsome woman, is she not?' he sighed. 'Alas, she is too involved in the healing arts to take notice of the warlord of her people.' There was more than a touch of regret in Conrí's voice.

'I thought as heir-apparent to Donennach that she was deeply involved in governance as well as her medical work?'

'Not really. The Uí Fidgente bloodline of Óengus survives only in Donennach and his sister. Most of them were killed when Eóganán and his evil family declared themselves rulers. They were almost wiped out, as you know, when your brother defeated and slew Eóganán on Cnoc Áine. Donennach became ruler as a popular choice. There was no one of consequence to name as his heir-apparent but Airmid. She says it will only be temporary until Donennach's son Ercc grows to manhood and proves himself worthy to take over. Ercc is undergoing his education among the Corco Duibhne and not yet at the age of choice.'

'What if Airmid marries and has her own children?' asked Eadulf.

Conrí's smile grew bitter. 'She says that one bad marriage was enough for her.'

'Then she has been married?'

'Many years back,' he said. 'Donennach and the family disapproved of the choice, for the man was unworthy. However, Airmid is a determined woman and she had to find out the hard way. Donennach was trying to get her to divorce the man.'

'On what grounds?'

'Oh, that he beat her. She once appeared with a blemish on her face where he had struck her. Donennach ordered her to take her *coibhe*, the dowry, and leave, demanding full compensation according to law.'

'And did she?'

'It was unnecessary, for the husband was then reported killed at the battle of Cnoc Áine, but—'

He was cut short by a guard entering the great hall together with Enda, who was looking strangely agitated. There was something in his stance that caused the warlord to excuse himself, then rise and hasten over to him. Conrí bent his head to listen to the guard's urgent whispering. Fidelma saw a worried expression cross the warlord's features and he turned towards Brehon Faolchair and beckoned to him. The Brehon immediately rose and went to join the warlord. It was clear that something had happened.

Brehon Faolchair stood still for a moment listening, his face a mirror of the warlord's grim expression. Then he shook his head from side to side as if in disbelief as he returned to the table.

'A problem?' queried Prior Cuán, looking up.

Brehon Faolchair looked straight towards Fidelma, addressing her with a voice that was now very grave.

'I am afraid that the attempt to buy time with a new investigation of Abbot Ségdae's murder has come to nothing, lady,' he said tightly.

'There can be no point in renewing the hearing, for Gormán has now demonstrated his complete guilt.'

Fidelma felt apprehensive as she returned the Brehon's angry gaze. 'What has happened?' she asked.

'Gormán has escaped from his cell and fled the fortress with the woman, Aibell.'

# CHAPTER SEVEN

&#x10cfa;&#x10cfa;

After Brehon Faolchair and Conrí had left the great hall and the clamour that had greeted the Brehon's outburst had subsided, Fidelma asked Enda what exactly had taken place.

'It is very confusing.' It was unusual for her to see the phlegmatic young man so utterly at a loss. 'This morning, as you know, I went with Ciarnat and saw Aibell to pass on your message. We were then allowed to visit Gormán in his cell. It was true that he and Aibell had been fretting because you had not visited or contacted them since our arrival. Gormán was morose, of course, but seemed thankful when I gave him your message and assured him that you were doing everything to help him.'

'So what has gone wrong?' Eadulf demanded.

'I don't know. Gormán was vehement that he was innocent but relieved that matters were now in your hands; he was anxious to speak with you. After that, Ciarnat and I left him. I did not bother to come and find you afterwards as there was no need. Your message had been passed on. I went to the barracks and was chatting to some of the warriors there. You can learn much in a barracks when warriors are relaxing and speaking freely.'

'Probably so,' Eadulf agreed. 'But when did you learn about the escape?'

'Just now. I was in the barracks when a guard came in looking

102

as if he had been in a fight. I recognised him as the guard from the prison. He shouted that the prisoner had escaped. Some of the men leaped to their feet and went haring off to give chase. I could not believe the guard meant Gormán, so I asked him what had happened. As he helped himself to a jug of *corma*, he told me that the prisoner's woman, Aibell, had come with a meal. As he bent to open the cell door, he was knocked sprawling by a blow from behind and was rendered unconscious. When he came to, the prisoner and the woman had disappeared.'

'Is he saying that Aibell knocked him out?' Fidelma sounded sceptical.

'The commander of the guard came in at that moment and I hurried here to find you but was overtaken by him – hence we arrived together in the hall.'

'Have Gormán and Aibell been caught? You say the warriors set off when the guard sounded the alarm. It would be hard to leave the fortress without being seen or to hide without being discovered.'

'I do not know, lady.'

'Where is Ciarnat?'

'That, also, I do not know.'

Fidelma put her hand to her head in disbelief. 'I do not understand it. Of all the stupid things to do!' She moved quickly to the doors of the hall, with Eadulf and Enda in her wake. 'Come, let us follow Conrí and Faolchair,' she called over her shoulder. 'Whatever possessed Gormán to do this? Things were difficult enough but now this action has made them impossible.'

'It is unlike Gormán,' Eadulf replied.

'But maybe not unlike Aibell.' Enda showed his bias. 'She has a mind of her own. And I haven't seen Ciarnat since I left her to go to the barracks.'

As they started to cross the courtyard, they saw Conrí hurrying towards them from the direction of the main gates. By his side was a dishevelled-looking guard.

'Have they been recaptured?' Fidelma demanded before the warlord could speak.

Conrí shook his head. 'It was a well conceived plan,' he replied bitterly. 'It seems that Gormán's wife had two horses ready at a side gate, just behind the prison house. That gate is usually locked. There is no sign of them but they can't have gone far. I have sent Socht and some men after them. Socht is a good tracker. They can't be allowed to escape.' He then added as if in apology, 'Even though I sympathise with Gormán's plight.'

'So they escaped through a side gate on horseback?'

'The cells for prisoners are entered by a separate entrance from the main barracks, lady,' explained Conrí. 'As I said, the gate there is usually locked and bolted. We don't often use it, since its main purpose is as a strategic exit for our warriors should the fortress be under attack at the main gates. A party of warriors can leave at the side to encircle the raiders at the main gates.'

'Are you claiming that Aibell had planned this and had two horses waiting outside with this gate already unlocked and unbolted?' Eadulf could scarcely believe this.

'Yes. They even used the horses they arrived here on,' the warlord informed them. 'My guess is that if Gormán is the warrior I think he is, then he will head south across the stony ground to hide their tracks, and then cross the river and follow it further south, hoping to disguise the tracks by riding in the shallows. He will think that we will expect him to immediately turn due east. We should be able to recapture them shortly,' he concluded with satisfaction.

'It sounds incredible,' Fidelma said.

'I doubt Aibell could have accomplished this alone,' agreed the warlord, and Fidelma noticed that his eyes flickered towards the guard at his side as he spoke. The man in question was an ugly-looking fellow, with overhanging brows, and hardly any neck to speak of. He was small and thickset, with a look of cunning about him.

'Are you the guard who was knocked out by a young woman?' she asked.

The man reddened as he defiantly grunted an affirmative.

'Explain what happened?' she demanded.

'The woman came with a meal for the prisoner,' the man replied sullenly. 'I bent to unlock the door to let her in and she hit me. I knew nothing more until I recovered my senses, by which time they had fled.'

'She arrived carrying food. You turned your back, bent to the door . . . and she knocked you out?'

'Exactly as I said. I had no suspicion, see, for the girl was always visiting the prisoner and bringing him meals. I had often opened the cell before in such a fashion.'

'It is difficult to believe a young woman would be able to give you a sufficiently powerful blow as to cause a burly man like you to be rendered unconscious.' Eadulf was suspicious.

The man looked sheepish. 'Nevertheless, brother, that is what happened. She must have hit me with something heavy. A cudgel – that's it! She must have used a cudgel.'

'So what happened to the tray of food that she was carrying while she was producing the cudgel from somewhere and preparing to knock you out with it?' Fidelma asked.

The guard hesitated, his face reddening even deeper. Then he dropped his gaze.

'What did the girl say to the prisoner after she paid you to let her into the cell?' Fidelma demanded brusquely.

'She said . . .' the man began, stopped and looked helpless.

'It was obvious you were bribed,' Fidelma continued. 'She needed help to arrange such an escape; to have the gate unlocked and horses ready. You were bribed, that is plain. Now I want to know what she said.'

The guard seemed to realise it was futile to make any further pretence. He muttered, 'I heard her say something about betrayal.'

Fidelma's eyes narrowed. 'Betrayal? Can you recall her precise words?'

The man frowned. 'I think it was "we are betrayed". Perhaps it was "we have been betrayed". Something like that. The rest was spoken in a whisper. I agreed to give them a good head start . . .'

'For a price?' Conrí was angry.

'Most things are done for a price,' the man replied sulkily.

'You will have time to meditate on that at leisure in the cells that you once guarded. We will hear what your commander has to say about your willingness to take bribes and betray our trust.'

As Conrí marched the man off at sword point, Fidelma glanced at Eadulf and Enda. '"We are betrayed!"' she quoted. 'What do you think Aibell meant by that?'

'Earlier this morning, she was content to leave the inquiry in your hands,' the warrior replied. 'Then in a short space of time, she had planned and executed a successful escape for Gormán. Why?'

'And why at this precise time?' Eadulf wanted to know. 'If such a plan was feasible, why had she not put it into action before? Nine whole days have passed since her man was incarcerated and more or less declared guilty, apart from the legal niceties. Why wait until after you had arrived and started an investigation? It just doesn't make any sense.'

'Things only make sense when we are in possession of all the facts.' Fidelma sounded resigned. It was clear that she could not find any logic for this new turn of events.

Brehon Faolchair had called a meeting in the great hall. Prince Donennach, looking more exhausted than before, sat in his seat of office and allowed Brehon Faolchair to conduct the proceedings. Prior Cuán and his steward, the tall and arrogant Brother Tuamán, attended but sat quietly. Abbot Nannid and his steward, Brother Cuineáin, had plenty to say on the other hand, muttering about conspiracy and Gormán's guilt. Conrí and Enda stood in the background. There was a tense atmosphere as Brehon Faolchair began.

'We have heard what happened,' he said. 'On my part, we admit our responsibility in that one of the guards was bribed. We are not without fault in this matter.'

'We also know why it has happened,' interposed Abbot Nannid. 'The man escaped to avoid punishment and has given us a clear declaration of his guilt. Further, we know now that his woman is as guilty as he is.'

'The escape is not so easily explained as there was no logical reason why Gormán should decide to escape now,' remarked Fidelma. 'It is strange.'

'Strange because you do not want to believe his guilt.' Abbot Nannid's voise was full of derision. 'I am sure that you have had time to work out some honey-tongued reason for the man's action. Come, Fidelma of Cashel. I am waiting for some excuse.'

'I am as perplexed as you are,' Fidelma returned heatedly. 'Perhaps even more so. The case against Gormán has yet to be heard in its legal entirety.'

As Abbot Nannid let out a bark of laughter, Prince Donennach stirred and said, 'Surely, Fidelma, the matter now speaks for itself? I am afraid that I now agree with the abbot that Gormán has declared himself guilty.'

'Yet a court must still legally try him and find him so. That is the law,' Fidelma insisted stubbornly.

'You may have beguiled those who wish to be beguiled last night by trying to gain time by making legal points. But now the matter is at an end.' Abbot Nannid raised his chin aggressively.

'Gormán will be returned for trial. Let us wait for that trial until we declare him guilty,' Fidelma said firmly. 'I promise you, he will return for trial.'

Brehon Faolchair smiled with sad cynicism. Even Eadulf stared at her in some amazement.

'How long will that be?' Abbot Nannid sniggered. 'We do not have eternity to wait for that promise to be fulfilled.'

'I do not expect to wait an eternity.' She turned to Conrí. 'Is there word from Socht yet?'

'There is none yet,' Conrí said.

Abbot Nannid's tone was disparaging. 'If you ask me, Gormán and the women had help . . . and I don't mean just one guard's greed. I mean the help of Gormán's friends. He won't be found easily when he has all the territories of the Eóghanacht to hide in.'

Fidelma bridled at the accusation. 'I hear Nannid is of the line of Coirpre, son of Bríon, who claimed to be seventh-generation descent from Eóghan Mór. So Nannid claims to be an Eóghanacht. If that is so, perhaps Nannid is hiding him?'

Prior Cuán was worried at the studied insult and tried to draw them back to the main point of the discussion.

'I am sure that the correct path is to persuade or attempt to bring Gormán back here for a hearing so that all the arguments can be properly presented before the prince and his Brehon. We must put our trust in Conrí's men to overtake him in this flight.'

'What if they do not overtake him?' Abbot Nannid jeered. 'I recall that Gormán has friends among certain warriors of the Uí Fidgente.' The barb was clearly thrown towards Conrí, who made an obvious effort of will not to take the bait. The abbot went on: 'What if he goes to ground like some fox? Do you expect us to calmly wait for ever and a day before we demand that Cashel make recompense for the action of the commander of the King's bodyguard?'

Fidelma turned her gaze to Prince Donennach. 'I ask for an adequate period of time to find Gormán and then persuade him to return here to answer the charges.'

'Even if you found him, do you think you could persuade him?' Prince Donennach asked in surprise.

'I offer no guarantee, but the consequences of the matter are such that we must go as far as we can to resolve it.'

'I object to such sycophantic behaviour to the Eóghanacht of Cashel!' Abbot Nannid thundered. 'These are just honeyed words again without substance. Of course she has no intention of persuading the man and his woman to return here!'

Prince Donennach ignored him even though Conrí had uttered a loud hissing sound at the suggestion that Prince Donennach was a sycophant. The prince held up a hand, as if to wave Conrí back, and glanced anxiously at Brehon Faolchair. 'Is there some precedent to our giving a ruling to this matter?' he asked.

Eadulf realised that most judgements were usually justified by reference to precedent or *fásach*.

Brehon Faolchair was hesitant. 'I have not heard of one. Nonetheless, perhaps it is time one was set, in view of the uniqueness of the situation. However, if it is done we must have some time limitation. Abbot Nannid has made his strong views known. What do you say, Prior Cuán? Would you agree that the *dálaigh* from Cashel be allowed a period of time to find and persuade Gormán to return for trial?'

Prior Cuán compressed his lips. 'I am no judge but a simple man of religion. I could not say what is right and proper in this case. Let those learned with the law make the decision.'

Fidelma glanced at Eadulf and grimaced. It seemed she didn't think much of the prior's attempt at diplomacy.

Brehon Faolchair held a whispered exchange with Prince Donennach then he turned back to Fidelma.

'We have decided to allow Socht the ancient time period of nine nights and intervening days. If Gormán is not brought back here by then, he will be judged in his absence.'

It was not the first time that Eadulf had heard reference to the mystical figure nine. In ancient times Fidelma had told him that her people judged the passing of the week as by nights, followed by days. The old week was therefore nine nights, and three of these weeks constituted the lunar month. The figure of nine seemed to occur in many stories of Fidelma's people as Eadulf had understood them. The High King Laoghaire had set up a nine-man commission to consider and render the ancient laws into the new Christian writing.

'I accept the terms,' Fidelma agreed, glancing at Conrí. 'Then all we can do is wait word from Socht.'

At that very moment, the hall doors burst open and two warriors came in dragging a struggling girl between them.

Fidelma turned, wondering if it was Aibell and whether she and Gormán had already been caught. But the struggling figure was the unkempt form of Ciarnat.

'We caught her outside the fort, lord,' one of the warriors addressed Prince Donennach.

Cairnat tried to shake her arms free but gave up and attempted to address the prince instead. 'I was returning to the fort when these idiots caught hold of me and dragged me here,' she panted. 'I do not understand the meaning of this. What am I supposed to have done?'

'Are you saying that you do not know that your friend Aibell and her husband have escaped from this fort?' Brehon Faolchair demanded sternly.

Fidelma saw the girl's features tighten. It was difficult to ascertain whether she was surprised by the news or not.

'I was visiting my mother in the township. I know nothing,' she said sullenly.

Abbot Nannid smothered a guffaw. 'Another chance to beguile us with some new expression of innocence?'

Fidelma moved to the side of the girl with a sympathetic look. 'You say that you have only just returned to the fortress. When did you leave it?'

'I left just after we delivered your message to Aibell and Gormán, lady,' the girl responded. 'We told Gormán to be patient, for you were reinvestigating the matter.'

'You left at that time? Why?' Brehon Faolchair wanted to know.

'To see my elderly mother, as I said.'

Abbot Nannid snorted. 'An elderly mother? I don't believe that for one moment.'

The girl turned with an angry scowl towards him. 'Anyone in this fortress will tell you that my mother, Étromma, served here as a cook for many years and therefore I followed in that service. She is elderly now and alone apart from myself. She lost two sons, my brothers, in the service of the Princes of the Uí Fidgente.'

'And I suppose you claim that you have no knowledge that your friend, the girl Aibell, was plotting the escape of the murderer, Gormán?' Abbot Nannid was unbending with his questions.

The girl's reply was equally pugnacious. 'My mother is elderly. She still dwells in the township in the shadow of this fortress. I left here earlier having no duties to fulfil here today, in order to visit her and break bread with her. I did not expect to be assaulted by warriors on my return to the fortress gates, nor to be dragged here as if I am some criminal without the law.'

Fidelma was watching the girl's features closely. She was keeping something back, Fidelma could tell. 'We do have to ask you some questions,' she said gently. 'This is because we cannot understand why Aibell should have arranged an escape for Gormán at this time, especially after the assurance I gave you this morning. I am told Gormán was content to let me handle matters. How was his mind changed so quickly?'

The girl shook her head. 'I cannot help you.'

'Well, I suppose your mother can support your story that you went straight there and remained there until now.' It was Abbot Nannid again. tone.

The girl immediately protested: 'My mother is elderly and frail. She should not be intimidated!'

'Very convenient,' remarked the abbot.

'You see,' Fidelma went on, ignoring him, 'there are difficulties for us, Ciarnat. Brehon Faolchair must be assured that you did nothing to aid the escape of Gormán and your friend, Aibell.'

'I have no understanding of what has happened.' Ciarnat was obdurate and yet there was still something that made Fidelma suspicious. 'I left the fortress at midday and have only just returned.'

'I will explain, Ciarnat,' Brehon Faolchair said easily, 'so that you may understand how we are thinking. Firstly, this escape seemed so well planned. Horses had to be made ready, they had to be led to the side gate of this fortress which, moreover, had to be unbolted and unlocked, ready and open for the escapers to flee through. If Aibell had accomplished all that by herself, it would have taken some time in the preparation, yet it seems she was able to do this in a very short time. The actual escape was easy enough. The guard admitted he was bribed. For the moment, the bribe continues to buy his silence – but a night in his own cell may release the stiffness of his tongue.'

Ciarnat stood silent, looking wretched and uneasy.

'But the most puzzling aspect of this escape was something which the guard let slip,' Fidelma added. 'He overheard Aibell tell Gormán that they had been betrayed. By whom were they betrayed – and about what? Was this so-called betrayal the reason for the escape?'

'You see now, Ciarnat, why we might need to ask questions of you,' pressed Brehon Faolchair.

'The girl is clearly the accomplice,' Abbot Nannid asserted. 'I am glad that the *dálaigh* appears to admit this. Those who help the murderer share the crime. We might not be able to hang Gormán but we can make an example of his accomplice.'

Ciarnat gave a small cry, a clenched fist raised to her mouth as she understood the meaning behind his words.

Fidelma glanced at him, infuriated. She felt sure she could have coaxed some more information from the girl, but the abbot's brutal tactic had spoiled any chance of that by scaring her.

'You have a way of distorting words, Abbot Nannid, and that can be a dangerous trait,' she reproached him. 'I have merely put some facts forward to seek answers and have yet to draw any conclusions from them.'

'The conclusions should be obvious,' returned the bellicose abbot.

'They might be to you, but not to one trained in law.' Fidelma was losing patience.

Ciarnat was trembling. 'I don't know what to say,' she began hesitantly.

'Say what you know and what you believe to be the truth,' Eadulf advised encouragingly, 'and you will not be at fault.'

'You told me that you would see Gormán and Aibell after the questioning of the witnesses. With the warrior, Enda, I took this news back to Aibell and Gormán. Enda is witness to this. Then I left the fortress and went to my mother's house. That is all I know.'

'If you didn't help your friends to escape, who did?' boomed Abbot Nannid.

'I have already told you what I know. I cannot invent anything else.'

'I for one do not believe you,' the abbot snapped.

'Thankfully, it is not up to you to believe the statements of a witness,' Eadulf suddenly exploded at the man. He had been feeling his temper simmering at the rudeness and disrespect to his wife from the Abbot of Mungairit ever since the previous evening. 'Your ability in the matter of belief has been questionable in the past. If I remember correctly, when we were uncovering the conspiracy against Prince Donennach in your own abbey, you were either gullible about believing people or you had your own purpose!'

The abbot wheeled round on Eadulf, his face livid, his mouth working. For a moment it looked as if the man would forget his religious calling and resort to violence.

Brehon Faolchair moved forward with a restraining hand to separate them.

'I do believe that all our tempers have become a little heated today. It is not often that we find our trust abused – and this can often lead to anger.'

Fidelma shot a warning glance at Eadulf. In a way, he had been right in that the abbot had either been an innocent participant in the conspiracy at Mungairit Abbey, or that he had played his part with knowledge. In any event, she was sure that Prince Donennach's sister Airmid had made a correct assessment that Nannid was watching the prince's office with covetous eyes. At Mungairit, Fidelma had decided that she could allow some leniency in her judgement and did so. But now Nannid seemed to have emerged in what seemed, if Airmid was right, another conspiracy to overthrow her brother.

'Brehon Faolchair is correct,' Prince Donennach was saying to his cousin. 'There is no need to be unduly harsh on the girl. I recall that Étromma, her mother, did serve our household well for many years. She has explained her absence from the fortress. It is easy to check.'

'But in the meantime, we should keep her in the cells until we are sure,' Abbot Nannid said eagerly.

'I do not think we need be so drastic,' Brehon Faolchair reproved him. 'Anyway, if she were part of the escape plan, why should she return here? She would have ridden off with her friends. Is this not so?'

He asked the question of Fidelma who bowed her head in response.

'The logic is unassailable,' she replied solemnly.

'Then I will suggest a compromise,' Prince Donennach offered. 'My sister, Airmid, will take her into her household, where she may feel safe. Then we can have time to consider matters.'

'Once again, I protest.' Abbot Nannid would not let it go. He said snidely, 'Surely we do not have to continue appeasing the Eóghanacht?'

However, Brehon Faolchair was nodding his approval. 'An

excellent suggestion. So be it.' He turned to the two warriors who had brought Ciarnat into the hall. 'Take the girl to the lady Airmid and tell her that she is to be treated as a guest in her household by order of the prince. I will come later and explain the situation in more detail.'

As the men escorted Cairnat from the hall, Prince Donennach rose. Abbot Nannid did not disguise his rage as he too rose and, with a swift jerk of his head towards the prince, strode away. His steward, Brother Cuineáin, followed – almost scampering behind him.

Prince Donennach looked after them as the doors of the hall were slammed shut with a force that shook the walls. He turned apologetically to those who remained. 'This prelate cousin of mine is a man of fixed vision. I fear he admits of no opinions, judgements or interpretations other than his own. Remember, you have nine nights to find the fugitive and return him to face trial, otherwise we face difficult decisions.'

With this comment he left for his private chamber, followed by Brehon Faolchair.

Brother Tuamán rose, bowing to Prior Cuán. 'Forgive me, I have more matters to attend to in respect of the debates between Imleach and the Mungairit.'

Prior Cuán regarded him in astonishment. 'Do you mean, after all this, that you expect there to be some sort of debate continuing between Imleach and Mungairit?'

'We should not abandon the work now.' The steward's voice rose slightly in admonishment. 'We can still achieve much.'

'For what purpose is this work when we have heard so clearly that Abbot Nannid will not retreat from his position? He and his acolytes will insist on keeping to the Penitentials and the argument that they should supplant the laws of the Five Kingdoms.' Prior Cuán concluded dryly, 'I, for one, would say that the only course was for us to return to Imleach.'

'Just because the abbot has been removed from the debate,' Brother Tuamán argued, 'there is no need to abandon it entirely. After all, Abbot Ségdae was reconsidering his view on this matter of church law.'

Fidelma could not contain her surprise at his remark.

'Brother Tuamám, I have known Abbot Ségdae since he became Abbot and chief ecclesiastical adviser to my brother. Are you seriously claiming that he was considering adopting the Penitentials? Is that what you mean?'

The tall man reared up and said in a pompous tone, 'As steward it has been my privilege to have discussed many of these matters with the abbot, and his attitudes were not as fixed as has been suggested. I hope, when I have gathered my notes, to have similar discussions with Prior Cuán, to carry on this momentous work with our brethren of the Uí Fidgente churches.'

With an all-embracing bob of his head to the company, he strutted off.

Prior Cuán then struggled to his feet, pausing for a moment, leaning heavily on his stick. 'I cannot believe Ségdae would have contemplated supporting the Penitentials,' he said.

'You seem as surprised as we are, Prior Cuán,' observed Eadulf.

'I have only been Abbot Ségdae's deputy for a short period,' Prior Cuán replied quietly, 'yet it is the first time that I have heard of any compromise on this matter. Abbot Ségdae and I discussed this topic several times together, as well as in the opening debate with Abbot Nannid. He was prepared to stand against the use of the Penitentials outside any religious community. Furthermore, he was even against their use within a community in which the entire *fine* or family of the community had not freely accepted them. I will have to tackle the subject further with Brother Tuamán. The fellow has an exaggerated idea of his own self-importance, as you may have noticed. It seems inconceivable that the abbot would reveal this change of attitude to him and not to me.'

'Do you know much about your steward's background?' Fidelma asked.

'About Brother Tuamán? Only that he has not been steward for very long. In fact, he arrived at Imleach shortly before me. He presented himself with good credentials, being well educated at the abbey on the island in Loch Léin. After Brother Madagan's betrayal, which you know about, the abbot was desperate for a good steward and Brother Tuamán seemed well qualified.'

Fidelma smiled ruefully. 'He is that. However, I shall look forward to learning what you find out about Abbot Ségdae's views and whether they had changed. It is an interesting point that the steward makes though,' she added thoughtfully.

Prior Cuán asked: 'Which point?'

'If Abbot Ségdae was about to make such a momentous decision with regard to accepting the rule of the Penitentials and bringing them into Imleach, then his sudden demise would seem providential to those arguing against them.'

Prior Cuán's face went pale, and an expression of anger flashed across his usually benign features.

'Are you accusing me of welcoming the death of the abbot!' he said hoarsely.

Fidelma held up a protesting hand, palm outwards.

'Forgive me, Prior Cuán. Eadulf here will tell you that I sometimes think aloud.'

Eadulf contrived to examine the floor for he knew that Fidelma's 'thinking aloud' was often designed to bring forth a reaction.

'I have a fault,' she continued, 'which is to examine matters from other points of view. If you look at all possibilities, no matter how ill conceived and odious they may be to one, then by either storing them in the mind or discarding them, one may well come to a better perspective.'

Prior Cuán stared at her for a moment, then gave a sound like an exclamation of disgust and limped off.

She stood for a moment before turning to Eadulf and commenting: 'Interesting. I'd like to find out a little more about the background of this prior.'

'So what now?'

'Now there are some things that I have neglected, having been sidetracked by Brother Tuamán. To accomplish them, we must return to the guest-hostel where Ségdae was killed.'

Eadulf's eyes brightened suddenly. 'You mean that even now, you have not completely condemned Gormán as guilty?'

'There are other ways of interpreting his flight from this fortress,' she said.

'Then you feel that there might be a way into Abbot Ségdae's chamber through which a killer could have entered in the manner Gormán claimed?'

'Not as such, but it behoves us to take a look.'

# chapter eight

There was no one about in the guest-hostel, not even a guard outside, when Fidelma and Eadulf entered. She paused and called loudly, just in case Brother Tuamán was in his room on the next floor. Before climbing the wooden stairs she took advantage of everyone's absence to glance quickly into the rooms on the ground floor where the two scribes had their quarters. It took only a few moments to see that they contained nothing of interest. Having checked, she ascended to the next floor with Eadulf behind her. To his surprise she went directly to Brother Tuamán's room and tapped on the door. There was no answer and so she tried the handle. It was locked.

'He seems to be a cautious man,' observed Eadulf.

'He might have reason to be,' Fidelma replied enigmatically. 'He said he was returning to transcribe some notes. He is certainly not doing so here.'

She turned and moved along to Prior Cuán's room, and again she paused to knock before entering. Nothing appeared to have changed since their earlier visit. Fidelma went to the table, picked up the book she had noticed previously, and opened it to glance at the title page. She gave a gasp of surprise.

'It seems he reads Greek, for there is an inscription in it. Ah – and guess what this is a copy of?'

'I am afraid that construing Greek is beyond me,' Eadulf said. 'I sometimes even struggle with the Latin in which the ancients put down their wisdom. I can cope with the colloquial form better.'

'The text is in Latin but another hand has written an inscription in Greek,' Fidelma pointed out.

'So why the surprise?'

'Firstly, the book is *Paenitentiaele Theodori.*'

'What? You mean Theodore of Tarsus? Has he written a book of Penitentials?' Eadulf asked.

'It is some years since you escorted Theodore the Greek from Rome to the Kentish kingdom where he was installed as eighth archbishop and claimed jurisdiction of all the churches of the Jutes, Angles, Saxons and also the Britons – even though the Britons rejected him. He was an ambitious cleric because he also started sending deputations to the Irish abbots to claim jurisdiction over them. Here his ambition met with stronger resistance.'

Eadulf remembered the tall ascetic Greek appointed by Vitalian, Bishop of Rome, to succeed Wighard, who had been murdered in Rome. His murder had been solved by Fidelma and Eadulf. Eadulf had then been appointed to escort Wighard's successor, Theodore, to his new seat in the town of the Cantware, as the people of Kent were called. He had never been comfortable with the man, who seemed to consider all the western churches as outlanders who should be brought firmly under his control.

'That was six or seven years ago,' reflected Eadulf. 'Thankfully, Theodore, to my good fortune, sent me here to bring messages to Abbot Ségdae of Imleach, which led to our being reunited and . . .'

But Fidelma was still peering at the volume. 'It doesn't surprise me that Theodore of Tarsus would support the adoption of the Penitentials, but it is an interesting choice of reading for our frugal prior in the circumstances.'

'Do you mean because he claims to stand against the Penitentials? Well, reading such a book is not incompatible to his views.

Remember the saying of the Romans? *Nosce hostem tuum* – know your enemy.'

Fidelma gave an irritated shake of her head. 'A good point, Eadulf, but that is not what I am reading from the Greek inscription here.'

'As I said, my Greek is not good enough to construe it. What does it say?'

'It says – "Theodore, a servant of God and of the Lord Jesus Christ, to my faithful brother in Christ, Cuán, scholar of Cluain Eidnech, since we rejoice in your faith in Christ Jesus and the word of truth".' Then she paused and added, 'The phonetics of the Irish names are spelled in Greek form but they are clear as to the meaning of the names.'

Eadulf was shocked. 'Then how did Prior Cuán come by such a book? He must have been known to Theodore of Tarsus to have deserved such an inscription, but how . . .?'

'A personal gift,' Fidelma mused. 'I knew Cluain Eidnach had a reputation for its scholarship but I did not think it extended far, even within the Five Kingdoms. I can recall only one Cuán named as a meritorious scholar but he was an abbot of Lios Mór. He died when I was a child.'

'Prior Cuán may have been on a mission to the kingdom of the Cantware,' suggested Eadulf. 'You know how many of your countrymen still take the word of the Faith to the kingdoms of the Angles and the Saxons?'

Fidelma replaced the book carefully on the table without further comment and glanced round the room.

'It is strange that there is little sign of writing materials for such a literate man, even a stylus and a *ceraculum* to make notes on, especially during what was a debate of some magnitude,' Eadulf said, interrupting the silence.

'Maybe the notes were taken by one of the scribes or Brother Tuamán,' suggested Fidelma. 'In which case, he would not need his own writing materials.'

'Perhaps,' conceded Eadulf. 'Anyway, we are still left with the evidence that only Gormán could have killed Abbot Ségdae. So how does investigating Prior Cuán help us?'

'Perhaps it does not, although it is important for both Imleach and my brother to know more about our friend Cuán and how he was appointed the *praepositus* or prior, as he likes to call himself. Still, we have learned enough here. Let us examine the other matters.'

They moved on to the chamber which was directly next to the one the abbot had occupied. They had not examined it before, nor did it help them. Its lay-out was almost an exact replica of the others, except that it was devoid of any furnishing. It had but one window and that, like its neighbour, was barred; when tested by Fidelma, she found the iron was immovable. She looked around carefully and even examined the wall separating the room from that of Ségdae's chamber for signs of weakness.

'We have to conclude that there was no other way into the abbot's chamber but through the one door,' she finally admitted.

'So what now?' prompted Eadulf.

'Now we still have a problem to resolve.'

Eadulf hunched his shoulders in a helpless gesture. 'It is a problem only if we accept Gormán's story – but what if he is not innocent after all? As incredible as it might be to us, that is a logical conclusion. The more we have considered the alternative, the more we come across the fact that Gormán's story is impossible.'

'Things are always impossible until they are achieved,' Fidelma said dryly, turning from the room and moving down the stairs.

Brother Mac Raith was standing at the door of one of the rooms on the lower floor, about to enter it. He looked up in surprise as they descended. 'Good day, lady . . . brother,' he greeted them.

Fidelma returned the greeting and asked his name. He told her, then said, 'Can I help, for I do not think there is anyone here?'

'I need to ask you a few questions,' Fidelma replied.

'I was not here when the abbot was killed, so cannot help you with any details,' the religieux offered immediately.

'So I have already heard. I believe that you and your companion are of the Muscraige Mittine?'

'That is so, lady,' he replied nervously. 'Brother Máel Anfaid and I are cousins. We received our education together and both decided to join the community at Imleach.'

'Why choose Imleach?' Fidelma queried. 'There are many other well-known scholastic communities that are nearer to your homeland.'

'But which one compares with the reputation of Imleach, founded by the Blessed Ailbe, the Chief Abbey of the Kingdom of Muman?' Brother Mac Raith responded with a note of pride.

'Then you were attracted solely by the scholastic reputation of Imleach?' She was amused by the adulation in his voice.

'I had developed a fair hand when I was young, lady, and wanted to became adept in calligraphy. Imleach was a natural choice.'

'How long have you been in that community?'

'Ten years – and now I am chief scribe. That was why Abbot Ségdae chose me to accompany him to this council.'

'You certainly have a well-chosen name for a member of such a community,' smiled Fidelma.

The young man hesitated with a frown until he realised that she was referring to the meaning of his name, which was: 'son of grace'.

'A better name than my poor kinsman, Máel Anfaid,' he replied with a grin. 'Alas, it is apposite in the circumstances.'

Fidelma answered the jest with a smile as the name meant 'follower of the storm'.

'It does appear that a storm has erupted here,' she conceded. 'But as chief scribe at these discussions, your task must be an onerous one.'

'It is a task that is not beyond the limits of my capabilities,' the young man answered with some pride. 'However, there has been little work for me to do in the circumstances. We were expecting a council of scholars and were faced only with the Abbot of Mungairit and his steward.'

'So Abbot Ségdae was expecting to attend a full council, not just some preliminary talks with Abbot Nannid?'

'We all thought there would be several leading churchmen of the Uí Fidgente to debate with,' confirmed the scribe.

'Have you kept a record of these discussions so far?'

'Little enough, lady,' Brother Mac Raith replied. 'We were only into the second day of discussions when the abbot was struck down.'

'Is it possible to see those notes anyway?'

'I do not have them, lady. The custom was that, at the end of the day, I would transcribe from the *ceraculum*, the wax tablets on which I make the notes. The record was placed on papyrus and would be handed to Brother Tuamán.'

'He keeps these records?'

'I suppose so. He doubtless shows or gives them to the abbot and Prior Cuán,' the man added. They would have to agree that I had made a correct summation of the discussions.'

'I will ask Brother Tuamán if I might see them. However, out of interest, can you recall what was discussed during those two days?'

Brother Mac Raith actually grinned. There was a lot of posturing.'

'Meaning?' Eadulf queried.

'The Uí Fidgente were determined to justify their cause even though their prince had signed a peace with King Colgú. Abbot Nannid was, indeed, the only spokesman during the entire two days, talking about the claims of his eponymous ancestor Fiachu Fidgennid. I have to say Abbot Ségdae was very patient.'

'What about ecclesiastical matters? Was anything mentioned about the Penitentials?' Fidelma asked.

'Abbot Nannid made the claim that all the abbeys and bishops of the Uí Fidgente were now agreed that they would adopt the Penitentials written by someone called Cuimín. He had based his rules on a text called *De Paenitate* by a Roman writer named Aurelius Ambrosius.'

'And who is this Cuimín?' Eadulf asked. 'Is he an Uí Fidgente scholar?'

'I believe that he is now dead. Abbot Nannid spoke of him in the past tense. It seems that he was from near Loch Léin where he had established a church. He was mentioned as being the son of Fachna, a chieftain of that area.'

'Abbot Nannid claimed all the Uí Fidgente abbots and bishops had adopted these rules?'

'That is so, lady. Yet I heard Abbot Ségdae remark that it was curious that only Abbot Nannid represented them at these discussions.'

There was something in his voice that made her say: 'You sound sceptical of the truth of this?'

The scribe thought for a moment, as if considering what he should say. 'It is just that the religious community here do not support Abbot Nannid.'

'Really? In what way?' she asked sharply.

'Brother Máel Anfaid and I have a kinsman in the Abbey of Nechta. From what he says, his community were more or less forced to accept the Penitentials by Abbot Nannid.'

She glanced meaningfully at Eadulf. 'Is this the kinsman that Brother Máel Anfaid and you went to see on the night the abbot was killed?'

'That is correct, lady. He is Brother Éladach who holds the office of *aistreóir*, doorkeeper of the community. It was never called an abbey before Nannid arrived and ordered it to be enclosed.'

'I recall that when we visited here about six or seven moons ago,' Eadulf remarked, 'there was a small community around the chapel. It was nothing so grand as an abbey. There were no walls, just a group of people who were part of the township but devoting some of their work to the chapel.'

'That is so,' agreed the scribe. 'Nechta was a local woman who became converted to the New Faith. She established the chapel. After Nannid arrived, I am told that there have been great changes which have displeased the entire community. A wall has been built enclosing them and the new rules have been imposed.' He suddenly paused and looked at them in warning. 'But Éladach's views must not be aired abroad, especially to Abbot Nannid. The community felt they had no option but to accept because of Nannid's rank, and he apparently threatened to use these Penitentials to punish them if he was not obeyed. But do not attribute this to Brother Éladach, please, lady.'

Fidelma offered him reassurance. 'Everything that you tell me remains strictly between us, unless it has a direct bearing as evidence in a criminal proceeding.'

'Something you said puzzles me,' Eadulf remarked thoughtfully. 'You speak as if Abbot Nannid has been here some time. Did he not come here just for this council only a week or so ago?'

Brother Mac Raith looked troubled. 'You must speak with Éladach on that matter. He implied that Abbot Nannid had been here a long time.'

'We will take it up with Brother Éladach,' Fidelma assured him. 'He is a kinsman of yours, you say?'

'He is Máel Anfaid's uncle and a cousin of mine. Éladach chose to join this community here long ago when it was just a group of folk, each pursuing their own professions – he was a carpenter. That was long before it was enclosed.'

'So you and Brother Máel Anfaid share Brother Éladach's thoughts?'

'We do.'

'So let me return to that evening – the evening when Abbot Ségdae was killed,' said Fidelma. 'You and Máel Anfaid both went to see his uncle, Éladach?'

'We did.'

'At what time did you return to the guest-hostel and hear the news of the abbot's death?'

'We stayed to join him in the last meal of the day and then the last service. We came back towards midnight and found the fortress awake and in uproar. That is when we heard the terrible news.

'How did you come back?'

The scribe frowned, trying to understand the question. 'How? How else but walk?'

'I meant, by which route?'

Brother Mac Raith was still puzzled. 'There is surely only one path from the township to the fortress. We walked up through the main gates.'

'I see. And who was at the guest-hostel when you returned?'

'There were many people milling around in great consternation. Prior Cuán was among them. Brother Tuamán, Brehon Faolchair, some attendants, some warriors and the female physician – I do not know her name but think she is related to the prince – they were all crowding around the hostel. The Brehon was trying to gather all the relevant facts, I think.'

'Where was Gormán at this time?'

'He had already been taken to the cells. I heard afterwards that his wife had also been taken to a cell in case there was some conspiracy. It is little enough that I can tell you. Neither of us can provide any details connected with the event as we were not here.'

Fidelma finished the conversation by thanking the young scribe. She and Eadulf left him at the guest-hostel and made their way across the courtyard. A flight of stone steps led up to one of the walkways around the walls of the fortress. 'Let's catch some of the breeze that is blowing. I need to clear my head,' Fidelma said. She went ahead up the steps to the parapet and rested against it, looking down at the River Mháigh below them. A gentle summer breeze ruffled their hair.

'It is best,' Fidelma murmured to her husband, 'to gather one's thoughts in a place where one is not overheard.'

'My thoughts are now concerned with the loyalties of the prior,' Eadulf said. 'We must check that he was with Brehon Faolchair at the time of the murder.'

'That should be easy,' she agreed.

'What of the book of Penitentials inscribed as a gift from Theodore of Tarsus?'

'More important is to know how, less than six months ago, he was able to come to Imleach from Cluain Eidnech and persuade Ségdae to make him Prior. That's a short time to establish himself.'

Eadulf said, 'I had forgotten your tradition that abbots and bishops are usually appointed from the ruling families, and that the communities they form usually follow the tradition of electing the officials of the abbey from those appointed.'

Fidelma nodded. 'It may be of concern that this Cuán comes from a territory that has no connection with my brother's kingdom let alone the Abbey of Imleach itself.'

'And what about his steward, Brother Tuamán? He said he came from an abbey on a lake west of here.'

'Inis Faithlinn, in Loch Léin,' Fidelma sighed. 'But the territory is an Eóghanacht one. Congal, son of Máel Duin, is ruler of the western peninsulas of the kingdom.'

'Yet we have just been told that someone called Cuimín had a chapel there and wrote a text of these Penitentials which Abbot Nannid now quotes.'

'You mean that Loch Léin is where Brother Tuamán also comes from?' Fidelma interrupted. 'The connection is so obvious that it probably means nothing. Don't worry – there are so many strands to this mystery and all of them appear so inviting to follow.'

'At least Prior Cuán stood up for the law while Brother Tuamán claims Abbot Ségdae was preparing to compromise on it. Surely that is another mystery to follow?'

They were interrupted by Conrí calling up to them from the courtyard. By his side was a warrior they had not seen before. They went down the steps to join them.

'I thought you might want to have a word with Ceit here.' Conrí indicated the man at his side. 'Ceit was the commander of the guard on the evening that the abbot was murdered. In fact, Ceit is the *cenn-feadhna*, commander of the *Lucht-tighe*, the household guards of Prince Donennach.'

The stocky warrior had thick, curly black hair and a beard to match, yet his eyes were a sparkling light blue in a weather-tanned face. He inclined his head towards Fidelma. 'Can I be of service to you, lady?' His tone was a deep bass that seemed to rise from the pit of his stomach.

'Indeed you may,' she told him. 'I was going to seek you out later but it is opportune that we meet now. Do you remember the events of the evening that Abbot Ségdae was killed?'

'It is not often we have an abbot stabbed to death in this fortress, lady,' replied the man. 'The events are embedded in my mind.'

'But this may be difficult as I am searching for information about people coming through the main gates.'

'I have a good memory, lady.'

'Do you remember, for example, the two religious from Imleach leaving the fortress?'

'My duty started just before the evening meal, lady. They must have left before I went on duty. I first remember Abbot Ségdae returning. It was still light then for, as you know, the feast of the *Grientairissem* is not far off. However, the two religious returned after dark.'

Eadulf knew that the feast of the *Grientairissem* or sun-standing, marked the longest day of the year and therefore darkness fell late in the evening.

'Did they need permission to leave?'

Ceit shook his head immediately. 'They had no reason to seek it, lady. I was instructed to give our guests from Imleach every consideration. I was here when they returned after dark and was able to tell them the news about the murder of the abbot.'

'You were not at the guest-hostel? I understand there were a lot of people there.'

'I had been there earlier, just after Lachtna raised the alarm. Brehon Faolchair had arrived and he took command so I was superfluous. However, I was there when Prince Donennach and the lady Airmid arrived. Lachtna was well able to take charge of any service warriors could give at that stage. Gormán had already been taken to the prison house, so I returned to my post at the gates. Brother Tuamán and Lachtna were the only witnesses to what actually took place.'

Fidelma thanked the man, who continued on his way across the courtyard to the main gate. Conrí, who had remained, asked: 'Is there anything else I can help you with, lady?'

'I am very interested in this side gate. Would you show it to me?'

The warlord smiled ruefully. 'I suspected it would play a prominent part in your thoughts, lady. I am still wondering how Gormán could have been so foolish as to destroy any hope he had of defending himself.'

They followed Conrí in silence across the courtyard to the stone block that housed the cells. It was a squat building squeezed between the stables and the *Laochtech* or warriors' barracks. Just by the side of it was a pair of large solid oak doors. While they were not as tall and wide as the main gates they were certainly tall and wide enough for a mounted rider, ducking over the neck of his horse, to pass through. They were now shut and secured by bolts. Fidelma also noticed that a large lock served as extra security. She glanced around.

'The big iron key,' she pointed to the key hanging on a hook on a wooden pillar by the right side of the gate, 'I presume that fits this lock? Does it always hang there?'

'It does,' Conrí confirmed.

'If the bolts were undone, it would require no great feat of strength to take the key and unlock the gates?'

'No strength at all,' confirmed Conrí. 'But, as you say, the iron bolts that also secure the doors would have to be released first.' One was at the level of Fidelma's waist and the other was just above the top of her head.

'Yet we are told that Gormán's wife had two horses, saddled and ready *beyond* the gates – which had been opened by her,' Fidelma observed. 'It needed a taller person to remove the top bolt. Even with bribing the guard, it would be difficult to accomplish everything that was needed. And I doubt the guard would risk deserting his post to perform those tasks.'

'Perhaps the horses were on this side of the doors and it was Gormán who undid the tougher bolt. Anyway, we can ask the guard who was well paid for his part in this matter,' suggested Conrí. 'He now inhabits the cell in which Gormán had been placed – so perhaps we should interrogate him now?'

There came the sound of a bell from the main building and Fidelma said, 'It is time to prepare for the evening meal. Let the guard languish in his cell overnight and we will speak to him in the morning when he has had more time to contemplate his future.'

The evening meal was not attended by either Abbot Nannid or Prior Cuán; nor was Prince Donennach present. Brehon Faolchair presided over the meal while Brother Tuamán was the only representative of the Imleach delegation there. When Fidelma enquired about these absences Brehon Faolchair explained that each absentee apparently had other matters to attend to. The meal passed mostly in silence albeit interspersed with brief exchanges about the weather, crops and the condition of the local game. The subject of Abbot Ségdae was studiously avoided.

The meal having been consumed, Fidelma and Eadulf, with Conrí and Enda, went to watch the final moments of the sun setting behind the western hills. At the main gates, flickering brand torches had been lit in preparation for nightfall, which was almost on them. As they looked, there was sudden movement – horsemen were arriving. Then a dismounted warrior separated himself from the shadows and came hurrying across the courtyard in their direction.

'It is Socht!' Conrí exclaimed.

Socht raised a hand and let it fall in formal salutation. There was light enough to see the disappointed expression on his face which revealed that his mission had been unsuccessful.

One part of Fidelma felt a surge of relief that Gormán had not been caught; the other filled with dismay that they had only nine nights in which to resolve the situation. It was not a good prospect though it was better than the immediate action threatened by Abbot Nannid.

'I do not have to remind you that Gormán is good at his profession,' Socht said with grudging admiration. 'He is an able warrior who knows how to disguise his trail.'

'There is no need to find a reason for failure,' Conrí told him glumly. 'I did not think it would be an easy task.'

'Easy or not, I was able to follow the tracks southwards across the river in spite of the stony ground.'

Conrí looked slightly mollified. 'So he took the trail I thought that he might?'

'There were a few signs on the far bank where he and the girl had no time to linger and cover all their tracks.'

'So they crossed the river?' Fidelma asked.

'They seem to have crossed it twice, lady. The river almost bends back on itself. So they crossed it again where it straightens and then followed its eastern bank. I went as far as the place where there is a smaller tributary called the "twisted river", An Luba, which joins the Máigh. I was trying to see where they turned due east. Yet there was no sign that they headed into Gormán's own territory, east towards Cashel. I would have expected some sign in the muddy grounds there.'

'But there was none?' asked Eadulf. As Socht was an expert tracker, the question did not even warrant a reply.

'He could have started to walk his horse west along the river bed,' Conrí suggested.

'Along the Luba?' Socht shook his head. 'You would eventually have to pass under Cnoc Samhna and he would be seen.'

'Why is that?' Eadulf asked.

'The Hill of Samhain is also known as the Height of the Kings because it is where the rulers of the Uí Fidgente are inaugurated. To protect the sacred site there are always sentinels there; it is also the site of one of our signal fires which are lit to warn the fortress of strangers,' explained Conrí. 'The sentinels there keep a sharp watch.'

'Also, it would be a dangerous thing to do,' Socht confirmed. 'Walking horses along the river bed at any length would slow him and his woman down. The muddy bottom of the river could bog the animals down, especially where one horse has to follow another. The first horse might be lucky but the second would be sinking in mud already stirred up and loose.'

'So where could they be heading?' Conrí mused.

'There was one thing that caused me some puzzlement,' Socht said. 'They had tried to ford the Máigh again but this time from east to west. This was just before we reached the Luba tributary. The river shallows there and the ford seems an easy route across. However, once on the west bank you can't get far into the dense forest and undergrowth at that point. There were some signs that they probably turned back and re-crossed to the east bank again, although the signs were unclear. It was then I lost the tracks altogether. With little daylight left, I decided to come back and perhaps search again at first light.'

'Why would he turn west?' enquired Conrí.

'I did wonder if this crossing was an attempt to confuse anyone following his trail. He would know east from west and realise that his best chance of finding safety was east among his own people. He would keep on the east bank and make his way further south before turning for home. Why, then, make a foray due west?'

'You may be right. He might have tried to throw us off his track,' the warlord said thoughtfully. He glanced across at Fidelma, who was quiet, as if her mind was elsewhere. 'What do you think, lady? You know the man better than we do.'

Fidelma raised her eyes and stared at him unseeingly for several moments. Then she shrugged. 'Gormán's home is east in Cashel, not in the west,' she said slowly.

'I will start searching again at first light,' Socht decided.

'Leave that task to one of the other trackers,' Contrí told him. 'I need you here tomorrow because Prince Donennach wants to discuss the disposition of our warriors.' He glanced awkwardly at Fidelma. 'Gormán must be back here within nine nights if we are to prevent Abbot Nannid from forcing the prince to declare his guilt and punishment.'

'We have already seen the position that Prince Donennach has been presented with,' Eadulf said.

'*A fronte praecipitium, a tergo lupi*,' Fidelma observed quietly.

Seeing Conrí's frown, Eadulf translated: 'A precipice in front, wolves behind. Whatever decision Prince Donennach makes, he will be faced with war; an internal war among the Uí Fidgente or a war against Cashel. And we have only nine nights to avert it.'

# CHAPTER NINE

'It is time we talked,' Eadulf announced.

The couple were alone in their chamber and should have been asleep but they were both finding it difficult to clear their minds and compose themselves. It was a warm summer night. Fidelma had been standing by the window gazing up at the star-sparkling sky above the distant hills which were lit by the white-blue haze of the moon. Eadulf was stretched on his back on the bed, his head pillowed by his clasped hands.

'I thought we had been talking most of the day,' she replied. Eadulf heard the faint amusement in her voice. He eased himself up to a sitting position.

'Every time I go over the facts as they have been told to us, I cannot see any way of escaping the inevitable explanation: that Gormán is guilty of this crime.'

Fidelma swung round from her position to face him. The light from the night sky through the window caused her to see him almost clearly whereas she stood against the light, showing only the silhouette of her figure.

'Do you really believe that he could do such a thing?' she asked.

'I would say no, but there is no alternative explanation,' he replied.

'One explanation is that someone is not telling us the truth.'

'But who?' Eadulf asked. 'The events, as we have been told them by witnesses, allow for no doubt or difference in interpretation.'

'Abbot Nannid would argue that it is because the facts are the facts, and Gormán is guilty.'

'Yet putting the facts together as we know them, together with Gormán's character, is difficult for me. We all have the capability of killing in the right circumstances. Gormán is a trained warrior, commander of your brother's bodyguard. It is true that he has killed in battle. But he is imbued with a warrior's honour code and in these circumstances . . .' He ended by raising his arms in a helpless gesture.

'So having reached an impasse between the facts and your assessment of his character, what would you propose?' Fidelma asked.

'I don't know, truly I don't. Maybe we must hope that Gormán escapes and that is an end to it.'

'You mean that Gormán simply vanishes into permanent exile?'

'That would be a solution.'

'But what kind of solution? Is it a solution for Della, his mother? Is it a solution for Gormán, or for Aibell? It would mean that they become fugitives for the rest their lives.'

'But it would be a means to stop the ensuing conflict.'

'That, I doubt. Abbot Nannid would say that Gormán's escape underlines his guilt, and force Prince Donennach to demand compensation from Cashel. Cashel would refuse and . . .'

'But according to your law any reparation should go to Imleach, not to the Uí Fidgente.'

'That is true to an extent. However, because the murder happened in the fortress of the Prince of the Uí Fidgente, it is an affront to his hospitality and he could demand compensation.'

'But would he?' asked Eadulf.

'As I said, he might be forced to it,' countered Fidelma. 'Abbot Nannid is already manipulating him into following his lead.'

'What do we have to defend Gormán with? Only our belief that it is not in his character to commit murder, especially to kill a churchman that he knew well.'

'That is a start,' she replied without enthusiasm.

'Faced with this situation, at what point does one abandon the search for truth to prevent conflict and bloodshed?'

'When truth is found,' Fidelma said firmly.

'So you do not think that we have heard the truth?'

'As you have just pointed out, when the facts are so cut and dried, but are in conflict with character, then something is amiss. Why do you think that Brehon Faolchair purposely created errors in preparing this case?'

'Because he also wanted to prevent conflict,' Eadulf said simply.

'Just that? I think he knows that something more sinister is happening here.'

'The overthrow of Donennach? Brehon Faolchair would not want to see the law of the land supplanted by these Penitentials from Rome.'

'You are right, Eadulf. I suspect that Faolchair believes the murder of Abbot Ségdae, especially the circumstances in which it happened, might have been done by design.'

'How is that possible?' Eadulf asked. 'Gormán's arrival here was not planned. He came to warn the prince about Gláed, and we are told that it was only when Donennach didn't show an interest that, on learning that Abbot Ségdae was here, Gormán went to protest to him. I believe that chance has more than a hand in this.'

'That is a puzzling thing. Where did the story that Donennach was not interested in the potential threat from Gláed come from? Both Donennach and Conrí have confirmed that Gláed was perceived as a real threat.'

Eadulf stirred uncomfortably. 'I had forgotten that with everything that has been happening. You do well to remind me.'

'So you see, not all is as cut and dried as we have been led to believe. There are still contradictory matters.'

'Even Gormán and Aibell's story does not come from a first-hand account but from Ciarnat.' Eadulf was beginning to sound excited. 'Didn't you find it strange that she was waiting for us along the road to tell us her account of events *before* we reached this place? Could she have gone to that spot in answer to the signal fires? When Conrí and his warriors came to meet us, why did she not wait but was on her horse and away into the woods so that she would not be seen?'

In the gloom of the bedchamber, Fidelma crossed to a small table, picked up a beaker of water and took a swallow.

'In retrospect, I wish I had gone to see Gormán immediately, and Aibell also, but the value of the well is often not realised until after it has dried up.'

'Then what can we do? We have examined all the witnesses.'

'There are still a few people that I would like to talk with. We will start tomorrow.'

'Who, for instance?'

'With the only member of the guest-hostel that we have not yet spoken to – Brother Máel Anfaid.'

'But he was not there at the time of the killing,' Eadulf objected.

'Neither was Brother Mac Raith, but the information he gave us was useful.'

As Eadulf gave a low puzzled sigh, she crossed to the bed. 'Now we must try to sleep for I am thinking we will have a long day tomorrow.'

The sun was already bright and the day promised to be very warm when Fidelma and Eadulf, having had the morning ablutions, went to the feasting hall. To their surprise only Prince Donennach and Brehon Faolchair were finishing their breakfast. Attendants approached but there was no need for them as the guests could help themselves. A jug of apple juice stood on the table. There was a choice of hard-boiled goose eggs, a hard cheese known as *tanag*, and a sausage that Eadulf had not encountered before.

'It is called *longin bóshaille*,' offered Brehon Faolchair when Eadulf hesitated, examining it. 'It's finely cut ox meat, stuffed in an ox gullet, spiced with wild garlic and thyme and cooked as a sausage. Often the meat is salted.'

Besides these dishes was *eorna*, the barley bread, and *gruiten*, salt butter. To finish was *logg di shubuip*, a bowl of wild strawberries and a pile of apples. They chose their food and took their seats. After some time had passed in silence, Prince Donennach glanced moodily at Fidelma and spoke.

'How are things proceeding in the resolution of my dilemma, lady?'

'I have been thinking of little else,' she replied.

'If you suspect an attempted plot against you,' chimed in Eadulf bluntly, 'I cannot see why you do not act first and move against those you suspect?'

Prince Donennach smiled grimly. 'Who do I suspect? You mean, make Abbot Nannid my prisoner?'

Brehon Faolchair was shaking his head. 'For what reason would one do that, friend Eadulf? The only grounds for suspicion are because he demands church law for a churchman's murder.'

'Abbot Nannid has considerable authority among my people, Brother Eadulf,' Prince Donennach added gently. 'There is nothing overt in his behaviour other than that. He kept a neutral stance when previous members of my family tried to seize power, as well you know.'

'It seems your family has more than their fair share of conspiracies and plots to wrest power,' returned Eadulf.

Brehon Faolchair frowned in disapproval but Prince Donennach replied only, 'That is fairly said, Brother Eadulf. I have devoted years of my life to attempting to put an end to it and arguing that we follow the law of inheritance, which is an estimable law, instead of wrestling in the mud for power. My own grandfather, Óengus mac Nechtain, was killed in a conspiracy just before I was born and that led to the rule of Eóganán and a time of turmoil. So it has continued.'

'We have managed to keep stability since Colgú defeated Eóganán at Cnoc Áine four years ago,' added Brehon Faolchair.

'And since you became ruler of your people, your efforts to maintain the peace have not gone unnoticed,' Fidelma confirmed.

Prince Donennach sighed. 'I made it my aim to prevent the internecine conflict among the Uí Fidgente as well as to end the conflict between us and the Eóghanacht. As I have said, we have a good law of inheritance. We cannot better the meeting of the *derbhfine*, the three generations of the family, to discuss and appoint the person who is the most worthy to succeed as the head of the family. Unfortunately, it is a failing of our kin that we seem to breed jealous, ambitious malcontents who will exploit and manipulate – and even murder – to achieve their ends. I would hate to see all my years of toil unravel.'

'You suspect that is the aim of all this?' Eadulf said. 'If so, I ask again, why not make Abbot Nannid a prisoner, since you seem to suggest he is behind it?'

'If I did so without plain evidence, under the very laws we aim to protect, the peace among the Uí Fidgente would unravel faster than a horseman can ride around this fortress at full gallop, my friend.'

'Let me put a direct question to you, Prince Donennach,' Fidelma said, regarding him thoughtfully. 'And you may answer as well, Brehon Faolchair. Do you think that the commander of my brother's bodyguard really went mad and killed Abbot Ségdae? Because madness would appear to be the only means of explaining what has happened.'

Prince Donennach gave a tired smile. 'If it was madness, then it was a convenient madness – convenient for Abbot Nannid, that is.'

Brehon Faolchair nodded slowly in agreement. 'I did what I could to postpone the inevitable. But Gormán was alone in the room with Abbot Ségdae. There were witnesses to his going in and the chamber being locked and secure without anyone else in it. Even Gormán admits to being in the chamber with the abbot and says the latter had a full view of what was behind him. So if Gormán was hit from behind, why didn't the abbot raise any warning?'

'So we are faced with a blank wall,' Prince Donennach summed up.

'Until we find a weak point whereby it crumbles,' Fidelma replied with optimism.

Brehon Faolchair stared at her. 'You think there is such a weakness? Unfortunately, Gormán seems to have already admitted his guilt by running away with Aibell.'

'I am sure we will find that weakness,' she told him. 'Meanwhile, there are some matters on which I should like clarification.'

Prince Donennach sat back and gestured for her to continue.

'I am told that the reason why Gormán and his wife came here was to give you a warning that Gláed of Sliabh Luachra had killed his brother. That he had declared himself chief of the Luachair Deaghaidh and might be a threat to you. As you know, he killed his own father before, and he was placed in the custody of his brother for trial.'

'Gormán came to give warning,' affirmed the prince.

'How did you react to it?'

Prince Donennach looked at her in surprise. 'Sliabh Luachra is not far from here. Gláed could raise a substantial raiding party. How would you expect me to react?'

'Tell me,' pressed Fidelma.

'I think you already know that a messenger was sent to Conrí, the commander of my battalions. He was at his own fortress down-river, at the Ford of Oaks. I asked him to come here straight away.'

'For what purpose?'

'To take command of a band of warriors to Sliabh Luachra to

find out whether the report was true and what support Gláed could count on.'

'And what was your intention?'

'To pre-empt any attack on the Uí Fidgente. I know what these robber chieftains are like and Gláed, without the restraint of his father or brother, will be a formidable enemy.'

'But why is Conrí still here?' Eadulf asked.

'He and his men arrived the morning after the murder of Abbot Ségdae. Frankly, I was not sure what to do. I felt it better to keep him and his men here until we could sort matters out. We posted sentinels in the countryside to give us warning of any threat.'

'So there was no question that you did not take Gormán's warnings about Gláed seriously?'

Prince Donennach was baffled. 'Why would I discount his warning? He knew enough about the war bands of Sliabh Luachra from your last visit here. I took the warning about them very seriously indeed.'

'One of the stories I heard is that you had treated the warning lightly and he had gone to Abbot Ségdae in an angry mood. I think it was offered as some way of proving a motivation . . . incriminating him by implying that he had an uncontrollable anger.'

'That was not so,' the prince declared.

'When Gormán came to see you about the matter of Gláed, were you alone?'

Prince Donennach thought back. 'As a matter of fact, Brehon Faolchair was with me as was Abbot Nannid and his steward, Brother Cuineáin.'

Brehon Faolchair agreed. 'That is true, Fidelma. I recall Gormán reporting that he had heard from some merchants that Gláed had deposed his brother and was rousing the robber bands of the Luachair Deaghaidh to join him to raid the countryside. On hearing this, Prince Donennach immediately instructed a messenger to ride to Conrí and request his presence to discuss a defensive plan.'

'Was Gormán content with this action?'

'Why would he not be content?'

'How did Abbot Nannid respond?'

Prince Donennach frowned and rubbed his forehead thoughtfully. 'I cannot recall any notable response from Nannid.'

'I would have expected some response,' Fidelma said. 'It was while we were uncovering the plot at the Abbey of Mungairit that Gláed was handed into the custody of his brother, Artgal. His brother was to take him back to Sliabh Luachra to answer to his own people for murdering their father.'

'Neither of us can recall any response,' replied the prince after exchanging a look with Brehon Faolchair, who shook his head.

Fidelma was rising when Ceit, the commander of the Prince's fortress guard came hurrying in. His features looked grim.

'What is it now?' Prince Donennach sighed wearily. 'Have you come with another tale of woe?'

Ceit was certainly nervous. 'I have to report, lord.' He cleared his throat. 'I have to report that the guard – the one who took the bribe to allow Gormán to escape – he has been released from his cell.'

There was a brief silence and then Fidelma repeated incredulously, 'He was released from his cell?'

'There was no sign that he broke out,' muttered Ceit. 'The door was simply unlocked.'

'He was a guard,' Prince Donennach pointed out sarcastically. 'Did he have a key when he was put into the cell?'

'Of course not!' Ceit retorted, and then, recalling who he was speaking to, added more politely, 'He was searched thoroughly before being locked up.'

'So you are saying that someone released him? And there is no sign of him?' Fidelma asked.

'I have already sent men to track him down.'

Prince Donennach scowled. 'It seems that this fortress has become an easy place to escape from. Let us hope it is far harder to break into if we are to be attacked by Gláed's marauders.'

'At least we now know one thing,' Fidelma told them. 'There is definitely some conspiracy at work here. I was going to question the guard this morning. Having taken a bribe once, it seems that he was not going to be trusted to endure our interrogation.'

'Trusted by whom?' Brehon Faolchair demanded.

'That is for us to find out, as soon as possible. I'll be surprised if you have more luck in finding this man than you have had finding Gormán.'

She left the hall with a thoughtful-looking Eadulf in her wake. Outside, they paused in the warmth of the sunlight. Eadulf spoke first. 'If the guard was allowed to escape simply to stop him from talking to us, why not make sure he would never speak to us? He could have been killed in the cell. Why just allow him to escape and risk recapture?'

'Unless he could be more useful as a messenger,' she replied.

Eadulf was perplexed and said so but Fidelma did not answer him directly.

'Any other thoughts?' she asked.

'Only that Prince Donennach has now confirmed what Conrí already told us – that he did take Gormán's warning seriously. So who spread the false story that Gormán went to see Abbot Ségdae in an angry mood?'

'Don't you think we should talk to Ciarnat?' Fidelma asked in a mild tone.

Eadulf was annoyed with himself. 'Of course! It was Ciarnat who told us the story.'

Enda was crossing the courtyard towards them. 'Have you heard the news?' he greeted them morosely.

'About the escaped guard?'

'Yes, him. I have been speaking to the warriors in the barracks this morning,' Enda said. 'It seems the man had only recently joined their company and there was not much love lost between them. Nobody liked him. They said he was from Sliabh Luachra . . .'

Fidelma nodded on hearing this, and they made their way to the physician's house in silence. They were greeted at the door by Airmid. The little grey terrier came bounding out, sniffed at them and then went off to examine more interesting scents.

'There is certainly a threatening atmosphere hanging over this place, lady,' Airmid said as she greeted them.

'Wherever there is death, there is gloom,' Fidelma replied. 'But surely, as an apothecary, you are used to that?'

Airmid was not amused by the levity. 'Well, this gloom seems to permeate the very countryside and our people. It seems to threaten our very existence.'

'So far as I feel it, the gloom emanates from Abbot Nannid,' muttered Eadulf.

'He is like a brooding storm cloud,' Airmid agreed. 'When he approaches, there is darkness. Everyone waits for the storm to erupt and only when he passes does the brightness reappear. My brother has been sunk in the darkness for many days – and I hear that you have been able to offer no solution.' She suddenly drew herself up. 'I suppose you have come to question young Ciarnat?'

'We have,' Fidelma acknowledged. 'Has there been any problem about submitting her to your charge?'

Airmid shook her head. 'She has been upset, of course. I have known the girl since her mother, Étromma, brought her here when she worked as a cook in the palace. I remember that Ciarnat used to play with that girl, Aibell, when they were little. So she was pleased to meet her again when Aibell arrived here with the warrior, Gormán. Ciarnat grew up to be an attendant here. She started in the days of Eóganán. I have found her level-headed and trustworthy, so I was glad when my brother suggested that she should be placed in my care instead of being incarcerated as Nannid thought she should.'

Airmid led the way through the apothecary to her living quarters where they found Ciarnat sitting sewing a garment at a table. She paused and stood slowly as they entered, looking fearfully from one to another.

'Just a few questions,' Fidelma reassured her, then paused and glanced at Airmid.

'I will leave you then,' the physician said, withdrawing.

Eadulf and Enda stood by the door while Fidelma sat down and motioned Ciarnat to reseat herself. The girl spoke first.

'You must believe me, lady. What I said was true. I did not know that Aibell and Gormán would attempt to escape. I really was with my mother. She is elderly and I often call and stay with her.'

'There are many matters that need sorting out, Ciarnat,' Fidelma told her gently. 'But it is not that which I have come to see you about.'

'What then?' The girl's chin came up a little defiantly.

'When you waited for us on the road as we were coming here, you told us how you met up with Aibell and Gormán and what they said to you.'

Ciarnat frowned. 'That is so.'

'It is a matter of clarification about something you mentioned. You told us that Gormán was disappointed because Prince Donennach did not take his warning about Gláed of Sliabh Luachra seriously?'

'Yes, I did.'

'Then you were present when Gormán spoke to Prince Donennach? You clearly heard the prince dismiss Gormán's concerns?'

Ciarnat said, 'No, I was not present, but was told about it afterwards.'

'Then Gormán told you?'

'I didn't see Gormán after he met with Donennach. In fact, I do not think I saw him again until the hearing before Brehon Faolchair.'

'Then who told you about Gormán's disappointment? Was it Aibell?'

Again the girl said, 'No. When Gormán went to the prince's chamber to speak with him, I remained chatting to Aibell for a while. Then I had to leave the fortress and go to the township to see my mother. I did not come back until the next morning and it was then I heard about the killing. Aibell was held until midday.'

'I must then ask you again how you heard that Gormán was disappointed with Donennach's response to his warning,' Fidelma repeated. 'If neither Gormán nor Aibell told you, then who was it?'

Ciarnat shrugged. 'It is no secret. When Gormán went to see Donennach, there were several people with him.'

'So we have heard,' confirmed Fidelma. 'Are you saying that one of them told you?'

'Apparently someone told a member of Abbot Ségdae's party – one of the scribes who attended him. Everyone was talking about Gormán and the news of the killing. It was said that when Gormán had left Prince Donennach, he was annoyed that his warning had been cast aside.'

Fidelma breathed out long and slow. 'I do not like this. Someone told someone who told someone else.' She turned back to the girl in irritation. 'Answer a straight question, Cairnat. Who told you?'

'As I said, it was one of Abbot Ségdae's scribes – Brother Máel Anfaid.'

There was a pause while Fidelma examined the girl thoughtfully. 'Brother Máel Anfaid? And he was told by whom?'

'He did not say.'

Fidelma slowly rose to her feet. 'Very well. We must ask you to remain in the custody of Airmid until matters are sorted out. Is there anything that you want us to do in the meantime? You mentioned that you are concerned about your mother, Étromma. Do you want me to call upon her to reassure her of your welfare?'

Ciarnat hesitated a moment and then replied: 'If you ask for the *aistreóir*, the doorkeeper, at the Abbey of Nechta. He also acts as *uaithne*.'

Seeing Eadulf's puzzled expression, Fidelma explained: 'Under the law of the *Crith Gabhlach*, an *uaithne* is legal officer appointed by the community whose task is to ensure the well-being of the poor and elderly.'

'In this case that office is held by the doorkeeper of the abbey?' Eadulf asked.

'Yes. His name is Brother Éladach,' confirmed the girl.

Fidelma was now growing used to surprises. 'Brother Éladach just happens to be the uncle of Brother Máel Anfaid,' she pointed out.

'He is,' confirmed Ciarnat without guile.

'Very well,' Fidelma said firmly. 'We will inform him and hope you will not be kept long from the care of your mother nor to the return to your duties in the prince's household.'

Enda opened the door and followed Fidelma and Eadulf back out into the sweet scent of the herbal garden. There was no sign of Airmid as they walked through it and into the main courtyard of the fortress. Fidelma was taking them to the guest-hostel where Abbot Ségdae had met his death.

'I presume we are going in search of Brother Máel Anfaid,' Eadulf hazarded after a few moments.

'Your presumption is correct,' she said.

As they approached the door, it opened and Prior Cuán came out, followed by Brother Cuineáin. They halted at the approach of Fidelma and her companions.

'We were looking for Brother Máel Anfaid,' Fidelma explained after polite greetings were exchanged.

'He is gone on some errand into the town, I believe,' offered the prior.

'To the abbey?' queried Fidelma.

'Possibly. I am not sure.'

She turned to Brother Cuineáin. 'As a matter of fact, I wanted to ask you a question. I believe you were in attendance on Prince

Donennach when Gormán warned him about the fact that Gláed of Sliabh Luachra was free again and making threats?'

The steward of Mungairit said, 'Yes, I was. Why do you ask?'

'I just wondered how Prince Donennach responded to the warning. Was he dismissive, or did he take it seriously?'

'How else would a responsible leader act?' the man replied testily. 'He gave orders for his guards to be alerted and sent for the warlord, Conrí.'

'There was no doubt in anyone's minds that Prince Donennach was seriously concerned on hearing this news?'

'No doubt at all. Now, if you will excuse me, I am due to meet with Abbot Nannid and Brehon Faolchair. There is still much work to be done.' The steward turned and hurried away towards the great hall.

A moment later, Fidelma and her companions continued to make their way through the main gate and towards the township.

Brother Éladach turned out to be an elderly, pleasant-featured man, with a permanent smile on his jolly face.

'No, lady, I have neither seen my nephew this morning nor Brother Mac Raith,' he replied after Fidelma had introduced herself and put her question. 'The meetings between the brethren of Imleach and Abbot Nannid have been delayed by the terrible events in the fortress,' he added unnecessarily.

'I understand that you are also the *uaithne*, appointed to look after the elderly folk of this township?'

'That is so, lady. I have enjoyed that post for the last five years.'

Fidelma then told him of Ciarnat's concerns about her mother.

'I regularly call on Étromma – I have known her for many years. I expect Airmid will do so too as she often comes by here.'

'Why does she visit here?' Eadulf intervened.

'Since Abbot Nannid has been here, he has suffered an ague from time to time, a shivering fever. Or so I'm told. It seems to come and go. The lady Airmid is a physician and so visits the abbot when needed.'

'I would not think Abbot Nannid was one who was prone to fevers,' Eadulf remarked dryly.

'An Mháigh is called the River of the Plains, brother. Mudflats, marshlands, with much water around. At this time of year the area produces a preponderance of *cuili conda* – insects and midges whose bite can produce fevers.'

Eadulf grimaced in sympathy. Having once studied the healing arts, he continually carried in his *lés*, or medical bag, a jar of ointments combining honey and apple-cider which, when applied to the midges' bites, was at least a solace and eased the irritation.

'I have no knowledge of Airmid's intentions,' Fidelma was saying, 'but Ciarnat was concerned that her mother would be worried and mentioned that you might consent to visit her.'

'Tell her to have no fear, lady,' Brother Éladach said kindly. 'I shall see to Étromma. She worked hard in the prince's household during her life, as does her daughter after her. She had two sons who were killed at Cnoc Áine when your brother's army defeated Prince Eóganán, and that deprived her of sons to attend her. So she relies on Ciarnat quite a lot.'

Fidelma felt a curious pang of guilt as she considered this news. However, Eóganán had been leading an insurrection against her brother and many good folk on both sides died during the battle. Indeed, Eadulf himself had been captured by one of the Uí Fidgente's supporters at the time and nearly suffered death. She decided to change the subject quickly.

'I have already spoken to Brother Mac Raith, who tells me that he is also a relative of yours.'

'A distant relative,' the doorkeeper agreed. 'When he and my nephew decided to enter the religious I tried to persuade them to join us. We were then a small open community. We had freedom. However, they decided to go to Imleach for training. The facilities to learn the art of calligraphy and illumination is renowned there.

Mac Raith succeeded in achieving excellence and is now chief illustrator and scribe.'

'I was told you were unhappy that this community had adopted the Penitentials as rules.'

Brother Éladach looked askance and gave a quick glance around as if to check that no one had overheard.

'Why should I be unhappy at that?' he parried.

Fidelma looked hard at the man. 'I thought that you were also unhappy that the laws of our people were being ignored by these new church laws?'

Brother Éladach cast a second worried look around him. 'They are the laws of God which supersede the laws of man,' he intoned in a carrying voice. He then lowered his head so that she could not peer into his eyes and murmured, 'It is not wise to speak of these things.'

'I presume it is not wise while Abbot Nannid stays with you?' She also lowered her tone.

'It was only in the month of Dubh Luacran, the moon of the dark days, that Abbot Nannid came from Mungairit and ordered us to construct the wooden walls that surround our community. Since then we must not speak our minds.' His voice now was barely a whisper.

Fidelma glanced meaningfully to Eadulf. 'When we were here last, this abbey did not exist. It was a small religious community that was just part of the township. There were no walls.'

Brother Éladach swallowed, hesitated – and then seemed to make up his mind.

'This is so. The holy lady Nechta had started to preach the New Faith under the shade of the old sacred oak in this township a hundred or more years ago. The early members of the community erected our wooden chapel close by that oak. Those who felt devoted to the Faith built their dwellings around it, each living in their separate houses, individually sustaining themselves but devoting time to the teachings of their spiritual mother, Nechta.'

'When Nechta died, she must have appointed someone to follow her as leader of the community,' Eadulf said.

'In accordance with our laws, it was the community who was her *derbhfine*, her kinfolk, who would gather and elect the best among them to preach the word of the New Faith to the community. That continued until the dark days, nearly seven months ago, when Abbot Nannid arrived.'

'Are you saying that he has been here nearly seven whole months?' Eadulf asked.

'Yes. Abbot Nannid came here and declared that it was wrong that we had no barrier between our homesteads and the people of the township. While we pointed out that we *were* the people of the township, he ordered that whosoever felt true to the New Faith must enclose themselves behind walls and become a *cenobium*.'

Enda, who had been a silent listener, was puzzled. 'Become a what?'

'It means a religious order regulated by rules,' Fidelma explained. 'A few centuries ago, a community of those believing in Christ was established in the deserts of Egypt by a teacher of the religion called Pachomius. That became the model for a *cenobium*.'

'That's correct,' Brother Éladach agreed. 'And Abbot Nannid said we should be a *cenobium*, a religious order regulated by these new religious rules – the Penitentials, as they are called.'

'Are you saying that he gave you no option?' Fidelma was astounded.

Brother Éladach shrugged. 'Abbot Nannid of Mungairit is a powerful man and the Chief Abbot and Bishop in the land of the Uí Fidgente. He not only ordered our workers in wood – I was a carpenter – to construct the walls, but told those of the township that it was their duty to help us if they believed in the New Faith. Within two months the walls, as you see, were built to surround our community and separate us from the people.'

Fidelma frowned. 'Let me be perfectly clear on this, Brother Éladach. Are you saying that Abbot Nannid and Brother Cuineáin came here seven months ago and ordered you to construct a walled community, a *cenobium*, and they have remained here ever since?'

'Exactly so.'

'Then Abbot Nannid and his steward did not come here recently just for the council with Abbot Ségdae of Imleach?'

'He had been settled here for many months before he suggested the council,' agreed the *aistreóir*.

'And you are also telling us that Abbot Nannid has more or less taken over as abbot of your community?' Eadulf pressed.

'I suppose he has. As I said, we did not have an abbot leading our community before. Nannid told me that I should regard myself as doorkeeper of the community and no one should be allowed in or out of the *cenobium* without his permission or without authority. In previous days, the townsfolk could move freely among us, and us among them. We were indivisible with the townsfolk. They even came to our little gatherings at the chapel and under the oak.'

'Is it not strange that the abbot of such a large community as Mungairit, which is renowned for its scholars, suddenly comes to your community, deserting his own community, and chooses to stay for such a long while, exerting his authority over you?' mused Fidelma.

'He is chief over all the monasteries,' sighed the doorkeeper. 'I suppose he can stay where he wants.'

'He is abbot of one of the great teaching centres of the Five Kingdoms. Does it not make you curious? Is there any communication between here and Mungairit?'

Brother Éladach shrugged uncomfortably. 'I am not aware of any messengers that he sends. I know he raised gold and silver from us to send there. I hope you will not tell him that this conversation took place?'

Fidelma saw the pleading look in his eyes. 'Of course. We merely came in search of your nephew,' she said. 'Is there any other place where he might go, outside of the fortress or this community?'

'Well, he often takes a stroll by the river, along where the trading boats are moored and some of the merchants conduct business.'

'We will look there. But should you see him before we do, kindly tell him that we are looking for him.'

'Is something wrong?' Brother Éladach queried anxiously.

'No. I just need to ask him a question or two,' she reassured him before she turned to leave.

With Eadulf and Enda, she strolled across the market square in the direction of the wooden quays. There seemed to be a lot of people moving among the boats tied up alongside, and the stalls. Women as well as men were making purchases from traders who were landing goods along the quays. Their cargoes mainly consisted of foodstuffs – sacks of grain, vegetables, fish and meat. However, there were other goods such as metalwork and pottery, although the visitors had already noticed that the township had its fair share of smiths and potters. There were a few places where one could buy food and drink, which apparently served the traders while they conducted business. These were hardly more than shacks and certainly nothing like the inns where people might stay the night.

Fidelma seemed deep in thought but Eadulf could no longer contain himself.

'I was wondering whether our trust in Ciarnat's word might be misplaced.'

Fidelma glanced at him. 'Do you think I have been trusting her completely, then?' she asked.

Eadulf pulled a face. 'I had. But the fact that two of her brothers died at Cnoc Áine might put a different complexion on matters.'

'In what way?'

'She might not be as supportive of the Eóghanacht as she pretends to be. Her brothers were killed by your brother's warriors. Now she has to support her elderly mother in their place.'

'Cnoc Áine happened several years ago and Eóganán's successor, Prince Donennach, has made peace with my brother.'

'Nevertheless, everyone except Ciarnat claims that Gormán's warning was taken seriously. If she was wrong about that, or if she lied deliberately, what else has she told us that might be wrong?'

'She says she was told this by Brother Máel Anfaid. Now we must find him and hear what he has to say.'

They moved on along the quays. They saw a few religious and questioned them but with negative results. There was no sign of Brother Máel Anfaid. One man, an ale-seller at one of the shacks, volunteered that he had seen the religieux from Imleach pass by some time earlier. He knew the brother by sight for he had often paused for a mug of ale on previous days. But there was certainly no sign of him along the riverbank now.

A sudden cry from behind made them turn. It was Conrí, on horseback. He came trotting up. There was an unreadable expression on his features.

'Lady,' he called down without dismounting, 'you must all come back to the fortress at once.'

'What is wrong?' Fidelma was alerted by the unusual note in his voice.

'It's Ciarnat, lady. She has been found hanged.'

# Chapter Ten

ℰ

Conrí, once dismounted, led them across the courtyard of the fortress, towards Airmid's herb garden and apothecary. They had barely entered the gate into the garden when Airmid emerged to meet them. Her attitude was one of anger and aggression.

'What did you say to her?' she almost shouted at Fidelma. 'What did you say that made that young girl take her own life?'

Fidelma halted, shocked at the verbal assault. The accusation that she had caused the death of Ciarnat stunned her for the moment.

'Nothing was said that threatened her – in fact, the very opposite,' Eadulf intervened, coming to Fidelma's defence. 'She was only depressed by her incarceration but we promised her that it wouldn't be long until we showed that she had not been involved in the escape of Gormán.'

Brehon Faolchair had now emerged from the living quarters behind the apothecary and apparently had overheard the exchange. He was shaking his head sadly.

'It is true, Airmid. I spoke to Ciarnat after Fidelma left. I was passing your apothecary and saw Fidelma and her companions leaving. Ciarnat came to the gate and we had a conversation. She did not seem troubled, nor was she unduly depressed.'

Fidelma turned to the Brehon inquisitively. 'What did you talk about?'

'She was asking how long she would be confined here in the house of Airmid. I told her that, in spite of Abbot Nannid, it would not be for much longer. She also asked if I had seen Brother Máel Anfaid. I wondered why she should be looking for him. She did not tell me . . . but it was the third question which I found most curious. She asked me the same question that you were asking this morning: had Prince Donennach taken Gormán's warning about Gláed to heart?'

'How did you respond?'

'I told her, as I told you that the matter had caused the prince grave concern. When she heard that, she seemed puzzled.'

'What did she say?'

'Nothing of consequence. She merely thanked me and passed back into Airmid's house. Meanwhile I went on to the *laochtech*. I wanted to see if there was anything I could find out relating to the release of the guard.'

Airmid had calmed down somewhat but she was still reluctant to accept that nothing had been said to upset the girl. 'Whatever made her hang herself must have happened soon after she saw Fidelma,' she observed suspiciously.

'Tell me the sequence of the events,' pressed Fidelma. 'When was she found? Who discovered her?'

Airmid gathered her thoughts before answering. 'I was working in the apothecary when my dog started to bark from the house. I waited a while, thinking that Ciarnat would deal with it, but the noise went on. So I finally left my work and went to the house, intending to chide the girl for not attending to the dog. It was I who found her. She was hanging from a roof beam with the dog at her feet, gazing up and howling.' She paused and sniffed loudly. 'I was not strong enough to take down the body. I rushed out and spotted Conrí and one of his men passing and called out to them. They came in and . . .'

Fidelma turned to Conrí. 'Better you should tell me what you saw.'

'I was with Socht,' he nodded to the warrior standing behind Brehon Faolchair. 'We accompanied the lady Airmid into the house and saw the girl just as she described. While Socht supported the body I stood on a chair and cut the rope. The poor lass had choked to death. I sent Socht immediately for Brehon Faolchair but, knowing your involvement in this, I came straightway to find you.'

'With your permission,' Fidelma said to Brehon Faolchair, 'I want to see where this happened.'

They moved to the house, Conrí leading the way. Ciarnat still lay on the floor, a coverlet over her body. Socht was standing nearby.

'Where was she hanging?' Fidelma asked, ignoring the body for a moment.

'From that roof beam,' Conrí replied, indicating one of the beams that crossed above them. Fidelma noticed a wooden chair, standing upright, below it. Seeing the meaning in her glance, Conrí added: 'The chair was on its side when we came in. I climbed on it in order to sever cord from which she had hanged herself.'

Fidelma looked at the height of the chair and then up at the beam. 'You examined the body, of course, Airmid?'

The apothecary nodded. 'Only inasmuch as I pronounced she was dead. That was after Conrí cut down the body, although I could see she was dead when I first came in and saw her hanging from the beam.'

'Just so.'

Fidelma now bent down by the body and, gently removing the covering, she stood back and gazed thoughtfully at the dead girl. Ciarnat lay on her back. Her eyes were closed and her features were not as badly disfigured from the effects of the hanging as Fidelma might have expected. When someone is throttled to death at the end of a rope, the face is usually discoloured and the lips blue, the tongue often protruding. But here, the girl's features seemed almost to be in repose, as if she were asleep. Fidelma stood up straight and turned to Eadulf.

'Have a look at the body, Eadulf. You also, Airmid.'

Eadulf moved forward and went down on one knee. After a moment, he was joined by Airmid, visibly put out at what she saw as having her judgement questioned by Fidelma.

'Strange,' Eadulf muttered as he peered at the girl's face and then the neck.

Fidelma guessed that he had spotted the very same thing as she had.

Airmid stiffened in annoyance. 'What is so strange?' she demanded.

'Help me turn the body over,' Eadulf instructed, oblivious to Airmid's angry tone.

The physician hesitated and then ungraciously helped him turn the body over, face down. Again, Eadulf paid particular attention to the girl's neck, parting Ciarnat's long hair so he could examine the nape and then moving up the back of the head.

Eventually, he gave a long sigh, and looking directly at Airmid, he said one word. 'Well?'

Airmid moved closer and parted the hair exactly as he had done . . . then gave a quick gasp.

'I did not examine her so closely before,' she said as if justifying something.

Fidelma had known there was something out of place. 'What is it?' she asked.

Eadulf glanced up. 'In my opinion, the girl was unconscious or dead before she was hoisted up on the beam. Judging by her relaxed features, I would say she was already dead. She had suffered a severe blow on the back of the head. There is an abrasion there, with some bleeding and evidence of bone fragments. Clots of blood are visible on the nape of the neck and blood has dripped on to the back of her dress.'

Fidelma turned to Airmid. 'Do you agree?'

The physician glanced up distractedly. 'I had not noticed it before,' she confessed. 'I just confirmed that she was dead. However, the injury could have been caused when Conrí cut her down. The body could have fallen so that—'

'Beg pardon, lady Airmid.' It was Socht who interrupted. 'You are forgetting one thing.'

They turned to focus their attention on him. He had stood silent all this time. For a moment he looked from one to another of them, slightly confused as to whom to address.

'You may recall that my lord Conrí and I came in to cut the body down. While he took the chair to climb up, I stood under the body of the girl to support it. When the body was cut loose, I took the weight and lowered it gently down on to the ground. I was careful, just in case there was still life left – but there was none.'

'In other words, the injuries were not caused after she was cut down but before she was hoisted up to the beam?' Fidelma summed up.

'That is the logical deduction,' Eadulf said, 'that she was dead before being strangled by the rope.'

'Do you agree with Brother Eadulf's observation?' Fidelma asked Airmid.

There was a silence and then: 'I agree,' she replied solemnly.

Brehon Faolchair moved forward to gaze down at the body, a look of horror on his face. 'Then we are now saying that this was *not* suicide, but . . .?'

'But murder,' Fidelma affirmed grimly. 'That is exactly what we are saying.'

She said to Conrí, who was looking bemused at these new revelations, 'You say that you stood on that chair to cut her down. Where was the chair exactly?'

'I picked it up from the floor just there,' Conrí pointed to a spot under the beam. 'She was hanging from there and the chair was lying on its side beneath her. I presumed that it must have been overturned by her when she kicked it free to hang herself.'

Fidelma nodded slightly. 'Yes, our killer certainly dressed the scene to mislead us. If Ciarnat had climbed there with the intention of hanging herself, tied the rope and kicked the chair from under her, it would have been overturned in that position.'

She paused for a moment and looked at the chair thoughtfully. 'Yet the killer made an important mistake.'

Eadulf had joined her now; he looked at the chair and then up at the beam. And then a brief smile of enlightenment crossed his features.

'Shall I demonstrate?' he offered. When Fidelma nodded, he said to Conrí, 'Would you oblige us by standing on the chair and showing us how you cut Ciarnat down?'

The warlord's brows came together in bafflement. Nevertheless, he obediently climbed on to the chair and stretched towards the beam.

'Your outstretched hand hardly reaches the beam,' Eadulf pointed out.

'As I said, I had to cut the cord that held her.' He drew his sword and reached upwards. 'See?'

'I see exactly,' nodded Eadulf.

Seeing everyone's puzzlement, Fidelma explained. 'You will note that Conrí is a tall man, yet he could not reach the beam on which Ciarnat is said to have tied herself. Conrí is, of course, taller than Ciarnat.'

Brehon Faolchair shrugged. 'You have already pointed out that she was murdered and then hoisted up to the beam.'

'Indeed,' Fidelma agreed. 'The killer tried to make it look like a suicide. Why he would do so is the important question. However, at the moment I am interested in how he reached that beam.'

'Where is the rope she was tied up with?' asked Eadulf, an idea occurring to him. 'If it was long enough, the killer could have simply swung it over the beam and hauled up Ciarnat's corpse without bothering to climb there.'

Conrí had dismounted from the chair and sheathed his sword. Now he was shaking his head.

'Not with this cord, friend Eadulf,' he commented, crossing to a table on which two pieces of cord lay. They had obviously once been one piece, now cut into two, and these ends were frayed by the stroke of the sword. The warlord picked up the pieces and held them out for all to see.

'What is that?' Fidelma asked, seeing them for the first time.

'That is the cord with which she was supposed to have hanged herself, lady. I severed it when I cut her down. Socht, as he has explained, stood below to support her body when she was released, so that she did not fall.'

'It is a short cord, even when put together,' Fidelma observed. She estimated it was longer than *déis-céim* in her native measuring system, perhaps nearly two metres.

'Just enough to hang someone,' Conrí muttered, looking rueful.

Eadulf pointed to the three knots tied at one end. 'But that looks like . . .' he began slowly.

'A religieux cord belt.' Brehon Faolchair's voice was grim.

'It is not a fashion that I have seen often,' Eadulf said, thankful that his own robes fastened with a leather belt. 'Yet I am sure that I have seen it worn recently.'

'Neither is it popular here,' the Brehon nodded. 'But I too have seen it worn and not so long ago.'

'You are thinking of Brother Mac Raith from the Abbey of Imleach,' Fidelma reminded them. 'He wears such a rope belt.'

'Just so.' Brehon Faolchair looked relieved. 'Brother Mac Raith but also his companion, Brother Máel Anfaid – both have adopted this form of *crís* or religious girdle.'

'It seems odd that if a murderer was going to attempt to disguise a murder to make it look like suicide, and go to all that trouble, why would that murderer leave behind such an obvious clue to their identity?' Eadulf mused. 'It would be the height of stupidity.'

'Unless it was just another attempt at disguising the real murderer,' Fidelma said.

Brehon Faolchair's eyes narrowed in thought. 'It could be that the man was in a hurry and this was the only rope to hand.'

'Yet he had time to get some means to climb up to the beam, tie the rope, descend and hide that means . . . unless, of course, he was an acrobat,' Fidelma replied.

Airmid was looking worried. 'There is a ladder that I keep at the side of the house. Some thatching needs to be repaired.'

'Then let us see if it is still there,' suggested Fidelma.

Led by Airmid, they left the house and went to the side of the building. The ladder was propped against the wall, as she had said.

'I suppose it is possible that it could have been used to gain an easy access to the beam,' Brehon Faolchair admitted.

Eadulf had moved to the ladder and examined it. 'More than a possibility,' he said. 'There are fresh bloodstains on the rungs.'

Fidelma went and looked at the spots he indicated.

Eadulf said: 'My opinion is that our killer, having killed the girl with the blow to the back of the head, which caused some bleeding, knew this ladder was here. He took it inside, propped it against the beam and then took the cord, fastened it over the beam, then dragged the girl's body up the rungs and tied the cord around her neck. The blood splattered on the rungs. The killer took the ladder back and returned to clean any marks of blood from the floor and arrange the chair in a clumsy attempt to make it look like suicide.'

'Clumsy, indeed,' nodded the Brehon. 'Because he forgot to clean the blood from the rungs.'

'I don't think he was too clumsy. There are only a few spots of blood on the rungs. He doubtless thought that even if we did make a connection with the ladder, the stains would have disappeared by then.'

'But surely the rest was clumsy?' the Brehon protested.

'Not so. I think he came fully prepared to mislead us with the religious rope belt.'

'I don't accept that,' snapped Brehon Faolchair. 'I find this bizarre. Someone comes to murder the girl. He then disguises the murder to look like suicide but does it in such a way that we immediately realise it is a murder because he places a piece of evidence that incriminates someone else. It is too complicated. Too fantastic.'

'Whoever did it knew that there was a ladder at the side of the house,' Eadulf stated. 'You can't see it even if you come into the herb garden around the apothecary. You have to come through the herb garden and then here to the house, which has its own fencing around it. So we are talking about someone with knowledge of the buildings.'

Fidelma turned to Airmid. 'Did you observe anyone around your house or apothecary this morning?'

Airmid shook her head. 'No one that I did not know.'

'Forgive me, that was not exactly the question,' Fidelma said sharply.

'Perhaps it would be best if you recount your morning and who you saw,' Brehon Faolchair said to keep the peace, as Airmid's eyes flashed angrily for a moment.

'Very well,' the physician said. 'Ciarnat had been handed into my safekeeping. She stayed with me in my house overnight. So when I awoke this morning, she was the first person I saw.'

'Was she awake or asleep when you awoke?' Fidelma asked with equal sarcasm, making the point that two could play at such a game.

Airmid let one shoulder lift slightly and then relaxed. 'As a matter of fact, I had to wake her. We broke our fast with fruit and water from my well. We had some little discussion and then I went off to prepare some cures in my apothecary. It was then that Fidelma and her companions came. After that I got back to work and knew nothing more until I heard my dog, came back to the house and found her hanging, just as I told you.'

'And you were in your apothecary all the morning?'

'I was.'

'You did not even notice Brehon Faolchair passing and speaking with Ciarnat?'

'I did not.'

'So, in fact, anyone could have slipped through the herb garden, entered your house and killed Ciarnat?' pressed Eadulf.

'Since that is blatantly what happened, then the answer is obvious.' The woman's rudeness caused Eadulf to blink.

'Thank you, Airmid,' Fidelma intervened quietly. 'You have been very helpful.' She then addressed Brehon Faolchair. 'With your permission, since you have noticed it is worn by the two scribes from the Abbey of Imleach, I would like to question them. However, I suggest that you take the cord as evidence, for it is best placed in your care than mine.'

Brehon Faolchair agreed, then asked: 'Do you really believe that the death of Ciarnat has something to do with one of the scribes from Imleach?'

'We shall find out. However, I am more certain that it is connected with the murder of Abbot Ségdae.'

'Then, as you already are pursuing an investigation into the abbot's murder, I will let you pursue the girl's murder also. Lady Airmid, I shall arrange for the poor girl's body to be removed to the Abbey of Nechta. Her mother is known there and Brother Éladach can carry out the obsequies.'

When Fidelma, with Eadulf and Enda, was crossing the courtyard again, Eadulf asked her: 'Why does Brehon Faolchair have to grant you permission to investigate the girl's death?'

'You forget we are in the fortress of Prince Donennach and that Faolchair is his Brehon,' replied Fidelma. 'This is his jurisdiction.'

'You seem to think that her death is connected with that of Abbot Ségdae,' Enda said. 'But what could the poor lass have known, that she had to be killed to silence her? And could one of the brethren from Imleach really have done such a thing?'

'You ask very pertinent questions, Enda,' Fidelma said. 'Perhaps it was something that Ciarnat had already told us that brought about her death.'

'I don't understand.'

'If we understood, we would probably know everything,' Fidelma answered with weary resignation. 'Anyway, no speculation without . . .'

'. . . information,' ended Eadulf, completing one of her favourite sayings.

She glanced at him in annoyance before allowing herself a whimsical smile.

'Very well, Eadulf. But I was always taught by Brehon Morann, my mentor, that speculation can be the enemy of a tranquil mind. If the mind is not tranquil it cannot perceive and question with the necessary calmness and control.'

'How else do we arrive at a conclusion to a mystery other than to speculate on possibilities with the information that we have? It is a human condition. Speculation is the art of life.'

'I did not realise you were such a philosopher, Eadulf,' she said, accepting that he had made a valid point.

'It's not much of a philosophy,' he returned moodily.

She was about to respond when they came to the door of the guest-hostel, which was opened by the haughty steward, Brother Tuamán. He seemed put out at the sight of them.

'You are becoming a frequent visitor to our quarters, lady,' he said, unsmiling.

'I believe Abbot Ségdae did not ask to die here,' she answered dryly. 'I am obliged to ask questions and you, I am afraid, are equally obliged to answer them.'

The steward inclined his head in grudging resignation and stepped aside to allow them to enter the hostel. Brother Mac Raith was inside, busy collating some vellum pages. He looked up from his task and on seeing them, stood up.

Fidelma's eyes immediately fell to the waist of his robe. There was the twisted hemp rope, tied on his right side and the two ends of equal length falling almost level to the hem of the robe. There were the three knots in the one end. She glanced at Brother Tuamán, who wore the more normal leather belt as did Eadulf.

'I merely wanted to ask about this new fashion that I have seen . . . the one Brother Mac Raith is wearing.'

'The rope girdle? I believe it is called a *loman*.' Brother Tuamán sniffed. 'I know nothing of it. Best ask him,' he added with a jerk of his head to the young man.

The scribe's brows had drawn together. 'It *is* generally called a *loman*,' he said, 'although I have also heard it called a *sursaing*. What can I tell you about it, lady?'

'It is unusual. Where does it come from?'

'From Gaul, I believe, lady. It is being adopted by the religious brethren there.'

'Can you tell me the purpose?'

The young man hesitated, seemingly embarrassed. Then he took courage. 'Many of the brethren not only spend time within the abbey in pursuit of their contemplation but many work in the fields to provide food and crops to sustain the members of their communities. Wearing robes in the fields, especially on rainy, wet days, presents a problem. So the Gaulish brethren have developed a custom of taking their long robes and drawing them up between their legs before tying them around the waist with a piece of cord. Some choose linen cord and some twisted hemp. Three knots are tied in the end in symbolism of the Faith – the Holy Trinity.'

'You say this idea originated among the brethren in Gaul?'

'So I am told, lady. Even those who no longer work in the fields but, like myself, work within the abbey as scribe and illustrator, have begun to adopt this form of dress.'

'You do not wear such a girdle, Brother Tuamán,' Fidelma said, addressing the steward.

'I am old-fashioned and prefer a solid leather belt and trews under my robes,' replied the steward. 'So do most members of the community at Imleach.'

'So it is not a new rule of the Abbey at Imleach?'

'Indeed it is not, lady,' he averred sharply. 'Abbot Ségdae did not believe in conformity of dress for members of his abbey, but people were free to choose.'

'So this is why only Brothers Mac Raith and Máel Anfaid wear the *loman*?'

Brother Mac Raith was frowning. 'Is there some rule which we have broken here by using this dress?'

'By the wearing of it? None that I know of,' Fidelma said. 'But I am interested to know why you decided to adopt this form. You have just admitted that as a scribe you did not have to wear it if it was only introduced as a practical aid for workers in the field.'

The young man hesitated again; this time he actually blushed.

'Come on, man. Answer the question!' Brother Tuamán ordered impatiently.

'We thought it made us look more distinguished. Few others at Imleach had adopted the fashion so we thought it would make us stand out.'

Fidelma was actually smiling broadly.

'*Vanitas vanitatum*!' Brother Tuamán sneered.

'Well, I suppose it is natural for a young man to have a certain vanity about his looks and dress.'

'Natural – for a member of the Faith?' Brother Tuamán was outraged. '"Turn my eyes from looking at worthless things," say the holy scriptures.' He whipped round to the young man, who had now gone pale. 'Remember the words of the Lord – "for the Lord sees not as man sees: man looks on the outward appearance, but the Lord looks on the heart." Remember that. You would learn that lesson in pain, if we followed the Penitentials of Cuimín.'

'I was not aware you knew of Cuimín's Penitentials?' Fidelma seized on his words.

'I know of their content. You may recall that I have told you that Abbot Ségdae was considering that content,' he said. 'Anyway, I was trying to show Brother Mac Raith that surrender to vanity is not the way to a good religious life. We must strive to follow the teachings of the Faith. I remind him of . . .'

'I know. A quote from the Psalms echoed by Samuel,' replied Fidelma, causing the eyes of the steward to widen in astonishment. 'Wanting to have a good appearance is a natural condition of men and women of all ages. Do we not have a proverb that cleanliness is part of the glory of this world?' Then she turned to the chastened young man. 'Still, it is wise to remember, Brother Mac Raith, that the tree with handsome foliage may look beautiful but it often bears bitter fruit, so good appearance may not be worth pursuing, after all.'

'There is one thing I would like to ask,' Eadulf intervened. 'How many of these *loman*, as you call them, do you and Brother Máel Anfaid possess?'

The young man looked bewildered. 'Why, we only have one each. The art of twisting the strands and tying the knot at the end cause them to be hard to come by, as well as expensive.'

'So you have one and Brother Máel Anfaid has one?'

'That is so.'

'I was told that you were looking for Brother Máel Anfaid earlier,' Brother Tuamán commented. 'Was this what you were seeking him for?'

'Not exactly,' Fidelma replied evasively. 'But you remind me, has he returned yet? I would still like to see him.'

'Returned?' The steward raised his brows a moment.

'He was not here when we came looking for him earlier. We

were told he had gone into town, perhaps to see his uncle at the Abbey of Nechta. But we could not find him. I just wondered if he had returned.'

'Not that I know.' The steward glanced at the young scribe, who quickly shook his head.

'Then we will trouble you no longer,' Fidelma said.

'Now what?' Eadulf asked as they left the guest-hostel and Fidelma turned towards the main gate of the fortress.

'I thought we should go in search of the missing brother and see if he still retains his *loman*.'

Enda said, 'If there were only two and Brother Mac Raith still wears his, then it seems obvious . . .'

'One thing I have learned, Enda,' she admonished. 'Never trust the obvious.'

As they approached the gate they noticed there was some excitement there. Two men, looking like boatmen by their clothing, were engaged in an agitated conversation with one of the guards. Fidelma recognised Ceit, the guard fortress commander. He glanced round as she came up.

'Have you seen Brehon Faolchair?' he asked.

'He is probably in the great hall with Conrí. Why, what's wrong?'

'There's been another death, lady.'

'You mean that of the girl, Ciarnat.'

'No, someone down at the riverbank.'

'Not the guard who escaped last night?' asked Eadulf.

'Not him,' Ceit replied scathingly. 'He's the sort that is deserving of death but is so sly and quick, I doubt death will ever find him.'

'Then who is it?' Fidelma tried to keep the exasperation from her voice.

Ceit gestured to the boatmen. 'These folk say that a body has been found in the river, a little downstream.'

'He wore a tonsure, lady,' muttered one of the boatmen, bobbing his head in respect. 'And the poor fellow was naked, save for the remnant of his robe.'

'A tonsure and a robe?' Fidelma said. 'It sounds as if the dead man was a religieux. Why didn't you go to see Brother Éladach at the Abbey of Nechta?'

The boatman shrugged. 'The religieux was a stranger to all of us, but one of my men said he thought he had seen him before, at the fortress. We knew there was a religious deputation staying there. Anyway, it is here that we knew we would find the Brehon.'

'These boatmen have seen this man walking along the river quays from time to time during the last week,' added Ceit.

A feeling of inevitability overcame Fidelma. 'Ceit, if you can't find Brehon Faolchair, tell Conrí of this matter. Say that we have gone with these men to see if we can identify this body.'

She instructed the boatmen to lead the way.

'Are you sure the body is not that of a local religieux, one from the Abbey of Nechta?' she asked as she fell in step with them.

'I would swear that he is a stranger here,' one of the boatman replied. 'But apart from that I cannot give much information. The only thing we can tell you for sure is that the man did not enter the water and drown by accident.'

Fidelma did not break her stride although it took a slight effort. Somehow she had already realised that it would have been no drowning accident that brought the boatmen hurrying up to the fortress. 'What makes you say that?'

'Because there was an injury to his head. He was struck before he entered the water.'

They greeted the statement in momentary silence. Then Eadulf moved closer to Fidelma, saying, 'Are you thinking what I am thinking?'

'Indeed,' she sighed. 'I think we have found the missing Brother Máel Anfaid.'

# chapter eleven

Fidelma, Eadulf and Enda accompanied the two boatmen to the wooden quays along the river. The area was still crowded with merchants, boatmen and buyers. No one took any notice of them, or seemed aware of their mission, as they pushed through the throngs. It appeared that the body had been found beyond the precincts of the trading quays or any habitation, for they walked until the track narrowed into a muddy footpath that was hard to follow through gorse, brambles and bushes.

'How was the body spotted so far along here?' Fidelma asked the leading boatman.

The man spoke over his shoulder: 'We had been bringing a cargo from the Ford of the Oaks – it's downriver from here. As we rowed towards the township quays, one of the crew noticed the body. It was face downwards, caught among some rocks. We edged in, and discovered that the man was dead. I left one of my men with the body and I came on to report the find to the fortress.'

He paused in mid-stride and raised his voice: 'Hoi! Linneáin! Are you there?'

From behind some boulders and bushes a voice answered.

The boatmen led the way round the boulders and they came across another man sitting morosely on a rock. Nearby, stretched on its back, was a body. The water-soaked robe had been arranged to make a decent covering. There was no sign of a belt or cord to fasten the robe. The seated boatman stood up hurriedly and nodded nervously to the newcomers.

'Has anything been disturbed?' Fidelma asked immediately, glancing at the scene.

'Not since we dragged him from the river here,' the man, Linneáin, replied, nodding to the rocks that bordered the nearby waters. 'I merely arranged the robe for dignity's sake.'

'Any sign of a belt or cord to fasten the robe?'

'He was in the river so perhaps it has been loosened and is somewhere in the water,' the man suggested. 'I didn't see anything like that.'

Fidelma was pretty sure that she knew the real reason why the belt was missing. She knelt down by the corpse. He was a young man, pleasant-featured in spite of the puffiness of the drowned features. He wore the tonsure of St John, his dark hair cut back from the forehead to a line from ear to ear and long at the back. With help from Enda, Eadulf turned the body over. It was obvious how he had come by his violent death as there were signs of abrasions and blood clotted at the back of the skull. The man had certainly taken a number of blows; he had been struck with great ferocity. Gently they returned the corpse to its former position and stood back.

There was a sudden movement along the bank and they could hear Conrí's voice calling them.

'This way!' Eadulf gave an answering cry. 'Keep coming along the path and you'll find us.'

A few moments later Conrí, followed by Brehon Faolchair, appeared around the rocks. The group moved back to let the newcomers view the body.

Brehon Faolchair took only one glance and sighed: 'That is Brother Máel Anfaid from Imleach. Any sign of the cord belt, the *loman*?'

'None,' she confirmed.

'So it seems that the cord that Ciarnat was hanged with was his.' Conrí's voice was almost relieved.

'Having killed Ciarnat and strung her up with his own *loman*, it seems that he came here and drowned himself in remorse,' Brehon Faolchair concluded.

'I think not,' Fidelma said with a touch of quiet sarcasm. 'Unless, in his fit of remorse, he was able to beat himself to death on the back of the head before jumping into the river.'

Brehon Faolchair was in no mood for irony. He immediately knelt to check the body, Eadulf helping him to lift the head. When he stood up, his face was a mask of dismay. 'Another murder? Ciarnat – and now the person that you think was set up to pay for her death. It is hard to comprehend.'

'This young man was killed in the same manner as Ciarnat – slain by violent blows to the back of the head. That reminds me – Gormán also said he was rendered senseless by a blow to the back of the head, just before Abbot Ségdae was murdered.'

Brehon Faolchair's eyes widened. 'You don't mean to say that the same person was responsible in all three instances?'

Fidelma did not answer.

'Let us go through it,' Eadulf offered. 'Ciarnat was murdered but her death was arranged to look like suicide – in such a way that it quickly became obvious that it was not. The clue was Brother Máel Anfaid's *loman*, or cord belt, a new fashion worn only by him and his companion Brother Mac Raith. It was placed there as a clue to mislead us. It was easily traced to Máel Anfaid.'

Fidelma was nodding in agreement. 'Máel Anfaid was dead even before Ciarnat. He was killed, the cord belt was taken, and then the body was dumped in the river. Then the murderer went to kill Ciarnat.'

Brehon Faolchair was still puzzled. 'There is a complicated mind at work here.'

'Complicated, indeed,' Conrí agreed. 'At the moment, these killings appear random; unrelated.'

'Yet there is a link. The death of Abbot Ségdae, of Ciarnat and of Máel Anfaid are all connected . . . .' Fidelma stopped abruptly.

Brehon Faolchair shook his head. 'I cannot see that.'

Fidelma turned to the three bemused boatmen. 'I have only one question more for you. I presume that you are all local men?'

'That we are, lady,' agreed the leader.

'You know this river well?'

The fellow could not help a smug grim. 'An Mháigh? I know the river well, lady, from the place where it rises and all along its sixty-two kilometres to where it empties in the sea estuary.'

'Its flow doesn't look powerful,' she said, looking at the almost calm waters.

'You should see it after a rainstorm, lady. The river drains the plains here and just north of where we are now is An Lúbach, the twisted river that reinforces it. Downstream at the Ford of Oaks the river becomes a tidal one and the tide often pushes against the flow downstream.'

'You say that you found the body in the water but snagged by these rocks here on the bank?'

'That is so.'

'So the body could have been pushed into the water further upstream and then floated down here in the current?'

The boatman held his head to one side as he considered. 'It depends, lady. Today the river is calm, the flow not great. I don't think a body would float far today. Apart from that, it could have easily been seen if it floated by the quays before reaching this area.'

It was a good point. 'How long do you think he has been dead?' Fidelma asked Eadulf.

'Not more than a *cadar*,' he replied, using the native measurement for a quarter of a day. 'Perhaps even less than that.'

'So it is likely that he was killed at this point rather than floating here from upstream?'

'Given the nature of the river and the quays, it is possible,' Eadulf returned thoughtfully. 'It cannot be said to be a certainty.'

'A short search of this area of the bank would be useful. We may find something,' Fidelma said. She then addressed the boatmen, telling them, 'You have been most helpful, and we are grateful for your service.'

'I know these men,' Brehon Faolchair added, 'so I will ensure their help is properly acknowledged and rewarded.'

With the boatmen dismissed, they made a search of the immediate surroundings, but it produced nothing unusual or that they could connect with the death of the religieux. Brehon Faolchair then asked Conrí and Enda to carry the body to the township, to the Abbey of Nechta. There, Brother Éladach, the young man's uncle, seemed too shocked to fully take in what had happened. Fidelma and her companions left the Brehon with Conrí to help him. Then she led Eadulf and Enda away, across to a deserted part of the river near the wooden bridge.

It was obvious to Eadulf that Fidelma had chosen this isolated spot as there was something on her mind which she did not wish to speak about in front of anyone else. Eventually, she found an old fallen tree, bleached into a grey-white log by the sun, to provide a seat for them by the riverbank. The two men sat down with her and waited while she stared moodily at the whispering river.

'It makes no sense,' she suddenly said aloud.

Eadulf shifted his weight on the log. He agreed entirely but he did not feel inclined to comment. It was Enda who spoke.

'Forgive me, lady. I am a simple warrior and only when playing *fidchell*, wooden wisdom, do I excel in solving conundrums. However, if there is a link between the three murders, surely one has to go back to the first murder as a starting point.'

'And so?' Fidelma said to encourage him.

'As you know, I do not believe that my friend, Gormán, killed Abbot Ségdae.'

'Belief is not knowledge,' Eadulf interrupted grumpily.

'That is true – but what if this plan to destabilise Prince Donennach's rule was not the result of Abbot Ségdae's murder but the *cause* of it?'

Fidelma was about to chide the young warrior but then she hesitated.

Enda went on thoughtfully, 'I was trying to think of a reason – a good reason – why Gormán would flee from the fortress, knowing that you had made a successful appeal for a new hearing.'

'And did you find an answer?' Fidelma wanted to know.

'What if Gormán was persuaded to escape by the same person who killed the abbot? As I said, what if the murder itself was part of the plot to cause such conflict?'

'That is rather far-fetched,' Eadulf objected. 'Aibell was the one who arranged for Gormán to escape from the fortress, she the one who bribed the guard and arranged the horses. Are you now saying . . .?'

'Then there is also the involvement of Ciarnat and Máel Anfaid,' Fidelma butted in. 'How does that fit into your plot?'

'Well, I still think that is the link, lady.' Enda would not give way.

A call interrupted them. It was Conrí, coming from the Abbey of Nechta.

'Brehon Faolchair has asked me to find you. There is to be a meeting with Prince Donennach immediately in the great hall.'

Fidelma was not enthusiastic. 'For what purpose would this meeting be? The investigation of the recent deaths has not yet truly begun.'

'It is Abbot Nannid who has demanded it, lady.' Conrí shrugged. 'He was with the prince when we reported Ciarnat's death. He was not happy about it and will be even less so when he hears of Brother Máel Anfaid's demise.'

Fidelma rose from her seat with a sigh. 'No doubt he will use the new deaths to put more pressure on Prince Donennach. We had better go and placate him.'

As she fell in step with Conrí, she said in a quiet voice: 'I have a request to ask of you, Conrí.'

'Which is? You have only to ask, lady.'

'Abbot Nannid and his steward have been absent from Mungairit for some months now. He must have left soon after we resolved the mystery there.'

'Ah, you've heard the story of how he arrived here and ordered the rebuilding of this little community of Nechta?'

'Don't you find that strange?'

'It's not strange that he should try to assert his authority over all the religious communities of the Uí Fidgente,' replied Conrí thoughtfully, 'but now that you mention it, it *is* odd that he should spend such a long time away from his own abbey.'

'One of the largest abbeys in the Five Kingdoms and one which must take a fair amount of work to govern,' added Fidelma.

Conrí rubbed his chin thoughtfully. 'What is it that you are suggesting?'

'I was wondering whether there have been any communications between here and Mungairit in recent months?'

'Mungairit is, as you recall, a closed community so little news comes from them as a rule. Anyway, I have spent much of my time at my own fortress at the Ford of the Oaks – where I have my own herds and fields to attend to. So I am not sure what has passed between here and there.'

'Surely messengers from the abbey would come to keep Abbot Nannid informed of events? Does he not send regular messengers to Mungairit?'

'Have you asked Brother Éladach?'

'He mentions that Abbot Nannid has gathered gold and silver from the community to send to Mungairit, but he does not seem to know about regular communication.'

'What are you thinking, lady?'

'How many days would it take a fast horseman to ride from here to Mungairit? Two or more?'

'A fast rider should easily make it within two days, avoiding the river route and going by way of the low-lying land to the east. In fact, I have such a warrior in my command. He is a great rider and his horse is a powerful beast. He could leave here immediately.'

'Could he do so without alerting anyone as to his destination or the questions he must seek answers to?'

'If so ordered, lady. What do you think he might learn if he rode to Mungairit? I cannot see that he would return here with information that would save Gormán or resolve these other mysteries.'

'I simply want to know why Abbot Nannid has spent so much time here.'

'Then I shall send him to Mungairit.'

'I am sure that you will be as interested in the news he brings back as I will be,' replied Fidelma softly. 'Now let us go and see what new strife Abbot Nannid wants to stir up.'

The atmosphere in Prince Donennach's hall was tense. The prince himself was presiding from his official seat on the dais with Brehon Faolchair just below and in front of him. Even Donennach's sister, Airmid, was present, seated to his right. Conrí had taken his place behind them. At the long table below them sat Abbot Nannid together with his steward, Brother Cuánáin, sitting beside him. Opposite them sat Prior Cuán with his steward, Brother Tuamán. Fidelma and Eadulf took their seats.

Without waiting for permission, Abbot Nannid rose and launched forth, his voice high and accusing.

'We now see what delays and prevarications have produced,' he screeched. 'We start with a simple murder. The identity of the culprit was obvious – but his punishment was delayed because our Brehon wrongly advised our prince that the King of Cashel must be informed before punishment was meted out. This Eóghanacht King must be allowed, it is said, to send legal representation to defend the murderer. So a week passes and the murderer's friends arrive – the notorious young advocate, Fidelma of Cashel, with her Saxon . . .' He paused as if searching for the right word. 'Her Saxon companion. Her honey tongue convinces our Brehon and our prince that the law has not been properly obeyed, even though the murderer has been found guilty. So we have another delay.

'And what does that delay result in? It results in the murder of an innocent serving girl of the prince's household. Then the murder of another religieux from Imleach, who just happens to be the nephew of the doorkeeper of the abbey of this township. It is time for us to search out the guilty ones and punish them as I have advocated all along. If we continue to delay, who knows how many more are to die?'

Throughout his harangue, for there could be no other description for his speech, there was a silence. The silence continued for a while after the abbot resumed his seat and sat back with folded arms.

Brehon Faolchair then slowly rose. His face, albeit expressionless, seemed drained of blood.

'I have no need to defend my actions. It is true, I did make some errors in fulfilling the legal obligations. Abbot Nannid, however, would have been quite happy for me not to acknowledge them as errors. It was our duty to send to Cashel in this matter, in accordance with the peace that has been agreed between the Uí Fidgente and Cashel.' He sat down suddenly and glanced to Fidelma as if inviting her to speak.

Fidelma came to her feet with her features set in a grim smile.

'We must forgive Abbot Nannid for his grammatical slip which has turned my reputation as an advocate into the pejorative form – notorious.' There were several guffaws of suppressed laughter as the meaning of what she had said sank in. The word *airdirc* meant well-known, famous, celebrated or renowned but, with a slight inflection, could be taken to mean notorious. Her inference that the abbot was ignorant of the grammatical difference seemed to appeal to the humour of many.

Abbot Nannid glared at her across the table, his mouth tightening into a thin line.

Fidelma continued with a growing confidence of tone. 'I also have to say that I am sad to see the abbot's memory fading. Eadulf and I were guests at his Abbey of Mungairit only months ago, and I must remind him that Eadulf is not a Saxon but from the Kingdom of the East Angles. Further, he is not my "companion" but my husband. Obviously, the abbot appears under some strain or he would not overlook the fact that such terminology could be taken wrongly. Even an abbot would be liable to compensate the husband of a princess for the affront to his honour.'

Prince Donennach had started to smile but then, taking note of the increasingly ferocious expression on Abbot Nannid's features, he intervened. 'I am sure that this was merely a slip of wording, as you suggest, Fidelma. Was that not so, Abbot Nannid?'

The abbot hesitated and then, accepting that his sarcasm had not produced the effect he had wanted, he muttered: 'A slip of grammar and of memory.'

'Then I am sure Eadulf of Seaxmund's Ham will accept the apology offered by Abbot Nannid?' Fidelma looked at Eadulf who rose, bowed to the abbot and said coldly: 'In the circumstances, the apology is accepted.'

It was clear to everyone that Fidelma had won her points. It was not in her nature to refer to the matter again.

'I am sure we all share the abbot's concern about the subsequent murders, and we all want to see the conspirator and his co-conspirators found and judged according to *the law of this land*.' She used a slight but challenging emphasis on 'the law of this land'. 'At this time, we do not have anything but suspicion by which to judge if the murders of Ciarnat and Brother Máel Anfaid are connected with that of Abbot Ségdae. So speculation there will lead us nowhere.'

'You use the word conspirator and not murderer,' snapped Brother Cuineáin.

'That it is because I choose my words more carefully than others,' she replied, barely glancing at Abbot Nannid.

'Surely, the culprit who killed Abbot Ségdae is obvious?' went on Abbot Nannid's steward, who had clearly been fretting at his abbot's retreat in the verbal battle.

'Nothing is obvious unless one is in possession of information that we currently do not have,' Fidelma replied. 'Do you have such information?'

'The girl Ciarnat, for example,' blustered the steward, 'she was involved . . .'

'Ah yes,' interrupted Fidelma. 'Ciarnat, who Abbot Nannid just described as "an innocent serving girl of Prince Donennach's household". When did you come to this view, Abbot Nannid?'

Startled, Abbot Nannid glanced up and said, 'What do you mean?'

'As I recall, last night you were all for locking Ciarnat in some cell and submitting her to vigorous interrogation. You were sure that she had helped Gormán and Aibell to escape from this fortress. You expressed your suspicion of her guilt quite belligerently, suggesting that if Gormán was a murderer, then if *he* could not be executed, you would contemplate Ciarnat being similarly punished. Or am I mistaken?'

Abbot Nannid thrust out his jaw. 'Her murder has absolved her from any connection with the matter.'

Fidelma's eyes flashed with an inner fire. 'On the contrary, we could argue that her murder means she had some information that she was neglecting to share with us and which her assailant wanted to ensure continued to be kept a secret. Innocence and guilt are but relative terms.'

She paused before turning to speak to Prince Donennach directly.

'I think we can safely say that we have proceeded under the law, and by that I mean the law of this land, in its right and proper course. If we had followed any other course, it would still not have prevented the deaths of Ciarnat or Máel Anfaid . . . or perhaps those that are yet to come. It is perverse to suggest otherwise. We follow the course of the law as handed down to us from the time beyond time when the High King, Ollamh Fodhla, ordered those laws to be obeyed in every corner of the land. We shall pursue the guilty through these laws for they are the laws of this land.'

Abbot Nannid rose again. For a moment it seemed as though he would challenge Fidelma. Then, surprisingly, he appeared to change his mind and addressed Prince Donennach instead.

'I spoke here to show my concern at the continuing deaths. That the death of another member of the Abbey of Imleach has taken place and remains unpunished does not fill me with confidence about proceeding under the laws that date from a period when our people walked in barbarism and the world of Christ had not yet penetrated beyond our shores. But having expressed my concerns, I will rest the matter until I return to this fortress.'

Prince Donennach leaned forward with a frown. 'Until you return? Are you leaving Dún Eochair Mháigh, Abbot Nannid?'

'I am afraid that my steward and I must depart for a few days,' Abbot Nannid replied.

'It is an odd time to leave,' Brehon Faolchair commented.

'It is a matter of my religious duties.'

'A matter of religion?' mused Brehon Faolchair. 'Are you returning to your own Abbey of Mungairit?'

'I am not,' snapped Abbot Nannid. 'I have a meeting at Cnoc Fírinne, the Hill of Truth. I shall return in a few days, by which time it is my prayer that the advocate from Cashel will have recaptured Gormán and resolved the murders that have attended her investigation.'

His glance at Fidelma was vicious. Then he bowed to Donennach with a quick 'By your leave?' before turning and, followed by his steward, striding out of the great hall.

Prince Donennach relaxed back in his chair; Fidelma could almost hear his sigh of relief. He whispered something to Conrí before turning to his sister, Airmid. They rose and left the hall together. Conrí made his way quickly to Fidelma.

'The prince says that you dealt with Abbot Nannid very well,' he smiled.

Fidelma shrugged. 'Abbot Nannid is in many ways a vain and silly man, but in that very vanity and stupidity is a danger. By the way, what is this Hill of Truth that he mentioned?'

'It's a hill north of here. For a moment, in view of what we agreed earlier, I was worried in case he had heard that I had dispatched my rider to Mungairit, and was leaving the fortress to go there.' Conrí's relief was obvious.

'But what is special about this hill?'

'Oh, it's one of the highest hills, about three hundred metres high, and situated just to the north-west of here. Not quite as far north as my fortress at the Ford of the Oaks. It is located well back from the river. I can't recall anything of interest except there is a small chapel there.'

'I wonder what religious problem there can be that calls the abbot to that hill?'

Conrí displayed a complete lack of interest in this question. Fidelma now found herself facing Prior Cuán. He looked worried as he limped over and leaned on his stick before her.

'You don't think Brother Máel Anfaid had a hand in the murder of this girl Ciarnat?' he said without preamble. 'My steward has told me about the matter of the cord belt.'

'I do not think so,' she reassured him. 'Trying to lay the blame on Máel Anfaid seems a little too clumsy. Have no concern, Prior. We shall get to the bottom of this matter.'

With the meeting over, the rest of the day passed in a mood of frustration. The more Fidelma mulled over the facts as she knew them, the less she could find any avenue to explore. There was not even a glimpse of a loose end, a tiny thread by which she could start to unravel the ball of twine that was this mystery.

It was later that evening, when they were preparing for the evening meal, that Fidelma returned from her bath. She came into the chamber in a hurry, throwing her toilet things on the bed, and causing Eadulf to glance up in surprise. Before he could speak, she stood before him, hands on hips, and declared vehemently, 'I am an idiot!'

Eadulf grinned. 'Oh, I wouldn't say that.'

'It's true.'

'What has brought on this self-condemnation?'

'The need to find some weak link in this mystery that will eventually lead us to the solution.'

Eadulf shrugged. 'Well, we have considered almost everything. There appears to be no lead at all.'

'Except for the one lead that we should have followed from the beginning.' Fidelma threw herself down on the bed. 'There was I, too busy thinking of protocol, of the correct legal methods, being too concerned in hearing the stories from the witnesses, before going to the one central person in this matter. That was my undoing.'

Eadulf stared at her, perplexity apparent on his features.

She sighed impatiently. 'I should have questioned Gormán first.'

'We have considered that already,' Eadulf pointed out. 'We knew from the hearing exactly what his defence was. However, it's too late now. Gormán has fled and God knows where he is.'

Fidelma sniffed. 'God may well know but I think I also have a clue.'

Eadulf blinked in surprise. 'How so?'

'Remember how Socht was saying that he tracked Gormán and Aibell and that he found tracks trying to cross the river to the west and that puzzled him? He thought it was a false trail because he had expected that Gormán would head back east to his own people. Well, I am sure that it was not a false trail.'

'You mean that Gormán and Aibell went towards the west . . . but where?' Eadulf's eyes suddenly widened. 'You don't mean he went to Rath Menma where Ciarnat said they were married?'

'Perhaps not as far as that.' Fidelma was confident. 'I think we will find them at the home of Aibell's uncle or somewhere in that vicinity.'

'Aibell's uncle – Marban the miller?'

'Where else would they find a natural support?'

Eadulf remained thoughtful for a moment or two. 'So you are suggesting that we go to Marban's mill, seek out Gormán and bring him back here?'

'Perhaps not bring him back immediately,' she replied. 'At least, not until we have heard his story from his own mouth.'

'Then we would have to be careful how we depart from this fortress. Conrí will probably want to follow us. Or, indeed, the real culprits may plan something for us. I wonder that we have not met with some accident to stop our investigation already.'

'I may be wrong but I do not think it is the intention of the conspirators to kill us but rather to trap me, as adviser to my brother, into a position where my advice leads to either Donennach being overthrown or committing his people to a war against Cashel. I am being used, Eadulf, and I do not like it.'

'But our deaths would also provoke your brother to descend on Prince Donennach with his war bands more quickly than this drawn-out game.'

'I don't think so,' she said. 'Whoever is behind this, they want to display some sort of moral right to argue before the High King. They would not want the High King to take Cashel's side. I am merely the cat's paw.' She remembered her brother's reasoning before they had left Cashel and took comfort in it.

'Let us proceed on the assumption that Gormán and Aibell are sheltering either in Marban's mill or thereabouts. Will Marban trust us enough to reveal their presence to us? Will Gormán trust us? After all, he fled the fortress rather than just leave matters in your hands,' Eadulf said. 'Why did he do that?'

'These are questions to which we must find the answers. I will inform Prince Donennach discreetly tonight that we intend to leave at first light to pursue our investigations. We owe him that. Meanwhile, ask Enda to prepare our horses and some provisions. He must not say a word about our intentions to anyone among the guards or at the stables. If asked, he should merely say that he only obeys orders and does not question them.'

'Prince Donennach will demand to know where we are going and for how long,' Eadulf pointed out. 'I am sure he will also confide this in Brehon Faolchair.'

'Indeed,' Fidelma concurred. 'I'll think of something. Perhaps imply that we are interested in the intentions of Abbot Nannid.'

A distant bell began to chime.

'We had better act quickly,' Eadulf advised. 'That's the summons to the evening feast.'

# CHAPTER TWELVE

❧

They left the fortress just as dawn was showing a faint white line above the eastern hills. Ceit, the guard commander, was standing under the flickering light of the burning brand torches by the gate. He raised a hand in salutation but did not stop them as they walked their horses through the gate and down the hill towards the main square of the township. Eadulf noticed that Fidelma had glanced over her shoulder several times.

'Anything amiss?' he asked.

'I think that Donennach has taken the hint that we have decided to shadow Abbot Nannid and passed that on, otherwise Ceit might have been more interested at our early departure. In fact, Donennach and Brehon Faolchair did not make any fuss when I told them we were going to be away for a few days.'

Eadulf asked Enda, 'When you were preparing our horses, you didn't notice anyone else in the stables – anyone particularly interested among the warriors there in what you were doing?'

'I did not,' the young warrior replied. 'Even the *echaire*, the stable-keeper, was obligingly asleep on a pile of hay and did not move while I was there saddling up the horses.'

Fidelma nodded. 'I suspect that Donennach and Brehon Faolchair believe that they might learn far more by sending Conrí to follow us discreetly. Perhaps they think that if we are not following Abbot Nannid we might even lead them to Gormán.'

In the desolate town square, a few brand torches were spluttering as the embers were dying. But with the coming dawn there was light enough to see that the square was empty and Fidelma looked around to make sure they were unobserved. She turned her horse to the right, towards the wooden bridge over the river. On their left were a number of storage huts lining the riverbank which provided an area of shadowy darkness. She increased the pace a little and then abruptly turned into the dark embrace of the buildings. Once hidden from the main area among the shadows, she halted. 'Stay quiet,' she ordered before slipping from her horse, handing the reins to Enda and hurrying back the way they had come.

Only a few moments later, the sound of a band of horses came to their ears. Even from where they had halted, Eadulf and Enda could hear hooves thudding hollowly on the wooden bridge across the river. They heard someone swear and a harsh voice rebuking the man who had broken the silence.

After a little while, Fidelma reappeared out of the darkness and remounted her horse.

'I was right,' she told them, but without satisfaction. 'That was our friend, Conrí, with six or more mounted warriors apparently trying to follow us.'

'So what now, lady?' asked Enda. 'It will be full light soon.'

'I remember the route we first took to Marban's mill. We followed the river to the south and crossed it over a ford to the west. I think that must have been the route Gormán took. Once over the river it was not too long before we reached the mill.'

'Then I suggest that we start immediately, before Conrí and his band of warriors realise they have been tricked and come back to find us,' Eadulf suggested.

*　*　*

It was with feelings of familiarity that they passed through some rocky terrain and started to smell the aroma of drying grains from the wood kilns. It was now a warm day with a cloudless blue sky. They followed the smells along a small path emerging from the trees on to a high rocky ground. It was not so many months before that they had been here and caught sight of the mill where they had once hidden from the murderous brigands of Sliabh Luachra. Marban's mill was a watermill, situated by a fast-flowing stream, a millpond before it and a spring behind it. At one side of the mill were storehouses and beyond them, two large stone-built kilns. Even against the bright cloudless sky they could see the heat haze rising and some smoke billowing now and then. Apart from the difference due to the change of seasons, it being mid-summer now compared with winter when they had first come to the mill, the scene appeared the same. There were several workers around the mill which, as they already knew, was a large and important one.

As they trotted their horses down the rocky slope, a shout told them they had been observed. A giant of a man appeared from the mill. He was shirtless but wore a leather apron that covered his great chest but left his muscular tanned arms bare. His large head was covered with a mass of dark red hair, and a bristling beard. He gazed at them for a moment, from light blue eyes, and then his face became wreathed in a broad grin.

He ran forward to help Fidelma dismount, although she did not need his attention.

'Fidelma!' he grinned, then: 'And friend Eadulf! Aibell suspected that you would turn up here sooner or later.'

'You know why we have come then?' Fidelma asked once the greetings had been exchanged.

Marban's grin disappeared and he motioned to the mill. 'Come and let me provide you with good apple cider and let us talk.'

As they walked across to the mill, Fidelma glanced around her. 'Are Gormán and Aibell here?'

'They are not,' Marban replied without hesitation.

'But you do know where they are?' pressed Fidelma.

To her surprise he shook his head. 'Not exactly.' He opened the door and motioned them inside. It was comfortable inside the slightly stuffy millhouse and the place brought back memories. Marban handed out some clay mugs and then went to the side door which gave access on the flowing stream beyond. A thin rope was attached to a basket that was balanced in the waters; from the basket he produced a large pottery jug and filled their mugs with an amber-coloured liquid. Enda tasted it immediately, licking his lips appreciatively.

Marban smiled. 'It's nice and chilled. Good apple cider.'

'It is that,' Enda agreed, wiping his mouth with the back of his hand.

Fidelma was inwardly chafing at the delay in coming to the point of their visit. Only the etiquette of hospitality caused her to raise the drink to her lips and take a sip before she spoke.

'Now you say you do not know where Gormán and Aibell are . . . *exactly*?'

Marban raised his own mug and swallowed, hunching his shoulders for a moment before letting them relax.

'You know that Gormán and Aibell are married?'

'We do. We had the story from her friend Ciarnat.'

'Ah yes. The girl who helped them escape from Dún Eochair Mháigh.'

Fidelma and Eadulf exchanged a quick glance of surprise. 'How do you know this?' Fidelma asked.

'Aibell told me.'

'She told you that Ciarnat helped them?' Eadulf clarified.

'She did,' confirmed the miller.

'Did she say why?' Fidelma wanted to know.

'Ciarnat said that you had betrayed Gormán and was not going to help to free him.'

'But . . .' Eadulf exploded and was stopped with a gesture by Fidelma.

'It is not true,' she said quietly. 'Why was this believed?'

'I thought it didn't sound like the *dálaigh* I knew, lady. But Aibell believed her friend.'

'I can think of no conversation that I had with Ciarnat from which she could have mistaken my intentions.'

'Unless . . .' Eadulf said, 'unless Ciarnat was told this by someone she trusted, then she would have been wary of checking the truth with us and Aibell would take her word.'

'It would fit,' Marban agreed slowly. 'Gormán was certainly reluctant to believe the story that you would abandon him, but Aibell was convinced. There was a necessity to move quickly and no time to debate the matter. So Gormán accepted it as the truth.'

'It might also explain the reason why Ciarnat was killed,' Eadulf pointed out.

Marban looked shocked. 'What? You say that Ciarnat has been killed?'

'Murdered,' Eadulf said heavily. Then, warming to an idea, he went on. 'What if the person who told Ciarnat that we intended to abandon Gormán had done so knowing that an escape would be made? Once the plan had gone as expected, what if that person then killed the girl to prevent her being a witness against him?'

Enda leaned forward. 'Why make it look as if Brother Máel Anfaid killed her?'

Eadulf was terse. 'We know the killer had tried to implicate him, hanging the girl with his *loman* after he had killed Brother Máel Anfaid. Perhaps it was simply to lead a false trail? If Brother Máel Anfaid had fed her the lie about Gormán's warning having been dismissed by Donennach, it is likely that he also told her that we had betrayed Gormán.'

'Did Aibell amplify on what Ciarnat told her?' Fidelma's question was aimed at Marban.

'She only said that Ciarnat had told her that you had accepted that Gormán's cause was lost and had given up on saving him. But . . . I am sorry, lady. I am trying to remember what Aibell said. Ciarnat mentioned that it was someone of influence. Anyway, it was felt that the only thing they could do in the circumstances was to flee the fortress and go into exile. Ciarnat arranged everything, having bribed a guard who showed them a gate in the fortress through which they could escape without being observed.'

'Brother Máel Anfaid was a part of all this?' queried Eadulf.

'It is hard to believe that Ciarnat would describe him as someone of influence,' Fidelma said thoughtfully.

'Many things are hard to believe,' Marban volunteered. 'Even the evidence against Gormán.'

'Ciarnat was given the wrong information on purpose, knowing she would pass it on. Afterwards, the poor girl was murdered to silence her. Máel Anfaid enters into the chain of information somewhere. It is my intention to find out the truth from Gormán and Aibell.'

Marban was unhappy about this. 'It is a heavy responsibility you are placing on me, lady. Can I be assured that you are still determined to defend Gormán? Aibell my niece has found happiness with him. I would not want to rob her of it as she has been robbed of her mother and most of her young life. You must promise me that you do not intend to simply drag him back to Dún Eochair Mháigh and give him over to the mercy of Abbot Nannid.'

Enda gave a low chuckle. 'The idea of anyone trying to drag Gormán anywhere he did not want to go . . .'

'You have my promise that I believe Gormán to be innocent of the murder of Abbot Ségdae. I knew it almost from the first moment I arrived at Prince Donennach's fortress.'

Marban hesitated only a moment more. 'I trust you, Fidelma. I trust you all,' he added, including Eadulf and Enda. He was silent awhile and then he made up his mind. 'I know where Aibell and Gormán have gone and will direct you there.'

'It is for the sake of truth and justice, Marban,' Fidelma assured him. 'When did they leave here?'

'They left yesterday because they reasoned that it was well known that I was Aibell's uncle and eventually someone would come here looking for them.'

'Where did they intend to go?'

'They had not decided on their final destination. The first place they intended going was to a cousin of mine. His homestead is north-west of here. He and his son have a farmstead but my cousin is a worker in wood and prefers to isolate himself in a woodman's hut in a dense forest on a nearby hill. That is where they will be, not at the farmstead. You can't miss the hill because of its length and it rises no more than three hundred metres. It is mostly hazelwood that covers the slopes.'

'To the north-west?' Fidelma was thoughtful. 'Would that take us towards the coast?'

'Not as far as that,' said Marban. 'It is no more than ten kilometres from here. Just a short ride. I will show you the track that will take you across the marshlands. Follow it, and then, keeping to the track through the forests, you will come to the hill that I speak of.'

'Will it also help if we know its name?' suggested Eadulf.

'I don't think I've ever heard it,' Marban said with a grin. 'Anyway, my cousin is named Corradáin and he is an *erscraidhe*.'

It was Enda who explained: 'That means a carver of wood.'

'Like I said, it is my cousin's profession,' Marban agreed.

'Is there any special reason why they should be going to stay with your cousin?' Fidelma asked.

'Only that Corradáin is an honourable person. He will hide them until they make up their mind where they should eventually go.'

'Before we leave I would like to know a little about what happened when Aibell first came here. I mean before Gormán turned up.'

'That was some weeks ago, when she arrived here with a man from Sliabh Luachra. He was called Deogaire and apparently had helped Aibell escape from the bondage of Fidaig. He did not stay long. Aibell wanted to meet me and talk about her parentage. I told her the story of how I helped her mother escape from her father Escmug to Rath Menma, and how I finally had to kill him to protect her mother. I kept nothing back from her.'

'That was good,' Fidelma said.

'It was not long afterwards that the warrior, Gormán arrived. At first they had a big row shouting at each other. Then the next thing they were in each other's arms.' The miller threw back his head and gave a loud shout of laughter. 'Young love!'

'So,' prompted Fidelma, 'they decided to go to Rath Menma . . .?'

'Yes. I went with them.'

'And they were married there?'

'And there they were married,' confirmed the miller. 'The old couple Cadan and Flannair, who farmed there, knew a local Brehon who came to ensure all was done according to law.'

'Then you all returned here?'

'It was while we were returning that we encountered a band of merchants who told us the news about Gláed. He had killed his brother Artgal and escaped, and was now leading the Luachair Deaghaid out of their burrows from Sliabh Luachra.'

'This is the point where I become confused,' Eadulf admitted. 'Why did that fact become of such concern to Gormán? Admittedly, he knew that Gláed was an outlaw, who had killed his own father among others and now his own brother. We all knew that. But all those who dwell in the valleys of Sliabh Luachra are thieves and robbers if not killers.'

The miller spread his hands. 'Gormán and Aibell had decided to return to Cashel. But one of the merchants said that he had overheard that Gláed had agreed to serve as a mercenary to some powerful person who was going to overthrow the Prince of the Uí Fidgente.'

'What?' Fidelma straightened with a startled look.

'We had heard about Gláed and his declaration to have revenge on those who had wronged him. But we did not know this particular detail,' Eadulf explained.

'But it is logical, now I give it thought,' Fidelma reflected. 'He was involved with the previous conspiracy to murder Prince Donennach, so why should he not be involved in another one?'

'I suppose the merchants did not tell Gormán the identity of this powerful person?' Eadulf asked.

They were not surprised when Marban gave a shake of his head. 'No names were mentioned.'

Fidelma sighed. 'When Gormán and Aibell came back here, did Gormán tell you any details about the murder of Abbot Ségdae?'

'Only that he had just entered the chamber to speak to the abbot when he was hit on the head from behind. When he recovered consciousness, the abbot was dead and he was accused.'

'When they turned up here with this story, did you offer them advice?' Fidelma asked the miller.

The big man gave one of his characteristic shrugs. 'As you know from my past, lady, I am not the right person to give such advice. I did not do well when Aibell's mother fled to me for protection from my brother, Aibell's father. In the end, I had to kill my own brother to prevent a greater evil.'

'It was a matter of *duinorcun*, manslaughter, for you acted in self-defence,' she told him. 'I judge you without legal blame.'

Marban looked awkward for a moment and then suddenly rose and stretched his limbs, glancing through the window.

'Let me remind you that the sun now stands at its zenith. I would not recommend you to commence your journey through the marsh-land now. This is the time when the insects are most active. Wait until the day begins to cool. Meanwhile, please join me and my workers in the *etar-shod*, the midday meal, albeit frugal. You will then have plenty of time to ride on to Corradáin's homestead and arrive there long before twilight.'

'Now that sounds like a good idea!' exclaimed Enda, who then looked embarrassed, for it was Fidelma's role to accept the invitation. Nevertheless, she did not rebuke him but indicated her acceptance.

'But we must not tarry too long, as I know that Conrí and a band of warriors will soon be on our trail.'

Marban raised his brows in surprise. 'I thought Conrí was a friend of yours, lady?'

'He is also warlord of the Uí Fidgente and his allegiance is to Prince Donennach and Brehon Faolchair. His duty is to track down Gormán and return him to the custody of the fortress. We must ensure that we reach Gormán first.'

'I understand,' the miller acknowledged. 'How far behind is he?'

Enda was the expert. The young warrior thought for a moment. 'It depends how far they went northwards over the bridge in the wrong direction. If they went to the Hill of Truth before they turned back, it could be as much as two days.'

'Let us hope that is the course they have taken, for we need to gain as much time as possible.'

Marban left the millhouse and they heard him shouting orders to arrange the food. The miller's idea of a frugal meal did not match their own. Usually the *etar-shod* was a light affair because the main meal of the day was in the evening. However, the aroma of roasting meat, baking bread and several other delicious odours they could not identify, soon assailed their nostrils. Several wooden tables were swiftly erected before the mill, on which the workers and their wives placed the feast, along with the inevitable jugs of apple cider, and were now seating themselves.

Marban escorted his visitors to the end of one of the tables and seated them around his own chair. The atmosphere was cordial. The millworkers, many of whom remembered Fidelma and Eadulf from the previous year, were friendly. There was no hierarchy here, unlike the formal meals given by princes and kings. Meat was cut from two nearby roasting spits, placed on dishes and brought to the table where those seated just helped themselves. Everyone lent a hand and no one was appointed carver or server as at formal feasts.

As Eadulf examined the dishes of meat, hesitating to make a choice, he found Marban at his side. The miller explained the dishes with pride. 'That is *muilt-fheoil*, mutton, and that is *fiadh-fheoil*, venison. The venison I particularly recommend, my friend. It is basted on the spit with honey and salt and is quite sweet.'

Also on the table were hard-boiled eggs, freshly baked small loaves, still warm, called *tortíne*, and some dishes of green vege-tables which Eadulf identified as a kind of kale or cabbage, whose taste had been enhanced by *crem* or wild garlic, as well as some other herbs. As these various dishes were pressed on him, he joked, 'If I succumbed to all these temptations, I swear I would not be able to ride out of the millyard, let alone to our destination.'

Fidelma cast him a disapproving look. 'Well, I would advise moderation, especially with the apple cider. A full belly is not a good travelling companion.'

Eadulf reluctantly pushed his platter from him, saying to the miller with a smile of regret: 'It is a good feast, Marban. I had not expected millworkers to eat so well.'

'We also work well,' Marban replied seriously. 'It's a hard day's work to keep the mill productive. Sometimes we work our kilns all night as well – and a man cannot fulfil such work and maintain his health on just a small bowl of gruel. These,' he waved a hand to encompass everyone, 'are my people. I am responsible for them.'

'That reminds me, Marban,' Fidelma said. 'You are not well protected here. Do you have plans if the news from the merchants proves true? What happens if Gláed and the men of Sliabh Luachra come riding down on your mill? It was here that we captured him after he killed his father in one of your sheds. Your mill also lies on the route to Dún Eochair Mháigh.'

'You make a good point, lady,' agreed the miller. 'And it is on that point that I decided I must remain here to protect my mill and ensure the safety of my people.'

Fidelma gazed around her. 'I see no defences,' she commented.

'Neither will Gláed, I hope,' the miller smiled confidently. 'The path to this mill from Sliabh Luachra is one that passes across the marsh plains. You see, lady, I have learned a few tricks since you were last here. There are eyes and ears that will alert us of any approach of Gláed and his marauding wolves.'

Eadulf had to think for a moment before remembering that *foilc*, the term for marauding wolves, was also used for bands of robbers and brigands.

'But even if you knew Gláed's brigands were on their way, you could hardly sustain a defence against an attack.' Fidelma remained concerned.

'We don't mean to,' Marban said easily. 'As soon as we get warning of Gláed's ravening wolves coming out of Sliabh Luachra, everyone will make for the forests.' He gestured across the stream to the south which, unlike the areas to the north and south-west, was a thick tangle of forest.

'Gláed could destroy the mill,' Eadulf pointed out.

'I have my strategy, lady. We'll retreat until the threat is gone, and if Gláed tries to follow us into the forests then it will be to his detriment. My people and I are forest-dwellers so we shall survive any attack.'

It was finally time to leave. They bade farewell to Marban, who showed them the track that led north-west across the flat plains criss-crossed by streams and watercourses. At first it was easy riding, although the atmosphere was close and humid. The track eventually became muddy even in this summer month. The area was, in effect, a marshland not too dissimilar from the stretches that lay east of Cashel and bordered on the lands of Osraige – and with the same amount of midges, so Eadulf morosely observed. There were no more little hillocks poking out to alleviate the flatness of the scenery and they had long since left the high trees to the south.

Eadulf disliked travelling through such terrain, if terrain it could be called for there was little of land in it. It was a treacherous wetland of bogs, waterholes and mires whose liquid traps could swallow men and horses if they mistook their way and deviated from the narrow, safe tracks that ran through it. The predominate growth through which they passed consisted of reed mace, or bulrushes, standing thirty centimetres high and reminding Eadulf of dark sausages on spikes. Here and there he saw what appeared as little sprouts of white on the green parts of plants: experience told him they were groups of white leeches, nasty little carnivores that it was best to avoid, as were most little insects that populated the area. Dragonflies, flea-flies, damselflies – each were irritants and bearers of disease. Now and then they had to flick away such creatures from their patiently plodding horses.

The area was strangely quiet to Eadulf's ears. He glanced up several times at the blue canopy above, shielding his eyes against the lowering but unprotected sun. There was not a cloud in the sky. Neither was there any sign of birds – and that seemed unusual to him. The only bird he had seen was a stately grey heron, standing on its long legs in some shallow water and, with its long sinuous neck, poised ready to stab its prey and swallow it whole. Once he spotted an otter marking its territory, appearing incongruous in the climate with its thick fur and webbed feet.

He was not sure how long they had been moving through this wilderness when Enda called, pointing before them.

'We are coming to the treeline. The land is beginning to rise. The forest is just ahead.'

'We'll pause a moment to rest the horses as soon as we reach the shade of the trees,' replied Fidelma.

It was not long before they could feel the ground hardening beneath their mounts and rising away from the low-lying marshland.

A short while later, they entered the shelter of the forest and paused by a freshwater stream. It gushed down the hill and emptied into the marshland. They dismounted and allowed their horses to drink while Eadulf took the opportunity to wash the taste of the marshland and its sticky odours from his mouth. Then he gazed around. They were surrounded by hazel trees but here and there, mainly along the borders of the marshes, were a variety of yew trees.

'There seems a good track this way.' Enda pointed to a narrow path that certainly wound its way through the trees in the direction they intended to go.

Without further conversation, they remounted and moved off in single file with Enda leading the way. It was pleasant to ride under the shade of the trees, and now their ears became attuned to more sounds – bird calls and the grunt of wild boar snuffling through the undergrowth – a contrast with the quietness of the marshland.

Enda turned in his saddle and informed them, 'There is an open stretch ahead and a hillock. We can probably see the hill where this man, Corradáin, has his hut.'

'So long as it's not the hill of *corrmíl*,' Eadulf tried to joke, giving the word for the tiny biting midges, as he was still suffering from their attentions during the trek through the marshes. No one laughed, nor had he expected them to.

They came to the area, a rocky rise where, it seemed, no trees could put down roots. The area was clear of tall growth and verdure. They halted and Enda immediately scrambled up on to a tall rock.

'I think I can see the hill that the miller means,' he announced excitedly. 'It shouldn't take us long to reach there.' Then he frowned.

'What is it?' Fidelma asked, looking up at him.

'I can see smoke. Smoke on the hill.'

'Just someone's cooking fire?' hazarded Eadulf. 'You don't need fires for warmth in this heat.'

'It just seems too large a pall of smoke for a cooking fire.'

'Let us move on directly,' urged Fidelma. 'I don't want us to be journeying through the forest at twilight.'

Enda gave a final glance in the direction of the hill before scrambling down and mounting his horse. 'It is not that far,' he said. 'We should have plenty of time to reach it before dark.'

'Reaching it is one thing,' Fidelma said, 'but then, somewhere on it, we have to find Marban's cousin Corradáin, and, hopefully, Gormán and Aibell.'

They were on a broader track now which meandered through the forest.

'I hope our reception by Gormán and Aibell will be a friendly one,' Eadulf fretted. 'Aibell believed Ciarnat's story and convinced Gormán – so they might not welcome our appearance.'

'We have to convince them otherwise,' Fidelma replied. 'They will see that Marban trusted us.'

It wasn't long before they arrived under the dark shadows of the long hill. It certainly looked like the one which Marban had described. From east to west, Fidelma's acute eye judged it was many kilometres in length. The western end was more densely covered by a forest of hazel.

'Which way now?' Eadulf asked.

Enda was looking towards an area at the western end of the hill. 'There is still that pall of smoke up on that ridge, lady,' he said, pointing, 'although it's not as heavy as it was when I first saw it. The fire seems to be dying out, whatever caused it in the first place.'

'Fire might be a sign of human habitation,' Fidelma responded. 'Let's explore that source first. We might even find someone to inform us where Corradáin has his dwelling.'

There was a straightforward track leading up to the ridge which Enda had indicated. It was simple to follow the treeline up the hill to where it opened on a large level area. They could smell charred wood as they came up to it. Thankfully the winds were blowing across the mountain, taking the noxious fumes away from them.

There was no mistaking the remains of a human habitation which had been the source of the fire. The wooden building and surrounding sheds had been almost totally reduced to charcoal. Stretched in front of the burnt-out buildings were two male bodies. They had been untouched by fire. One of them had a woodsman's axe still buried in a smashed skull. The cause of the death of the second man was also clear. Two arrows were embedded in his chest.

Eadulf glanced round nervously for a potential threat but Enda was already dismounting.

'Whoever did this must have set fire to the buildings and are long gone,' he reassured them quickly. 'There are signs of several horses having been here.' He gazed about, a grim expression on his features. 'From the remains of the tools, lady, this looks like a woodman's workplace and there are some newly carved pieces over there.'

Fidelma's mouth was dry. 'You think that this might be Corradáin's place?'

Enda went over to the bodies and stared down at the man with the axe still buried in his head. Then he did the same to the body with the arrows.

'I am afraid that this one seems familiar, lady.'

Fidelma and Eadulf dismounted and joined Enda. In life the man had been tall and muscular, with a mass of dark red hair and a bristling beard.

'He and Marban could have been brothers,' Eadulf commented.

'But they were cousins.' Fidelma's voice was tight. She stood back and peered around the clearing.

'I wonder who attacked him and why?' Enda asked.

Fidelma suddenly raised a finger to her lips. Her head was to one side as if listening. They did not hear anything beyond the trilling of birds in the surrounding trees. She leaned closer to them. 'I thought I heard a sound like something falling, coming from behind that burnt-out cabin.'

'Woods are full of sounds,' Enda whispered back.

'This was like pottery falling and breaking. Did you not hear it?' They shook their heads in unison.

Fidelma gestured for them to follow her. Such was the intensity of her demeanour that Enda unsheathed his sword. He knew that she was not given to imagining things. She led them to an area at the rear of what had been the wooden cabin, where she halted. The land hereabouts had clearly been planted, mainly with herbs. Gorse bushes which were just ceasing to flower formed a border against the tall hazel trees.

Yet there was one gorse bush that caught Fidelma's eye. It stood incongruously apart from the others; not in the borderline at all. In fact, she could even see a gap where it had been cut and moved; the glint of white cut roots showed clearly. She moved quietly towards it and glanced down. Then she waved her companions forward and pointed. There were dried blood splatters on the soil around it.

Finger to her lips, she gestured to the gorse bush with a motion as if pushing it aside. Enda nodded, and pointed to Eadulf in an elaborate pantomime to show that he should shove the gorse aside. Then he motioned to his sword. It was over in a matter of movements. With the bush dragged aside, a wooden trap door was revealed, its boards level with the surrounding earth. An iron ring formed a handle on it in the middle.

Eadulf exchanged a look with Enda and then bent to the ring, heaving it up. Enda sprang forward, sword poised ready. Below them was revealed a small underground chamber. It was easily recognisable as a *fotholl* – an underground cavity lined with wood, in which food was stored to keep it fresh as long as possible. In larger houses it was called a *talam*, or cellar.

As the dying rays of the sun struck the entrance and lit up the hole, they saw a figure lying at the bottom, staring up at them with terrified eyes. The features were bloodstained but easily recognisable.

'Aibell!' Fidelma gasped.

# CbApTER TbIRTEEN

❧

For a moment Fidelma had a sense that she had witnessed this scene before. Then she recollected that her first encounter with Aibell was when they had found her hiding in a woodsman's hut. She had stared up at them, her tousled blue-black hair cut short and quite dirty, scattered with dead leaves and wisps of straw. Now, instead of patches of dried mud on her face, there were streaks of blood, yet her features were still as attractive, symmetrical with discernible freckles on her cheeks. Her dark eyes were wide and her lips parted in fear.

'Aibell, it is I, Fidelma. Are you injured?'

The girl shivered and stirred herself. 'Have they gone?' she managed to get the words out.

'They have – whoever "they" are,' confirmed Fidelma. 'Let us help you out of there.'

Eadulf reached down, caught the girl's outstretched arms and drew her from the hole. As she emerged, he saw the abrasion on the side of her head and another on one bloodied arm. 'You are hurt,' he said. 'Those wounds need attending to.'

The girl was looking round at the devastation with a horrified expression.

'Where is Corradáin?' she asked hesitantly, gazing at the smoking remains of the cabin.

'If he had red hair and looked like your uncle, Marban, I am afraid that he lies dead in front of the hut.' Fidelma spoke the words gently but there seemed no other way of telling her the truth.

The girl gave a single sob and lowered her head, staggering a little as if she would fall. Eadulf steadied her and said to Enda, 'Can you find something she can sit down on?'

Enda spotted a short log, obviously cut for the purpose of sitting. It had been placed so that anyone sitting on it could rest their back against a hazel tree that grew directly behind it. He helped Eadulf guide the girl to it. Then Eadulf darted back to his horse to fetch his *lés*, the medical bag. He had noticed a spring nearby which rose from the hillside and bubbled down, passing the buildings. This must have supplied Corradáin with his water source. Taking a clean cloth from his bag, he soaked it, and also filled a mug of the crystal clear water before returning to the girl.

No one had spoken to her or questioned her, waiting for Eadulf to tend to the girl's injuries first. He gave her the water to drink and she swallowed it eagerly. Then he peered at the abrasions and started to wipe away the blood. She winced once or twice as he did so but did not cry out during his administrations.

'You had a nasty blow to the side of the head and another you seem to have deflected with your arm,' he observed. 'The blood has ceased to flow from the wounds so they are not deep, but I expect that you will have bruising for some time.'

He put a salve on the wounds and used clean linen strips, also taken from his *lés*, to bandage them. Then Eadulf returned to the spring, filled a second mug of water and took it back to the girl. This time she sipped it more slowly.

Fidelma, who had been standing watching, now seated herself on the log beside the girl.

'Where is Gormán?' Fidelma asked.

'I pray that he has escaped,' replied Aibell.

'Escaped from whom? What happened here?'

Eadulf felt the question was too blunt and tried to preface it with more tact. 'Marban told us why you and Gormán felt the need to escape from Prince Donennach's fortress. We guessed that you would seek shelter with him but he explained that you both felt it best to . . . to vanish. He said you would stay awhile with his cousin Corradáin while you were making up your mind where to go.'

Aibell's expression was despondent but her voice held a note of bitter reproach aimed at her uncle. 'How did you persuade him to tell you? He was meant to protect us.'

'And he did so,' Fidelma returned in a firm tone. 'Once he heard that the story Ciarnat told you was not true, that we were *not* abandoning you and Gormán to the mercies of Abbot Nannid, he realised that you were in more danger than ever.'

The girl's dark eyes flashed momentarily.

'Are you asking me to believe that Ciarnat lied? She is a friend from my childhood.'

'Ciarnat has been murdered,' Fidelma told her brutally. This was no time to be delicate: the truth had to be revealed.

The girl sat back, shocked. Eadulf frowned at Fidelma in disapproval of her forthright approach.

'She may have lied to you or, as we believe, she was told a lie herself,' he explained kindly. 'That is why she met her death – so that she would not reveal the identity of the person who told her that lie.'

Aibell was quiet for a moment. 'Are you saying that you would not have abandoned us . . . abandoned Gormán? Abbot Nannid was so certain that Gormán would be executed under these new church laws. Every time it was argued that it was not our law, he replied something in Latin saying execution was demanded by the Holy Scripture.'

'*Qui percussent et occiderit hominem, morte moriatur,*' Eadulf muttered. 'And he that kills any man shall surely be put to death.'

'A line from Leviticus.' Fidelma was dismissive. 'Abbot Nannid is very fond of quoting that line. He should remember the words of the Christ Whose religion he claims to follow. "Do not judge, so that you may not be judged. For with the judgement you make you will be judged and the measure you give will be the measure you get." Abbot Nannid will one day find himself judged accordingly.'

Eadulf smiled encouragingly at Aibell. 'All we are saying is that we are here to help and to uphold the law so that the truth of what happened is known.'

'Gormán did not kill Abbot Ségdae,' Aibell said quietly.

'And that is why you must help us to prove it,' affirmed Fidelma.

'Now, if you are up to it, tell us what happened here,' Eadulf coaxed.

The girl hesitated and then seemed to gather an inner strength. 'As Marban has told you, we came here yesterday and Corradáin gave us hospitality. He was so much like my uncle – full of the joy of life, in love with the forests that he tended. He was a fine carver of wood. He asked no questions and made no condemnation of us.' A great sorrow was upon her, but she bravely continued to speak.

'This morning, Corradáin was up at first light because he wanted to mark some trees for felling. We had barely awoken and broken our fast, when he came back, out of breath and looking worried. In the valley below runs one of the main tracks along the south side of the hill; it then swings north through a valley.'

Enda spoke for the first time. 'We crossed it. It seemed to be more of a *ro-shét* than just a track.'

A *ro-shét* was a class of road which, as defined by law, accommodated the passage of many horses and carriages and hence was called a 'great-way'.

'And so?' prompted Fidelma.

'Corradáin had been near the track when he heard the sound of approaching horses. Thinking that they might be searching for us, he hid. He counted about forty horses passing by. The riders were fighting men but he said they did not have the look of professional warriors.

'At their head rode a young man with barely the stubble of a beard on him. Corradáin described him as having cruel, wolf-like features, and the starved look of someone in need of a meal. In spite of his youth, he carried himself with an air of great self-importance.'

'Gláed!' Eadulf almost shouted, recognising the description.

Aibell nodded. 'Gormán and I realised at once who it was. I had seen Gláed many times when I was his father's bond-servant.'

'If they followed the track below this hill to the east, would that bring them to Prince Donennach's fortress?' asked Eadulf.

'Corrdáin told us that the main track swings around the hill and goes northwards through a valley, but a small track does branch due east to the great river.'

'Then what happened here?' Fidelma pressed.

'Gormán was agitated. He told me to wait here with Corradáin, and he would follow them for a while to see which track they took. He felt he owed allegiance to Cashel to prevent any uprising.' Her voice broke. 'I fear for my husband.'

'So Gormán went off to follow Gláed and his men . . .' Fidelma prompted.

The girl pulled herself together. 'Time went by and we began to grow nervous, but then I heard a horse ascending the track. Naturally, I thought it was Gormán returning. I ran from the cabin to greet him . . . and at once, I saw it was not he.'

She paused and licked her dry lips. Without asking, Eadulf went to get more water from the spring. The girl took the mug and drank.

'I presume it was one of Gláed's men?' Fidelma said.

'Not only that, but the man was one of those who had served Fidaig when he was alive. He was a brutal fellow. He saw me, and recognised me as the escaped bond-servant who used to work in Fidaig's household. Giving a roar, he jumped from his horse, grabbing me by the hair as I turned to run. He threw me to the ground, striking me a couple of times.'

'How did you escape?'

'I heard him say something about taking me to Fidaig's son for punishment – but that first I would have to amuse him. I know I lay helpless with the man bending over me and then I heard him squeal, a terrible animal-like squeal ending in a grunt as you hear when a wild boar is slaughtered. His body was heavy on me and then I felt it being dragged off. There was Corradáin trying to help me to my feet. I saw my attacker lying on the ground with one of Corradáin's great wood axes embedded in his head.'

She shuddered and took another swallow of water, her shaking hands making her spill some of. Then she tried to continue in a more controlled fashion.

'Corradáin was anxious. He said that there might be comrades of the man about as he could hear the movement of horses below. I was dizzy from my injuries and scarce knew what I was doing. He led me around the back of the cabin, opened the wooden hatch door into the *fotholl* and told me to hide inside. He said he would try to disguise the entrance.'

'That he did,' muttered Enda. 'He spread gorse over the trap door.'

'After I hid I could hear a lot of shouting. I heard horses and excited movement – and then I heard the sound of crackling flames. I could feel the heat even down in the *fotholl* but, of course, thanks to my uncle, I was well protected from the flames. I have no idea how long I was there. I kept feeling dizzy from the blows the man gave to my head. Perhaps I passed out. Then I heard horses again. I was frightened. Suddenly the hatch was wrenched open, and . . . and you were standing there.'

Fidelma was nodding slowly. 'We can only guess at what happened after Corradáin hid you. Once he had attempted to disguise the entrance to your hiding place, he must have run back to the front of the cabin. Unfortunately, he did not have the chance to find another weapon by the time your attacker's companions arrived. One of them, perhaps two, shot him with two arrows in the chest and he was killed instantly. Having found their companion dead with the woodsman's axe in his head, they decided to wreak their revenge by setting the cabin alight. We saw it burning from a distance and by the time we reached here it was smouldering and destroyed.'

'That seems to be the truth of it,' agreed Eadulf. 'What concerns me is that Gormán left here early this morning. It is now nearly twilight and he has not returned.'

'Could he have come back while you were hiding and you did not hear him?' Fidelma asked the girl.

'I heard your horses so I think I would have heard his returning,' Aibell replied in a troubled voice.

'Maybe not,' intervened Enda. 'If he returned at the height of the fire, the crack of the flames would have been deafening.'

'Yet, if he did, then he would have encountered the attackers whom we can safely identify as Gláed's men,' Fidelma said.

'Were they stragglers following Gláed, or were they part of his main band?' Eadulf wanted to know. 'There are too many things unknown to start forming conclusions. The main question is: what has happened to Gormán?'

Enda pointed to the darkening sky. 'Perhaps an even more pressing question is: where should we camp for this night? It will soon be too dark to see anything and, if these marauders are still about, we daren't light a fire.'

'But if we don't light a fire, and Gormán is seeking to return, he will miss us,' Aibell protested.

'I am afraid it seems inevitable that something has already delayed him,' Eadulf told her gently.

'We must accept the realities of the current situation,' Fidelma stated. 'We can do nothing until first light. The only place we can pass the night is here. We can utilise the smouldering cabin for warmth by sleeping near it – we could even light a fire behind the remaining walls. I don't think it would be seen from below this hill, but I would not advise it since it is not necessary. It won't hurt us for one night to drink water and eat something cold.'

'Well,' Enda suddenly rose, 'before I cannot see a hand in front of me, I'll check out Corradáin's *fotholl*, in case he has stored something edible there that we could use.'

'We should also attend to the horses,' Fidelma said, looking around. 'I suppose they made off with your horse, Aibell?'

'It appears so. Corradáin had an ass but kept his other animals at his son's farmstead on the northern side of this hill.'

Eadulf had nearly forgotten that Marban had mentioned a farmstead run by Corradáin's son.

'Have you been there?'

The girl shook her head. 'Corradáin told us about it. His wife is long dead and his son and daughter-in-law look after a farmstead down on the plain. Corradáin preferred to dwell in the forest. His love was trees and the wild game of the woods.'

Enda reappeared, carrying some items. 'Corradáin was storing jugs of cold apple cider down there and there are apples a-plenty. Oh, and I found a jar of dried hazelnuts, some already-roasted acorns and a good supply of sweet chestnuts. We shall not starve.'

'You are sure that they are sweet chestnuts?' Eadulf was particular. As a child, he had once mistakenly thought all chestnuts were the same and ate an inedible horse chestnut. He was sick for a day.

Enda's voice was pained. 'Friend Eadulf, I would hope you thought better of my knowledge.'

'We will have to share what covering we can,' Fidelma said, changing the subject. 'While the days are warm, the nights can be cold, so I suggest that as soon as we have the horses tethered safely, you find a suitable spot near the remains of the cabin to bed down. Tomorrow we shall have a lot to do.'

'A lot to do?' queried Eadulf.

'There are two bodies to be buried,' she replied. 'And in the light we must find forage for the horses. Then, of course, we must decide what to do next before we move on.'

Eadulf had almost forgotten about the two bodies, and with the moon now rising, he suggested that he and Enda move them to the farthest side of the smoking ruins from where they intended to sleep. Night had fallen but the crisp white glow of the moon was such that their gruesome task was made easy. The only thing the moonlight could not do was differentiate the colour of the vegetation to identify any good forage for their horses and so they tethered them near the lower end of the brook so that at least the beasts had water enough.

Although they settled themselves, and ate sparsely of the nuts and apples, sharing in turn the apple cider, it was clear that they were not ready to sleep. They sat with ears tuned for any sound among the trees that might alert them to danger. Finally, it was Eadulf who made a suggestion. 'We might as well discuss our next step now since sleep is not forthcoming yet.'

'We must find out what has happened to Gormán,' Aibell declared at once. 'I am not going back to Dún Eochair Mháigh until I know.'

'I would support that,' Enda said. 'Gormán was not only my commander, he was my friend. I am duty bound to find him.'

'We set out from Dún Eochair Mháigh to find Gormán and I think that task should be fulfilled,' Eadulf said. 'The only decision to make is: where do we start? Gormán went to follow Gláed and the brigands. He promised to return as soon as he found out in which direction they were heading, but he hasn't done so. The only course open to us is to set out in the same direction and hope to pick up his trail. Enda here is said to be a good tracker. If he cannot follow the brigands' tracks then no one can.'

'You make it sound easy.' Fidelma felt more caution was needed.

'Often when things appear hard, they can be rendered down into manageable stages. Everything is achievable if one is not afraid to take the first step.' Eadulf paused and they heard him chuckle in the gloom. Then he added: 'That philosophy was once taught to me by a talented young *dálaigh* some years ago. I learned much from her.'

'You have convinced me,' Fidelma said, smiling in the darkness at his compliment.

'Then we are agreed?' Eadulf asked. 'Tomorrow, when we have interred Corradáin and the nameless brigand, and checked the area, we shall set off to follow Gláed's marauders.'

'And while we do so,' added Aibell's soft, slightly reproving, tone, 'we should find the farmhouse of Corradáin's son, to inform him of his father's death.'

As it was dark she could not see the guilty expressions on her companions' faces because they had forgotten all about Corradáin's son.

They woke up, cold and shivering, just after first light to the raucous sound of birdsong and the curious cry of a solitary fox. In spite of the still smouldering ruins of Corradáin's cabin, it had been an unusually cold night for the time of year and they found themselves stamping their feet and waving their arms to regain some degree of warmth. The first task was the burial of Corradáin and the other body. It was done in a respectful silence, with Eadulf ending the ritual with a murmured prayer.

He and Fidelma went to check the horses while Enda scavenged from the *fotholl*. He managed to get a small fire going from some of the embers of the hut and, with this means, he was able to prepare a passable meal. By this time the sun was now warming the air and, so far as they could see, looking up between the surrounding trees, there were few clouds in the sky. When they had finished the tasks, Fidelma made a final examination of the area, in case there was anything salvageable that they were overlooking. The attackers had taken not only Corradáin's ass but Aibell's horse with her *setan*, the saddlebags, as well. There was nothing else left.

'You'll have to ride double with one of us, Aibell, until we catch up with Gormán.' Fidelma phrased it purely as a means of comforting the girl. Privately, she had come to the conclusion that Gormán must be dead. He would not have abandoned his wife, therefore if he had been unable to get back to Corradáin's cabin, some ill fate had clearly befallen him during his tracking of the Sliabh Luachra men.

'Aibell can ride behind me, lady,' Enda offered. Then, lowering his voice: 'Friend Eadulf is not so good a horseman as to cope and . . .'

Although Eadulf's horsemanship had improved greatly – out of necessity – and these days he could even take their young son Alchú riding, he was still not completely at ease on horseback. Aware of his limitations, Eadulf offered no protest.

'No – I'll need your eyes as a tracker, Enda,' Fidelma told the warrior. 'Aibell can ride with me.'

With Enda leading, Fidelma and Aibell came next with Eadulf following behind. They left the clearing that had once been Corradáin's home, and made their way down the hill, between the dense trees to the broad track that skirted the elongated hill. Fidelma rode cautiously, eyes and ears alert. The raiders from Sliabh Luachra might well have passed through on the previous morning, but that did not mean they had gone for good. As broad as the track was, it wound through a forest and there could be many hidden dangers.

Eadulf eased his cob forward until he rode alongside Fidelma's sturdy mount, Aonbharr.

'This raiding party seems a long way from Sliabh Luachra, if I recall the geography,' he commented.

'Your memory is correct,' she nodded.

'If Gláed is serving as a mercenary to some Uí Fidgente noble with the intention of overthrowing Prince Donennach . . .'

'It bodes ill,' Fidelma cut in.

'Then you believe he is part of this mystery at Donennach's fortress?'

'He has appeared at an opportune time. If his band *is* following this track eastward, he must be moving directly towards the River Máigh. I think that might have been what Gormán feared – and he followed just to make sure.'

They rode onwards. Every now and again, Enda would stop to examine the ground.

'Still signs of a large number of horses passing here,' he would call out, to assure everyone that they were following the right path. In this manner, they continued to move along the wide track for a considerable distance. In different circumstances it would have been a pleasant ride through the forest, with the warmth of a summer's sun falling on them through the canopy of branches and leaves. Now and again they heard the howl of a she-wolf warning her cubs, and once there was a scuttling sound as a wild boar suddenly burst through on the track ahead of them. The animal paused, grunted – and then, to their relief – trotted off back into the cover of the forest. Birds kept up a constant exchange of calls. Even Eadulf almost found the ride relaxing.

Then the track suddenly came to a fork. One branch led straight on to the east while the other turned north through a small valley. They halted while Enda dismounted and surveyed the earth. Finally he announced: 'The horsemen have turned north.'

'So they are not going to Prince Donennach's fortress.' Eadulf was puzzled. 'Why go north?'

'I passed along this road a few times as a child,' Aibell said. 'That was before . . . before . . .' They did not have to be reminded again of the bitterness of her childhood and how her own father had sold her as a bond-servant to Fidaig, then chief of the brigands of Sliabh Luachra.

'Do you have any idea where the northern road leads to?' Fidelma asked.

'If you swung more easterly then you could reach the Ford of the Oaks.'

'That would mean going back towards the river – or is it that the river turns to flow more to the west there? Can you remember any other important place on that northern road if you were not heading as far as Conrí's fortress?'

The girl searched her memory and revealed: 'There is another fortress and township at Cromadh, the bend of the river on An Mháigh. It belongs to an important Uí Fidgente chieftain named Donnabháin.'

Fidelma was immediately interested. 'Do you know what sort of person he is?'

Aibell gave a whimsical smile. 'I cannot remember very much, as I was taken to Sliabh Luachra when I was just a child, but Ciarnat told me once that you have already met his son.'

'His son?' Fidelma repeated, baffled. 'How would Ciarnat have known that – and where did I meet his son?'

'He is Ceit, the commander of Prince Donennach's guard at the fortress.'

Fidelma exchanged a surprised glance with Eadulf.

'It is tenuous link,' he pointed out. 'Gláed and his cut-throats might not even be going to Cromadh.'

'True enough,' Fidelma said. 'Although Ceit would know of all our comings and goings from the fortress. I agree that his father might be a fragile connection but we should not discount it.' She paused. 'Let us remember this fact. By increasing our information we can make better speculations. Don't the scriptures say – *Vir sapiens et fortis est vir doctus robustus et validus*?'

'A wise man is strong, a man of knowledge increases his strength,' Eadulf translated.

Fidelma turned to Aibell. 'Is there nothing else of importance lying in that direction that you know of, and to which these raiders might be heading?'

'Not really. Once we pass north through the valley between these hills, the land is almost flat with a few simple homesteads. There is only one prominent landmark as I recall from my childhood. That is Cnoc Fírinne.'

Fidelma tried to disguise her look of excitement. 'Cnoc Fírinne?' she repeated.

'The Hill of Truth, though why it was called that I do not know.'

'Is it the site of some religious community?'

Aibell shook her head. 'I have not heard it to be so, but as I have already said, my childhood memories are lazy and many things may have changed since then.'

Eadulf said gloomily. 'If not a religious site why would Abbot Nannid go there?' Could he really have an assignation with Gláed and his band of raiders?'

'If he did,' Fidelma replied, 'why would he name the location of his meeting in front of Prince Donennach and Conrí? He would surely be more circumspect about it.'

'A good point, although he only said he was going there on some religious errand. Perhaps the name of the hill slipped out inadvertently? He would not expect anyone to make a connection with Gláed.'

'Is this Hill of Truth far from here?' Enda wanted to know.

'If I remember correctly,' said the girl, 'we should see it as we come through this pass ahead of us. The hill is said to be so high that it can be seen from great distances over the flat northern plains of the Uí Fidgente territory.'

'Very well,' Fidelma said. 'We have no choice but to follow Gláed's band – but if there is little shelter available we must proceed with caution.'

They turned northward along the path, and eventually entered the valley between the two hills. After some time, including a stop by a gushing brook to rest their horses and consume a frugal meal of fruit, they left the shelter of the hills to pause on a rise and stare out across the broad plain before them.

The first thing they noticed was a large hill around four kilometres due north of them. There was a small hillock before it but the large hill was a gorse-covered mound of nearly three hundred metres high, with a curious limestone bald patch on its highest peak.

'I presume that is Cnoc Fírinne,' Eadulf stated.

A moment later, Aibell cried, holding out her left hand to point. 'Look, oh look!'

Across the plain to the immediate west, past ploughed fields and among some sparsely spaced trees, was what seemed to have been a group of buildings. They were now only black smudges in the landscape, and a pall of smoke hung low in the hot summer air above them.

'A farmstead on fire, or nearly burned out,' muttered Enda. 'I can hazard a guess at who is responsible, since the men of Sliabh Luachra have passed this way.'

'I see no sign of horsemen on the plain down there,' Fidelma noted. 'Let's check to see if there are any survivors of this attack.'

Eadulf licked his dry lips. 'Shouldn't we be a little more careful and not just ride straight up . . .?' But his companions were already moving off. Shrugging philosophically, he followed them.

The smell of burned wood was pungent as they approached what had been a number of barns and animal pens. Beyond these were the ruins of the farmstead itself. They halted before the main building.

Eadulf, observing no danger from any lurking raiders, dismounted and began to examine the ruins. The first thing he saw was the body of what he took to be the farmer. The man had been tied to a tree at the back of his property. He had not been long dead for the blood was still seeping from the spear thrusts in his chest and stomach. To one side, lying on the ground, hands stretched out imploringly was the body of a woman – no doubt the farmer's wife. The couple were both fairly young. The man was tall, well-built with a mass of dark red hair. The pretty young woman was suntanned, with fair hair and callused hands indicating that she worked with her husband on the farmstead.

Eadulf sighed deeply as he gazed around. More devastation – cruel destruction of people's homes and lives. There was little left standing and certainly nowhere this time for anyone to hide in the charred ruins. Meanwhile, Enda had been searching the outbuildings.

'Definitely a raid,' he reported. 'There are pens for cattle and sheep but no sign of them, so I think they have been driven off to provide food for the raiders.'

He paused and looked about. 'Wait here,' he said, climbing back on his horse. 'I'll circle around and see in what direction they have driven the animals off.'

'I don't suppose Corradáin ever told you the name of his son?' Eadulf asked Aibell after he had gone.

The girl shook her head. 'All he said was that his son and his wife had a farm on the northern side of the hill where he worked and . . .' She stopped, her eyes wide with horror. 'You don't think . . .'

'Red hair seems to run in the family,' Eadulf said sadly, pointing to the farmer's body. 'There is no need to tell Corradáin's son about his father's death. The poor young man and his wife have met the very same fate – and at the very same hands.'

Aibell did not reply. Her features were deathly pale and her mouth clenched tight in a rictus of grief.

A few moments later Enda appeared and swung down from his horse.

'I am sure it was a raid for supplies. There are signs of a wheeled cart that is heavy in its tracks. They will have loaded it with whatever they could find. Also, they took several cattle and pigs, and I should imagine the cart was hauled by mules, judging by the tracks. I think they killed the chickens and any other birds, as I could see a large amount of feathers strewn on the path back there. It's easier for them to transport dead birds than live ones.'

'Which way were the raiders heading?' Eadulf asked.

'They were heading to that northern hill,' Enda said. 'There's no attempt to disguise their tracks. However, they appear to have lost one of the horses.' He jerked his head in the direction from which he had come. 'There is a carcass back there. A good-looking animal, a grey with a white mane and more like a warhorse than a workhorse. I can't think why they would want to kill it. It's been shot with several arrows, so it was deliberate.'

Aibell suddenly let out a scream, and was running in the direction that Enda had indicated.

'Wait!' cried Fidelma. 'Aibell, wait!'

The idea had occurred to her only a moment after Enda had spoken, but Aibell had already got there.

Fidelma, followed by Eadulf and Enda, set off after the lithe form of the girl. They could not overtake her before she came to the carcass of the horse. She halted before it. Her body shook for a moment and then she sank to her knees beside its head.

'Gormán!' she moaned. 'Gormán! It is my husband's horse!'

# CHAPTER FOURTEEN

∽

I t was Enda who tried to offer comfort to the girl first.

'Because it is Gormán's horse that has been killed does not mean to say that he is also dead. If he were killed here, where is his body?'

'That is so,' Fidelma immediately agreed. 'There are other possibilities. He might have managed to escape and hide, or they could have taken him captive.'

Aibell raised a tear-stained face to them.

'If he is captured, he would not be alive long,' she declared bitterly. 'Gláed has sworn vengeance on those who thwarted his plans to help Lorcán overthrow Prince Donennach last year. Gláed knows Gormán. He will kill him.'

'There is no sign that Gormán is dead or captive,' Enda said crisply. 'It would take more than a band of marauding wolves from Sliabh Luachra to finish him off.'

'That is true.' Eadulf was trying to sound more positive about the matter than he truly felt. He had witnessed the brutality of Gláed before and knew there was little by way of cruelty that he and his followers would not inflict on their enemies.

'So do we intend to follow Gláed to the Hill of Truth?' he asked.

'If Gormán is still able to follow these raiders, or even if he has been taken captive, that is the place where we will find him.' Enda looked across the vast plain towards the hill. 'The trouble is that it is the highest point on the plain. If Gláed is anything of a military leader he will place watchmen on the hill who could easily spot our approach.'

'There is a smaller hill between us and the larger one,' Fidelma said. 'The small hill is not high but there appear to be patches of woods and shrubland around it. If we make for that it should provide us with some cover as we approach.'

'There is one thing that I must know,' Enda requested.

'Which is?'

'Given that Gláed has some forty men with him, what is your intention if we catch up with him?'

'I do not intend to do anything more than observe,' Fidelma told him. 'Only when we have information will we discuss what can be done.'

'If Gláed is meeting with Abbot Nannid on the Hill of Truth, it means that we actually made a mistake at Mungairit last year by giving Nannid the benefit of the doubt about being involved in the conspiracy with him and Lorcán,' reflected Eadulf.

Fidelma's expression was grim. 'I was the *dálaigh* who made the decision, not you,' she reminded him. 'As such, it was my mistake and that decision cost the life of Gláed's brother, Artgal. Also, it was my decision to send Lorcán to Prince Donennach's fortress. As we heard, Lorcán almost escaped.'

'But was mortally wounded in the attempt.'

'The important point is that he did so.'

'He was helped to escape,' Eadulf said, trying to appease her.

Enda was restless. 'I thought we were going to bury the bodies and get on as fast as we can,' he said, his eyes signalling to where Aibell was still wandering around the smoking ruins, looking utterly lost and desolate.

'Of course.' Eadulf was immediately contrite. 'Let's find a spade and get on with our task.'

It was some time before they left the ruined farmstead of Corradáin's slain son and his wife and rode towards the woods that Fidelma had identified lying between the small hill and the higher rise of the Hill of Truth. Enda led the way again, using his knowledge of woodcraft and the natural cover of the terrain, gathered during his training as a warrior, to help them approach in safety.

They passed another farmhouse which was deserted but undamaged, although most of the livestock there had also vanished. They halted in the shelter of some outbuildings, while Enda dismounted and made a quick search of the main dwelling.

'It looks as if whoever was here saw the approach of Gláed's marauders and fled.'

'Taking most of the livestock?' Eadulf asked.

'Maybe not. Maybe they were taken as more spoils for the brigands.'

'Is there a spring or well that we can use?' Fidelma wanted to know. 'The sun is well past its zenith now and the horses could do with a drink. We might as well take the opportunity to refresh ourselves, since no one is here to offer us hospitality.'

'Farmers always know best where to place their farms for fresh water,' Enda offered. 'There should be a spring at the back of the building there. I just want to scout round on foot before I join you. Would you mind taking my horse with you? Maybe you'll find some food still left in the house.'

'Scout round for what?' Eadulf queried.

'Oh, for this and that,' Enda replied airily. Fidelma realised that he did not want to alarm them but needed to check in case some of the raiders were still lurking in the vicinity.

It was some few minutes before he rejoined them, by which time they had found fresh bread, presumably baked that morning, cold meats and cheeses. They helped themselves and washed the meal down with cold water from the spring, although they found containers of apple cider which Fidelma decided they should leave untouched. They needed completely clear minds.

'What signs did you find?' Fidelma asked as the young warrior dropped into a seat before the table and cut himself a slice of the bread and a piece of cheese.

'From the tracks, the main body passed by here a short distance away, on the other side of that treeline. Six riders came to the farmstead here and doubtless it was they who searched it. They don't appear to have done much damage, as you can see.'

'What about the farmer?' Eadulf asked.

'I saw tracks of two adults and some children heading east. They had some animals with them.'

'Do we know if Gláed is still making for the Hill of Truth?' Enda nodded.

'And Gormán?' Aibell demanded. 'What sign of Gormán?'

Enda shifted uneasily. 'No sign, but if he was on horseback with them, then there would be none. Certainly there were no tracks of a man on foot following the horsemen that I could find.'

'Then you believe he is a captive?' she said, her voice trembling.

'Belief is difficult without facts, Aibell. Once he left the farmstead of Corradáin's son, he could either be hiding, following on another route or placed on one of the horses whose tracks I have seen. Perhaps he is even heading in a direction other than this one.'

Enda did not mention the other possibility, but Fidelma and Eadulf knew it well and certainly did not want to share it with Aibell. Fidelma wished to press on, so as soon as they had finished their meal, they set off again. Enda was becoming more cautious. There were stretches where the trees and shrubland did not adequately cover their passage, and one or twice Enda left them while he went ahead to scout the land.

They had almost reached the wooded area of the small hill and moved away from the track that skirted it, which would have brought them out into the open view of the Hill of Truth. Beyond the trees they found a curious passage through some large limestone rocks. Enda had suggested that this cover of high birch trees would be a good place to halt. Beyond the rocky barrier and among the trees they found a small glade – a perfect spot. A brook tumbled through the glade, having risen from some spring further up the hillside.

'We can make this our base and leave our horses here before we climb up to see what is happening on the Hill of Truth,' Fidelma announced with satisfaction.

Enda had returned to the main track on foot to make a quick survey of the terrain and ensure that their tracks were not discernible. They had barely dismounted when the young warrior came racing back.

'There are horsemen riding this way,' he said urgently. 'The trees should provide cover here, but try to ensure the horses are quiet.'

Crouching behind a boulder, Fidelma whispered: 'How many riders?'

'Four, or maybe six.'

'What did you make of them? Are they more of Gláed's brigands?'

'They are heading for the Hill of Truth,' he said as if that answered the question.

'I'd like to see who they are,' Fidelma suddenly decided.

'No, lady. It's best for you to remain here. I will move closer and take a look.'

Without another word, crouching low, the young warrior moved stealthily away while the others held on to their horses, praying the animals did not cause any noise or make a movement that would alert the passing riders to their presence. In silence they waited, dreading the sounds that would announce that the riders had discovered them. When Enda came back, it was clear that something was troubling him.

'They've passed on. However, I'd like to show you something, lady,' he said. 'Best keep the horses here, Eadulf. Aibell can help you.'

Fidelma gave Eadulf a shrug to show she had no idea what was going on before she followed Enda without another word.

They had gone a little distance, out of earshot of the others, when the warrior turned and, keeping his voice low, said: 'I didn't want Aibell to hear.'

At once Fidelma asked: 'Was it Gormán?'

Enda quickly shook his head. 'The riders were definitely from Sliabh Luachra – not professional warriors but dirty, ragged men whose weaponry would not pass inspection among the warriors of the Golden Collar. The thing is, I recognised the man at the head of them . . . he was old Brother Conchobhar's nephew. I often saw him at Cashel when he was with Aibell.'

'Deogaire!' Fidelma exclaimed loudly in her surprise.

'The very same,' Enda confirmed. 'Black hair and that strange multi-coloured coat – I'd know him anywhere.'

'So Deogaire is here and joining Gláed?' She gave a shake of her head as if she could not believe it.

'I was saddened when Aibell rode off with Deogaire,' Enda said. 'You recall how upset Gormán was, and how he rode after them? But Marban said Deogaire had left her at his mill and then gone back to Sliabh Luachra, to his home. Well, now he seems to be in command of some of Gláed's marauding wolves.'

'But Deogaire claimed to be one of the Druids, still battling to retain the Old Religion, claiming to have the gift of prophecy. He used to irritate poor Brother Conchobhar beyond measure. He is the last person I would have thought would join Gláed's marauders.'

'Well, now he bears a blue shield with a raven's image on it. I saw his weaponry. And one of the men at his side carries a blue silk banner with a similar raven's image.'

'Are you sure that they are heading to the Hill of Truth?'

'Where else does that track lead?'

Fidelma was silent for a moment. Then she said: 'You are right,

Enda. It is better that Aibell does not know of this development for the time being.'

As they returned to the others, Fidelma raised her voice a little. 'There was not much to tell from the horses' tracks,' she announced brightly, as if that had been the reason why Enda had asked for her to come and express an opinion. 'Anyway, I think they were just a group hurrying to catch up with Gláed's main body. Now let us proceed. We can leave the horses here then two of us shall climb the hill. From the top we should be able to see across the little valley to the Hill of Truth.'

Eadulf knew when Fidelma was disguising facts that she did not want others to know. What others? He glanced at Aibell and realised that it must have some connection with her. Was it a sighting of Gormán? He was determined to find out at the first opportunity when the girl was out of earshot.

It was agreed that Aibell would remain there with Eadulf while Enda and Fidelma climbed the hill to spy out the land. The first intention was to see if Gláed and his men were camping on the hill or had passed on. Before they left, noticing that Aibell was pre-occupied in bathing her head and her arm, which still needed some attention after the attack on her, Eadulf quickly asked Fidelma what she had seen with Enda.

'Deogaire?' he whispered in surprise. 'I knew he came from Sliabh Luachra but he was surely no fighting man? All that mysticism and magic show and belief in the pagan gods and goddesses . . .'

'Maybe we should not dismiss Deogaire so easily,' Fidelma replied, then recalled that she had reacted in almost exactly the same way. 'What I mean is that he rescued Aibell from being Fidaig's bond-servant and led her out of Sliabh Luachra with Fidaig's men chasing after them. I would never under-estimate his physical courage.'

'But having rescued her from Fidaig, why would he join the war band of Gláed?' protested Eadulf.

'If filial allegiance stands for naught in Sliabh Luachra, one can easily change other allegiances.'

Aware that Aibell had left the brook, they fell silent on the subject and continued to make a camp.

A short time later, Fidelma and Enda left to ascend the hill, leaving Eadulf and Aibell waiting anxiously. It was approaching twilight when they returned. They were looking disappointed.

'There wasn't much to see,' confessed Fidelma. 'Gláed's men are certainly encamped there for the night. They have erected *bélscálán* across the hillside and we could see smoke from their fires.'

Eadulf frowned, uncertain of the word that she had used. 'Erected what?' he asked.

'Travelling tents,' she explained. 'They are encamped on the southern lower slopes below the high point of the hill. We also saw a wooden building that appears to be a chapel on the eastern slopes.'

'A wooden chapel?' frowned Eadulf.

'Perhaps Abbot Nannid was meeting a religieux there, after all.' Fidelma sighed. 'Anyway, we saw no sign of him or his steward, although there were a lot of horses tethered nearby.'

'We decided that the only thing to do is wait until nightfall and then see if we can get closer,' Enda said. 'We need to get near the chapel because that would be a natural point where Gláed would be camped and, if Gormán has been caught by him, he would also be nearby.'

'That's dangerous,' Eadulf protested. 'Would it not be better to—?'

Fidelma cut him sort. '*Periculum in mora!*' she said sharply, resorting to one of the aphorisms of Publilius Syrus whom she was so fond of quoting. Eadulf grimaced. There was, indeed, 'danger in delay' especially if Gormán was still in the hands of Gláed.

'It will be dark soon,' said Enda. 'We had better decide on a plan of how to get near their camp.'

'I was thinking that one person might elude the sentinels that Gláed will have undoubtedly set up to patrol their camp, but not all of us,' Fidelma said.

'You cannot go on your own,' Eadulf asserted. 'I'll come with you.'

'Eadulf, you and lady Fidelma are not trained at infiltrating an enemy encampment,' Enda argued. 'I am, and I should go alone.'

'It is my duty to go as a *dálaigh*,' Fidelma contradicted him.

'Then the three of us must go,' Eadulf said.

'I do not wish to remain here on my own wondering if you are caught or not,' Aibell protested.

'It is best if Enda and I go, Eadulf.' Fidelma was determined to have her own way. 'You and Aibell will remain here again.'

It happened without warning. There was a sound like a rush of air followed by two thuds. The quivering arrows stuck in a tree just above head height behind Enda. He was reaching for his sword when a nearby voice rasped: 'Stop or you are dead, warrior. The next arrows will be aimed at you and not as a warning. Hold your hands high, away from your weapons.'

They all froze, hands rising reluctantly in obedience to the harsh command.

Then, to Eadulf's surprise, there came a strange 'churring' sound. It took him a moment to recognise it as the call of a nightjar – a bird that was rarely heard, and only in summer. It must be a signal from one of the men hidden in the trees around them. A signal to whom?

'Who are you?' Enda called, trying to recover his dignity, because he felt he should have been aware of any hostile approach. After all, he had just boasted about his warrior's training and then he had let them down.

'You will find out shortly,' came the uncompromising voice from behind the trees.

There was a movement through the shrubbery, a whispered exchange and a tall man appeared, then halted with an exclamation of surprise.

Fidelma looked at the newcomer and said wearily, 'May we put our hands down now, Conrí?'

The warlord of the Uí Fidgente turned towards his hidden companions and called: 'You can put your weapons down.' Then he said to Fidelma, shaking his head, 'Yes, you may all put your hands down. However, I am in no mood to be tricked a second time.'

'A second time?' Fidelma asked, slightly amused, as four of Conrí's warriors emerged from the trees.

'We thought that you were heading directly after Abbot Nannid to the Hill of Truth. But you eluded us.'

'We took a more circular route,' Fidelma replied mischievously.

'And still you managed to meet up with Aibell. Where is Gormán, by the way?'

'We believe that he has been captured by Gláed.'

Conrí's expression of surprise said it all.

'It is a long story which I hope to make short.' Fidelma told him as sparsely and as quickly as possible without losing its sense. When Conrí had a chance to absorb the story, Fidelma prompted: 'Now it's your turn. How did you come here?'

'Brehon Faolchair ordered me to take some men and follow you to ensure that you brought Gormán back to us. He wanted him safe at the prince's fortress so that we can resolve the matter under the law. You managed to elude us almost immediately after we left the fortress. That was clever. So we came up along the river road and found Nannid, but no sign of you until just now.'

'Are you saying that Abbot Nannid is here?' demanded Fidelma with unconcealed excitement.

'There is a small chapel and habitation on the east slopes of the hill. We followed the abbot and his steward, keeping well back so as not to be observed. They stayed there last night and then around midday today we saw a large body of men arrive. That was Gláed and his brigands.'

'So Abbot Nannid had gone to meet Gláed?'

'We kept well out of sight, hidden in the woods. I decided

to wait until nightfall to see if I could get closer and find out what was happening.'

'That is exactly our plan,' Fidelma said.

'But we were having some difference of opinion over it,' Eadulf added.

'As a *dálaigh* it is essential that I witness what is happening,' explained Fidelma. 'I was taking Enda with me.'

'I insist on going.' Eadulf was still assertive.

Conrí scratched his head for a moment. 'And I must go as an unbiased witness.' He saw the dangerous glint in Fidelma's eyes and her mouth open ready to protest, and held up his hand, saying, 'I know that you, as a *dálaigh*, are sworn to be without bias, lady. I do not question that you serve only the law. But you know that tensions have risen between the Uí Fidgente and the Eóghanacht, especially over this matter that threatens dissension between us. I must go. But we would put ourselves in danger if more than two people went.'

'I have to go,' Fidelma said stubbornly. 'It is my duty as a *dálaigh*.'

'I was about to agree to that,' the warlord said, surprising her.

'If Fidelma goes,' Eadulf was immovable, 'I go.'

The warlord heaved a sigh to express his irritation. 'Friend Eadulf, I must agree with Fidelma and insist that you stay here. You are no warrior and frankly your presence will put us at a disadvantage. I will take Enda but you must stay here with Aibell and my men. We will be back long before first light.'

Eadulf was still reluctant, but Fidelma told him, 'You know that I will be in safe hands with Conrí and Enda.'

He saw that her mind was made up and so bowed to the inevitable.

'Very well, but I do not like it, Fidelma,' he said. 'But if you are not back at first light – what then?'

'My men will take you to Socht,' Conrí answered for her. 'I have left him and another man watching the main highway to Dún Eochair

Mháigh in case Gláed tries to make a sudden attack along it. He will decide whether we are at war with the men of Sliabh Luachra and act appropriately.'

'Do you really think Gláed would be so foolish as to attack the fortress?' Eadulf was dubious. 'Ceit has twice the men Gláed has guarding the fortress.'

'You are counting the men encamped here, but what if there are other encampments elsewhere?' Conrí said. 'What if this is not the main force out of Sliabh Luachra? What if there is some strategy to attack us from two points? More worryingly, what if there are more conspirators within Prince Donennach's fortress? Remember the guard who released Gormán and Aibell there? It is better to be prepared than to spend time regretting one's lack of foresight.'

Finally, when the time came, Conrí led the way with Fidelma and Enda into the encroaching darkness. They skirted the small hill, finding themselves on rising ground as they climbed towards the larger hill beyond. They could now see several campfires in the distance. It was difficult terrain to move across without a light for it was not cleared for farming purposes and there were many obstacles. They had to make their way through bushes and closely growing trees. Even though they were still in the phase of the full moon, *An Gealach* – the 'great brightness' as the country folk referred to it – the light was not entirely adequate.

It was to their advantage that the trees grew almost up to the area they were making for, the spot just below where Conrí had identified the wooden chapel and some smaller buildings; the higher elevations of the hill were gorse-covered or fairly bare. As they neared the end of the treeline, Conrí turned and made a lowering movement with his hand at the same time as dropping to one knee. Fidelma realised that they had come to the edge of the forest and were just below a shoulder on which one of several campfires blazed. This was just in front of the wooden chapel building. Unfortunately the fire was between the building and themselves and they could only see faint outlines of figures behind it.

Conrí turned to Fidelma who had positioned herself alongside him, with Enda on the other side. The warlord pointed wordlessly to his right. Some distance away was a clump of gorse and small boulders further up the rise. If they could get to that spot, they would have a better vantage-point to observe the figures on the other side of the fire. Conrí pointed to himself and then to the position, but Fidelma shook her head and indicated herself and then Conrí. The warlord hesitated and then nodded agreement. He turned to Enda and, again using his hand, motioned him to remain where he was.

Crawling flat on their stomachs they left their shelter and moved slowly and diagonally up the hill towards the boulders and gorse. The sloping hill was not even and there were many bumps and ridges, even molehills that, with odd clusters of gorse and tufts of tall grass, actually made excellent concealment from anyone looking down the hill. Conrí knew that, even in daylight, someone peering down a hill slope with such a terrain would not be able to see very much. High ground was not always the best ground to observe someone approaching so close. Luck was on their side. They reached the boulders without any alarm being sounded.

Now they could see the area between the fire and the entrance of the wooden chapel. The first person she saw, seated on a chair just outside the door of the chapel, was the gaunt figure of Abbot Nannid. The sight took Fidelma's breath away. He seemed relaxed and held a pottery mug in his hand. To one side of him stood the easily recognisable form of Brother Cuineáin. In front of him was a strange, bearded man, hands on hips, who looked vaguely familiar.

Fidelma peered, searching for Deogaire, but there was no sign of him. She felt Conrí tap her arm and allowed herself a soft gasp, for into the firelight strode a man she recognised immediately. Even in the flickering light he was still as she remembered him with his youthful air and confident stance. It was Gláed; Gláed the Howler, Lord of Barr an Bheithe, the murderer of his father and of his brother. Gláed, who now called himself Lord of Sliabh Luachra.

As they watched, the brigand chief seated himself in front of Abbot Nannid, and the other familiar-looking man stepped forward and filled the goblet Gláed held and then stepped respectfully back. There was nothing menacing between Gláed and the abbot. Both seemed relaxed. At one point, Abbot Nannid even laughed, an unusual event for him. For a while they engaged in some deep conversation. Then Abbot Nannid turned to his steward and gave him instructions. The steward nodded and disappeared into the wooden chapel. More drinks were poured and consumed as the two men seemed to wait for the reappearance of the steward.

Eventually, Brother Cuineáin came out of the building with a small sack in his hand. Abbot Nannid motioned towards Gláed who set aside his goblet, took the sack and peered into it. He nodded slowly as he examined the contents. Then he stood up, as did the abbot. Gláed's hand thrust out to take that of Abbot Nannid in a firm handshake. Then they turned together and walked out of sight towards the main encampment. Left alone, Brother Cuineáin lowered himself into the chair vacated by the abbot and stretched his legs before the fire. Then he peered around surreptitiously and reached down to the ground. When he straightened, they saw he was holding the goblet discarded by Gláed. He wiped the lip with the sleeve of his robe and tilted it back, swallowing back the contents with an apparent smack of his lips that they could almost hear.

A long time passed and it seemed that Brother Cuineáin had fallen asleep in the chair. Then the abbot returned alone. The steward came awake with a start. The abbot said something, pointing to the night sky, before the two of them entered the wooden chapel. More time passed, and finally Conrí touched Fidelma's arm and motioned back to the forest. She gave a nod of her head. There was not much more they could observe, though unfortunately they had not seen

Gormán. Back in the cover of the forest, they paused to catch their breath.

'Well, at least we have seen some sort of bargain being made between Abbot Nannid and Gláed,' Conrí commented.

'But what bargain?' queried Fidelma. 'By the way, the man who was pouring the drink seemed familiar but I can't place him.'

'No? That was the guard who was bribed to let Gormán escape.'

They finally decided that the only thing to do now was to return to the others and then work out a plan of action after they had rested. Aibell was distressed that there was no news of Gormán, but Eadulf was excited to hear about the involvement of Abbot Nannid and his steward.

'The trouble is,' Fidelma observed as they prepared to snatch some rest, 'there are questions. The merchants told Gormán that Gláed was hiring himself as a mercenary to a powerful person who intended to overthrow Prince Donennach. Is that person Nannid?'

'It seems obvious to me,' Conrí said.

'The fact that Abbot Nannid is involved with Gláed and his murdering cut-throats is good enough for me too,' agreed Eadulf.

It was well after first light when they were sitting down to a simple meal. Eadulf heard it first. The cry of the nightjar again; the curious 'churring' sound. There was a pause and then the call was repeated – this time closer to hand. Conrí turned, hand cupped to his mouth, and imitated the call. A short while later, they heard a figure approaching through the undergrowth and Socht emerged. His eyes widened in surprise on catching sight of Aibell and then Fidelma and her companions. Quickly composing himself, he took Conrí aside and had a swift exchange with him. The warlord listened with a stony expression.

A few moments later, he turned to them, addressing Fidelma.

'I have good news and bad news, lady.' It was obvious that he was trying hard to control his feelings.

'What is it?' she asked.

'Socht and his companion have just spotted Gormán alive and looking comparatively well.'

Aibell gave a little scream, hand to mouth.

'That is, indeed, good news.' But Fidelma did not give way to relief. 'So let us have the bad news?'

'Gormán was seen on the road back to Dún Eochair Mháigh. He was a prisoner on horseback. Abbot Nannid and Brother Cuineáin were leading the escort, which comprised four of Gláed's men.'

'Then the abbot is making no secret of his connection with Gláed by openly riding with his men?' Fidelma was clearly puzzled.

'It seems that Gláed has handed Gormán over to Abbot Nannid to take back to Prince Donennach's fortress as a prisoner,' Conrí said.

It made no sense. 'Why would he do that!' Eadulf exclaimed. He received no answer but Conrí and Fidelma exchanged a worried look.

# CHAPTER FIFTEEN

❧

T hey arrived back at Dún Eochair Mháigh, exhausted in the heat of the late afternoon. Ceit, the commander of the fortress guard, came running forward to greet them as they dismounted. He was obviously bursting with news, but Fidelma got in first.

'Has Gormán been taken back to the cells?' she demanded.

The expression on his face told them that Gormán's recapture was part of his news. Then he surprised them by shaking his head. 'He has not, lady.'

She stared at him. 'Where is he then? I presume that he has been brought back to the fortress?'

'I was about to tell you,' Ceit replied with dignity. 'It was at noon that we saw Abbot Nannid and his steward returning to the Abbey of Nechta. He was escorted by four unknown warriors . . .'

'Warriors!' Conrí snorted. 'They were brigands from Sliabh Luachra.'

Ceit's jaw dropped in astonishment. 'Are you sure?'

'Continue,' Fidelma snapped in irritation. 'They went directly to the abbey, you say? Do you mean that Gormán has been taken there?'

'He was.'

'Where is he now?' she wanted to know.

'Still in the abbey – they did not bring him here. I alerted Brehon

238

Faolchair, of course. He waited a while, thinking the prisoner would be returned to him, but when no word came from the abbey, he asked me to accompany him there.' He paused for a moment. 'It was the *aistréoir* – the doorkeeper, Brother Éladach – who opened the gates but he said he had strict orders not to admit anyone. I could see that Brother Éladach was unhappy at this for I have known him for some time and know that he is an honourable man.'

'I presume, Ceit, that you will eventually come to the point.' Conrí's voice was slow and studied.

'I am telling you,' complained Ceit. 'Brehon Faolchair demanded to see Gormán as it was his duty by right of law. Brother Éladach appeared to agree with him on his rights as a Brehon but could not let him pass. Abbot Nannid had issued strict orders. He had declared governance of the community by the rules of the Penitentials. Therefore, Brother Éladach said he could admit neither the Brehon nor me.'

Fidelma was almost speechless. 'He refused a Brehon entrance?'

'At that moment,' went on Ceit, 'the abbot's steward arrived – a smirking man whom I dislike. He confirmed that Brother Éladach was obeying the wishes of the abbot, who was then resting from the ardours of his journey. When Brehon Faolchair pressed him about Gormán, he replied that – I quote his words – "the murderer was being held under guard until such time as the abbot disposed of him".'

Aibell almost fainted and would have fallen, had not Eadulf caught her.

Fidelma turned to Eadulf and said, 'Take Aibell to our chamber and see she is attended to. Don't leave her.' She watched as he helped the girl across the courtyard and then turned back to Ceit. 'In what way did he mean "disposed of"?' she asked.

Ceit grimaced. 'I only tell you what was said. The abbot's steward added that the abbot would explain matters to Prince Donennach after he had rested from his trip. Brehon Faolchair felt there was nothing to be done until the abbot makes an appearance and explains himself.'

Conrí was grim-faced. 'It seems we must prepare.'

'Prepare?' Ceit echoed uncertainly. 'For what?'

'You saw the four men who provided escort for Abbot Nannid?' Conrí said. 'We have told you they were brigands. Well, Abbot Nannid met with their leader at Sliabh Luachra.'

The guard commander looked from Fidelma to Conrí, an expression of bewilderment on his face.

Conrí put it in simpler terms. 'I think we are going to be attacked by the men of Sliabh Luachra. We know they are now within the vicinity of this township.'

'What? You really believe that Gláed intends to attack us?' Ceit was incredulous. 'Even my *lucht-tighe*, the household guard, could defeat the brigands of Sliabh Luachra if they come out of their lairs.'

'I do not question your training or your courage, Ceit,' said Fidelma. 'However, I do question the fact that we do not know exactly how many men Gláed has, nor his exact purpose; nor – which is worse – who else he is in league with in this fortress other than, it seems, Abbot Nannid.'

'How many men do you have here, Ceit?' Conrí enquired.

'The household guard are not currently up to full strength but are a company of maybe fifty. The rest are posted on the hills as sentinels.'

Conrí was worried. 'And I have fewer than ten fighting men.'

'Should we ask the prince to issue a summons for a *slúagud*?' asked Ceit.

The *slúagud* was the general summoning of clansmen raised by individual chieftains when the territory and its prince was under threat.

'I doubt there is time for that,' Conrí said. 'But as we know where Gláed's marauders are, I would advise that sentinels be doubled.'

They left Ceit as the guard commander set about following the orders of the warlord, and they went to the great hall.

Prince Donennach and Brehon Faolchair were just entering the hall as they came in.

'Have you heard?' were Brehon Faolchair's opening words.

'I have,' replied Fidelma grimly. 'Abbot Nannid has imprisoned Gormán in the abbey and refuses to hand him over.'

'For the time being,' Prince Donennach added.

'Eadulf has just told us that Abbot Nannid had a secret meeting with Gláed and his marauders, and that it was Gláed himself who handed over Gormán as prisoner to him,' said the Brehon.

'The escort that Abbot Nannid brought into this township were four of Gláed's men,' Conrí said curtly. 'We should prepare for the worst.'

Prince Donennach slumped into his chair. His pale and strained features showed his apprehension.

'How do you know this?' he asked.

'We saw them together,' replied Conrí.

'We have witnessed the destruction wreaked by his marauders,' Fidelma told the prince. 'A woodsman was killed and his cabin burned. A farm was likewise fired, animals stolen for food for the band, and the farmer and his wife both killed. We managed to rescue Aibell, but Gormán was captured by Gláed and then handed over to Nannid, who seemed most friendly with the robber chief.'

'And the guard who was bribed to help Gormán escape from here, and then escaped himself, is also one of Gláed's men,' put in Conrí.

'So Abbot Nannid is working in collusion with Gláed to overthrow Prince Donennach?' It was a terrible shock. Brehon Faolchair was aghast.

'The abbot has the right to be called to account and explain his own involvement,' Fidelma stated. 'He must now release Gormán to the custody of Brehon Faolchair.'

'I have already been to the Abbey of Nechta to demand custody,' Brehon Faolchair said helplessly. 'He refused.'

'I heard the story from Ceit.' Fidelma was angrier than she had ever been in her entire life.

Brehon Faolchair's cheeks assumed a red glow of mortification as Fidelma ignored him and spoke directly to Prince Donennach. 'I suggest that you send your bodyguard to disturb Abbot Nannid's rest.' Without waiting for an answer, she added: 'I will withdraw so that my companions and I can refresh ourselves after our journey here. On my return I shall expect to see Abbot Nannid and his steward here before you, explaining themselves, and Gormán placed in your custody.'

She did not even wait for an acknowledgement from the depressed-looking prince but stormed out of the hall and made for the guests' rooms. Eadulf and Aibell were waiting for her; they had been joined by Enda. A young female attendant was standing by, looking nervous.

'We want water for washing,' Fidelma demanded in ill-humour and when the girl had hurried off, she said to her companions, 'Eadulf, you and Enda will share the room next to mine. Aibell will stay here with me. I do not want any of us separated until we have sorted out this mystery.'

They had washed and changed by the time there came a discreet knock on the door of their chamber. It was the young girl attendant.

'If it please you, lady,' the young girl mumbled, 'Prince Donennach requests that you and Brother Eadulf join him in the great hall.'

'Is Abbot Nannid in attendance?' she asked.

'He is, lady,' confirmed the girl.

'Is the warrior Gormán there also?'

'I overheard Ceit saying that Abbot Nannid has refused to hand him to the custody of Brehon Faolchair. But will you come, lady? They are waiting.'

'We'll be there directly.' Fidelma turned to Enda, saying, 'Aibell had better stay out of the way. If Abbot Nannid has presented himself without Gormán, then he must have some secret plan, so if you think there is any danger, I'll leave it to you to exercise good judgement.'

'You may trust me, lady,' the young warrior replied.

As they went down to the great hall, Fidelma confided in her husband, saying, 'I am not sure what astounds me more – the fact that Abbot Nannid has the boldness to present himself before Prince Donennach or that he apparently defies him.'

'Something is not right,' Eadulf agreed. 'As you say, it seems that he has some strategy of which we are ignorant.'

The atmosphere of the gathering in the great hall was tense.

Prince Donennach, still looking exhausted, slumped in his chair of office. His sister, Airmid, sat next to him; Brehon Faolchair in front and just below the dais as protocol dictated. Conrí stood behind his prince as usual, but there were several other warriors stationed in the hall, with Ceit among them. At the table, predictably, were Prior Cuán with his steward, Brother Tuamán, seated to the left, while to the right sat Abbot Nannid and his steward, Brother Cuáneáin. The abbot did not seem a whit abashed and wore a complacent smile on his thin features.

'Where is Gormán?' Fidelma demanded immediately, barely glancing at Abbot Nannid.

It was the steward, Brother Cuineáin, who replied. 'Where he should have been all this time. In a cell awaiting punishment.'

'You have no right to hold him in the abbey,' Brehon Faolchair told them. It sounded as if he had raised the point before.

Abbot Nannid rose to his feet. 'Since you have been negligent in pursuing the interests of justice by allowing a base murderer to escape, it behoves me to protect our people, both physically as well as spiritually,' he declared.

'Does your spiritual and physical protection involve dealing with a bunch of brigands, thieves and cut-throats?' Fidelma decided to get straight to the heart of the matter. 'There are witnesses to your meeting with Gláed of Sliabh Luachra at the Hill of Truth. Following that meeting, Gláed handed you his prisoner, Gormán, and you came here with four of Gláed's ne'er-do-wells as your escort.'

There was a moment's silence and then, to everyone's surprise, Abbot Nannid started to chuckle. Even Brother Cuineáin looked puzzled for a moment and then, as the abbot continued to laugh, he seemed to feel that he should join him with a wan smile.

Brehon Faolchair finally leaned forward and said firmly: 'This is a serious charge, Abbot Nannid. Gláed is not only a thief and killer but he is an enemy to the Uí Fidgente and a threat to the peace of this princedom. Do you admit that you met with him and his marauders and had dealings with him?'

Abbot Nannid said, 'I mean no disrespect to you, Prince Donennach. I am simply amused by the feeble attempts of the sister of the King of Cashel who, a few years ago, waded in the blood of the Uí Fidgente on Cnoc Áine, to claim that *I* am an enemy to my own people!'

Prince Donennach raised his head to look long and hard at the abbot. 'You deny that you met Gláed and had dealings with him?'

'I have every intention of telling you the truth of that encounter.'

'Then before you do,' intervened Brehon Faolchair, 'let me say that it is not merely the lady, Fidelma of Cashel, who brings evidence of this event but Conrí, warlord of the Uí Fidgente, who was with Fidelma and her companions as a witness.'

Brother Cuineáin made a lewd sound. 'It is well known that lord Conrí of the Ford of Oaks has been an intimate of the lady Fidelma for many years.'

Eadulf was on his feet amid the gasps of disapproval from those present. He was so enraged that he ignored the protocol that he could not speak until invited.

'I could forget I wear the cloth of the New Faith long enough to

disobey the ruling of Our Lord and not turn the other cheek,' he
snarled.

Abbot Nannid rose to his feet and threw out a protective arm as
if to shield his steward from attack.

'Peace, Brother Eadulf,' he said mockingly. 'You misinterpret the
words of poor Brother Cuaineán. Let us put it down to your Saxon
lack of fluency in our good tongue.'

It was Conrí himself who responded. 'I did not misinterpret the
words, Nannid, so do not accuse *me* of a lack of fluency in my
mother's speech. Also, friend Eadulf speaks our tongue as well as
any native of the Five Kingdoms.'

'I would also point out once more that I am an Angle, *not* a
Saxon,' Eadulf hissed. 'I am an hereditary *gerefa* of the Land of
the South Folk in the Kingdom of the East Angles.'

At this point, Abbot Nannid gave his steward a slight but mean-
ingful nudge and the man reluctantly stood up.

'Forgive me for my poor use of words, Conrí of the Ford of the
Oaks,' he said, trying to sound sincere but only succeeding in
sounding sycophantic. 'I meant no offence to you. But is it not
well known that you have often helped the *dálaigh* from Cashel?
Did she not win your friendship when she solved the murder of
your brother, Dea, and the murders at Rath Raithlen many years
ago? Did you not help her when the Venerable Cináed was murdered
in the Abbey of Ard Fhearta? And were you not on hand when she
came here in pursuit of a would-be assassin of her brother, the
King—'

'Whose assassin came from the Abbey of Mungairit,' Eadulf
interrupted, angered further by being omitted from the apology.

'. . . when she discovered a conspiracy against Prince Donennach,'
Conrí continued. 'A conspiracy that came out of Mungairit and
involved Gláed.'

Abbot Nannid's eyes narrowed at the implication but he allowed
his steward to respond.

'The point I was making in my own clumsy fashion,' he blustered, 'is that you may be considered biased under law.'

'Under whose law?' Conrí asked pleasantly. 'The law of the Five Kingdoms – or that of Abbot Nannid?'

Abbot Nannid turned to Prince Donennach with a smirk on his face that Eadulf would have liked to remove with his fist.

'I am sure that this company will accept that my steward spoke without thought,' he said in oily fashion, 'not realising his words could be misinterpreted.'

Prince Donennach waved an impatient hand. 'Nevertheless, Abbot Nannid, it does not answer the fact that Conrí was a witness. Do you deny that you met Gláed, leader of the brigands of Sliabh Luachra, and from him secured the prisoner to bring him back to Dún Eochair Mháigh with the help of his men?'

'I do not deny it,' replied the abbot, unperturbed.

Fidelma felt Eadulf look at her. It was obvious that the abbot had some excuse ready but she could not see what, and this put her at a disadvantage.

Brehon Faolchair was clearly troubled. 'As you do not deny this, perhaps you will explain.'

'Of course,' the abbot said coolly. 'That has been my intention all along until we were sidetracked on a matter of ego.'

'Proceed,' Brehon Faolchair instructed quickly, aware that Conrí had clapped a hand to his sword hilt.

'When I left this fortress, after the murderer of Abbot Ségdae demonstrated his guilt by absconding from his cell and fleeing with the woman, Aibell, my only intention was to go to Cnoc Fírinne, the Hill of Truth, on a church errand to meet with a Brother Feradach. He has a chapel on the slope of the hill.'

'What urgent need did this Brother Feradach have that you had to leave here with your steward?' Fidelma asked.

Abbot Nannid hesitated but Brehon Faolchair said: 'It is relevant information to your story.'

'Brother Feradach served me at the Abbey of Mungairit. You may know that I have remained here, at the Abbey of Nechta, for a while. I have presided over its transformation from a loose group of believers in the New Faith to an enclosed community which will one day become influential and will bring prestige and wealth to this place. However, I am still aware of my duties as Abbot of Mungairit. Therefore, I have been collecting the dues owed to my abbey and took a small amount of gold and silver to Brother Feradach, who was going to carry it on safely to Mungairit. This was to save me making the arduous journey myself.'

It was Fidelma's turn to sound amused. 'Are you trying to tell us that you went to this Brother Feradach's chapel on the Hill of Truth bearing gold and silver for him to take on to Mungairit? That, purely by chance, you fell in with Gláed, whom you already knew from the conspiracy at Mungairit? Gláed with forty or fifty marauders from Sliabh Luachra whom you just happened to meet? Did they greet you as an old friend and give you charge of their prisoner with warriors to guard him because they believed in the law?'

'It does not sound plausible,' Prince Donennach sighed.

'Put in such a way as the honey-tongued advocate from Cashel likes to paint the story – and, of course, she does it for effect – it is not plausible,' Abbot Nannid agreed carelessly. 'Nevertheless, truth is often implausible. But it is a simple story. While I was at the Hill of Truth, Gláed and his warriors did arrive by chance. They had a prisoner, Gormán of Cashel, whom they were determined to kill. I intervened, explaining the circumstances as to why I sought him, and asked that the prisoner be released into my custody.'

At this Conrí gave a low chuckle. 'And did Gláed say – "Of course you may have my prisoner, Lord Abbot. I have always obeyed the Church and the law." Then you bade each other farewell and went your respective ways?'

Abbot Nannid was unruffled. 'You have obviously learned the

art of *tábhachtach* . . .' He paused to savour the word which Eadulf knew meant the art of sarcasm. 'No doubt you picked it up from your friend, the *dálaigh*. The truth is that we had a long negotiation and we were able to make a bargain. I bought the prisoner and the services of four guards for a period of three days.'

'You use the word "bought". You have proof of this exchange?' enquired Brehon Faolchair.

'My steward here was witness to it.'

'He would be,' muttered Fidelma in a low voice but one which everyone heard.

'As good a witness in truth as your own,' Brother Cuineáin replied angrily.

'May we ask what sum did Gláed settle for, in exchange for handing Gormán over to you and for hiring out the services of his killers?' Fidelma wanted to know.

But no insult or question seemed to unsettle the smug abbot. 'I have nothing to hide on that account,' he said airily. 'I offered him five gold pieces and some silver, to the value of five *sed*s.'

'Not thirty pieces of silver?' Eadulf asked mildly.

Abbot Nannid flushed but still managed to keep his temper.

'Five pieces of gold and some silver,' he repeated heavily. 'I would also reject the term "killers" for the men I have employed. I would call them hired warriors.'

The word Abbot Nannid used to correct Fidelma was *amhus* which Eadulf recognised as a respected term for a mercenary.

'How is it that you had such a large sum on you?'

'As I said, we were on our way to meet with Brother Feradach, taking with us the dues that the Abbey of Nechta owes to Mungairit.'

Conrí whistled disbelievingly. 'You had the sum with you and travelled without protection. And Gláed knew you had such valuables with you to purchase his prisoner? Then, by the gods, knowing Gláed, why did he not slit your throats, take your gold anyway and—'

'As you see from my presence,' Abbot Nannid boomed, 'he did not. The bargain was made – and it was made with the protection of the one God. Am I to believe that you, warlord of the Uí Fidgente, reject the Faith when you refer to "the gods"?'

It was a clever way of trying to turn the tables on the warrior, side-stepping the point, and Conrí fell into the trap.

'It is a common phrase,' he replied tightly. 'You cannot wipe out a thousand years of ancient sayings in two centuries.'

For the first time Airmid, Prince Donennach's sister, leaned forward and whispered something in her brother's ear. He nodded and raised his hand to still the muttering.

'This meeting does not seem to be getting us anywhere but is merely continuing to sow the seeds of discord among us.'

'Yet these matters need to be answered,' insisted Fidelma.

'If you remember, Gláed was once a cleric.' Abbot Nannid's tone was even. 'He studied at the Abbey of the Blessed Machaoi on the island of Oen Druim and even won the degree of *freisneidhed* in law. That much was made clear in your previous encounter with him; even Conrí will bear witness to that. For whatever else he has done, Gláed still respects the Church and my person as Abbot. That is my explanation of how I met Gláed and secured possession of the murderer of Abbot Ségdae.'

There was a whispered exchange between Brehon Faolchair and Prince Donennach before the Brehon turned to Fidelma.

'Fidelma of Cashel, Abbot Nannid has given an explanation of his behaviour at the Hill of Truth. Before you speak, remember that he has admitted that he was there, spoke with the rebel leader Gláed and has returned here with the escaped prisoner, Gormán, having purchased the services of mercenaries. Do you have any evidence or witnesses that disprove his account?'

'It is a story as unlikely as believing a cat is innocent after shutting it in a room with a bowl of cream and then entering to find the cream has vanished,' Eadulf said contemptuously.

Brother Cuineáin grinned in derision at him. 'Evidence is needed, Angle, not speculation.'

Fidelma stood silent for a moment, head bowed. Then she heaved a sigh. 'We admit our observations were made from a distance. All we can swear to is that Abbot Nannid and his steward met Gláed and his marauders. And all we can give evidence to are the facts and not their interpretation.'

Brehon Faolchair waited a moment, looking uncertainly from Fidelma to Abbot Nannid as if expecting further argument. Then he had a whispered exchange with Prince Donennach before announcing: 'We must first deal with the implied question of Abbot Nannid's disloyalty to me in meeting with the brigand Gláed. The arguments have been listened to. The evidence presented by Fidelma of Cashel is deemed inadmissible inasmuch as it is too circumstantial and indirect. I take my authority from the *Berrad Airechta*, which clearly states the case. I am sure, Fidelma, you will have also considered this matter as it relates to what you have said?'

Fidelma conceded the reference, knowing what was about to happen.

Brehon Faolchair went on. 'In view of Abbot Nannid's explanation of his behaviour, and there being no clear evidence in contradiction to that explanation, then, indeed, the authority I quote must stand as the judgement on the matter of implied disloyalty.

'There is then the matter of compensation for tarnishing the reputation of the abbot,' intervened Brother Cuineáin with an air of triumph. 'It is well known that the law system stipulates compensation for making accusations which damage the reputation of a person. The compensation for doing so for an abbot or bishop of high degree, whose honour price is seven *cumals*, the worth of twenty-one milch cows . . .'

Brehon Faolchair held up his hand to silence the gloating steward.

'Brother Cuáneáin feels the law should consider restitution or compensation since the abbot's honour has been besmirched. Do you share your steward's opinion, Abbot Nannid?'

The man shrugged indifferently. 'My steward raises a good point.'

'He raises it under the law of the Brehons, not under your proclaimed Penitentials.' Brehon Faolchair's voice was bland but his eyes glinted. 'And if I pronounce a judgement now, you will not object?'

'Do so and let us get it over,' Abbot Nannid grumbled as if unconcerned.

Brehon Faolchair turned to Fidelma. 'I ask the same question of you, Fidelma of Cashel.'

Eadulf muttered something under his breath but Fidelma held the eyes of the Brehon steadily. 'I have accepted your ruling that the evidence does not completely sustain my interpretation of it. I will accept your judgement on restitution to Abbot Nannid's honour.'

Brehon Faolchair's lips formed a grim smile. 'Very well. Both parties being willing to accept judgement, I shall now give my ruling under the laws relating to *aircsiu*.'

Eadulf frowned, not having heard the word before. 'What's that?' he whispered.

Brehon Faolchair must have heard him for he went on: '*Aircsiu* is the law of "looking on", and I will explain that. Fidelma and Conrí came to the Hill of Truth and, because of the presence of Gláed and his brigands they wisely hid themselves. So they became onlookers to the scene. Now the law says that everyone who witnesses an offence and does nothing consents to it. The onlooker is obliged by law to intervene. For example, to put this simply, if a farmer sees that his neighbour's cattle are in danger, he must go to help them or pay a penalty for not doing so. Similarly, if he does intervene but is unable to prevent danger, he is not liable for the result. If the farmer is mistaken in his observation and intervenes when it turns out that the cattle are *not* in danger, he has fulfilled the obligation of the law and is also not liable for the result.'

Brehon Faolchair smiled briefly at Fidelma. 'What I rule under this law is that Fidelma and her companions saw what they thought was a crime being committed. They had not the ability to intervene immediately but intervened as soon as they were able – that is, when they returned to Dún Eochair Mháigh and reported the matter. The evidence has been examined and it has been judged that there was no sustainable evidence that wrongdoing had been conducted. Following on, under the law relating to *aircsiu* there is no argument for compensation.'

There was a silence and Eadulf could not help grinning broadly at the infuriated Brother Cuineáin opposite.

'Is there any objection to this?' Brehon Faolchair demanded. His question was aimed more at Abbot Nannid than at the obviously satisfied Fidelma.

The abbot's features showed little emotion apart from a certain tightening of his thin lips. He shook his head.

'*Si finis bonus est, totum bonus erit.*' Prior Cuán smiled, speaking for the first time during the proceedings. If the end is good, everything will be good.

At that point, Airmid rose from her seat and inclined her head towards her brother.

'I bid you excuse me from any further counsel, brother. I am sure that I have heard the essential matters that affect my position as your heir-apparent. But as a physician, other duties now call me.'

'You are so excused, Airmid,' Prince Donennach replied. They waited until she had left the great hall before resuming. The atmosphere was still tense.

'Can we proceed now to the more important matter that arises since Abbot Nannid has returned with the prisoner Gormán?' the prince suggested.

'Abbot Nannid admits that he holds Gormán of Cashel a prisoner,' Brehon Faolchair stated. 'We are grateful that Gormán has been recaptured. However, the abbot holds him captive in the Abbey of Nechta. It is now his duty to hand Gormán into my custody as Brehon to Prince Donennach, so that we may formally complete our hearing under the laws of the Brehons and, if now proven guilty, decide what is to be his punishment.'

Everyone now looked expectantly towards the Abbot. The thin face of the religieux twisted as he spoke.

'Not so,' he said.

There were puzzled looks and Brehon Faolchair leaned forward, saying, 'I do not understand.'

'I have already made my views known. My duty is to a greater authority than yours. I say that you have failed in your duty to keep your prisoner safe. You allowed him to escape: that cannot happen again. The man who killed Abbot Ségdae is judged guilty according to the law of the Faith. He is now my prisoner and will remain my prisoner until . . .' he paused dramatically '. . . until he is executed tomorrow at noon in accordance with the Penitentials that have now been adopted as the rules of the Abbey of Nechta and the New Faith.'

## CHAPTER SIXTEEN

~~~

The gathering was in danger of breaking up in confusion. Fidelma was stunned at Abbot Nannid's defiance of the law. It was hard to believe the man could be so confident of his position. She was aware that Prior Cuán had risen, hobbled over to Brehon Faolchair and engaged with both him and Prince Donennach in a hurried exchange. Then he returned to his seat and was about to speak to her when Brehon Faolchair called for silence. Prince Donennach wished to address them all.

'I have been asked by Brehon Faolchair to convene an extra hearing.' The prince's words were uttered in a tired monotone. 'This is not a court to assess the guilt or otherwise of Gormán of Cashel but to settle a more fundamental matter. It is an appeal lodged by Prior Cuán.'

'We are here to try to resolve the matter of legal authority over the prisoner,' explained Brehon Faolchair. 'Prior Cuán of Imleach argues that the law of this land is the arbiter of all legal matters and that Gormán should be handed over immediately to the custody of the prince for trial.'

At once Fidelma was on her feet. 'I support Prior Cuán in his appeal.'

'I contest it.' Abbot Nannid also rose. 'Since we have adopted the New Faith, the laws of the Brehons were only temporary laws until we accepted those of the New Faith.'

'Where is the proof that the laws of the Brehons were only accepted as a temporary measure?' Fidelma challenged him. 'In what text does it say so?'

Abbot Nannid ignored her outburst. 'My argument is simple. The prisoner, Gormán of Cashel, killed an abbot of the Faith and should now be punished under the law of the Faith. Indeed, not only should he be, but he will be. My authority is in Holy Scripture. Does not Genesis say – whosoever sheds the blood of man, by man shall his blood be shed?'

Brehon Faolchair looked unhappy. 'Are you claiming that your authority as an abbot is greater than that of your prince?'

'I am.'

No one was actually expecting such a clear answer and they turned with gasps of astonishment. Prince Donennach shook off his exhaustion and sat up straight, his mouth slightly open in an almost comical expression.

Abbot Nannid smiled thinly at Brehon Faolchair. 'At the recent Feast of Beltane there was a law council, was there not?'

'There was a council to consider amendments to the laws,' Brehon Faolchair admitted slowly. 'The council meets every three years to consider the working of the laws.'

'Obviously, you did not attend it?'

'I did not. If you remember, there was unseasonal weather at the Hill of Uisnech when the council was held. It prevented many from attending.'

'So you are not aware of the amendment to the laws of the *Crith Gablach*?'

Brehon Faolchair looked nervously towards Fidelma but she shook her head, as puzzled as he was.

'I presume that you will enlighten us on this amendment?' the Brehon said to Abbot Nannid.

'The new ruling is that an abbot, uniting the office of a bishop of the territory, is nobler than a king because the king has to rise before him on account of the Faith. It further amends that the honour price of an abbot is the same level as a provincial king.'

'Where did you get this news of the amendments from?' Brehon Faolchair asked, astounded.

Abbot Nannid caught Brother Cuineáin's and eye gestured for him to speak. 'I attended the council and heard the amendment proposed and accepted,' the steward told them all.

'Fidelma, do you have a comment to make?' The Brehon appealed to her.

'I know there are many abbots and bishops who argue that they should be treated as the equal and even as the better of the rulers of the Five Kingdoms,' she responded heavily. 'I have also heard that there was talk of an intention to reconsider their status in the laws on the matter. Certain abbots and bishops were proposing that it be enshrined in the *Críth Gablach*. I believe the idea was to argue that an abbot is nobler than a king, as Abbot Nannid has just said. I have also heard that not all the leading abbots and bishops, and certainly not all the kings of the provinces, and their Brehons, were in favour and many were not able to attend this council. Therefore, whatever was decided could never have been given the authority of a full council and received the High King's approval.'

'What are you saying, Fidelma?' queried Brehon Faolchair.

'Simply, if Brother Cuineáin was in attendance and has reported accurately, the council did not have proper legal authority to amend nor to circulate such decisions.'

'Do you wish to amend your position, Abbot Nannid?' demanded Prince Donennach.

'I have made my argument. Even if you declare the council invalid, I have the authority to carry out the laws of the Faith as Abbot.'

'As I see it,' went on Fidelma, 'even had it been accepted that you are as noble as or nobler than Prince Donennach, that does not give you the right to claim that your authority outweighs the law.

Kings, abbots and even Brehons have to answer before the law on equal standing.'

'I argue for the law of the Faith,' Abbot Nannid declared. 'Gormán killed an abbot. Leviticus says that if anyone takes a life, then he must be put to death.'

'Leaving aside the crucial matter of whether Gormán is guilty of the death of Abbot Ségdae or not,' Fidelma said tersely, 'and I argue that it has yet to be proved – we are discussing whether the rules of an abbot can overturn the law of the land. It is obvious that they cannot. It remains against the law of our people to execute anyone. From the time of the High King Eochaid, who was known as Ollamh Fodhla, our laws have stood for compensation to the victim and the rehabilitation of the perpetrator. How can the victim and the victim's family be compensated by a dead, corrupting body? How can a corpse be rehabilitated?'

'There is a New Faith in this land, Fidelma of Cashel. You are neglecting the Faith for the old pagan laws.'

'What is your justification for ignoring the laws of our country?' insisted Fidelma.

Abbot Nannid shrugged. 'Do I need a justification? I am Abbot of Mungairit, Chief Bishop of the Uí Fidgente. I repeat that we have been guided to the New Faith and embraced it. It is the Faith and its laws to which we are now answerable.'

Fidelma shook her head sadly. 'When the High King Loéguire mac Néill embraced Christianity, he took the New Faith to a council of law-makers, just as we have done for over a thousand years since Ollamh Fodhla organised the first council. The purpose of Loéguire's council was to examine our laws to see if they were compatible with the New Faith.'

'Is this history lecture relevant? We have heard it all before,' the abbot appealed to Prince Donennach. The prince did not respond so Fidelma answered.

'Then you should know your history well, Nannid of Mungairit.

You know that the learned men of our people sat and studied the laws and finally had them committed to writing. Of those who sat on the council there was Loéguire the High King himself; my own ancestor, Conall Corc, King of Muman, and Dáire, King of Ulaidh. They were the three most important of the kings, and they were advised by three of our most senior judges: Dubhthach Mac Ua Lugair, the Chief Brehon and Chief Bard of the Five Kingdoms; the Brehon Rossa mac Trechim, and Brehon Fergus an Bháird. They also sat with the Blessed Patrick, with his greatest convert and successor at Ard Macha, Benen mac Sessenen; he who had also been a prince of our people was converted by Patrick and took the name Benignus. Lastly there was the Blessed Cairneach. These last three were considered the greatest teachers of the New Faith at that time.'

'Most of us know our history,' Abbot Nannid said arrogantly. 'We don't need a lesson in what happened from you, Sister Fidelma.'

'But you obviously do need a lesson to know the meaning of what happened,' she corrected him. 'You should know that when that council put our laws into writing, it was stated in the introduction to the great text: "What did not clash with the word of God in the written Law and in the New Testament, and with the conscience of the believers, was confirmed in the law of the Brehons by Patrick and by the ecclesiastics and the princes of Éireann in this, the *Senchus Mór*." The laws of the Brehons are therefore clearly the laws of the Faith.'

Brehon Faolchair, amid the murmuring of approval from several, began to smile broadly at the point. 'So you argue that our law, as approved by Patrick and the first Christians here, is a Christian law for it did not clash with the word of God or the Christian Gospels?'

Abbot Nannid made a cutting motion with his hand.

'Since those days we have had more contact with the scholars of the Christian world in the east. We have sat too long beyond its borders. The scholars there have pointed out to us the errors of our early assumptions. It is to the Penitentials that we must now turn, as they have revised the old laws.'

Prior Cuán now rose, leaning on his stick, and hobbled towards the Abbot of Mungairit.

'Errors?' he repeated in a shaky voice. 'Do you accuse the Blessed Patrick of error? In Muman, the Faith was even brought here before Patrick by great scholars and teachers like Ailbe who founded my own Abbey of Imleach; by Ìbar, Abbán, Declan and Ciarán. Were these saintly scholars in error – and were the generations of great and holy men who followed them?'

'Yes, they were in error,' replied the abbot, unabashed. 'How many had time to sit and reflect on the great work ordered by Damasus, the Bishop of Rome, who commissioned Eusebius of Stridon to translate the texts in a form which the faithful priests of Christ could understand? In those scriptures you will find the laws of God, the Patriarchal Laws which the followers of the Faith must obey and not question. I presume that you, Cuán, who call yourself a scholar of the Faith, have read these laws which now must supersede the laws of the unenlightened?'

Prior Cuán chose his words carefully. 'I have studied the texts, Abbot Nannid of Mungairit. You often quote the Old Testament rather than the teachings of the Christ. So let me ask you, what is the Old Testament to us? It is a collection of texts about the ancient people of Israel whose language and culture are barely intelligible to us, even if we have studied it. We are told that the Christ emerged from such a people and their culture. At the same time, the disciples, such as Paul of Tarsus, and the Church Fathers that followed him, tell us that Christ's people rejected him and had him executed. His people did not want his teachings which had replaced so many of their laws and concepts.

'We are told by the Blessed Paul that the words of Christ were to be brought to those not of the culture of the Old Testament. So we ask ourselves why are these texts part of our scriptures unless merely to show us the history and the type of people who came to reject the Christ? Why are we so confused by these old texts that many Christian councils cannot even agree on what texts constitute the Holy Scripture that we should adopt as our own Faith?

'You remind us that Damasus the First, the Bishop of Rome, commanded Eusebius to translate the ancient texts into Latin. We find that this very act provoked arguments between Eusebius and Augustine of Hippo at the Council of Carthage . . . everyone had different opinions as to what should be left in and what should be left out of the final work.' Prior Cuán paused, shaking his head in disgust. 'What has the *Tanakh*, the Hebrew history of the Israelites and their battles, their philosophers and religion, to do with our equally ancient history, law and philosophies? Why should we accept the history and legends of the Israelites as more worthy than the history and legends of our own people? Instead of the *Tanakh*, why not accept the *Lebor Gabála Érenn*? Why should we throw away our very being for a culture from the other side of the world?'

The Prior of Imleach sank back on his seat. Fidelma gazed in amazement at the quiet passion of Cuán. Here was erudition indeed.

Abbot Nannid was now white-faced with anger. 'You are speaking heresy,' he shouted when he could no longer contain himself.

'He is denying the Faith!' Brother Cuineáin echoed his master. Even Brother Tuamán, the prior's steward, appeared to be troubled.

'Not so!' Prior Cuán replied, still seated. 'I fully accept the word of Christ and the founding fathers of the Faith. What I am saying is that the texts of the ancient history and religion of the land in which Christ came into this world, and whose people rejected Him, are of no more worth than any other. What is more important is what Christ actually taught and the teachings that have been passed on to us in the manner of His New Faith.'

'The words of Christ can only come from an understanding of the history of His people and their religion,' declared the abbot.

'But Christ is divine and above a product of one nation, one language and one culture. Is this not so?' demanded Prior Cuán. 'Aren't we taught that?'

'It is following the law of God that gives us the Faith,' replied Abbot Nannid. 'The law of God can only be that of his chosen people.'

'So what are you saying?' Prior Cuán asked. 'Is it that the newfound law of the God of Israel must now be the sole arbiter of all our lives, just because we accept Christ? Yet Christ Himself did not accept this law but questioned it.'

'We are talking about the murder of Abbot Ségdae. A life for a life! It is clearly said in the Old Testament.'

'We are not arguing Gormán's case,' Brehon Faolchair reminded him again, 'but whether the New Faith has abolished our laws.'

Prior Cuán would not let the matter alone and surprised Fidelma by his vehemence. 'You demand more than a life for a life, Abbot Nannid. Is it not so? You argue that whatsoever is ordered in the Holy Scriptures is now the law we must obey. That is what you claim as the Penitentials.'

'The sacred scriptures are there to be obeyed,' the abbot agreed dourly.

Prior Cuán shook his head as if in sorrow. 'The people of the Five Kingdoms hold most of their wealth in cattle, is it not so? Sometimes there are accidents with bulls, indeed, with other animals that become fractious, escape confinement and injure and even kill people. When this happens, in our law, compensation is made to the injured or their family. But the scripture known as Exodus says that not only must the animal be put to death but the owner as well. There is no choice in the matter. Do you follow that law?'

'The law of God is the law,' Abbot Nannid returned stolidly.

'And a man gathering wood for his poor fire on a holy day, as recounted in the Book of Numbers: God instructed that he be put to death for his impudence. Do you agree with that?'

'The judgement of God is not to be questioned.'

'So we must follow these laws without question because they are written in scripture?'

'That is what they are there for.'

'This morning in the marketplace in the township, I saw a group of boys making fun of a merchant struggling with a bag too heavy for him. Often boys and even girls have a cruel sense of humour. But would you put them to death?'

Abbot Nannid frowned momentarily. 'Why should I?'

'Because you say the judgement of scripture must be obeyed. In the second Book of Kings you will find that when the prophet Elisha was entering a town, a group of boys gathered round and made fun of his bald head. Elisha immediately had God strike them all dead for their impertinence. Do you find justice in that?'

Abbot Nannid hesitated a little. 'That law is the law,' he finally mumbled.

'Your law – not mine,' Fidelma declared.

Prior Cuán was not finished. 'There are many things in the Old Testament scriptures that merit death according to your lights, Abbot Nannid. Even acts of kindness are punishable by death. Yet doesn't Christ demand that we are all kind to one another?'

Abbot Nannid was on the defensive now. 'I have no knowledge of what you mean.'

'I see. Yet I had assumed that your knowledge of scripture would have been extensive for one who advocates such a blind obedience to the law written there.'

'Acts of kindness aren't punishable by death.'

'Then what of the story in Samuel when the Ark of the Covenant was being transported by ox cart down a hill and was in danger of falling off the cart because one of the ox team stumbled? Did not young Uzzah reach out a hand to steady it, to prevent it from falling into the mud and being damaged? For this offence it says that God struck him dead.'

'He was punished for daring to touch the Holy Ark.'

'To save it from being damaged. Did he deserve death as a reward for his act?'

'It is God's judgement. We must obey the law which is instituted by God. The judgement of death is mandated by the Old Testament.'

'Then many of us are worthy of being put to death,' Prior Cuán said with mock resignation. 'We must execute those who are disrespectful to their fathers or mothers, we must kill fortune-tellers, and women who are not virgins on their wedding night, we must slay adulterers . . . the list is endless. Will there be anyone left to inhabit your sort of Christian world, Abbot Nannid?'

'Only those worthy of God's infinite goodness will be saved.'

'And you have appointed yourself God's judge?'

'God has already made judgement, and those judgements are in the scriptures that comprise the Old Testament.'

Fidelma made one last attempt to bring reason into the discussion. 'When I was young, I was taught by Brother Ruádan of Inis Celtra. That venerable old man told me that we are Christians because we are followers of the teachings of Christ, but we are not like the slaves of the ancient laws of the Israelites. The principles of our Faith were set forth by Christ.'

'Did Christ not tell us in the scripture of Matthew that His mission on this earth was *not* to abolish the Law of Moses?' The abbot proposed this with a look of triumph on his face.

'Paul told the Galatians that the whole of the law is summed up in a single Commandment – that you shall love your neighbour as yourself,' Prior Cuán replied. 'Your Commandment seems to be that you will kill and punish as many of your neighbours as you see fit.'

Abbot Nannid reared up in anger. 'I have done with this. You will not move me from what I know to be right.'

Prince Donennach belatedly intervened. 'Abbot Nannid, have you considered where this matter might end?'

'I have only considered what is right and wrong.'

'Is there nothing I can say to you as Prince of the Uí Fidgente, as your prince, to persuade you to hand back the Cashel warrior to the custody of my Brehon so that he might be tried according to law? Will it avail me nothing if I plead with you not to go forward with your threat?'

'It is not to make a point that I make this stand, Donennach. I argue that I must support what is right according to the Faith.'

'Nannid, we are both descendants of Fiachu Fidgennid, both of the Uí Fidgente. My desire is to prevent our people descending headlong into war.' The plea was almost a cry of despair. 'For the sake of peace and our people, Nannid . . .'

'You are the ones who will not see peace if you allow this matter to go unpunished. Does it not say in the writings of Deuteronomy that if you reject the words of a priest, or judge of God's holy laws, you will also be put to death?'

His words brought a shocked intake of breath from the assembly.

'Be careful, Nannid of Mungairit,' Prior Cuán intervened fiercely. 'That clearly seems a threat against your lawful prince. Is it not said in Galatians, whatever a man sows, that shall he also reap?'

'My faith and my duty are clear. Gormán of Cashel killed an abbot. Tomorrow at noon, he shall meet with the penalty prescribed by the Faith which has been embraced by our people.'

Abbot Nannid now turned and, followed by his steward, Brother Cuineáin, he left the chamber.

Prior Cuán looked apologetically at Prince Donennach. 'I have done my best to argue with him on the grounds of the Faith, but I have failed. He is not moved. Nor will he be.'

Prince Donennach raised his hands helplessly. 'I thank you for your service. I thank you as well, Fidelma. I thank you both for trying to find some peaceful way of resolving this matter.'

Fidelma, however, was still angry. She felt that Prince Donennach had shown weakness in actually pleading with Abbot Nannid. 'You cannot allow this man to flaunt your authority and the ancient laws of this land.' Her voice was icy.

'What more can I do?' Prince Donennach almost wailed.

'You have your warriors here.' She pointed at Conrí. 'Send them to the abbey to bring Gormán here by force. Abbot Nannid has only four of Gláed's murdering brigands to defy them and they are no match for trained warriors.'

Brehon Faolchair felt he had to defend the prince. 'And what would happen then? The word would spread among the Uí Fidgente that their prince dishonoured his most senior abbot by sending warriors to attack an abbey. That is against all the rules of the Faith as well as our laws. It would be rumoured that Donennach did this in order to release a murderer. Whether judged rightly or wrongly, it would be claimed that he did so because he feared retribution from the King of Cashel. How long would it be before the people rose up against him?'

'Gláed and his men are encamped not far from here,' added Prince Donennach. 'I have no doubt that Gláed is waiting to intervene in this conflict. It may even be that this is planned. It could provide the very excuse that Gláed wants so that he can take advantage of the tumult that will ensue. If we thought our land was devastated after the defeat of Cnoc Áine, then it will be seen as paradise compared to what will follow if civil war is followed by war with Cashel.' Prince Donennach rose abruptly. 'My regrets, Fidelma. Truly, my regrets. If we are to descend into war, whether it be between Uí Fidgente and Uí Fidgente, or whether it will be against our old enemies, the Eóghanacht, we must prepare. I suggest that you and your companions make ready to leave our territory as soon as you can, for your own safety's sake. Return to Cashel and tell your brother, the King, that I have tried my best to choose the peaceful road. Prior Cuán, you and your companions should also return to Imleach. I can do no more.'

Brehon Faolchair after a moment's hesitation, followed him from the hall. Conrí, with bow to Fidelma, went after them.

Prior Cuán looked ruefully at Fidelma. 'I hear you are fond of quoting some of the Latin philosophers, lady. As Virgil says – *fata obstant*. Fate has opposed us.'

Fidelma thrust out her chin, a habit she had adopted when she was arguing a case that was not going to her liking. 'There is a saying that we should not willingly surrender to fate.'

'Abbot Nannid is an immovable object,' the prior lamented. 'Well, we will not be able to depart for Imleach until tomorrow. We'll wait until . . . until the afternoon.' He cleared his throat. 'Perhaps I should make a representation to Abbot Nannid that we might take Gormán's body with us so that he can be interred in his own territory?'

Prior Cuán did not meet Fidelma's eyes as he limped towards the doors of the hall. His silent steward, Brother Tuamán, with the scribe, Brother Mac Raith, followed despondently.

Fidelma sat staring at the table before her as the hall emptied. Eventually there was a curious stillness. Eadulf had remained at her side, numbly contemplating the inevitability of what was to happen.

'What now?' he asked, breaking the silence. 'Nannid has managed to get out of any accusation of being involved in a conspiracy with Gláed, and, he has even forced Prince Donennach to capitulate to his will.'

'Abbot Nannid is determined to execute Gormán and I don't doubt he will carry out his threat,' Fidelma said.

'So what can we do?'

Fidelma glanced around to make sure they were not overheard. 'There is only one thing left that we *can* do.'

Eadulf met her gaze for a moment and then nodded, his expression grim. 'So we'll attempt to rescue him tonight?'

# CHAPTER SEVENTEEN

At the doors of the great hall they found an agitated Enda waiting for them.

Fidelma looked at him with a frown. 'I thought you were taking care of Aibell in the guests' rooms?'

'We could not help wanting to know what has happened. We heard that your arguments did not go well, lady. And we heard the worst.'

'So where is Aibell?'

'She had an idea and has left the fortress.'

'Alone?' Fidelma groaned.

'She said she would be quite all right and will meet us shortly by the bridge off the town square.'

'You let her go unguarded?' she demanded incredulously.

'She is a hard person to argue with,' replied the young warrior. 'Come, we must go and meet her.'

Fidelma raised her eyebrows at Eadulf. His amused expression told her that he knew someone else who was similarly stubborn. They passed swiftly through the main gates and went down to the square. Only a few people were standing about and the atmosphere was uneasy; there was a mood of fearful anticipation. The three hurried on towards the bridge, wishing they could make themselves inconspicuous.

It wasn't long before Aibell emerged from the township to join them. Patience was not one of Fidelma's virtues and she greeted the girl with irritation rather than relief.

'What on earth do you think you are doing!' she snapped. 'It is very dangerous to be wandering alone out here.'

Aibell looked her straight in the eye. 'Anyone could have told you that Nannid is as cruel as he is narrow-minded. That is why I have been discussing a plan.'

Fidelma was astounded. 'Discussing a plan with whom?'

'Come, follow me,' urged the girl, instead of answering. 'We do not want to be seen here.'

Before Fidelma could question her further, the girl had disappeared into a small passageway. She set off at such a quick pace that there was nothing to do but hurry on after her. The girl hastened with ease among the buildings until she came to a little house on the southern edge of the township. It was shrouded by trees on the edge of thick woodland. The girl paused before the stout wood door and knocked on it, calling as she did so: 'It's Aibell.'

The door was opened by an elderly woman, her slightly bent shoulders covered by a thick woollen shawl and her long grey hair tied away from her forehead. She glanced at Aibell's companions with sharp grey eyes, then stood back for them to enter without a word. The door closed behind them and they found themselves enveloped in warmth. Although it was summer, the central hearth was obviously not used just for cooking.

Aibell laid a hand on the elderly woman's arm and looked at the others.

'This Étromma, Ciarnat's mother.'

They stood awkwardly for a few moments before the woman.

'I do not understand,' Fidelma said.

'Aibell was my daughter's friend,' Étromma said as if this explained matters.

'I know, but . . .'

Aibell broke in. 'You told me that Ciarnat was purposely given the wrong information to pass on to me, Fidelma. I have asked Étromma about it, and she has confirmed that it was part of a plot to make me persuade Gormán to escape so that he looked guilty.'

Fidelma was taken aback. 'How were you able to confirm this, Étromma?' she asked suspiciously.

The elderly woman lowered herself into a chair. 'I was born in this township and worked in the fortress all my life. I have many friends.'

'I don't doubt it, but how . . .?' prompted Fidelma again.

'I have a good friend at the so-called abbey here, and he over-heard something which worried him. You know that Abbot Nannid has taken up residence there? Well, my friend was passing a half-open door when he heard a voice saying that my daughter, Ciarnat, had been told to warn Aibell that you planned to abandon Gormán to his fate in order to preserve the peace with Cashel and your brother, the King. The person said that it had been suggested by a third party to Ciarnat that she must advise Aibell and Gormán to flee from the fortress. The same person also said that Aibell and Gormán would be tipped off that the guard could be bribed. Once they had fled, then Gormán's guilt would be clear to all.'

'I suspected as much,' Fidelma said.

'That was why poor Ciarnat was murdered,' Aibell said passionately. 'You were right about that.'

'It is all very well hearing voices – but whose voices were they?' Eadulf brought them back to reality. 'We need to know the name of the intermediary who told her.'

The old lady's features were twisted in anger. 'That we don't know. Brother Máel Anfaid was told the lie first; he then told Ciarnat. Ciarnat passed the lie to Aibell, and then Brother Máel Anfaid and Ciarnat were both killed to keep the secret of who told them.'

'So who was it that your friend heard speaking?' Fidelma pressed.

'Unfortunately, my friend said the voice was one he had not heard before,' replied Étromma.

'Could your friend not have entered the chamber in order to identify the speakers?' Eadulf asked.

'The half-open door was that of the chamber used by Abbot Nannid but it was not his voice.'

'That does not surprise me,' Eadulf sighed.

'Anyway, at that moment, the abbot's steward came along and my friend thought it wiser not to tarry outside the door.'

'So are we to believe that it was Abbot Nannid who was being told, or was he telling someone else?' asked Fidelma.

'Nannid must be in league with Gláed,' Aibell said. 'How else did all this come about and why?'

Eadulf was in agreement. 'Nannid must be trying to use Gormán to cause dissension among the people here. But how did Nannid manage to persuade Gláed to hand Gormán over to him?'

'You are right about them using Gormán. That has been obvious for some time,' confirmed Fidelma. 'Nannid would like to see a return to a more aggressive leader of the Uí Fidgente either under himself, for he is of the bloodline, or he is working with someone else who is prepared to break the peace that Prince Donennach has agreed with my brother.'

'There is dissension enough among us,' muttered the old woman. 'I have seen two fine sons march off when Eoghanán was our prince. They marched to Cnoc Áine on behalf of Eoghanán and perished there fighting against your brother, lady – fighting the King of Cashel.'

Fidelma sighed. 'That should be history now that Eoghanán is dead and Donennach rules in peace from this place,' she said softly.

'But now I have seen my fine young daughter, Ciarnat, killed for a lie,' Étromma went on, as if not hearing her. 'It is time to make a stand and accept that these lies and deceptions must not be ignored if ever there is to be true peace in this land.'

'This is interesting information against Nannid, but I fail to see where it may lead us,' Fidelma said restlessly, turning to Aibell. 'Tomorrow Gormán is due to be hanged.'

'I know,' Aibell said gravely. 'He must be rescued from the abbey tonight.'

'We had already come to that conclusion,' Eadulf told her. 'However, the way to make the thought into reality is much harder to devise.'

Aibell gestured to the elderly woman. 'Étromma has a plan but it will require the involvement of you, Brother Eadulf, and Enda.'

They looked at the elderly woman in surprise.

'What have you in mind?' Eadulf asked. He could not help the sarcasm in his voice. 'Do we walk up to the abbey, knock on the door and be admitted by the doorkeeper, who will then show us the way to the cell where Gormán is being held, unlock the door, and then we all walk happily forth into the night?'

Aibell ignored his scepticism in her excitement. 'That is exactly it . . . if the plan succeeds.'

Before the smiles began to form on their faces, Étromma said sharply: 'My daughter was murdered. So was the nephew of a dear friend of mine who not only hates those he suspects are responsible but knows them to have corrupted the community of Nechta. He will help and—'

She was interrupted by a knock on the door.

'That should be him now,' the elderly woman said, indicating that Aibell should answer the door. The girl opened it a fraction, peered out and then opened it more widely.

Brother Éladach, the doorkeeper of the Abbey of Nechta, came swiftly in and the girl closed the door behind him. His eyes swept round the company before he greeted Étromma.

'Have you told them?' he asked.

'I was just about to,' confirmed the elderly woman.

Fidelma greeted the doorkeeper. 'I presume you are the one who overheard the conversation in Abbot Nannid's chamber?'

'I did so, lady,' the doorkeeper nodded. 'And as the death of young Máel Anfaid was connected, it is obvious that he, too, was sacrificed by those who told him to pass the lies on to Ciarnat. The rest you know. They were both murdered by the same evil person who is intent upon executing an innocent man tomorrow, based on the spurious rules which he has forced upon our once peaceful community.'

'We are told that you have some sort of plan to thwart Abbot Nannid?' Fidelma said.

'It is a simple plan,' the man replied, looking sheepish.

'Often simple plans are the best,' she encouraged him. 'What do you suggest?'

'I once told you that I was a carpenter. To my shame, I helped construct the walls that surround our community. But that now works to our advantage. As well as the main gates of our so-called abbey, there are two small side gates, one to the west and one to the east. My plan is that after the moon reaches its zenith, the warrior here will come to the west gate. The only other man of strength that we can rely on is the Saxon brother here . . .' Eadulf did not bother to correct him. 'I will unlock the gate and then lead you to the cell where the warrior Gormán is incarcerated. It is a hut standing by itself. There are two men guarding him – they are men of the Sliabh Luachra, so be wary. They must be dealt with. After Gormán is released, he must be taken back to the west gate and I will secure it after you leave.'

Fidelma was about to ask the obvious question but Étromma pre-empted her. 'The young man will be brought here and hidden for a while. I have a special place to hide him until it is safe. I do not think anyone would believe he would continue to hide in the township, especially with me. They will assume that he has fled directly to Cashel.'

'For this we are much indebted, Étromma,' Fidelma acknowledged.

'It is a just revenge for what they have done to my daughter.'

'The plan sounds simple,' Fidelma allowed. 'But with this west gate being opened and then closed behind us, you, Brother Éladach, will be the obvious suspect.'

Éladach smiled grimly. 'I will prepare the east gate, to show that someone must have broken in through it. After you have left with Gormán, I shall make some adjustment to show that he also escaped by that east exit. Thankfully, we have no guards patrolling our walled community.'

'But you have men guarding the place where Gormán is imprisoned,' Eadulf said.

'Men of Sliabh Luachra, as you said,' Enda pointed out. 'They are cold-blooded killers. Trying to overcome them might result in a frenzied struggle that could raise the alarm.'

Eadulf looked uncomfortable. 'Are you suggesting that they are to be killed?'

'They would have no compunction in killing you,' replied the young warrior.

'We should not descend to their level,' Fidelma admonished. 'But these men would have to be rendered harmless.'

'Yet I have no skill as a warrior,' confessed Eadulf.

Fidelma ignored him. She turned to the doorkeeper. 'Do you know how Nannid plans his execution?'

'The buildings of our community are arranged around an old, sacred oak. I have been told that at noon, the brethren of the community will be ordered to gather to hear a homily from the abbot on the Penitentials and on the punishments that merit death as approved by the sacred scriptures. Then he intends to hang Gormán from the tree.'

Fidelma pursed her lips. 'I would know more of the lay-out of this abbey.'

Brother Éladach went to the hearth where ashes from the last fire lay on the raised flat stones. Using his hand, he spread the grey ash on the top of one of the stones. Then, taking a half-burned stick from the dead fire, he traced a rectangle in the ash.

'These are the outer walls. As you know, the entire outer walls are built of wood. Here is the main gate facing the square. On the east side is a side gate while, on the opposite west side, is another. The reason I chose the west gate for you to enter by is because it is closer to the cell where the warrior is contained.'

He bent and drew a small square in the centre and marked a little cross.

'That is the centre square and the cross marks the sacred oak tree where the Lady Nechta used to preach to convert people.'

'And where Nannid plans to hang Gormán,' Enda muttered.

'Where is his cell?' Fidelma pressed.

Brother Éladach indicated a point at the north-west corner of the smaller square.

'Inside the wooden walls of the abbey, everything is open. It is not one building for, as I told you, it was a series of homesteads, just like the rest of the township. At the east side of the interior courtyard is the chapel. On the opposite side are the buildings which are occupied by Abbot Nannid and his steward. The men he brought to guard his prisoner are also there.'

'How many members of your community live there?'

'We have about forty men and women and a dozen children. They live in huts across the entire site and between them are many storage huts. My own quarters are by the main gate. We have workshops and we have built ourselves a small library. You see, we are not a large community and until Abbot Nannid arrived and started to interfere with his new ideas, we were a contented one.'

'Aren't we neglecting what we are here for?' Aibell said anxiously. 'The night approaches and now each moment is precious.'

'These questions must be asked,' Fidelma assured her.

'It is also important to know that our community is not content with the rule of Abbot Nannid and his steward,' Brother Éladach stated. 'I am sure that you will find no one among the community who supports him. But while Abbot Nannid has legal authority over us, we must not be seen to be acting contrary to his wishes.'

'It is a simple plan,' Enda agreed thoughtfully, 'but I can see no alternative, and it may work. Eadulf and I will deal with the guards – but what are the conditions of his incarceration?'

'Conditions?' Brother Éladach was confused.

'Is he free within his hut, which is presumably locked or bolted, or is he tied up or what?'

'There are two bolts on the outside of the door of the hut,' replied Brother Éladach. 'However, his hands are tied.'

'Are you sure of this?'

'I went to take water and food to him earlier today. The guards were cruel and refused him food, saying what good was it to someone who was to be hanged the next day? However, they allowed me to give him some water.'

'What sort of physical condition was he in?' Enda said.

'While his hands are bound, his feet are free. I fear he might find his hands hard to use because of the constriction.'

'So we would have to overpower the guards, unbolt the door and then cut off his bonds?'

'The bolts are easily withdrawn. The guards are so confident that Gormán is bound and secured in the hut that they don't check on him regularly.'

Enda smiled with satisfaction. 'One good thing is that the men guarding him are lazy. They are not professional warriors, just thieves and robbers. I am feeling more confident now.'

Brother Éladach appeared pleased by the young warriors self-assured attitude. 'I tried to give your friend a message of hope when I gave him the water. I presumed the brigands were ignorant of Latin, but a commander of the King of Cashel's bodyguard would have some knowledge. I spoke briefly just in case. 'I said – *nil desperandum. Libersondum. Durate et vosmet rebus servate secundis.* The guards asked me what I said so I told them I was giving him a blessing as he was soon to die.'

'Did they believe you?'

'I am sure they did.'

Aibell was puzzled, for she had no knowledge of simple Latin. 'Did Gormán understand – and what did you say?'

'I roughly told him not to despair. I mentioned the word "rescue" and told him to wait and prepare himself.'

'That was good,' Fidelma said.

Enda gave a long sigh. 'That's it then. A simple plan. Friend Eadulf, we have no choice but to enter the community as Brother Éladach here has indicated, free Gormán and get away as fast as we can. You must have no compunction in dealing with the men guarding him.'

Eadulf drew himself up a little. 'I have fought my way out of more threatening situations before,' he reminded Enda solemnly, 'even though I have no warrior training. I have seen enough not to be that squeamish.'

Enda clapped him on the shoulder in approval. 'Now let us prepare. We do not have long.'

'I'll come with you,' Aibell announced. 'I can be of help.'

'Absolutely not,' Enda said firmly. 'In the matter of rescue and possible fighting, Eadulf and I will undertake this. You will stay with the lady Fidelma here, until we bring Gormán back with us.'

'But . . .' began Aibell.

'Enda is right,' Fidelma declared. 'I too would have liked to take part in this. However, he is a trained warrior.'

Brother Éladach nodded approval. 'I will go back now and attend to my duties as *aistréoir*. You will hear the little bell in the church sound, calling the community to gather for the last prayers of the day. After that, I will ensure that the bell is sounded three times, marking the end of prayers . . . three clear notes. Wait a little time after that, allowing for the community to go to their rest. Then come to the side gate. I will be there and shall guide you inside.'

'What if you are discovered?' asked Eadulf.

Brother Éladach said bravely, 'I must take that chance. If there is no other choice, then it is better to fight evil than sit and wait for it to multiply.'

'Good man,' approved Enda.

'There is one other thing,' Fidelma said. 'Enda and Eadulf will wait here with Étromma for your signal. But Aibell and I must return to the fortress so that people think that we have all gone back to rest there. Questions would be asked if it were known that tonight, of all nights, none of us were to be seen in the fortress. Once you have carried out the task, Eadulf and Enda must get back into the fortress to appear early the next morning to claim an alibi when the alarm is raised.'

Enda hit his left palm with his right fist. 'I had not thought of that. We will need a diversion to cover us while we do that. But how do we get back into the fortress?'

'Before I retire tonight, I will pretend to go for a walk in the courtyard,' Fidelma said. 'What has been done once, can work again. During the walk I shall make sure that the side gate is unlocked so that you may sneak in without going through the main gates. As for a diversion this evening, Aibell and I will provide it.'

She waited until they were all in agreement before she glanced round and said earnestly, 'Let us all go to our tasks and may luck be our companion this night.'

# CHAPTER EIGHTEEN

෯

As Fidelma and Aibell approached the fortress gate there was no sign of Ceit but the warrior on guard just waved them through. They were moving across the courtyard towards the great hall when a tall figure emerged from the shadows. It was Conrí. He halted in the flickering light of the burning brand torches.

'A gloomy night,' he greeted – but it was not to the weather that he was referring.

'Melancholy enough,' Fidelma replied, making her voice sound despondent.

'Is Eadulf not with you?'

'He has already gone to our chamber with some disturbance of the stomach. Probably something he ate earlier,' she lied. She hoped the warlord could not read her expression in the fading light. Then, sensing that Conrí wanted to say something more but seemed inhibited, she said to Aibell, 'Perhaps you could go to our chamber to see how Eadulf is feeling? And ask if he intends to join us in the hall before we retire.'

The girl nodded and they watched her scurrying away across the courtyard. Then Conrí turned to Fidelma.

'My rider has returned from Mungairit,' he announced quietly. 'He is accompanied by someone he met who had just fled from the

Hill of Truth. You will meet them both tomorrow. I think you'll find his news interesting.'

'You had best tell me now the essence of that news,' Fidelma instructed him, excited in spite of herself.

'In short, Nannid is no longer the Abbot of Mungairit. Neither is Brother Cuineáin his steward there. They left the abbey six or more months ago having been dismissed by the *derbhfine*. After the conspiracy that you uncovered, the abbey council decided that they could not place their trust in Nannid or his steward.'

Fidelma felt a growing relief. 'I had begun to suspect as much since Nannid has spent so many months here trying to create a new community in the township. But this does not help us in the current matter. Nannid is an astute debater. He will doubtless argue that he is now Abbot of Nechta and can still claim entitlement to demand punishment under these Penitentials. Don't let your rider relay this news to anyone else, not even Prince Donennach or Brehon Faolchair. I will know when the time is right.'

Conrí said in surprise, 'Don't you think it might help at all? You realise that Gormán's death is inevitable at noon tomorrow?'

'Even if Nannid can only call himself Abbot of Nechta, he still has enough influence among the Uí Fidgente to stir them up against Prince Donennach. I think that has been his intention all along.'

'But surely this might make some difference?'

'No, not of itself. You mentioned that your messenger encountered someone on his return – someone from the Hill of Truth?'

The warlord nodded grimly. 'It was the religieux, Brother Feradach. He confirms that he had gone there on behalf of Mungairit to meet with Nannid. However, he saw the encampment of the men from Sliabh Luachra and fled.'

Fidelma said thoughtfully, 'That just supports Nannid's version of why he went to the Hill of Truth. Again, it does not help the situation with Gormán.'

'I know, I know.' Conrí hunched his shoulders in a despairing gesture. 'There must be some way to help him!'

'I wish there was.'

'Perhaps there is. I mean . . .' Conrí spoke awkwardly. 'Well, when Gormán escaped from here, I had my duty to fulfil, my allegiance to Prince Donennach to try to recapture him. When Gormán continued to evade us, I began to realise that it was probably the best solution to this problem.'

'But it was not a permanent solution. The dilemma would still face Prince Donennach.'

'I mean, what I am trying to say is that if Gormán could escape again and go back to Cashel, it would be better than being killed here. I do not think Prince Donennach would insist that his warriors should pursue him too diligently.'

'It would still be a problem.'

The warlord looked anxious. 'This evening I have been speaking with Prince Donennach. If Gormán does hang tomorrow, I don't want there to be another war between us.'

'That prospect is one that must be avoided,' she agreed.

'Yet I am warlord of the Uí Fidgente and must make preparations for that very prospect. I do not want to send out my riders bearing the fiery cross to summon the clans to the service of Donennach. But once the news of Gormán's death spreads to Cashel, your brother will have no option but to gather his fighting men. Then he will march on our borders.'

'My brother is no hothead, Conrí,' Fidelma replied. 'He would be open to reasonable negotiation – but he would want restitution under the law, and I mean the laws of the Five Kingdoms. I think we both know well that someone is trying to provoke a war here, and it is not the Eóghanacht. However, I have understood what you have said.'

'Very well, lady. I shall say no more about the news from Mungairit until you tell me that I may do so.'

'For that, I am grateful. But I fear things will not end until we have resolved this matter under law and discovered the causes behind it.'

Conrí raised a hand to his forehead in farewell as she continued on her way to the great hall. There, she rejoined Aibell.

The only other people in the hall were Prior Cuán and Brother Mac Raith; while in one corner sat Airmed, the physician, with Brother Tuamán, the steward of Imleach. Between them was a *fidchell* board, the popular game of wooden wisdom, which needed a sharp eye and plenty of concentration. They were sipping at drinks as they played. Fidelma crossed to examine the arrangement of pieces on their board; she was particularly adept at the game.

'Have a care, Brother Tuamán,' she warned, seeing the alignment of the pieces. 'You will be in danger soon from Airmid's defence.'

They looked up and acknowledged Fidelma. Then, with a frown, Brother Tuamán peered closely at his opponent's pieces and spotted the danger that Fidelma had observed. 'Airmid was always good at defensive play even when she a student,' he beamed.

Airmid stood up abruptly. 'Enough of the game,' she said, glancing to the door. 'Where is Brother Eadulf?'

'He has retired early to our chamber. Something he ate earlier disagreed with him,' responded Fidelma.

'Do you want me to attend him?' Airmid asked at once.

'I think Eadulf has enough healing knowledge to deal with his condition,' Fidelma said to deflect Airmid's concern. 'He always says that water is a great purge but sleep is a greater healer.'

'The girl also seems unwell,' Airmid said, casting a glance to where Aibell fidgeted restlessly at one side of the hall. Fidelma was concerned. It was a matter of Gormán's life or death. If his young wife remained in the hall, she would certainly draw more attention to herself.

'No doubt she is feeling the strain of her husband's fate,' Fidelma said carefully. Then, going over to Aibell, she said in a carrying voice, 'You look tired, Aibell. We don't want you going down with an illness like Eadulf. I suggest you withdraw to our chamber and try to rest. You can do no good here.'

The girl muttered something inaudible and stumbled off towards the stairway to the guests' rooms.

Fidelma was aware of Airmid standing at her side. 'She is young,' Fidelma said, 'and these despondent days will gradually fade. It is often said that the passing of time is a great help.'

'Such advice is difficult to accept when your husband is about to be executed.' The dry comment was made by Brother Mac Raith, who had moved to warm himself by the fire.

'I agree,' Airmid said. 'It is sad that such things have come to pass.'

'Your brother could intervene,' observed Prior Cuán a little sourly, entering the conversation. He had been sitting before the fire, absorbed in watching the dancing flames.

'I will not argue with you on that,' agreed Prince Donennach's sister. 'If it is worth anything, I did advise him to take a stronger stand on the matter. He seems fearful of another effusion of blood, given that too much of ours has been shed over the years of the conflict with the Eóghanacht.'

Fidelma flushed slightly. 'Such conflict has never been of the Eóghanacht making,' she replied defensively.

Airmid put out a hand to lay it on Fidelma's arm for a moment.

'My dear, I meant no rebuke to you. But it is the truth that I am telling. The wars that we have been engaged in have achieved nothing but more bloodshed. Many, like my brother, want to avoid war among our own people at any cost. Others believe that my brother's policy of conciliation with Cashel is wrong.'

'You appear to place yourself as a neutral in this matter, lady,' observed Fidelma. 'Yet you are the heir apparent to your brother. You must have a say on his council.'

Airmid threw back her head and laughed. 'My brother tolerates my presence since there is no other heir to his bloodline. The council always look to a man to lead them.'

A look of annoyance crossed Fidelma's face. 'The law is clear on that: women can fulfil any role.'

'But not usually fulfil the role of kingship.'

'On the contrary, as you wander the kingdoms and princedoms of this island you will find several women leaders among them, and not only leaders of their people but commanders of war. Did not Macha of the Red Tresses rule all the Five Kingdoms from Tara in ancient times?'

Airmid smiled thinly. 'I do not possess your passion or your knowledge, lady,' she replied. 'I simply know that I, like my brother, would prefer peace.'

'Is your brother not joining us this evening?' queried Fidelma.

Airmid shook her head. 'There is much on his mind this evening,' she replied.

'Much on everyone's mind,' Prior Cuán said bluntly. 'There'll be no peace if we abandon the laws that have been with us since the time before time, and just accept these alien concepts coming from Nannid.'

'For my own part,' Airmid sighed, 'I want nothing more than to be allowed to carry on as a practitioner of the arts of healing. But I suppose Nannid could argue that there is a difference between abandoning our old laws and abandoning our old religion?'

Prior Cuán frowned. 'I am unsure what you mean, lady.'

'Simple enough. We were once firm in the Old Faith. We worshipped the gods and goddesses as, indeed, our people had done since the time when Féinius Farsaid led us out of the primeval mists. We remained constant to our gods and goddesses, who shaped our lives for century after century. Then some of our people heard stories of a new God, a single God worshipped among a people in the east. This God, they were told, had sent His Son to bring them to the Faith. Some of our people believed in the New Faith – Ailbe,

Ciarán, Declan and others and then, eventually, the leader of this Faith in Rome sent a former hostage of the Uí Néill to convert us.

'It was two centuries ago that the High King, Laoghaire, son of Néill of the Nine Hostages, decided to leave the Old Faith, abandon the gods and goddesses that we had worshipped for millennia, and accept this strange New Faith from the east. So, having abandoned our own Faith, a New Faith has shaped and sustained us. We abandoned our old Faith, so what would be wrong with abandoning our old laws? What is the difference?'

There was a silence after Airmid had spoken.

'Put in that form, lady,' Fidelma said eventually, 'it is an interesting comparison in support of what Nannid argues now. Are you in favour of his Penitentials?'

Airmid gave a quiet laugh. 'If it were left to me, I would be content with both the old religion and the old law. What has worked for centuries seems hardly worthwhile amending, much less spilling blood over. But I thank the powers that it is not my responsibility. All I do is point out that times change and often we have to change with them. But left to myself, I am certainly no reformer.'

Brother Tuamán looked up from where he still sat at the *fidchell* board.

'I am sure that Abbot Nannid would agree that the road to what is right and proper is a righteous one to tread, and it is worth sacrifices to attain an end to it. It is right and proper that we have cast away our superstition for the light of knowledge of the True Faith. We have attained much but we must seek more and come nearer to the Great Truth. That is why I entered into the life of the religious.' He paused and glanced round, realising they were staring at what, for him, was an outburst. Then he gave a shrug. 'Indeed, that is why I entered the great Abbey of Imleach and was proud to serve Abbot Ségdae as I will now be proud to serve his successor.' He dropped his gaze back to the *fidchell* board.

Airmid looked at Brother Tuamán in amusement for a few moments before saying to Fidelma, 'So what will you do now, lady?'

'Now?'

'Now all is lost here, I mean. I suppose you will head back to Cashel tomorrow. Will you attempt to persuade King Colgú that my brother had no choice but to act as he did? I mean, by not interfering in the execution of his warrior.'

Fidelma pursed her lips in a thoughtful expression before speaking. 'I suppose I would start by saying that perhaps, all is not lost until it is lost. But certainly I will report to my brother, Colgú, and his Chief Brehon, what I have seen here.'

Prior Cuán leaned forward slightly, his brow creased in perplexity. 'We must do all in our power to prevent any thoughts of vengeful bloodshed, lady. If we must face the consequences of tomorrow, let us hope we can persuade Colgú not to seek reparation on the field of battle.'

Fidelma suddenly felt mischievous. 'Alas, is there not an old proverb which says that there was never a more just judge than the field of battle?' she said dryly.

Prior Cuán looked at her in disapproval. 'It must be a very old saying – from barbaric days. I, for my part, will be riding straight for Cashel tomorrow to admit that my poor scholastic knowledge was unable to move Nannid, who is equally firm in his beliefs. But Fidelma, I will be telling your brother, the King, that he must remember that vengeance is to be left in the hands of God.'

'Waiting for divine vengeance is a tedious process,' Airmid said tartly. 'I recall that in the past, the Eóghanacht have shown us the efficacy of acting more swiftly in such matters.'

Fidelma knew it was a provocation and a reflection on the long history of rivalry between their two families for the Kingship of Muman.

'We believe it is the King and his council who will make a response once all the facts are known,' she said quietly.

Airmid seemed surprised. 'Are they not already known? Do you still insist there should be yet another hearing after the warrior admitted his guilt by fleeing from here before you had time to offer a defence for him?'

'It would seem that not all the facts have been allowed to come to light,' Fidelma replied, but she did not elaborate.

Prior Cuán rose from his chair and reached for his stick. 'It is time I retired,' he announced.

Fidelma crossed to his side. 'I need some exercise before I retire,' she told him. 'A walk across the courtyard of the fortress will be sufficient. I will accompany you as far as your quarters, if I may, Prior Cuán?'

As they moved towards the door of the hallway, Fidelma glanced at his stick. She frowned, trying to remember something about walking sticks. 'You seem to have changed your stout blackthorn. Have you lost it?'

Prior Cuán chuckled. 'I indulge myself by carrying two different sticks when I travel, lady. This one is good for use when I am within the abbey buildings or places such as this. It's made of chestnut wood. But sometimes I use the other one. To be honest, it often depends which I have left nearer the door of my chamber when I leave it.'

As they left the hall, Prior Cuán glanced back in disapproval at Brother Tuamán, who was indulging in a goblet of some strong liquor as he gazed down at his *fidchell* pieces. Airmid re-seated herself opposite him, toying with her own drink. Outside, the prior paused and said: 'I do not think that drinking intoxicating liquids figures in the austerity plans of those who subscribe to the Penitential rules.'

'Abbot Ségdae never approved of the Penitentials being adopted at Imleach,' Fidelma commented. 'It is difficult to believe Brother Tuamán when he said that our friend was considering making concessions on their use.'

'Abbot Ségdae was a wise man . . . I do not believe in the adoption of the Penitentials.'

'Nannid argues that they should replace the Law of the Brehons.'

'It was the very reason why Abbot Ségdae agreed to lead this delegation to meet with Nannid. Indeed, it was why Ségdae chose me to accompany him as adviser, for I have studied these Penitentials.'

'I presume that you have heard how Nannid enforced his rules on the community here?'

Prior Cuán grimaced. 'Nannid is fond of rank and authority. He is a vainglorious man and I am sure he would do anything for power. If he was sent into the wilderness for forty days and nights, within the first few minutes he would accept a deal with Lucifer and settle not even for all the kingdoms of the world but for a small part of a bogland.'

Fidelma answered him with a wan smile as she bade him good night. Then, ensuring that he had entered the guest-hostel where the delegation from Imleach was staying, she moved on towards her real objective. A bell was sounding from the Abbey of Nechta. It was time to play her part in the plan to rescue Gormán. She hoped that she would succeed. The guards were gathered at the main gates standing under the brand torches. There were sounds of music from the *laochtech*, the warriors' quarters, where they were noisily entertaining themselves.

She passed the stone building in which Gormán had been incarcerated. It was entirely in darkness now that there were no other prisoners housed there. Fidelma paused and took a careful look around her, listening as well as examining the shadows with her sharp eyes. Satisfied, she moved swiftly to the tall wooden gates through which Gormán and Aibell had fled some days before. Now it was not to supply a means of exit that Fidelma had come there but the reverse – to ensure a means of entrance. The iron key was hanging on the wall to one side of the gate and Fidelma took this and eased it into the lock and turned it. Then she found the two bolts and drew them. To her relief, frequent use had made them draw easily and without a sound. She stood up and leaned against the wall for a few moments, breathing a little quickly after her exertions. She took the iron ring handle and pulled it towards her. The gate swung open a little. Then she pushed it back.

She had done her part now. All she could do was pray that no one came by and noticed that the bolts were not thrust home and that the gate was unlocked. She paused to replace the key on its hook before hurrying back across the courtyard towards the main buildings.

What she did not see, after she had left, were the two shadows emerging from the stables and coming to stand before the gate.

'Interesting,' Conrí, warlord of the Uí Fidgente, remarked softly to his companion Ceit, the commander of the guard.

'Interesting, indeed,' nodded his comrade. 'I presume that the lady has accepted the hint you gave her?'

'I hope she has.' Conrí was thoughtful. 'I can't imagine how she will achieve it, but we'll keep a watch on this gate tonight. I imagine that come dawn tomorrow we will be faced with more than a little excitement.'

# ChAPTER NINETEEN

∾

The soft tolling of a bell came clearly through the night air. It sounded distinctly three times.

Étromma sprang to her feet with surprising agility for one of her age. 'That's the bell to mark the extinguishing of all lights in the community. It is time to prepare yourselves, lads.'

Enda rose with a studied languor, attempting to show how calm he was. 'We are prepared enough,' he said, easing his sword in its scabbard and checking the knife which hung in its leather sheath on his left side. He gazed at Eadulf critically. 'I wish you had armed yourself with something more powerful than a blackthorn stick, friend Eadulf.'

He was referring to the weapon that Eadulf now clutched determinedly. It was a thick stick with a knob at one end, and it had been well tempered in the smoke of a fire until the stick was almost blackened. It had apparently belonged to Étromma's dead husband. She had handed it to Eadulf to use when it became obvious that he was no swordsman and, indeed, was unsure of his resolve to kill a fellow human with sharp steel. As a member of the religious he had often tussled with the idea of turning the other check, rather than resorting to violence to prevent further injury or death at the hands of an aggressor. However, he had seen enough death recently to know that the men of Sliabh Luachra would have no compunction about using violence on him.

'It's my late husband's *maglorg*,' Étromma had explained. 'In his day, fighting with the sticks was a way of settling an argument of honour if you didn't feel like calling a Brehon and pleading your case. You would challenge the person who did you wrong and the better man at plying the stick would win.'

Eadulf had stared at the stout stick with wide eyes. 'Were many people killed then?'

The elderly woman had chuckled. 'Bless you, Brother Eadulf, none at all. The purpose of the stick-fighting was to get the other to submit – not to kill them. But you could give them a sore head with a tap of this.' She pointed to the knob end of the stick.

Enda looked serious. 'In this instance, friend Eadulf, I think you should be aware that our opponents will not settle for just a tap on the head.'

As the chimes faded, Étromma went to the door and peered out.

'There is darkness across the township,' she reported, closing the door. 'Bide here a short while and then go – and may God go with you.'

Eadulf found himself wondering whether God would approve of such a mission to secure Gormán's release. He grinned at the thought – and then straightened his features as he realised that Enda was looking at him with some concern.

'Don't worry, Enda,' he said. 'I'll not let you down.'

'I am not worried that you would,' the young man replied. 'But this is a job for a warrior.'

'I think you should go now,' Étromma advised. 'Éladach will be waiting for you.'

Enda led the way into the darkness. Outside the door of the elderly woman's homestead, they paused to allow their eyes to adjust to the night. Then the young warrior set off without hesitation, Eadulf close on his heels. Enda appeared to have a good grasp of the route through the now darkened cabins and homesteads. Hardly any time passed before they reached the wooden wall that encompassed the so-called Abbey of Nechta and eased their way along it. Enda spotted the wooden gate easily.

He paused, ensured Eadulf was with him and then tapped softly, once only. The gate immediately swung inwards and they passed inside.

The shadow that greeted them did so in Brother Éladach's reassuring tone.

'Follow me closely. There are no lamps now that the community has retired to bed. However, you'll see a faint glow further along this path. That is by the central square of the community. There is a lamp burning outside the hut where Gormán is incarcerated.'

Enda allowed a faint hissing breath to escape him. 'But that means that we have no element of surprise emerging from the darkness,' he whispered. 'The guards will see us approaching. If we have to make a frontal attack, friend Eadulf, both men must be rendered unconscious or eliminated.'

'I understand the problem,' Eadulf whispered back. 'Even if we could silence one guard, the other will raise the alarm. They must both be dealt with at once.'

'Let us hope that fortune will be with us, my friends,' muttered Brother Éladach.

'Then the sooner we observe the situation for ourselves, the better,' Enda said.

Led by the doorkeeper, and keeping well within the shadows of the line of huts, they crept stealthily towards the centre where they could see the flickering glow from a lantern.

A few moments later, they halted by a hut. Brother Éladach pointed to the next one along. He did not have to tell them that it was where Gormán was imprisoned. Two men were on guard outside the hut on which a lantern hung. Other lanterns lit up the square beyond. One man was standing warming himself before a brazier, which added to the glow of light. It was a cold night in spite of being summer. Another man was sitting, whittling at a piece of wood with a knife. Eadulf found himself perspiring in spite of the chilly air; his heart thumping.

'Stay here, my friends,' Enda breathed. 'Keep out of sight. I'll be back in a moment.'

He moved forward at a crouch into the darkness towards the back of the hut. Both of his weapons were now out of their sheaths and ready for use, sword in one hand and knife in the other.

It was not long before he reappeared.

'I'll go to the other side of the hut and make a soft noise,' he whispered, outlining his plan. 'Hopefully that will catch the attention of the guard who is standing up and he'll come to investigate. I think I can deal with him. But you, Eadulf, will have to get close to the one sitting down and incapacitate him before he realises something is wrong. Understood?'

Eadulf muttered an acknowledgement. Then Enda crawled away. Eadulf moved up to the corner of the hut, gripping the blackthorn stick in both sweaty hands. He peered round at his quarry. The man still sat on a bench and continued to whittle away at his stick. His companion was stretching himself before the brazier. Eadulf drew back quickly and tried to mentally prepare himself.

'What the hell are you doing?' came a gruff voice.

Eadulf nearly jumped, his heart pounding. He was about to swing round to see who was threatening him when he realised that it was one of the men speaking to the other.

A lazy voice replied, 'It helps to pass the time. Better than doing nothing.'

The first voice swore. 'I'll be glad when this is over, so that we can rejoin Gláed. Better to be riding with sword in hand. Blood and booty. That's the life.'

'We have to do what Gláed tells us,' the other replied. 'He tells us to act as bodyguard to this abbot, so that is what we must do.'

'Why do we have to wait until tomorrow to kill the man? I could end it with a single sword-thrust now if the old man wants him dead so badly.'

'Old man or not, he is an abbot,' reproved his companion. 'And we have been ordered to do what he tells us.'

'And as an abbot he must be a bigger thief and killer than any of us,' his companion sneered cynically. 'Although it does not take much strength to dominate this lot of sad rejects . . .' The voice went silent all of a sudden. Eadulf had not heard anything but the voice then continued, 'Did you hear that?'

'Likely just a cat or dog,' hazarded the second man.

'We were told to be careful.'

'Go and look then. I say it is nothing.' The guard resumed his whittling.

Eadulf heard the first man curse and the sound of him moving. Easing his blackthorn to shoulder level, Eadulf sprang forward. It seemed to happen so slowly, as if his limbs had become weighed down with lead. The seated man heard him, looked round in surprise; his mouth started to open to shout an alarm while at the same time the hand holding the knife rose in self-defence. Grunting with the effort, Eadulf swung the cudgel and struck the man hard on the side of the temple.

He stood over the fallen man breathing heavily for a few seconds.

Then there was movement from the far side of the cabin. Eadulf tried to raise the blackthorn again, ready to defend himself against the unconscious man's returning companion. But it was not him. Enda emerged from the shadows, sword in hand, and Eadulf almost collapsed in relief. Enda glanced at the fallen second man. He did not say anything but went to the door of the cabin and examined the bolts on the door. As Éladach had said, there were two of them and they slid back easily, making no sound.

Even as they prepared to open the door there was a sudden gasp of agony from behind them. They whipped round to find the man that Eadulf thought he had knocked unconscious was struggling erect, a sword in his hand. But his eyes blurred in the lamplight as if unable to focus. Blood gushed from his mouth. Then he fell forward on his face. They saw the hilt of a knife buried in the man's back.

Behind the body stood the shaking figure of Brother Éladach.

'*Deus miseratur*,' he prayed. 'May God have mercy on me.'

Enda quickly realised what had happened. 'I am sure God will forgive you,' he whispered, regaining his sense of humour. 'Meantime, silence.'

He turned back to the door and with Eadulf they pulled it open. In the shadows a figure had risen awkwardly into a sitting position on the straw palliasse.

'Is it time?' muttered a familiar voice.

Eadulf replied in a light-hearted whisper, 'Yes – time for you to leave this den of evil.'

There came an audible swallow. 'Is that you, friend Eadulf, or am I hearing things?'

'You are not hearing things and I am with him,' Enda said, moving forward with his sword. 'Now keep quiet and still, while I cut those bonds.' He sheathed his sword and took out his dagger.

'Enda? What is happening?' gasped Gormán and was immediately told to be quiet again.

'What is happening,' hissed Eadulf, 'is that you are being rescued. Now save your questions until we get you away from this place.'

Gormán knew enough to turn and hold out his bound wrists behind him so that Enda could get to work on severing them. Having done so, it being the work of a few moments, Gormán began to rub his wrists to restore the circulation. 'I wondered what Brother Éladach meant by his cryptic Latin,' he croaked.

Enda now motioned to Eadulf and Brother Éladach to help him carry the bodies of the two dead guards into the hut. He closed the door on them and noiselessly pushed the two bolts back into place. Brother Éladach waved at them to follow him and they trod softly back to the side gate through which they had entered.

Before they went through it, they paused, listening in the darkness. Apart from the distant bark of a dog and the mourning cry of a night owl, it was quiet.

'I regret I had to kill that man,' Brother Éladach whispered. 'But he was about to raise the alarm.'

'You did well,' Enda assured him. 'If no one notices that the guards are not on watch, it might not be until first light before their bodies are found.'

'Are you sure that you want to stay?' Eadulf asked Éladach. 'Nannid is of a suspicious mind and he will work out that Gormán had help from someone here.'

Brother Éladach shook his head ruefully. 'I have already prepared the east gate so it looks as though Gormán has fled in that direction. But I must stay to try to help my people. *Deus vult*. God wills it.'

'Then it is time for us to move. The sooner we are away, the better,' Enda said.

'Go with God and I will secure this gate after you.'

With quick gestures of farewell, the trio hurried silently along the wall and, with Enda leading, were soon swallowed by the shadows. As they passed the darkened houses, moving away from the newly constructed walls of the so-called Abbey of Nechta, Eadulf felt thankful he could rely on Enda, with his warrior's training, to guide them with such certainty towards the house of Étromma. The sudden bark of a dog from a nearby building caused them to halt, breaths catching in their throat. There came the rattle of a chain and then a masculine voice swore and shouted at the animal to be still. There was a further bark, then a clatter as if something had been thrown, followed by a protesting whine before silence descended again. No one spoke as the men moved on.

Only once did Gormán signal that he needed to halt. It was then that Eadulf realised he was barefoot. 'It's all right, friend Eadulf,' Gormán said, wincing. 'I can manage awhile but the stones are hard. They took my shoes from me to make sure I did not run off.'

Eadulf knew that most warriors of the King's bodyguard wore *máelan*, shoes of fully tanned leather with hard soles and heels. Warriors needed the comfort of good footwear and were unused to going barefoot.

'It won't be long now,' Enda promised his friend. 'Just to that corner.'

'Where are we going?' Gormán asked.

'A safe house. Aibell has arranged it.'

Gormán grunted but said no more. A moment later, they arrived at Étromma's house on the border of the township. Enda halted and rapped softly on the door. It was opened immediately and they entered. A lamp was lit and Étromma came forward.

'So you have him. Did all go well?' she asked.

'Yes, but I am afraid that we had to kill the guards – the two men of Sliabh Luachra,' admitted Eadulf.

'May their troubled souls find rest in the Otherworld,' the old woman muttered, but it was only a formula without meaning. 'What of Éladach?' It was clear that she was concerned for the doorkeeper.

'He is fine. Everything went as planned,' confirmed Enda.

'As soon as they realise this man is missing they will start searching,' the elderly woman said.

'We are hoping they will think he has fled eastwards, thanks to Brother Éladach.'

'But realising that you are on foot, Gormán, they will still search the township,' the old woman pointed out. 'I have a place ready for you, but it may be a little uncomfortable.'

Gormán grinned. 'It will not be as uncomfortable as where I was during the last day. Anyway, to whom do I owe this hospitality?'

'I am the mother of Ciarnat, who has been murdered by your enemies.'

Gormán gazed at her in amazement.

'There is a lot to explain,' Eadulf told him hurriedly, 'but I am afraid that Enda and I must leave it to Étromma to do so. We have to ensure that we are back inside the fortress before daybreak.'

'One question,' insisted Gormán. 'Where is my wife? Is she safe?'

'Aibell is with Fidelma in the fortress,' Eadulf said. 'They are making sure that their presence is recorded there, for I don't doubt that there will be much happening tomorrow morning when your escape is discovered.'

They left Gormán looking bemused as the old woman showed them to the door, carefully extinguishing the lamp before opening it.

With a whispered 'good luck' they slid once more into the shadows of the township. Again, Eadulf was happy to let Enda take the lead but the way was easier, for this time they kept along the riverbank, passing the entrance to the bridge after checking that the town square remained deserted.

Instead of attempting to follow the main track up to the fortress gates, which stood invitingly open, but with the entrance lit with burning brand torches, Enda took them up the slope above the riverbank to the towering fortress wall. At the foot of the wall was a small ledge-like pathway. The wall enclosed the fortress and palace complex. First, they had to follow the northern wall. Then they must turn to follow the path that curved round the contour of the hill on the eastern side of the fortress, towards the side gate.

'Let's hope Fidelma's plan has worked,' whispered Enda as they approached it – the very gate through which Gormán and Aibell had escaped from the fortress only a few days ago.

Their heart in their mouths, they pushed against it. It moved quietly inwards and they slipped through, all feeling a sense of elation that they had got away with it.

'Take care – there's too much light here,' Enda hissed in disapproval, for several brand torches lit up this area of the fortress. He put his weight against the wooden gate to swing it shut while Eadulf fumbled with the bolts. He took the large key hanging on the nearby hook and turned it in the lock before replacing it on its hook. Then he paused and wiped the sweat from his brow.

'It's a chilly night to be out for a walk, my friends,' came a familiar voice, filled with amusement.

Eadulf and Enda turned with a start. In front of them stood Conrí and the guard commander, Céit. Both men were smiling broadly.

'We . . . we were unable to sleep because of what's happening tomorrow,' Eadulf stammered, knowing he sounded ridiculous. 'We needed some air.'

'Of course you did,' Conrí assured him nonchalantly. 'The lady Fidelma told me you were unwell, friend Eadulf. What better than a walk in the cool night air to regain clarity of thought and purge the evil?'

Céit at his side was nodding agreement as if pleased at his companion's wit.

Eadulf stood silent, wondering if he could bluff it out.

'I hope Enda was of help in resolving the problem and that the breaking dawn will bring a better day,' went on the warlord mildly.

Eadulf frowned; it was as if there was some other meaning in Conrí's words.

'I certainly hope so,' he mumbled.

'Well,' the warlord said pleasantly, 'we had best be on our way; we have duties to perform, Céit. Try not to disturb anyone when you return to your chambers. I am sure the lady Fidelma is anxious for you.'

Eadulf and Enda watched the warriors in bemusement as they turned and strolled away.

Fidelma was not the only one anxiously waiting for them in the guest chamber. Aibell was present, and trembling with anticipation.

'Gormán is safe with Étromma,' Eadulf told her straight away. 'Brother Éladach carried out his tasks exactly as we planned. But when Enda and I returned to the fortress and entered by the side gate, we found Conrí and Céit waiting for us. Their behaviour was very curious.'

'What did they say?' Fidelma frowned. She did not seem surprised when he told her.

'It seems,' she reflected, 'that Conrí was not misleading me when he told me earlier this evening that the last thing Prince Donennach wanted was to see Gormán executed. In fact, he implied that if we could devise a plan of rescue without implicating Donennach, he would look the other way.'

'But will they look the other way when Nannid finds Gormán missing at first light and comes looking for him here?' Enda wanted to know.

'We'll deal with that in the morning. Were you able to subdue the men guarding Gormán?'

'I am afraid we were forced to kill them,' Enda replied bluntly.

'Was there no other alternative?'

Enda shook his head. 'No. It was a case of their lives or ours, lady. Brother Éladach dealt with one. Eadulf thought he had rendered the man unconscious, but he recovered and was about to raise the alarm. I dealt with the other. We left the bodies locked in the hut where they had kept Gormán. With luck they might not be discovered until morning.'

'But is Gormán safe with Étromma?' Aibell pressed anxiously.

'He is as safe there as anywhere,' Enda said. 'The plan was followed and, hopefully, it will be thought that Gormán has fled eastwards towards Cashel.'

Fidelma was not completely convinced. 'Remember that Nannid is not a stupid man,' she cautioned them. 'He must know that Gormán would not leave Aibell behind here. Where Aibell is, there too will Gormán be. I fear that Nannid will descend on Donennach's fortress with such rage that Nebuchadnezzar in his fury will seem like a lamb by comparison.'

Aibell looked bewildered. 'Neb . . . who?'

'Just a story from the old scriptures that Nannid is so fond of,' Fidelma told the girl. 'More importantly, tomorrow is going to test my ingenuity and I shall need all your support.'

# CHAPTER TWENTY

⊘

E ven before Fidelma and her companions had completed their morning toilette, they had heard a bell ringing frantically from the abbey in the township. Pandemonium had erupted.

'You had better remain here in this chamber,' Fidelma told Aibell. 'Keep the door locked. That is, until we discover what is going on. You will obviously be the first target for Abbot Nannid if he is as angry as I think he will be.'

Fidelma, Eadulf and Enda made their way down to the great hall. They were surprised at how few people were gathered there. The next thing they noticed was that the food, which the attendants had laid on the table, had been left more or less untouched. A worried-looking Prince Donennach was standing having an anxious exchange with Brehon Faolchair, while Conrí stood by with a look of suppressed amusement on his face. Prior Cuán and his steward Brother Tuamán were seated with Brother Mac Raith, who was absently picking at a bowl of fruit. All eyes turned on them at their entrance.

The sound of the abbey bell was still resounding in discordant notes. Before they could speak, Prince Donennach burst out: 'Have you not heard? Gormán has escaped!'

'We have just risen,' Fidelma replied blandly, whilst attempting to look absolutely dumbfounded. 'Gormán has escaped?'

'Yes, and he has killed his guards in the process.'

Brehon Faolchair intervened. 'Where is the girl Aibell?'

'Aibell is upstairs in the chamber I am now sharing with her and where she has been all night,' Fidelma replied carefully. 'The poor girl has passed a terrible night. I must run and tell her the news. Why do you want to know?'

'I was asked to find her and to constrain her,' explained the Brehon.

Fidelma looked at him coldly. 'Who asked you to do such a thing?'

'Abbot Nannid,' Faolchair said hesitantly.

'Surely you do not take orders from Abbot Nannid!'

'You give me your word that she has been with you in your chamber all night?'

'I am a *dálaigh* and sister to the King of Muman. Do you doubt my word?' Fidelma bridled. 'I shall defend any threat made against her.' She turned to Enda and gave him instructions in a firm tone. 'Take some food for Aibell and yourself, and stand guard at the chamber. No one is to enter without my permission . . . *no one*.'

Prince Donennach looked embarrassed as Enda hurried away to carry out her orders. 'There is no need for that, Fidelma. We accept your word.'

'I am concerned that Abbot Nannid is allowed to make free with his orders, telling your Brehon what he should do.'

'I merely wondered where the girl was,' protested Brehon Faolchair. 'You must admit that it is reasonable for Abbot Nannid to wish to know her whereabouts in the circumstances. The fact that Gormán has escaped again – and this time killed his guards – puts a serious complexion on this matter.'

Fidelma spoke clearly and coldly. 'I would remind you, Brehon Faolchair, that under our law, Abbot Nannid has acted illegally. Gormán should have been handed back to your custody yesterday until such time as we made a proper examination of the facts. The abbot refused to release him, even when given a clear order and opportunity. He held Gormán illegally and threatened to execute him illegally.'

'But Gormán killed his guards!'

'The deaths of two mercenaries – thieves and doubtless murderers themselves, men from Gláed's bunch of ravening wolves – does not overly excite me. I would argue that these killings were lawful as a means of self-defence. These men were part of the group that killed a peaceful woodsman, his son and the son's wife. Do not ask me to have sympathy for them. Had there been an opportunity, I would have had them apprehended for the killings under our law and not Nannid's law. Anyway, under our law, I would argue that by killing them, Gormán, who was going to be illegally executed, was only acting in self-defence, so no crime has been committed.'

Conrí had begun to grin in approval at her response but stopped as Brehon Faolchair glared at him.

'I am sure that Abbot Nannid will bring accusations of conspiracy in this matter,' the Brehon said heavily.

'Let him do so,' shrugged Fidelma. 'What does he think? That I and Eadulf, Enda and Aibell rose in the middle of the night, went to his so-called abbey, tapped on the door, were admitted, went and released Gormán, killing the guards by the by, and then came back here and went calmly back to sleep again?'

Eadulf erupted in a bout of coughing.

'No chance of that,' Conrí piped up. 'I was with Ceit in the fortress last night and know you were all here during the night.' The warlord actually allowed one of his eyelids to half-close in an approximation of a wink.

'Personally, I hope Gormán is well on his way to Cashel.' Prior Cuán spoke for the first time, helping himself to an apple.

His steward, Brother Tuamán, gazed at him aghast. 'I must ask you to remember that this Gormán murdered Abbot Ségdae.'

At that moment, there was a disturbance at the doors of the great hall which were flung open. The gaunt figure of Abbot Nannid stormed in – there was no other expression to describe his entrance, so Eadulf thought. His black cloak was flapping like giant raven's wings, his thin features were twisted in a scowl. Almost running behind him was his steward, Brother Cuineáin, clearly out of breath. Behind them came Ceit, the commander of the guard. Ceit started to make an apology to Prince Donennach but the abbot cut him short.

'Where is he?' the man thundered, coming to a halt before Prince Donennach. Brehon Faolchair moved forward to stand between the abbot and his prince as if some physical threat was taking place.

'Remember that you are addressing the Prince of the Uí Fidgente,' he warned, but his tone was nervous.

'The murderer could not have overcome my guards without help,' the abbot shouted. 'He is being hidden somewhere and I shall personally track him down. Where is his woman?'

The last question was directed specifically at Fidelma, who decided not to reply.

Brehon Faolchair's face reddened. 'I must ask you to speak in tones of respect before your prince, Nannid of Mungairit. As for the wife of Gormán of Cashel, she is in a safe place and has been so since last night.'

The abbot blinked rapidly as if he were not expecting the response.

'I demand that she be turned over to me,' he snarled. 'I'll soon make her tell me where the murderer is hiding. I demand it by the law.'

'To which law do you refer?' Fidelma said. 'I seem to recall that you have rejected the ruling of our law in favour of your own rules.'

'What were your rules, Abbot Nannid of Mungairit?' It was Prior Cuán who met his fellow prelate's bluster with a raised eyebrow. 'You held Gormán captive and so you declared it was you who could decide his fate. *Qui tenet teneat, qui dolet doleat*,' he murmured. 'He who holds may go on holding. He who complains may go on complaining. In other words, the law is with the person who is in possession, not those seeking possession. That is your declared law and you must accept it now that it applies here.'

'There has been a conspiracy.' Abbot Nannid's voice was still high-pitched in anger. 'I will get to the bottom of it.'

'Abbot Nannid has finally said something with which I agree,' Fidelma rejoined. She went to the table and calmly poured herself a mug of apple cider.

Uncertain looks were cast in her direction. Even the abbot seemed confused and his angry rantings died away.

'What is it that you agree with?' asked Prince Donennach, puzzled.

'That there is a conspiracy here,' Fidelma stated.

There was another pause before Brehon Faolchair spoke. 'Are you saying that there was a conspiracy to help Gormán escape?'

'That was not what I had in mind,' replied Fidelma. 'I refer to the wider conspiracy to overthrow Prince Donennach.'

'Are you accusing the Abbot of Mungairit of such a conspiracy, apart from his disagreement with us about the law?' Prince Donennach demanded.

'I am not accusing the Abbot of Mungairit,' replied Fidelma with emphasis. 'I am accusing Nannid, a *former* Abbot of Mungairit.'

There were gasps of astonishment.

'What folly are you bent on now?' the man sneered.

'I am accusing you, Nannid, of conspiracy. I am not accusing the Abbot of Mungairit.'

'Fidelma,' Prince Donennach was torn between annoyance and intrigue, 'I would have a care with your words. Nannid is distantly related to my own family of the Uí Fidgente and has been Abbot at Mungairit for many years.'

'But not for six months.' It was Conrí who intervened.

PETER TREMAYNE

Everyone swung round to the tall warlord except Fidelma, who carried on sipping her drink.

'Explain yourself,' Prince Donennach snapped.

'I'll do better,' replied Conrí, and he motioned to Ceit with the words, 'Bring in our latest arrival.' Then he turned back to the prince. 'It was Fidelma who finally prompted me into doing something which one of us should have done long ago. The abbot has been with us here for six months, together with his steward.'

'I undertook to build up the religious community here and create an abbey that Prince Donennach would be proud to have under the walls of his palace!' Abbot Nannid exclaimed but with less confidence than before.

Conrí heaved a sigh. 'Had we done what the lady Fidelma suggested, we might be in a different situation today.'

'And what did she suggest?' asked Prior Cuán, obviously intrigued.

'That we send someone to Mungairit to ask some questions.'

'But for what purpose?' Brehon Faolchair appeared baffled.

'Will you explain, lady?' asked Conrí.

'It's very simple. I was surprised that the religious community close by the chapel founded by Nechta in the township had suddenly surrounded itself with walls. The last time I was here, it was an open community indivisible from the township. I asked Brother Éladach the reason. He told me that Nannid and his steward had arrived six months ago, claiming authority as Abbot of Mungairit and senior bishop of the Uí Fidgente. He instructed walls to be built to enclose the community, renaming it the Abbey of Nechta. He then imposed the Penitentials as its rules – those rules we have been discussing so laboriously. The community accepted them solely because of his proclaimed authority, and on that basis alone.'

'But we know that he is Abbot of Mungairit,' pressed Brehon Faolchair.

'He *was* Abbot of Mungairit,' emphasised Fidelma. 'Did no one think it strange that the abbot of such a great and reputable abbey was spending so much time here?'

'Dún Eochair Mháigh is the capital of the Uí Fidgente,' Prince Donennach protested. 'He had the right to spend time here.'

'He had the right as abbot and senior bishop of this territory. Yet is it not strange that he spent so long away from his abbey? That thought occurred to Brother Éladach, but when he raised it, Nannid came up with the notion that he was going to use this venue to invite Abbot Ségdae to come here to discuss the ecclesiastical problems of our people following the peace agreed by Prince Donennach and my brother, the King.'

'Are you saying that the council was merely an excuse for him to remain here?' Brehon Faolchair asked.

'Not an excuse but a justification. And yet it did not ring true. Imagine abandoning Mungairit, that great abbey and school founded by Nessan, who had been appointed by Patrick. Yet Nannid came here to spend an entire six months trying to make an open community into an enclosed one.'

'Why shouldn't I do so?' demanded Nannid, summoning up an effort to defend himself.

'Several days ago I asked Conrí to send to Mungairit to make inquiries. Last night he reported that the rider had returned.'

At that moment, the doors of the great hall opened and Ceit entered. By his side was an athletic-looking young man, together with a young religieux. Brother Cuineáin's features had assumed a ghastly pallor. And Abbot Nannid's thin lips were almost invisible.

'Do you wish to hear the words from Mungairit?' asked Fidelma.

There was a silence which Conrí took as permission to speak.

'My messenger will confirm these words, as will the young brother from Mungairit who arrived with him. This is Brother Feradach. You will recall that in the month of Cet Gaimrid, the first of the winter months, Fidelma uncovered a conspiracy which emanated from Mungairit. The plan, as you know, intended the assassination of both Prince Donennach and King Colgú of Cashel. Gláed was part of that plot but the main instigator of it was Lorcán, son of Prince Eóghanán.

'It had been wrongly assumed that Eoghanán and his two sons were slain at the battle of Cnoc Áine. But Eoghanán had a third son, Lugna, the identical twin brother of Lorcán, who had entered Mungairit as a pious youth. Lorcán had in fact survived Cnoc Áine. To further his ambitions, he then slew his brother, Lugna, and assumed his role at Mungairit while concocting his evil plot of revenge. The lady Fidelma and Eadulf were there, as was I, when the final revelations were made.'

Brehon Faolchair was nodding irritably. 'Yes, yes. This is known and has been recorded by our scribes.'

'It is also recorded that Gláed was handed over to *his* brother Artgal to be taken back to Sliabh Luachra for punishment. We now know that he escaped and killed Artgal – and now leads his band of ravening wolves, who are currently encamped only a short distance from the walls of this fortress,' pointed out Conrí.

'Furthermore, it is known that Lorcán was brought here to await my judgement following my return from my visit to the High King,' added Prince Donennach. 'Yet before I reached here, he contrived to escape . . .'

'And was mortally wounded by my men, when he failed to surrender,' ended Conrí.

'That is all very well,' snapped Brehon Faolchair. 'But my understanding was that Fidelma judged that Abbot Nannid was innocent of any involvement.'

'I could find no direct link to Lorcán's conspiracy,' agreed Fidelma. 'I did, indeed, give Nannid the benefit of the doubt.'

'However,' Conrí continued, 'the *derbhfine* of the abbey, the council of Mungairit, later met and decided that there were many other questions to be answered by Abbot Nannid and his steward. The council decreed that Nannid was not worthy to continue as

Abbot, nor was Cuineáin worthy to act as steward under such circumstances. Both were to be banished from the abbey and should seek their own salvation.'

'Why was Prince Donennach not informed of this?' demanded Brehon Faolchair. 'Mungairit is not at the ends of the earth.'

'It was learned that Nannid had come to Prince Donennach and, with some naivety, it was thought that Nannid would have explained all to his relative. The question of sending a special messenger to the prince did not occur to the council of the abbey.'

'Prove I am not the Abbot of Mungairit!' Nannid challenged them, making a final attempt at dominance.

Conrí pointed to the young religieux at the door. 'Perhaps we shall hear more from Brother Feradach of Mungairit. By the way, he is the religieux whom Nannid was to meet at the Hill of Truth. He tells me that the purpose of his meeting there with Nannid was to receive money that Nannid owed to Mungairit.'

The young religieux moved forward. At that precise moment, the sound of urgent trumpet blasts shook the hall. A warrior burst in, saw Ceit and spoke urgently to him. Ceit rapped out some orders and sent the man running off. The guard commander then turned to them with an expression of dismay.

'You will have to delay this matter. Gláed's ravening wolves are gathered at the opposite side of the river. They are ready to cross the bridge; lined up for an assault. I've ordered the fortress gates to be shut and our warriors to turn out.'

Prince Donennach's warriors were gathered along the walkways at the top of the walls that fronted the fortress, each armed with bows and quivers of arrows. The main gates had been shut and barred. Prince Donennach had climbed to the walkway above the gates with Conrí and Ceit at his side. Whatever weakness he had displayed in handling his kinsman, there was no doubting the young man's courage in battle. He was a fighting prince who preferred to lead his men. Brehon Faolchair had nervously taken shelter nearby. Fidelma and Eadulf, having sent word to Enda to continue to guard Aibell, had decided to take their positions with Donennach. Brother Tuamán and Brother Mac Raith had also joined them to observe the threatening marauders. Only Prior Cuán remained below in the courtyard for it was difficult for him to climb up to the walls with his disabled leg.

Conrí had ordered some of his warriors to confine Abbot Nannid and Brother Cuineáin in the great hall to await the outcome of what was about to happen.

Fidelma viewed the scene with some foreboding. There was no way of defending the township or the walled community of Nechta. Already there was panic and confusion as men, women and children ran hither and thither to find shelter. Mothers were screaming at their wandering children, others seemed to be standing, paralysed in despair. There would be nowhere to hide once the marauders crossed the bridge. It was obvious that the township would be attacked first.

The question of how the marauders had managed to get so close to the town was answered as they scrutinised the lines of mounted raiders on the far side of the bridge across the river. A line of nine men with arms bound behind them were being marched in front of a couple of horsemen across the bridge and into the main square. They were made to turn in a line facing the fortress and halted. Ceit viewed them bitterly. 'My sentinels, each one surprised and caught. That is why we had no warning. Gláed is obviously mocking us by bringing them here to slaughter them in front of our eyes before he attacks.'

It became clear that the marauders intended no surprise attack, for three riders now detached themselves from the main body and trotted their horses across the bridge, swinging round to the path that led up to the fortress gates. One of the three riders was a *techtaire*, a herald, who rode in front of the others. He carried a long blue silk banner dancing in the wind from its staff – and on the blue silk they could make out the figure of a raven. Behind him rode a second man carrying a bronze war trumpet which he now blew several times as they approached. The third rider was obviously their leader.

'That's unusual,' Conrí muttered. 'The ravening wolves of Sliabh Luachra don't usually announce their presence before they strike.'

'What are they doing?' Prince Donennach asked, licking at his dry lips.

'I think they want to speak to us,' replied Conrí in surprise.

'Keep the gates closed.' Prince Donennach was suspicious. 'They can talk from below.'

The three horsemen halted as they came abreast of the tall pillar stone with its ancient Ogham inscription naming Dún Eochair Mháigh as the 'house of kings'. The riders positioned themselves before the tall wooden gates.

'The leader seems familiar,' Fidelma started to say when her words were interrupted by another blast on the war trumpet.

Conrí leaned over the parapet to call down: 'We can see you. We do not recognise your standard although you proclaim on it the Goddess of Death and Battles; clearly you are men of Sliabh Luachra. What do you seek here?'

'My lord wishes to speak with Prince Donennach of the Uí Fidgente,' called the trumpet-bearer.

Prince Donennach moved to Conrí's side after the warlord made a careful sweep to identify any hidden bowmen; there were none.

'I am he,' called Prince Donennach.

The leader moved his horse forward a little. He wore a bright, multi-coloured cloak. He removed his polished metal war helmet, revealing a mass of long black hair which had a shimmer of blue in the early morning sun. The man was handsome, with pale skin, bright blue eyes which stared up, fathomless like the restless blue of a summer sea.

Fidelma let out a gasp, followed by an exclamation from Eadulf, for it was Deogaire, the nephew of Fidelma's old mentor Brother Conchobhar. It was Deogaire who had once rescued Aibell from the fortress of Fidaig, father of Gláed of the Sliabh Luachra. But Fidelma knew enough not to intervene in the ritual that was unfolding.

'Who are you, who threatens my fortress?' called Prince Donennach.

The young man sat back on his horse and chuckled. 'I am no threat to you or to your fortress, nor to the township behind me, Donennach, Prince of the Uí Fidgente. I am Deogaire, lord of the people of the Sliabh Luachra.'

They saw that he held a sack in his left hand, and this he abruptly tossed to the ground so that something bloody and gruesome rolled out of it to lie in the dust of the track before the fortress gates. Heads strained to see what it was.

'In life, my friends,' Deogaire called up, 'that was Gláed, brigand chief of the Sliabh Luachra. I bring you his head, Donennach, to show that he is no longer a threat to you.'

'How did Gláed meet his end, and for what cause did he perish?' questioned the prince.

'He died because he was a usurper; a murderer of his own father and his own brother. He raided, raped and murdered, and led his people into suffering and slaughter. He died because I recently returned to Sliabh Luachra seeking justice for myself and all those he had wronged. I wished to seek account of the effusion of blood that he had caused and the lives made wretched by him. When I caught up with him at the Hill of Truth, I challenged him to the *fír cómlainn*, the truth of combat. One man and one sword pitted against another. The gods were on my side.'

'The gods?' exclaimed Brother Tuamán with an exaggerated expression of shock. '*Deus salva nos*! This man is not a Christian! We cannot trust him.'

'I do not hold to the New Faith,' Deogaire called back, overhearing the steward's exclamation. 'I adhere to the ancient Faith and am possessed of the *imbas foronsai*, the gift of prophecy which sustains and comforts me.'

Fidelma grimaced at Eadulf. 'At least that is the Deogaire we know of old,' she whispered.

'So why do you approach this fortress with the ravening wolves of Sliabh Luachra?' demanded Prince Donennach.

'To show you that these are now *my* ravening wolves and they will return to their lairs. The gods helped me defeat the pretensions of Gláed in token of which, I bring you his head to dispose of as you will, in respect or contempt. If you have memory of our old religion, it is believed that the soul resides in the head. Thus our ancestors, when they slew their enemies, cut off the head so that the soul might freely speed to the Otherworld and no longer haunt the living.'

'I have heard of the custom, Deogaire of Sliabh Luachra, and so we accept your token,' replied the prince. 'But I see you hold nine of my warriors bound in the square behind you. What is your intention with them?'

Deogaire raised his hand. One of the horsemen guarding the prisoners leaped from his horse, drew his sword and went along the line, swiftly cutting their bonds before remounting. The former sentinels stood rubbing their sore wrists and looking around in confusion and shame.

'Poor sentinels though they may be,' Deogaire called, amusement in his voice, 'I return them to you so that you may train them more thoroughly.' Then he untied a smaller bag from his saddle bow and this he also threw to the ground as he had Gláed's head.

'This is for the community of this township. It is the gold and silver pieces paid for the person of Gormán by an unscrupulous cleric. It is returned to show that no longer will those who now serve me accept blood money. Had I reached the Hill of Truth earlier, it would not have been paid in the first place and Gormán of Cashel would simply have been freed. You may also rest assured that the men who supported Gláed and were responsible for the death and destruction visited by his raids have met the consequences of their actions. One of them was once a guard in your fortress. Your trust in him was wrongly placed. Truly, Prince of the Uí Fidgente, what with your useless sentinels and your treacherous guards, there is a lack of judgement in your fortress. I do not need the gift of prophecy, the *imbas forasnai*, to tell you that you should have a care of those you deem close to you.'

Prince Donennach was speechless. It took him a few moments before he called down to Deogaire: 'The gold and silver is accepted and will be returned to those it belongs to.'

'Then I will depart with my men, but before I do . . .' Deogaire drew his sword from his sheath and held it aloft. 'This is the sword of Deogaire of Sliabh Luahcra, by which I have claimed the chieftainship of all the people who dwell there.'

Still holding aloft the sword, Deogaire nudged his horse close to the Ogham-inscribed stone pillar and with a quick downwards sweep, he smashed the broad blade against it. The blade snapped in two. Deorgaire then dropped the half that remained in his hand.

'Witness, Prince Donennach of the Uí Fidgente – witness that I have broken my war sword against the pillar of your fortress and declare the *cáirde chlaidib* . . . the agreement of the sword. This is done in symbolic act to show that there is a pact of peace between us. Is it peace?'

Prince Donennach had understood the ancient ritual. 'Let it be peace,' he echoed gladly.

Deogaire lifted his hand in salute. He seemed about to turn away, then, as if in afterthought, he raised his head back to those looking down on him.

'I see that the lady Fidelma is with you.'

Fidelma moved to the side of Prince Donennach and called down: 'I am here, Deogaire.'

'I heard that you were here to defend Gormán from the charge of which he is unjustly accused. I know it is unjust for I knew Gormán at Cashel and my *imbas foronsai* tells me that he is innocent.'

'Unfortunately, prophecy is not a witness,' Fidelma returned with a wan smile.

'But it tells me that you will triumph in your defence. Word has reached me that he is safe from the unscrupulous cleric. Is Aibell also safe with you?'

'She is safe.'

'I heard that she had married Gormán. She deserves a good life after the anguish and ordeals suffered as a bond-servant in Sliabh Luachra. Gormán is a good man and they have chosen well of each other. Give them my good wishes and, when you have secured Gormán's innocence, should their paths come to Sliabh Luachra they will find mention of my name will ensure hospitality.'

Fidelma hesitated, wondering whether to explain the situation, but then decided against it, for she felt that the situation would not be resolved.

'I will do this,' she promised him.

'Then give my salutations also to my venerable uncle, Conchobhar. Tell him how things fare with his sister's son, who will no longer be an embarrassment to him.'

With that, Deogaire turned, and with his trumpeter and standard-bearer at his sides, he trotted back down the slope to the township square. The three rode back over the bridge across the river. The waiting men of the Sliabh Luachra moved aside to let them through and then joined their horses in a column behind them. Inside the fortress, no one said anything until the band of men had finally disappeared along the track to the south-western hills.

Eadulf was shaking his head. 'I hardly imagined young Deogaire as a noble and leader of men. I looked on him as just a mischief-making mystic.'

'Stranger things have happened,' Fidelma commented. 'Although we should have had some fore-knowledge of his capabilities after

Aibell told us how he had rescued her from the slavery of Fidaig's house.'

'Is what he said about souls and heads truly your ancient belief before the New Faith?' Eadulf asked.

'It was central to the belief of life in the Otherworld. Some in remote places still cling to the old beliefs. We are told that our great heroes in ancient times would ride into battle with the heads of their foes dangling from their war chariots. But those days are long distant.'

'Not so long ago, it seems,' observed Eadulf as Conrí was ordering one of his men to go and collect Gláed's head. 'And is there truly meaning in that agreement of the sword business?'

Fidelma nodded. 'Some of the ancient rituals of our past are still there to remind us of what we were. At least the threat from Sliabh Luachra is no longer a problem.'

Brehon Faolchair overheard her. 'That is so,' he said, 'but there is still the matter of Gormán to be resolved. You might have diminished Abbot Nannid's authority but you have not eliminated his influence. There is the question of Gormán's guilt remaining and how he should be punished. As Abbot Nannid has said, he may no longer be the Abbot of Mungairit, but now he claims to be Abbot of Nechta. More importantly, he is still of the Uí Fidgente bloodline and influential in this territory.'

Fidelma glanced up at the summer sky.

'When the sun reaches its zenith, call all those with an interest in this matter to assemble in the great hall. It should be declared that a Brehon court is convened. At that time and place I will argue the truth of what really happened in Abbot Ségdae's chamber, how he met his death and why.'

Brehon Faolchair stood in astonishment for a moment. 'Are you ready to put forward such arguments?'

'I knew how the killing was done almost immediately.' Fidelma sounded positive, and Eadulf knew she would not sound so without good cause. 'The real problem was also trying to show why, as well as identifying who else was involved, apart from the killer.'

'Who else?' The Brehon frowned.

'Do not worry. I presume that Gormán can attend as the accused protected by the court and without fear of harm from Nannid?'

'So you do know where Gormán is?'

'Let us just say that I will pass the word that he should attend and I am sure he will.'

'I understand,' the Brehon acknowledged. 'And yes, he will be protected.'

'I'll go to fetch him,' Eadulf offered.

'I will go also, lady,' said Conrí, who had been listening. 'Don't forget that Nannid still has two of Gláed's men in the abbey complex. There were four of them and two were slain, so we must find the others. I'll get some of my men to flush them out.'

'I had forgotten that,' Fidelma confessed.

'What do you want done with them?'

'Just strip them of their weapons, and send them along the track in the direction of Sliabh Luachra,' Fidelma instructed. 'You can inform them that they have a new chieftain in Deogaire.'

'Then we will deal with them first and I will inform friend Eadulf once it is safe to show us where Gormán is.' Conrí raised his hand in acknowledgement and called to some warriors to attend him before setting off to the Abbey of Nechta.

'Do you really know what happened?' Eadulf asked Fidelma as they headed back to the great hall.

'I can show that Gormán is innocent,' she replied confidently.

'Although Nannid is no longer Abbot of Mungairit, can you prove he is behind this conspiracy?'

'On the contrary,' Fidelma replied with a slight smile. 'Nannid is *not* at the centre of this web of intrigue.'

'What? You mean there is someone else?'

'Of that, I was never more certain,' she replied with emphasis.

# CHAPTER TWENTY-ONE

❧

The great hall of Prince Donennach was not exactly crowded, but those who attended made up for the numbers with vociferous excitement. Ceit the commander of the household guard had placed ten of his men in strategic places throughout the hall. He and two of his men were stationed behind the official carved oak chairs of office on the dais. The right-hand one was for the prince, and the left-hand one for Airmid, his sister in her role as *tanaise*.

Just below the dais, Brehon Faolchair sat as usual. He would formally conduct the business of the gathering as it was now a court of law.

The long table reserved for the feasting had been removed to one side and benches had been placed to the left of the hall. On these were gathered the potential witnesses and behind them, observers. The elderly Étromma had taken her seat alongside an anxious-looking Aibell. In the same group of seats sat Prior Cuán, his steward Brother Tuamán, the scribe Brother Mac Raith, a scowling Abbot Nannid, his steward Brother Cuineáin and Brother Éladach, the doorkeeper of the Abbey of Nechta. Next to him was the young Brother Feradach of Mungairit and the warrior, Lachtna. On the right hand of the hall, Fidelma and Eadulf were seated at a small table alongside a scribe appointed by Brehon Faolchair to record the hearing.

Gormán, looking pale and strained, had been escorted from his hiding place. His appointed seat was directly opposite Brehon Faolchair. Conrí and Enda stood on either side of him, with Socht behind. Aibell kept looking towards him with a desperate combination of love and fear. Apart from an initial reassuring glance to her when he had entered, Gormán now stood with his gaze fixed on Brehon Faolchair.

Brehon Faolchair scrutinised the occupants of the hall before he had a whispered exchange with Prince Donennach. The latter, looking tense, raised a hand in signal and a trumpeter at the far end of the hall put his instrument to his lips and gave three resounding blasts. The clamour of the gathering died almost immediately. Brehon Faolchair then rose to his feet.

'May I remind all present that this is a legal hearing which has been called according to the law of the Five Kingdoms. The first business of the court is to hear the charge against Gormán of Cashel as to his guilt or otherwise of the murder of Abbot Ségdae of Imleach and any other matters arising from that death such as the deaths of Ciarnat of this place and Brother Máel Anfaid of Imleach. This court has admitted that its preliminary hearing of Gormán for the murder of Abbot Ségdae was not constituted in the proper manner and hence we have accepted Fidelma of Cashel's plea for this retrial. All legal niceties have now been made and agreed upon.'

At once Abbot Nannid rose in protest. 'If we must go through this farce again, there are two other deaths connected with this matter that need to be considered. The accused killed two guards when he escaped from the custody of my abbey last night.'

Brehon Faolchair was not sympathetic.

'Since Gormán was being held illegally under the law of the Five Kingdoms, it has been rightfully argued that the killing of the two brigands from Sliabh Luachra who held him was an act of self-defence. Should Gormán be judged guilty, there may be a possibility of appealing this matter later. Are you ready to state your case, Fidelma?'

Faces turned expectantly as Fidelma rose to her feet and bowed her head towards the Brehon.

'My mentor, the renowned Brehon Morann of Tara, often used the maxim: truth is great and will prevail,' she began slowly. 'In this matter, the truth has taken a while to prevail. What was the basis of the charge against Gormán? Let me remind you. Gormán was found in a chamber claimed to have been locked from the inside because the key of the chamber was found still inside. There was a dagger by his hand and before him was the bloody body of Abbot Ségdae of Imleach. Gormán says he was knocked out from a blow that came from behind him. There is evidence by bruising on his head that he did receive such a blow. This was discounted, according to witnesses, because there was no way another person could have entered the room. The blow was explained away as having been made by Abbot Ségdae as he tried to defend himself with his staff of office. Even mortally wounded, it is said that he gave Gormán that blow. No logical motive for the killing was presented – except that it was claimed that Gormán had arrived for that fatal meeting in an angry state.'

She paused and looked thoughtfully at the witness benches. Eadulf was aware that, in presenting her cases, Fidelma liked to make dramatic pauses.

'Within a short time of my arriving here I found there was another way in which Abbot Ségdae could have been slain in that room which was supposedly locked from the inside.'

Loud murmurs of surprise rose from the onlookers.

'If Gormán was innocent then it became fairly obvious as to the identity of the killer – the one person who had the opportunity to do the deed. But I had to question whether it was a deed done by a single person? If so, what was their motive? If several people were involved, then the motive grew even more dark and ominous.

Instead of simply clearing Gormán, the purpose of my investigation had to be to pursue the questions that then arose. It is often easy to find out "how", but harder to find out "why" – and it was the "why" that became essential to revealing the complete truth. Without answering the "why" it would not have been possible to clear Gormán to everyone's satisfaction.'

She paused again as if to consider her arguments before resuming. 'It is easy to see the purpose of implicating Gormán in this crime. It was to create dissension between the Uí Fidgente and Cashel once more. If Abbot Nannid had had his way and had Gormán executed under these alien Penitentials, it would certainly have provoked a demand for retribution from Cashel. If Gormán was released, it could provoke internal conflict among the Uí Fidgente and perhaps the overthrow of Prince Donennach, who would be presented as someone afraid of incurring Cashel's displeasure. That was at the basis of a curious conspiracy.'

Abbot Nannid had been sitting rigidly, staring at her. Now he rose, his stance threatening. 'Are you accusing me of Ségdae's murder?' he thundered. 'If so . . .'

Brehon Faolchair interrupted sharply. 'You will be silent while the *dálaigh* is stating her case. That is her right under law. You will have plenty of opportunity for rebuttal later.'

Ignoring the outburst, Fidelma went on: 'Let us go through matters carefully. Gormán and his wife Aibell while visiting her uncle heard some disturbing news from travelling merchants. The news was that Gláed, by killing his brother, had made himself chief of the brigands of Sliabh Luachra and was preparing to raid the Uí Fidgente territory. More importantly the merchants told Gormán that Gláed was involved in serving some Uí Fidgente noble in a plot to depose Prince Donennach.

'Gormán came here to warn Prince Donennach but, as he could not identify the noble, he kept that matter back to seek further advice. By coincidence, having heard that Abbot Ségdae was staying here, Gormán, who knew him well, went to see him for that advice. Meanwhile, the prince sent for his warlord, Conrí, to organise his troops against Gláed.

'The plot was so complicated that I have had to consider whether I should begin with the act itself or with the conspirators – or even with the motivation of those conspirators.' She decided: 'I shall begin with the act.'

In the deathly silence that had settled in the hall, Eadulf could imagine one might hear a beetle scuttling over the floor.

'Gormán went to see Abbot Ségdae as a friend to ask what he should do about a conspiracy involving a noble of Prince Donennach's house. It was nothing to do with Prince Donennach dismissing his warning about Gláed. Stories that the prince had done so and thus angered Gormán were completely untrue. It was a lie that was purposely told to Brother Máel Anfaid, who then told Ciarnat so that it would create a picture of a man in frustration and anger entering the abbot's chamber. It was a weak attempt at a motive.

'Gormán entered the chamber and almost immediately the plot swung into action. The door had been left unlocked. The killer entered immediately behind Gormán. It was said that if the killer had been behind Gormán, the abbot would have seen him and uttered a warning.'

There were mutterings of agreement from some of the witnesses.

'Well, the abbot *did* see his killer and was not alarmed, for that person had every right to be there. We are told that the abbot said, "Oh yes, you want these?" and glanced down at his table. That was the last thing Gormán remembered before he received a blow on the head – back or side, it had the same effect. He was knocked out.

'This tells me that Ségdae knew the person who had entered the chamber and was standing behind Gormán. Not only did he know the person, but it was someone who the abbot thought had come to pick up some document or letters. He looked for them on his table – hence his words.

'As Gormán fell unconscious, the assailant went forward and stabbed the abbot to death. Then the scene was arranged. The dagger was placed by Gormán's hand and the abbot's staff was prominently set so that it looked as if he had tried to defend himself, managing to stun Gormán before he succumbed to death. Eadulf and I examined that staff and realised it could not have been the weapon that knocked Gormán out for it was incapable of inflicting the injury in the manner he received it. Having arranged the scene, the assailant left.'

'The main weakness in your account, Fidelma,' interrupted Brehon Faolchair, 'is that the door of the chamber had been locked from the inside. There was nowhere to hide when Ségdae's steward and the warrior Lachtna burst into the locked chamber. Lachtna found the key behind the door where it must have fallen when the door was forced open.'

'The door was locked from the outside,' Fidelma contradicted with confidence.

'But the key was on the inside!' Lachtna shouted from his seat. 'I found it. Do you call me a liar?'

He was immediately rebuked for the interruption by Brehon Faolchair, who said to Fidelma, 'The key was certainly found on the inside of the locked chamber. You will have to explain this miracle.'

'It was no miracle,' Fidelma assured him. 'It was a clever idea but not clever enough. The door was old and had several knot-holes in it. I borrowed the key from you, Brehon Faolchair, to experiment with my idea. Sure enough, I was able to close the door, push the key through a knot-hole and find it fallen in exactly the same place where Lachtna found it – where he was *meant* to find it by the real killer.'

'You said the abbot's staff could not have knocked Gormán out,' Brehon Faolchair said, when he could make himself heard above the noisy reaction of the gathering.

'True. Another mistake by the killer. Had the silver top impacted on the flesh hard enough to render Gormán senseless, it would have lacerated the skin and caused much bloodshed. In fact, there was just a bump and a bruise, as witnesses swore – but no blood. Had the wooden end been used, then such a blow would have splintered it. This did not happen. The staff was made of a thin yew wood.' Again she paused before announcing, 'I can tell you that the actual implement that knocked Gormán unconscious was a blackthorn stick.' She glanced at Prior Cuán. 'I am afraid it was Prior Cuán's blackthorn stick.'

Prior Cuán turned a shocked face to her.

'Are you accusing . . .?' he gasped, becoming speechless.

'No, of course not,' she said at once. 'You have two sticks, so you told me. One is the knob-headed blackthorn and the other is of chestnut wood. Can you remember which one you were using, the evening Abbot Ségdae was killed?'

Cuán glanced down at his stick with a puzzled frown. It was Brehon Faolchair who intervened.

'I must bear witness here, for on that evening Prior Cuán was discussing some matters with me. I remember I had previously seen him with a blackthorn – but that evening he was using the stick he carries now, which is made of chestnut wood.'

'That blackthorn was left in your chamber that evening,' Fidelma nodded. 'You had left it leaning in a corner. You have a habit of leaving whichever one of your sticks that does not come readily to hand propped up in a corner when you leave your chamber. It was so easy for the killer to pick it up, use it and replace it in your chamber afterwards.'

'A plausible story – but without witnesses it is still conjecture,' warned Brehon Faolchair.

'We will get there,' Fidelma assured him. 'Yet it is a long and complicated path that I have had to travel. Very well we have done with the "how" and we must turn our attention to the "why" before we come to the "who". As I have said, these events were part of a conspiracy to draw the Uí Fidgente into war – either among themselves or with Cashel. In whichever case, this would ensure that Prince Donennach would be perceived as a weak ruler and one that needed to be replaced.'

'So you are claiming that Abbot Nannid was behind this?' intervened Prince Donennach. 'He is of the bloodline and yet was the person stirring up the dissension?'

'He certainly became the obvious suspect,' Fidelma said. As the abbot started to rise from his seat, his face choleric, she smiled cynically and went on, 'But he was too obvious. Abbot Nannid is not a subtle man. It is true that he is a descendant of the Uí Chóirpi Aebda and therefore could claim to be a legitimate successor to Prince Donennach. But, as we know, Nannid is also a religious fanatic. He holds these new Penitential concepts dear. He has demonstrated that he does not accept the laws of this country – therefore why would he accept its laws of succession?'

'I protest!' shouted Nannid.

'Your protest will be noted but, for the moment, it is the truth that we are after,' replied Brehon Faolchair. He motioned Fidelma to continue.

'We now know that Nannid was dismissed as Abbot of Mungairit six months ago after the first conspiracy was discovered at that abbey. At the same time, Brother Cuineáin was also dismissed as steward. I had not judged them guilty of involvement in that conspiracy but only being ignorant of it. The council of the abbey later decided that this brought the abbey into disrepute and thus they were both dismissed from office and sent into exile. But note – the council only dismissed them because of bias and incompetence, not because of conspiracy.

'The council at Mungairit also imposed a fine on you, Nannid. Let me guess. Was it not a fine which you then raised by demanding monies from the community of Nechta here? You arranged to take the sum to Brother Feradach of Mungairit at a rendezvous – the Hill of Truth.'

Brehon Faolchair leaned forward with a quick motion. 'Are you saying that Nannid told the truth about his encounter with Gláed?' he asked incredulously. 'He intended to meet Brother Feradach but Gláed had arrived there by chance?'

'Sometimes even a liar will tell the truth,' Fidelma replied. 'He actually intended to pay the reparation to Mungairit so that he could declare himself free of constraints, should Mungairit raise questions as to what he was doing here. Brother Feradach, however, saw Gláed encamped on the hill and, wisely, decided not to proceed. Nannid did meet Gláed by chance and saw that he held Gormán as a prisoner. It was then that his fanaticism overtook his long-term ambition: Nannid's zeal to show his new power by keeping his promise to execute Gormán overcame his desire to pay off the reparation to Brother Feradach, who was waiting to take it to Mungairit.'

'But why would Gláed hand his prisoner to him? Just for the gold? He could have killed Gormán and taken the gold anyway.'

'Because one of Gláed's men, the very man who had been a guard here and was involved in this conspiracy, had probably drawn Gláed's attention to the fact that the execution of Gormán for the murder of Abbot Ségdae was an essential part of starting the unrest that would topple Prince Donennach. It was a key element of the plan of the noble who was employing Gláed as a mercenary in the plot.'

'This doesn't make sense. Are you arguing that this conspirator helped Gormán escape the first time and then wanted him recaptured the next?'

'When Gormán escaped with Aibell, it was intended to emphasise his guilt. But it was anticipated that he would be swiftly recaptured and brought back. Gormán was to be the focus of the conflict.'

'You say that the money Nannid paid Gláed for giving Gormán to him was money he intended to give to Mungairit in payment of fines?'

'It was money falsely raised from the community of Nechta,' affirmed Fidelma. 'We should thank Deogaire that the money will now be returned to the community.'

'It will be returned to me!' cried Nannid, standing up. 'I am still Abbot of Nechta.'

'I doubt that you will even be that when this matter is known,' Fidelma pointed out coldly. 'You imposed yourself on the community by virtue of an office you no longer held. Now you are neither more nor less than an ordinary member of the community. You know how office is awarded. The *derbhfine* or council of the community must meet and elect its leader. Judging from what I hear, I doubt whether it will be worth you or your steward even attempting to put yourself forward for the office after Brother Éladach has summoned the council of the community.'

'My voice is still powerful among the Uí Fidgente. I will ensure that they obey me,' Nannid blustered.

Socht left his position and actually placed a hand on Nannid's shoulder. 'Your voice will fall silent, Nannid, especially a voice which conspires against his prince.' His voice was firm and authoritative and Nannid found himself sitting down, blinking.

'But you were saying that Nannid was too obvious as a conspirator,' Brehon Faolchair prompted Fidelma. 'Do you say that he was not in this conspiracy?'

'You have my exact meaning,' affirmed Fidelma. 'I will say that as pedantic as Nannid is, with his rigid ideas and adherence to alien religious concepts and laws, he was *not* one of the conspirators. However, he was actually used in this conspiracy. His character was assessed accurately by the conspirators and he was manipulated so that it would deflect suspicion from them as the real culprits.'

'I confess, Fidelma, I am now finding this hard to follow.' The Brehon was shaking his head.

'It is simple. Ambition, power and the need for revenge on Mungairit played a dominant role in Nannid's intentions. He and his steward were exiled from Mungairit and came here hoping to open an abbey in the principal township of the Uí Fidgente. He wanted to claim the abbacy of this community and make it as powerful as Mungairit. It sounds impossible, but stranger things have happened. However, the community here was an intrinsic part of the township: it was not what they call a *cenobium* or closed community. So Nannid had to fall back on the authority of Mungairit – which he no longer had – when he ordered walls to be built around it and make it into a close community, as well as fraudulently demanding gold from them.'

'So Nannid was simply being manipulated. But by whom?' demanded Brehon Faolchair.

'I have said it is a complicated plot and one that sadly led to several deaths, beginning with that of Abbot Ségdae. Nannid had been persuaded to invite Abbot Ségdae here by those conspiratorial interests. It had probably been suggested to him that if he invited Abbot Ségdae here, it would help assure his prestige. In short, Abbot Ségdae was lured here to his death.'

'You are saying that Nannid was merely a tool, used to bring Abbot Ségdae here. So he was as much a victim as Gormán.' Brehon Faolchair sighed. 'It is a story that is hard to digest, let alone believe.'

'I trust that I shall lead you into the belief,' Fidelma replied solemnly.

'You have to account for the deaths of Ciarnat and Brother Máel Anfaid,' Prince Donennach interposed for the first time. 'You also have to account for the false story that Ciarnat told her friend Aibell, which was passed on to Gormán and then caused them to engineer Gormán's escape – which confirmed, in most of our eyes, that he was guilty.'

'That I shall do,' Fidelma said. 'False stories are easily spread. It is a human weakness that untruth is more readily believable than truth. Brother Máel Anfaid was told the story by someone he trusted and whose word he believed implicitly. He was informed that I had decided to abandon the defence of Gormán. He repeated this to

Ciarnat who, as it was expected, immediately told her close friend Aibell.' Fidelma smiled encouragingly across at the girl. 'Aibell is a person of quiet determination, and when it was also whispered that the guard was susceptible to bribery, she seized the chance to seek his help – the irony being that he was in fact part of the conspiracy and had already been ordered to engineer the escape of Gormán from his prison.

'This is where our conspirators became clever again; perhaps too clever. They guessed that I might be able to track down this line of false stories to its source, as they knew that I had already shown that one false story that had been spread was untrue. The false story was that Prince Donennach had dismissed Gormán's warning and that Gormán had gone in a rage to see Abbot Ségdae to protest.'

Brehon Faolchair rubbed his chin thoughtfully for a moment. 'Ciarnat was the innocent instrument of causing Aibell and Gormán to panic and leave this fortress so that we might assume Gormán was guilty,' he said. 'How were the conspirators too clever in this?'

'It was what followed. They no doubt assumed that Ciarnat would flee with Aibell and Gormán. However, the care of her elderly mother kept her here – and that was to be the poor girl's death sentence. I think our conspirators first killed Brother Máel Anfaid, who alone could identify the real source of the story. He was walking by the river when he was killed and his *loman*, his corded belt, was taken. It was a new style adopted by him and Brother Mac Raith and so easily identifiable. The killer then paid attention to Ciarnat, who staying under the protection of Airmid, your *tanaise*. Ciarnat was killed by a blow on the head and then hanged from a roof beam with the stolen *loman*. This was the clever piece – initially it was made to look like suicide.

'I was confused. Was it either a badly executed attempt at disguising the murder, or it was done in an intentionally clumsy fashion so that it was easy to draw the conclusion that it was murder? The person who had killed Brother Máel Anfaid and then killed poor Ciarnat was the same person who had killed Abbot Ségdae. But I think they were told exactly how to arrange Ciarnat's death because the chief conspirator wanted me to think that it was a badly executed disguise of a murder and would thus implicate the second conspirator.'

'You have now mentioned two conspirators,' Brehon Faolchair observed. 'Are you drawing close to naming those responsible?'

'I am,' stated Fidelma, as a wave of murmuring swept the hall. 'So let us get down to identities. Who is the killer of Abbot Ségdae, Brother Máel Anfaid and the girl, Ciarnat? Who would then be expendable in the eyes of the leading conspirator?

'I said at the start that if Gormán had not killed Abbot Ségdae, there was only one other logical culprit.'

She now looked across at the pale face of the steward of the Abbey of Imleach. The tall, muscular man rose from his seat with a cry of rage but found Socht at his side with a drawn sword.

'More often than not, the truth is in the obvious,' Fidelma said. 'Brother Tuamán took Gormán into the abbot's chamber. He pretended to leave but went outside, grabbed Prior Cuán's blackthorn from his chamber and returned. The abbot thought he had come back for some papers, so he looked down at his desk and uttered those words: "Oh yes, you want these." It was then that Brother Tuamán hit Gormán before stabbing the abbot and arranging the murder scene. He locked the door, posted the key through the knot-hole and then called Lachtna, the guard outside, saying he had heard the sound of arguing and a noise like a body falling. What followed was a logic based on these lies.'

'Can I ask a question?' It was Gormán who sought permission of Brehon Faolchair before he turned to Fidelma.

'I understand from what you say that Abbot Ségdae was lured here to be killed in order to start a conflict. But I came here purely by chance. I had just arrived at the fortress and no one expected me. How, then, was I drawn into this?'

'A good point,' conceded Fidelma. 'As you say, it was pure chance. The conspirators would doubtless have arranged for someone else to be blamed. I suspect that it would have been Prior Cuán whom they chose. But what better than the commander of the King of Cashel's bodyguard to be seen as the murderer? It was a great opportunity for them that you just happened to be in the wrong place at the wrong time.'

Brehon Faolchair was regarding the steward of the Abbey of Imleach thoughtfully. 'So it would also be Brother Tuamán who told Brother Máel Anfaid that you, Fidelma, were abandoning the case? His word would have been trusted implicitly by the young scribe. Certainly, Brother Tuamán is a tall man and one of some strength, which would have been needed in arranging Ciarnat's hanging.'

'It was felt that I was already dangerously near working out the reality of the situation,' Fidelma agreed. 'A distraction was needed which would confirm the guilt of Gormán. What better than if he escaped, even for a short period? It would serve as a definitive confirmation of guilt.'

'So Brother Máel Anfaid would have no cause to believe his superior was lying and he duly passed the story on to Ciarnait,' Brehon Faolchair summed up, clarifying the argument. 'When that plan worked, both Máel Anfaid and Ciarnait needed to be silenced for they were the essential links to the source of the false story.'

Prior Cuán rose unsteadily from his seat, leaning forward on his stick. He seemed bewildered. 'But Brother Tuamán is steward at Imleach and surely owed service to Abbot Ségdae. Why would he become involved in this Uí Fidgente conspiracy?'

'Because he was either fully or part Uí Fidgente. He told me that he had come from the Loch Léin area to the south of Sliabh Luachra. That is borderland between the Uí Fidgente and the territory of Congal of the Eóghanacht of Loch Léin. He studied at Inis Faithlian. Many Uí Fidgente studied there. It is one of the three great teaching abbeys in the area.'

'You mention Inis Faithlian as if it had importance?' the prior said.

'I believe that is where Brother Tuamán met his fellow conspirator when they were students. Perhaps they formed a relationship there. Was that relationship used to inveigle him into this conspiracy once he arrived with Abbot Ségdae? Perhaps it had even been arranged before he went to Imleach. Perhaps his task was to persuade Ségdae to come here. Tuamán's rise at Imleach was remarkably quick.'

'We have heard that Brother Tuamán was one of the conspirators but he is in no way connected with the bloodline of the Uí Fidgente,' Prince Donennach said. 'Surely the very basis of the conspiracy that you are arguing rests on a person having the claim of succession if I were displaced?'

'Now we have come to the heart of the matter.' Fidelma smiled grimly. 'You may have often heard me quote the wise Roman judge, Cicero. In dealing with all such mysteries as these I start with the question – *cui bono?* Who benefits?'

'Who would benefit if Prince Donennach was overthrown in some coup?' Brehon Faolchair said. 'Nannid is the only possible claimant I know of, and he is now discredited from any office. He would not be acceptable. So there is no one.'

'No one?' queried Fidelma innocently. 'Is there not one who has often been overlooked because the Uí Fidgente boasts a line of warrior princes? Is there not an heir apparent, a *tanaise?*'

'This is outrageous!' Airmid, Donennach's sister, had risen white-faced from her chair. 'The woman lies – she is an Eóghanacht spy sent to sow dissension among us. Ceit, have your men arrest her!'

'Airmid?' Prince Donennach was clearly shocked to the core. 'But that is ridiculous! She is my sister and cares nothing for matters of statecraft.'

'She is also your heir apparent, the single eligible successor.'

'It's all up! She knows all!' the burly figure of Brother Tuamán suddenly burst out. 'Help me, Airmid. You have the power to save us both.'

'Shut up, you fool. Can't you see all this is just words – words and no substance. The woman is just an Eóghanacht bitch sent to . . . she can't prove anything.'

'Remember, Tuamán, she was prepared to sacrifice you,' Fidelma said. 'You would have been blamed for the murder of Ciarnat, and no doubt her idea was to blame you for all the deaths if anything went wrong.'

The steward collapsed back in his chair, muttering. Then he peered round helplessly. 'I obeyed her – it was out of love. She promised to raise me by her side . . .'

'I think confession counts as evidence,' Brehon Faolchair said to Prince Donennach, his heart heavy for the young prince.

Suddenly, a knife appeared in Airmid's hand – one of her sharp surgeon's scalpels – and she had whirled round on her still-seated brother, who sat frozen in shock. She was in the act of throwing herself on him, her brother, screaming with hatred, when Ceit struck. Later, it emerged that he had merely meant to disarm her knife hand, at the very worst sever it. But Airmid was moving so swiftly, her right hand raised, that the sharp point of his sword went in, under the arm, through the ribcage and into her heart. Almost without a sound, the sister of Donennach collapsed to the floor at her brother's feet, blood gushing from her hate-twisted mouth.

Prince Donennach sat paralysed with horror, looking down at his dead sister.

# L'ENVOI

The body had been taken away. In a broken voice, Prince Donennach had called for the hall to be cleared but Brehon Faolchair had countermanded the order and told the guards to remain where they were. He gently explained this to the prince.

'I hate to contradict you,' he said, 'but this is a court of law and must conclude in a legal manner. It is essential, under law, that we hear what else Fidelma was going to say about the motivation of your sister to this treacherous act.'

Prince Donennach collapsed back into his chair and gave a listless assent.

Fidelma regarded the Prince of the Uí Fidgente with sympathy. 'I am sorry that it has come to this, Donennach. But many things caused me to pose questions that brought me to this conclusion. When we first met, Airmid told me she had studied the healing arts at the Abbey of Inis Faithlian. I wondered why Tuamán, who had studied at Inis Faithlian at the same time as Airmid, pretended not to know her, or her very name, when she was called upon to examine the body of Abbot Ségdae. It was Conrí who told me the name of the physician who attended. Yet when I came upon Airmid and Tuamán playing *fidchell* last night, in this very hall, and Airmid was winning, what did Brother Tuamán say? That she had always been an excellent player even when she was a student.

334

'I do not say it was conclusive. But then I recalled something else. Your cousin Eoganán was Prince of the Uí Fidgente when Airmid left her studies to practise her healing arts. Your family had been displaced by Eoganan. I was told that your sister fell in love with someone that your family did not approve of. In spite of their protests, Airmid married that person. Now what family would be powerful enough to stand up to your family's disapproval? The only one would be the rival branch of the royal line. The man she married was a son of Eoganán . . . that son was Lorcán. Lorcán, who had survived his father's defeat, killed his twin brother – the religieux, Lughna – and hid for some years in the Abbey of Mungairit, plotting the death of my brother, Colgú, and your overthrow, Donennach.'

There was an icy silence in the hall.

'During all that time,' Fidelma continued, 'you were led to believe that Airmid was a widow. Six months ago, when I uncovered the truth that Lorcán was alive and plotting in Mungairit, he was captured and sent by me as a prisoner to this very fortress to await your pleasure when you returned from your visit to the High King. I learned that he had escaped from his cell, but that the watchful guards had mortally wounded him. He died being nursed by Airmid who then became his widow in reality and swore vengeance on you.

'One more thing,' she concluded. 'It was thought he had help to escape. If we speculate that it was his wife who helped him, I do not think we would be far wrong. You had been so used to thinking of her as a widow during the years that had passed since Cnoc Áine that it did not occur to you that she might still be infatuated with him.

'Conrí was mid-way through telling me the story when we were interrupted before he could name the man that she had married. Had I insisted on the end of that story, in spite of my distraction, we might have achieved a quicker resolution to this matter.'

'At least the matter is resolved now,' Brehon Faolchair said with satisfaction. 'Needless to say, Gormán of Cashel leaves here without a stain on his character and reparation will be offered according to law. Tuamán will not be allowed to return to Imleach and his punishment will be decided later. As for Nannid and Cuineáin, they will be handed to the community of Nechta for their council to decide what is to become of them.'

Prince Donennach rose from his seat almost like a sleepwalker and stared round at those assembled in the hall.

'I take the burden of my sister's guilt on my shoulders and ask for your forgiveness,' he said slowly. 'I assure you that reparation of the honour price of each of those who met their death at the hands of her evil plot will be swiftly paid – the honour price of Abbot Ségdae, that of Ciarnat and of Máel Anfaid. This I have said and so it will be done.'

Brehon Faolchair waited a moment and heaved a sigh before announcing: 'This court, this hearing, is now terminated.'

As Fidelma and her companions rode through the gates of Dún Eochair Mháigh, she silently prayed it would be for the last time. Conrí, Socht and Ceit stood at one side of the gates and raised their hands in salute as they rode by. The atmosphere at the farewell feasting in the great hall during the previous evening had been mixed with sadness. Prince Donennach had not attended, but took his farewell of Fidelma privately. He continued to be visibly devastated by his sister's treachery and violent death whilst trying to kill him. For Fidelma and her companions there was a mixture of relief – and even happiness – at the prospect of returning to Cashel. She and Eadulf had missed their son. Prior Cuán and the young steward Brother Mac Raith were certainly relieved that the truth had been uncovered, but contemplated the future with uncertainty. There were, of course, notable absences at the feast. Brother Tuamán now occupied the cell once occupied by Gormán, while Nannid and Cuineáin had been taken to the Abbey of Nechta to be heard before the community.

Prior Cuán and Brother Mac Raith had left earlier that morning in a mule cart, joining a group of travelling merchants heading for the great Abbey of Imleach. However, Fidelma and her group had slept long past the usual hour and now, with Enda leading the way, followed by Fidelma and Eadulf, with Gormán and Aibell bringing up the rear of their small group, they finally left the fortress. Passing down the slope into the main square of the township, they heard the sounds of sawing, hammering and happy raised voices. On the far side of the square, the forbidding wooden walls of what had been the Abbey of Nechta were being hauled down with a joyous will.

Brother Éladach was hurrying across the square to speak to them.

'I had to say farewell, lady,' he gasped, 'and to give our thanks to you for preserving our way of life.'

Fidelma halted her horse for a moment and smiled down at him.

'You were not long in making a decision, my friend, as to whether to adopt the pretensions of an abbey or simply become part of the community of this township again.'

'It needed no great thought, lady. We can do without abbots and bishops to tell us how to live our lives, or walls to separate us from the knowledge and friendship of our fellow citizens.'

'What of Nannid and his companion, Cuineáin?'

'At the same time that our community decided to rejoin the real world, we informed them that they could leave at once, taking only whatever they had arrived with. Even that was more than they deserved.'

Eadulf pulled a face. 'With any luck, they took *less* than they arrived with. I am referring to the weight of their arrogance, their pretensions and their fanaticism.'

Brother Éladach chuckled and said sagely, 'One cannot ask too many miracles of God at the one time. Thanks to the lady Fidelma here, we have seen miracles enough.'

'Do you know where they will go?' She was curious.

'They were last seen heading south-west. The further they go, the better. And for all this, thank you, lady.' He raised a hand in blessing. 'May your journey be without hardship. Until the end of the road may you enjoy peace and safety.'

With a smile and a wave, Fidelma and Eadulf rejoined their companions moving eastwards towards Cashel.